THE
BODY
THIEVES

A NOVEL

The Body Thieves
By Christopher Bowron
copyright 2018 Christopher Bowron
ISBN—978-1-9994413-0-2 (Print) EBOOK—978-1-9994413-1-9

All rights reserved. No part of this publication may be reproduced, stored in a retrieval system, or transmitted in any form or by any means – electronic, mechanical, photocopy, recording, or any other – except for brief quotations in printed reviews, without the prior written consent of the author.

This is a work of fiction. The characters are both actual and fictitious. With the exception of verified historical events and persons, all incidents, descriptions, dialogue and opinions expressed are the products of the Author's imagination and are not to be construed as real.

Published by:
SOUTH SHORE PUBLISHING
7330 Estero Boulevard
Ft. Myers Beach Florida, 33931

THE BODY THIEVES

A NOVEL

CHRISTOPHER BOWRON

South Shore Publishing

CHAPTER ONE

HIS SUMMONS TO the Pentagon took Dom Tavano off guard. For those in the upper echelons of the military, it might be a daily occurrence - expected. For a disgraced military doctor, the call was very improbable, something that didn't happen unless you had attracted attention, wanted…or unwanted.

His heart thumped in his chest as he unlocked his black Jeep Renegade and slid into the driver's seat. Civilian pay might afford him a fancy Mercedes, but he didn't have a problem with that. Dom was a down-to-earth guy and enjoyed the anonymity the more pedestrian vehicle provided. He was a Jeep guy. Dom navigated through the streets of Bethesda, passing the Uniformed Services University Hospital, a few blocks from his house. There were many privileges to being a military doctor that most military officers did not receive, stability being one. He could work under the radar until he turned fifty, away from the stresses of normal military duty, then collect an excellent pension, but he didn't want that. His ass had been planted in Bethesda since he'd been declined active duty, and his medical license revoked seven years ago. He hoped enough time had passed to wash away his transgressions. In the back of his mind, he suspected the meeting would have something to do with his past; the man who summoned him was well known to Dom.

He turned onto the 495 Beltway, the highway that was crowded no matter what time of day or night. Within ten minutes, he merged onto the George Washington Memorial Parkway, which would take him to Pentagon City.

Loving Washington in the spring, he enjoyed how the trees sprang to life with baby leaves and blossoms just starting to form, but he was not happy. He didn't join the military to be support staff. What part of his psyche wanted to be torn from his cozy posting to a hellhole combat zone? If he hadn't always thought this way he might have wondered if this might be midlife crisis.

He didn't feel that he needed structure any more in his home life. He'd been married and frankly, it wasn't for him. Dom was an adrenaline junkie. The endorphin rush of working out, his only relief over the past few years, was no longer enough for him. He needed to get back in the game, and prayed Tom Williams would supply him with good news.

He'd been stationed in Iraq with the General during the pullout where he'd saved the man's life. The General had a ruptured appendix, nothing too terribly heroic, but it had been problematic and in unsatisfactory circumstances. As Dom drove, his mind wandered to his last weeks in Iraq. The upcoming meeting would no doubt be tied to them.

***

After seven years, Dom could vividly remember the concussion from the detonating warhead. It had slammed his jeep and the passengers flew backwards with little warning except for the whine of an incoming missile. The night sky erupted in bright orange and white light. A vacuum created by the bomb sucked the last remaining air from Dom's lungs. He heaved, trying to get a painful breath before dropping to his hands and knees and willing his chest to expand. As he regained his breath, the sound and smell of war became his immediate reality. All around were the screams of men down on the ground inside a cloud of dust…and gunpowder…and death.

Dom and his intern, Derek Webb, accompanied a British led, U.N. mission through the northern suburbs of Mosul. The Iraqis were still pushing back, which led to an upswing in dissident activity over the past few weeks. Protocol dictated the company stays on alert but no amount of awareness could account for a handheld RPG-18 Mukha fired from the window of an abandoned building.

He remained on his hands and knees, and waited for the dust to settle, no point in moving, until he could see and hear. The ringing in his ears had just started to subside. The troop carrier in front of Dom's vehicle took the direct hit. The result was a total debacle. He closed his eyes, rubbing dirt from his lids and tried to listen. *Screaming men! Where?*

He remembered methodically examining his own body, making sure he wasn't in shock or hit by shrapnel. Then he felt around to account for all his limbs. Having seen it hundreds of times, shock and endorphins can mask the worst pain and injuries. When everything felt okay, he opened his eyes and saw the air clearing. Feeling around for something to lean on, his right hand found a quivering body. He reached for the neck to check for a pulse. No neck! Only a gaping hole where the head had once been attached. Now, there was only blood, bone and tissue. *Dammit!*

Men continued to yell. He could hear footsteps…running feet. *Where is the commanding officer?*

"Medic!" A panicked voice screamed.

Dom searched for his field kit…he found it lying a few feet away, and slung it over his shoulder. Things became clearer as he moved from behind the wreck of the Jeep. The Brits appeared to be pulling things together quickly and were returning fire from behind cover of a low stone wall close to the troop carrier. He could see the incoming fire came from an abandoned building on the other side of the square. Pushing forward, he moved towards the screams. It didn't take long to find them.

Crouching down behind the low wall, he found the source of distress. He touched the shoulder of a soldier, bent down on one knee, hovering over a panicked man while trying to calm his fear. Dom could see more wounded flayed about on the ground; his quick assessment revealed he needed to deal with the screamer.

The kneeling soldier looked up. "Damn good thing you're here Major. Donoghue isn't doing so well."

"Move over!" Dom said in his distinct Brooklyn accent, the letter R replaced by a strong A sound at the end of *over*. Dropping to his knees, he handed a flashlight to the soldier. "Hold this, but shield the light. We don't need any more fire."

"Got it, Major." The young man used his hand to cover the top of the light beam.

Dom examined Donoghue's wounds, going over the A, B, Cs of trauma protocol. Still breathing…there was no doubt of that, as the man moaned in agony. A large piece of metal protruded through the upper chest just under the right shoulder blade…probably red hot on entry. The patient looked like he'd grabbed the metal, searing the skin on the insides of his hands. His lower left leg didn't exist below the knee, blood kept slowly spurting from the open wound. He put his face close to the screaming man, placing his hand over his mouth. "Son, you gotta' stop that. You'll draw fire. I'm a Doctor. You're badly hurt, but I'm going to make sure that you live. Got that?"

The young man nodded.

Dom jabbed him in the arm with morphine from his field pack. "This'll make you feel a hell of a lot better, and it'll hit you quick." Dom could see relief relax the features of the wounded man's face instantly. He turned to the soldier standing at his side. "We're not going to be able to remove that piece of metal out here on the field. I'm gonna' immobilize the site. Tie it tightly just below the knee…got it?"

The soldier nodded as Dom handed over a tourniquet from his pack along with another the dose of morphine. "I want you to stay with him until we can get backup. Just stab and squeeze, but not for another two to three hours…or you'll stop his heart."

The young man looked nervously at the small morphine package covered with a protective capsule. "Okay."

Dom put his face close to the wounded man. "Donoghue, Corporal Lee is gonna' look after you. You'll be okay if you don't move, and that means no screaming. I'll be back to check on you. There are a few more sons of bitches out there that need my help."

The downed soldier getting high on morphine nodded.

"Good boy." Dom placed a calming hand on the man's head to extend a touch of comfort.

Moving away from the wall, Dom shouted. "Webb!"

Corporal Derek Webb, his resident in training, must have flown farther from the Jeep than Dom expected. He'd been sitting beside Dom when the explosion hit the truck. A quick scan of the area proved his resident was not in sight. Webb wasn't the one without his head, that one had been a Brit. He moved to the next man on the ground. A hot piece of metal protruded from his stomach. The soldier sat stoically, obviously in pain. Dom unbuckled his field vest, and cut away his shirt. Closer inspection revealed the shrapnel had turned on contact, deflected by the soldier's heavy belt.

Dom looked at his nametag. "Foster, you're one lucky son of a bitch." Dom jabbed the man with morphine. "The metal turned at the last second and it's not in there too deep." He prodded the wound with his fingers. "I'm gonna' pull it out."

Foster grabbed Dom's arm. The wound was superficial. There was no fear in Dom's estimation of a tamponade, where the piece of shrapnel might be pushing on an artery, holding something together inside.

"Foster, be a man and let me get it out. There are more men out there needing my attention." Dom put a gauze pack around the metal and pressed as he pulled out the thin object. Dropping it to the ground, he dabbed iodine on a cloth and cleaned the wound. He handed a gauze pad to the man. "Hold this here until someone tells you not to…a nurse or a doctor."

Dom did a quick count. There were ten dead and eight wounded. He took care of the remaining injured men, pleased to see Webb leaning against the wall of a building. He'd been knocked cold on impact, having been blasted more than twenty feet away from the Jeep. Webb had been fortunate to have suffered only minor bumps and bruises.

The sound of reinforcement troops arriving lifted Dom's spirits as he finished up with the remaining wounded. Three armored trucks and a troop carrier rolled into the street. The threat from the warehouse across the plaza neutralized quickly.

***

Dom shook his head, seeing the off ramp from the Parkway - reality. Navigating the Jeep through the maze of parking lots and roadways circling the vast edifice of the Pentagon and its subsidiary buildings, he turned into a security checkpoint. The armed guard inspected his ID. "Good afternoon, Major."

Dom acknowledged the man with a short nod and accelerated. He did the same for checkpoints 2 and 3, then looked for a spot to park as he neared the complex designated for Army Services. Extremely rigid and anal, described Pentagon Security since 9/11. He would pass a couple more checks, including a bomb and retina scanner before he reached the office of General Williams, located in the bowels of the incredibly vast edifice.

CHAPTER TWO

Metlatonoc Region Mexico

ROSA ROSALES LOOKED up into her son Carlos' lean face as he prepared to leave their small hut. Although he'd called the place home his entire life, her heart felt heavy, she knew he would leave. She'd seen young men from their town and from the towns around San Vicente do the same, and never return…ever; the promise of work in the big cities like Guadalajara and Mexico City were far too enticing. The youth needed something to keep them there, but there wasn't anything meaningful to hold them in the awful living conditions. Without jobs, there was only intense poverty.

The Metlatonoc was a horseshoe shaped municipality, west of Acapulco, in the State of Guerrero. The region was exceptionally poor, and to make things worse, the war between the drug cartels accentuated the devastating poverty seen only in the poorest locations of the globe. If the Banditos perceived something to be of value, they took it…including flesh.

Carlos knew if he stayed in the house much longer, he might be tempted to change his mind. "Momma, I'll send you money. Hector and Ramón say that we will be making good money in no time at the resorts. Acapulco is less than a day away…I come back soon. Say goodbye to my sisters."

Carlos knew they didn't need to be looked after. They were hard working, and the eldest was heavy with child, which meant her husband was responsible for her now. He worried about his mother getting too old to live in such a place. He wondered what the region was like a hundred years ago, were things this bad, or was it the realization of how good things were on the outside that planted the notion of escape in young men like Carlos? If he kept thinking along those lines, he'd soon talk himself out of the adventure. He couldn't see any future for him here, working for the Cartel seemed the only feasible way out. The gangs ruled the area and they needed young men and women. Carlos was strong, smart, good looking, and the Cartel's men told him that there would be a bright future for him. He looked around the crude building. They didn't have modern conveniences; no running water, sewage, television, only a small radio receiving a few stations. He shook his head, trying to clear away any doubt. He would bring his family from this hellhole to Guadalajara, maybe to the States…once there was money in his pocket.

"You'll not come back." Rosa said, tears welling in her eyes. "No one ever does. You will die fighting for them. Drugs, it's just the drugs. They are evil, Carlos. Would you leave your poor old mother alone?"

Carlos let his eyes rise to the ceiling, trying to maintain his resolve. "Momma, I'm gonna do this. You know I need to do it… there's nothing here. This is a dead end, and you know it. I'll come back with some money. I'm strong, no one can hurt me. I'll be one less mouth to feed." He backed up, flexing his biceps in a mock show of strength.

"You *are* strong. That's why I worry. I remember when you were a baby. I couldn't keep you in one place. You were always trying to escape. I guess this is fitting." She turned her eyes to the ground, not able to look up at his handsome face.

Carlos kissed his mother's forehead, not wanting to see the tears he knew would be rolling down her cheeks. He threw his satchel over his shoulder and walked out the door.

***

The day's heat hit him like a slap in the face. *Mexico is always so hot!* He was sick of it being so damn hot. His shirt, instantly moist, would smell of body odor soon like the old men in the square. He'd become accustomed to the smell of dirty men. Carlos read how it was not the way in the United States. He sighed. Supposedly the temperatures were cooler in the mountains and along the coast.

With his mother's house behind him, Carlos walked away and never looked back. He kept his head down and stayed deep in thought as he walked towards the center of the town. He could not look back. San Vicente wasn't much, a ragtag conglomeration of ratty huts covered with signs advertising Coca Cola and Marlboro cigarettes. The town was dusty, hotter than the outlying areas and where their dwelling sat in the lee of a large hill. For half of the day, there was shade. You couldn't find a patch of shade in the town, unless you clung to the walls of the disheveled buildings. There were no trees, they'd been cut down years ago; only devastating heat. He tightened the bandana which most of the men wore around their necks to keep the sweat and dirt from running down his back and chest.

Carlos saw the men he'd come to meet. They were smoking by the town's central well. They both waved at him as he approached. His friend stood with them. Hector was tall and lean, strong as an ox; an imposing figure. The men had agreed to take the two of them to meet the bosses on the coast.

Carlos prided himself on being a hard worker and a devout

Christian. What he endeavored to embark on went against his strong morals, but desperation often drives people to do things out of character. When younger, Carlos dreamt about going to school. His teachers told his mother how smart he was with his schoolwork.

One day, he would make some money and buy himself an education. *To better yourself, you need to have an education.* Carlos could read and write, but that wasn't enough, and he knew it. He would work hard, then go to the States. If you worked hard in the U.S., you could attain anything; the sky was the limit. But first, he must deal with the men from the Cartel and he would heed his mother's words, knowing they were evil, but necessary to attain his goal.

One of the Cartel's men, Abel, greeted him and extended his right hand. He shook Carlos' hand enthusiastically. "Hey Carlos, como estás? You will not regret this, Carlos. Your future is ahead of you. Pacifico looks out for its own. I started out like you, ten years ago. Now, look at me."

Carlos didn't want to become like Abel, and he didn't trust the man whose eyes wandered whenever Carlos tried to meet them. The two older men had been hanging around the town for the past couple of weeks, looking for young men to work for the bosses. They offered good pay for a one-year contract, at least that's what they promised. If Carlos was a loyal worker, he would be rewarded. It felt like a sales job, yet Carlos needed the opportunity.

The men did impress Carlos at a certain level. They owned their own Jeep, not many could afford a vehicle in the Metlatonoc. Hector and Carlos jumped into the back of the vehicle. "Where's Ramon?" Carlos whispered to Hector.

"He's not gonna come, watch."

After a time, when their younger friend, Ramon, didn't show up, the men became tense. Their eyes looking all around, scowls formed on both of their faces. Since Ramon had always been a momma's boy, it didn't surprise Carlos that he didn't show. The driver, Henry, pronounced *Ehnry*, yelled over the rumble of the rough idling engine. "Can't wait any longer."

The older men fired up the jeep and soon they were on the road leading out of town. After about twenty minutes Abel yelled over the engine. "We take you for medical first. The bosses want strong workers. We will go see the doctor now."

Hector nodded and smiled as if seeing a doctor seemed like a luxury. Carlos wasn't so sure. He yelled back. "You said nothing about a doctor the other day. I'm not sick, I don't need no effin' doctor."

Henry turned around, his lips tight across his half-rotten teeth. "You don't seem to *fucking understand*. You see the doctor, or you face the wrath of the Cartel." He pulled a rusty looking handgun out of the glove box, resting it on his lap.

Hector jabbed him in the ribs with his elbow. "You're not sick, no worries man. Besides, I'll beat you up if you bail on me." He smiled at his friend.

Carlos still didn't like the sound of it.

***

They traveled down the winding dirt highway, the hills rolled by; the ground dry with rag tag vegetation starved for water. He elbowed Hector. "We're doing this!" He said more to ease his own nerves than anything, the pangs of guilt hitting him from leaving his family behind.

Hector turned to Carlos. "Your momma's not happy?"

Carlos nodded, knowing that Hector's mother had died a few years ago, leaving him to live with his sister and her abusive husband. Hector had no problem leaving. In fact, he couldn't wait to get out of there. Carlos smiled at Hector. "I'm glad you pushed me, I couldn't have walked out that door if I didn't know you'd never let me forget it."

"I wouldn't beat you, Carlos. You're the smart one, I need you as much as you need me. Together we'll be okay. We're friends for life. We're gonna be rich!"

Taking a deep breath, not so sure about the rich part, Carlos turned back to look at the stark hills as they passed by.

Within a couple of hours they reached a larger town. Carlos had been to Nuevo a few times with his uncle, but didn't recognize where the driver was heading once they left the main road. After several minutes of nervous driving, the Jeep pulled into a side street, the buildings pinched in on the road making it passable for no more than one vehicle. The Jeep followed the lane for a few hundred yards, when the driver abruptly applied the brakes, forcing the vehicle to a screeching stop in front of an old brick and stucco building. "We're here," yelled Abel over the roar of the engine.

***

The two young men were escorted into the interior of a surprisingly modern building. The marble floors were polished, and the walls were tall and recently painted. An antiseptic smell permeated the place. Carlos recognized the scent from when his uncle would pour disinfectant on the wounds of the family's meager livestock, and the children's feet, after stepping on the broken glass that littered their village streets. Abel took them to a room, empty of much besides a row of wooden chairs and a faded picture of Christ on the wall. They were offered a couple bottles of Corona beer, and were told to strip down to their underwear. Both Carlos and Hector complied, but wore nervous, tight-mouthed looks. Carlos could not help but feel a bit funny sitting in such a place in his underwear. "Mother Mary, I don't like this, Hector."

The door opened and a man in a green pajama-like-outfit motioned for Hector to follow him. Carlos assumed the man to be the doctor as Hector gave Carlos one last look leaving the room with the man.

After an hour, Carlos began to grow restless. How long could a simple medical examination take? He ran his fingers through his hair, rhythmically tapping his foot to an irritating melody repeating in his head.

After a time he'd wondered if he'd been forgotten. He started to put his clothes back on, feeling very uncomfortable. As he was pulling his pants over her hips, the man in the green outfit reappeared at the door and beckoned Carlos to follow. He didn't seem like a happy man, not looking Carlos in the eye, his walk stiff, urgent to get where they were going.

"I want to go home."

The man looked at his sideways. "You crazy? The cartel will bring you wealth." He pointed at the pants Carlos had just put back on. "You no need them."

Carlos nodded nervously, dropping his pants to his ankles.

The man led Carlos down a long sterile hallway with dim flickering lights in the ceiling, finally stopping in front of a door, pushing it open. With a curling finger, the man motioned Carlos to enter.

Carlos followed hesitantly.

The bright lights in the new room hurt his eyes. Large overhead beams, like he'd never seen before, lit up the small space, a sharp contrast to the dark hallway. In the middle of the space was a large table with medical equipment flayed around it. Somehow, Carlos figured a doctor's office might have a higher degree of organization. The room smelled of metal and disinfectant, only much stronger than in the other room. A tall man stood in front of the metal table, dressed in similar pajamas with a mask tucked under his chin.

"Please lay down." There was no question in his voice, he pointed to the table.

Carlos assumed him to be the doctor.

He couldn't contain the question. "Where's Hector?"

The man began to organize the medical tools on a side table.

"He's resting. Sit on the table." He wasn't a patient man. "This won't take a minute."

Carlos felt the hair stand up on the back of his neck.

Carlos started to back away towards the door. He was stopped by Abel, the muzzle of his pistol pressed into the small of his back. He would have bolted for the door if the man hadn't been there. "Why did it take so long with Hector?"

The doctor turned sharply to look at him. "There were others. You're not the only ones." He motioned again for Carlos to lay down, impatience etched across his face.

Others?

When Carlos got on top of the table, the doctor moved him to the middle and hooked his arm up to a monitor.

"I'm Dr. Degas and your name is?" He raised his eyebrows, waiting for the answer.

"Carlos Rosales."

Degas wrote down his name on a piece of paper, and attached it to a clipboard on the bottom of the table. "I'll need to do some blood work. It's required by the insurers." He motioned to the other man who had ushered he and Abel to the bright room, who was now standing beside the table. "The nurse is going to attach a drip."

Carlos didn't understand, but nodded in total innocence.

The male nurse held his arm down on the table and took a long metal needle out of a dirty looking pan sitting on a small metal stand with wheels. "This won't hurt for more than a second," his voice terse and short.

Carlos flinched as the needle pierced a large vein on his forearm; it burned slightly. The nurse quickly attached a long coiled tube to the needle and taped the apparatus to his arm.

When the doctor inserted a needle into the tube he asked, "You're in good health Carlos?"

He tried to respond, but his mouth refused to move. In fact, his whole body felt numb. He couldn't move at all! Panic ran through him. He tried to take a deep breath, but couldn't. He turned his eyes to follow the men's movements, but that was all he could do, besides worry.

"That's it. You won't feel a thing. Just try to relax, and this will be all over in a few minutes." He looked to his assistant. "Roll him onto his side."

Carlos couldn't stop the nurse from turning him over. His arms flopped helplessly. His body wouldn't respond. It was as if someone had taken control. His panic increased hearing Degas slip on a pair of plastic gloves and snapping them in place.

"Scalpel."

Carlos knew what a scalpel was used for. His eyes rolled in horror.

The nurse handed a small pen-like instrument with a thin blade to the doctor. Carlos couldn't see when the men moved behind him, but he could feel a tugging sensation on his side below his ribcage. The procedure continued for no more than a couple of minutes.

"Ice…here…hemostat…he's hemorrhaging."

"He's losing a lot of blood, Doctor."

Carlos swooned in his helplessness, his vision began to blur. "Losing blood." *This was supposed to be a checkup. What were they doing to him?*

Carlos closed his eyes slowly, and drifted into a dreamless sleep.

CHAPTER THREE

GENERAL TOM WILLIAMS sat at the end of a long wooden table, his build that of an NFL lineman, not what one would expect of an aging military commander. The man's stature and stern face demanded respect. When he spoke, especially in the confines of his tight, stuffy office, people listened. There were no windows in the room that could only be accessed via a long elevator ride into the bowels of the Pentagon. With thousands of tons of cement piled on top, the space seemed more of a bunker. Four people sat along the length of the table.

Colonel Dr. John Burrows, Under Secretary to the Surgeon General, broke the silence, which had grown uncomfortable. "Sir, before Major Tavano arrives, we need to discuss whether or not he's the correct choice for the mission? I have my concerns." Burrows did things strictly by the book. In his mind, Dominic Tavano was not mentally fit to practice medicine, let alone head a covert operation. He wanted to keep the man on the hook for his past transgressions. "He's crossed the line too many times. The incident in Iraq put us all under some serious heat. "You sat on the board seven years ago, and together, we revoked his license."

Williams folded his hands on top of the table. "Yes, we did, and at the time I agreed with the decision. Tavano needed some time to step back, time to debrief. He's a fantastic surgeon, perhaps one of the best to come out of the military system in some time. A hundred and fifty years ago, they would have called him a hero. Today, everything is put under a goddamned microscope, and he's branded a pariah."

"For Christ sake, Sir, he shot two British officers in the head."

Williams hesitated for a moment, looking up to the ceiling. "Euthanized is the correct word, John, not shot."

"That's open for debate." Burrows shook his head, his mouth taught.

"I'd have him in my corner, Colonel. He thinks outside the box, smart as hell. That's why I recommended him for the posting. He's been rotting in the University hospital for seven years. He's still with the corps, and looking for a chance to redeem himself. And we have something he wants: a chance to get his medical license reinstated. He knows if he leaves the Army, it won't happen. We can offer him clemency." Williams took a deep breath. "Look, he saved my life back in Iraq, I owe him one. I've seen him work under hellish conditions, he's unflappable and damn good at what he does." He stopped talking, put his hands down on the table and stared everyone in the eye. "We don't have any other medical doctors in his position and… he's the only man available who speaks fluent Spanish."

Burrows nodded slowly. "You're saying he's expendable and really our only choice?" He placed his palms on the table.

Williams hesitated. "No one's expendable, but I'll admit from time to time we have to put people into situations that may present a higher level of risk." He stood clasping his hands behind his back. "This is the goddamned army, John, we fight wars, and this is a war. Tavano will understand the risk and I can guarantee he will assume it."

"Why isn't the CIA looking after this?"

Williams smiled. "It's a matter of personnel. The CIA isn't going to find a civilian doctor willing to take on the risk, nor is there anyone available within those agencies qualified to do the job. Major Tavano is still on the payroll and basically has no choice, unless he wants to face a court martial."

Next to Burrows sat a woman in her early sixties with sun-wrinkled skin. Dressed casually, her long gray hair pulled back into a ponytail, she spoke with a South African accent, and an air of authority. "We understand his credentials are excellent, General Williams, but I didn't know the military was big on granting favors?" She paused looking him directly in the eye. "I hope that our candidate is the correct choice, and not politically motivated. Will Dr. Tavano be able to negotiate with the Mexican mob, and the medical conglomerate, we think is the link in the U.S.? I hear the man is brash. He will need to be tactful. We don't need a hot head, someone who'll cause an international incident. At the moment, the issue of human organ trafficking is politically sensitive."

Williams turned to the woman. "Dr. DeRosnay, I can only vouch for his character, and credentials. I've never seen anyone function in a tight situation like Major Tavano. He can be abrupt, but he is a smart man. I have faith that he'll be able to figure things out. In the end you have to trust the people you put in place. He won't let us down. If he can't accomplish what he's sent to do, he'll die trying. That's how Tavano is built."

"We were told the same thing a year ago."

The General smiled. "There you go. That was the CIA; they put an intern into a compromised position. The Gulf Cartel smelled a rat before he could perform one extraction. Thankfully, the State Department and Central Intelligence passed this on to Military Intelligence where this type of mission should have been handled in the first place." He paused. "We're putting a failsafe into the equation. Should Tavano cross the line and start trouble, we'll have him removed. His field nurse is the Canadian equivalent to an American Navy Seal…Vandoo. She's a trained killer. She'll be given orders to take him out if he fumbles."

He turned back to Burrows. "I don't know what you're worried about, Colonel. If Tavano is successful, mission accomplished. If he fails…" He stared at Burrows to make his point. "You've never been a big fan of Tavano, but he's the right man for the job, the decision is made."

Burrows conceded the argument with a slight nod. "Tom, it just goes against my better judgment. I've said my piece and will obviously defer to your authority." He hesitated. "I may not like what he's done in the past, but I don't want to throw him to the wolves either."

"Thank you, John, I appreciate the input. This is what Generals are paid to do – make hard decisions."

After a soft knock, General Williams' secretary stepped in. "Sir, Major Tavano's here."

"Show him in Wendy."

CHAPTER FOUR

DOM WASN'T A nervous person, but his instincts warned him the meeting would be important, and he could feel his pulse racing. You don't get called to the Pentagon to be given your marching papers. The powers on high don't waste their time calling people in for that. He refused to speculate, loose thoughts would only lead to more anxiety. He closed his eyes, and cleared his mind, pushing away all negative thoughts. Instead, his mind drifted back to Iraq as he waited for his audience with The General.

***

Dom finished his rounds, pulling the latex surgical gloves off his hands with a loud snap, tossing them in a waste bin. He'd taken the metal piece of shrapnel out of young Donoghue's shoulder. It would heal up nicely, but the man would surely miss his leg. The stump required sewing up and pressurized gauze padding. A heavy dose of antibiotic would also need to be administered, through his IV drip. The rest of the wounded were lucky to suffer superficial injuries. He could do nothing for the dead.

Very tired, he shuffled his way to the officer's mess and sat down with a shot of whiskey and a pint of English ale. He had only finished two sips when he heard the incipient voice of Colonel Gregory Fields coming up behind him, conversing with a couple of young British officers. Dom could feel his blood begin to boil before Fields reached the chair where he sat down. Dom thought Fields acted like a pompous asshole and a bully. Dom made no bones about his dislike for the man.

Fields commanded the British 6th Regiment, and as he was stationed with the 6th, Dom fell under the Colonel's command. For some reason, Fields didn't warm to him, and Dom wouldn't back down from the frequent confrontations with the man that often arose from Fields' persistent antagonism.

"Major Tavano. I hear you made a balls up today. Beckham here says if you'd acted quicker, some of my men would still be alive. For the life of me, I can't understand why the UN insists upon the cross pollination of our resources."

Dom smiled, turning to look up at him, his Brooklyn accent a foil as Fields put on a snobby English drawl. "They do it so assholes like you can't screw up a situation, which is basically under control. You're a corrupt bastard. I'm here to keep an eye on you, and you know it. That's why you don't like it. If that ain't the reason, then I'm making it the FUCKING REASON. What happened today was under your goddamned watch, and you know it. I'm not taking the blame because you chose to stay back at the base playing with yourself."

Fields took the jab without reaction and sat down beside Dom. The other two remained standing, their faces uncomfortable with the ensuing exchange. "You see, the problem with you Yanks is you all think you know everything, especially you, Major Tavano. You are a bloody know-it-all, but really, you're dumber than a damned plank.

I don't think you could change a diaper in an old folk's home. You're a hazard to our company, and frankly I want you out, and believe me…I'll find a way."

"How long have I been here, five weeks? You've been busting my balls since day one. You are a pompous prick and you give the Brits a bad fucking name." Dom gulped down half his beer in one swallow. "I'm not gonna play your game, Fields. You're just yanking my chain to get a reaction outta me…to get rid of me. I'm not gonna do it. I'll say one thing though, you'd better not be third in line at a triage." He downed his whiskey and stood up.

Fields stood up at the same time and faced him toe to toe, his face turning red. Clearly, Dom's comment hit a soft spot. They eyed each other for what seemed like a minute, neither wanting to back down. When Fields shoved Dom, it took every ounce of resolve for Dom not to split open the man's nose. Instead, he wisely turned and left the mess. "Prick!" He said loud enough to be heard by all.

"Watch your back, Tavano."

***

Dom's thoughts jolted back to the present and he bounced in his seat hearing the General's secretary calling him. "Major Tavano, the General will see you now." She could not hide her chuckle seeing his nervous reaction.

"Thank you!" He rose from the uncomfortable wooden chair and followed her to the door. He opened it and stepped in. He'd been in Tom William's office a few times and recognized the long wooden table running the length of the room. He also remembered Williams telling him how the General didn't like desks, preferring a table so he could spread his work out in front of him.

Dom saluted the General and looked over to John Burrows. He felt no love for the man, who'd been instrumental in stripping him of his license, but this was the Army and he saluted per protocol.

"Colonel Burrows." They locked eyes for the briefest of moments before Dom turned to the other three at the table. He didn't recognize any of them and only one was in uniform.

"At ease, Major." Tom Williams said, "Please take a seat." He motioned to the lone empty chair at the opposite end of the table.

The General waited for Dom to be seated before he stood. "Major, let me introduce you to my colleagues. He motioned to his left. "You know Colonel Burrows from the department of the Surgeon General."

Dom nodded, resisting the urge to make a snide comment.

Williams gestured to the gray-haired woman. "Dr. Joanna DeRosnay, professor and anthropologist from Georgetown University."

Dom nodded to her and she returned the gesture, wearing a slight frown on her brow.

Williams moved his gaze to the other side of the table, waving at a forty-five-year-old woman, dressed in a blue pantsuit. "Christine Pendergast, from the Department of State."

Dom nodded.

"And finally, Major Chris Bachman, Military Intelligence."

The man looked more like Special Ops, Dom could tell from the way he carried himself. Bachman looked to be six foot, dark hair, full dress uniform, and well decorated as indicated by several bars of varying color on his jacket lapel. "Major Bachman is in charge of your mission, you will report directly to him."

Dom did his best not to smile. *Mission?*

Williams didn't waste any time. "Major Tavano. I brought your name forward to lead a task force." His deep-set eyes stared him down.

Dom's heart skipped a beat. Again, he tried his best to show no emotion.

"What do you know about human trafficking?"

Still in shock, Dom took a moment to gather his thoughts.

"Sir, as it pertains to the sex trade and slavery, or to the sale of human organs?"

Williams wasn't surprised Dom might know something about the topic. The man was renowned for having a photographic memory. "The organ trade. Professor DeRosnay has spent most of her life following it in Latin America, if memory serves me right, she's written a couple of books and dozens of papers on the subject. She's seen the process from the bottom up." He gestured to DeRosnay.

Dom recognized the woman now.

"Thank you, General." She turned to Dom, and stood up from the table, motioning to a digital display covering most of the wall behind her. It depicted a map of Central America, Mexico, and the United States.

"Dr. Tavano, please tell us what you know of the organ trade."

Dom smiled. "Which article of yours would you like me to cite? I haven't read them all, but I did particularly like your book on Human Traffic in the African Sub Continent."

Caught off guard, DeRosnay hesitated. "What do you know about Mexico?"

Gazing at the ceiling, Dom smiled inside. He hadn't read the book. Still, he remembered the cover and enjoyed the look of surprise on the faces of those around the table. "As far as the organ trade is concerned? Not a lot, except for the fact that some regions rival the poverty found in Bangladesh, Haiti and Somalia. Hard to believe, with the country being so close to the States. I would surmise the trade in human flesh is alive and well."

"It is alive and well. The proximity to the U.S. border makes the illegal transport of harvested body parts much more alluring to those involved. The recipients want organs that are fresh, and they pay big bucks for them."

DeRosnay motioned to Pendergast. "I've been fighting for the poor and impoverished in third world countries for over thirty years. Finally, the State Department has seen fit to do something about the problem…though I think it's due to pressure from the UN. You can't fight the trade in organs unless you cut off the source of funding. Unfortunately the funding source comes from richer countries: the U.S. in particular." She stared at Pendergast.

Pendergast's brow drew down and her cheeks reddened before she responded tersely. "Dr. DeRosnay. This is an initiative drawn up by the Secretary, created with no connection to your influence, nor the United Nations. You're here as an advisor; let's be clear on this point. We want this mission to be a success, not a failure like we've seen in the past. If you feel you can't be part of it in a supporting role, I think you should step down before we go any further."

DeRosnay nodded, her eyes looking down at the floor. Dom could tell there was no love lost between the two women. Irritation and tension evident in her voice. "The list of potential organ recipients in the western world is large. Slightly less than 80% will receive an organ through conventional means. The remaining 20% die, or find what is required illegally. There is a huge black market, strongly represented in the United States. The West has the money, the impoverished regions have the organs, be they from willing or non-willing donors."

She walked over to the screen, which with a tap to the bottom corner, now depicted a map of the world. She pointed at Iran, expanding the image with her fingers. "The Iranians are the only nation to embrace the organ trade openly, but they find their clientele strictly from the Middle and Far East. There is nothing that we in the Western world can do about Iran.

"There are laws in place in most first and second world countries, but they don't have any backbone. No one wants to police the infractions, nor are they willing to take the next hard step to take down the big corporations propagating the business."

She walked back to the table and sat down. "The problem? It's become big money and big money in most modern first world countries is a strong lobby. People's lives are saved, and that remains the bottom line. Public officials are bribed. Doctors make lots of money, coroners, morticians, etcetera and the list goes on. The sad thing is, as I've alluded to, there are no international laws in place that bear any clarity. The edicts conveniently allow law enforcement to turn a blind eye. There have been many international symposiums over the years, but no one is willing to do a damned thing. The poor continue to be exploited. Tens of thousands are killed each year for their flesh. An even greater number are coerced, lied to, or robbed of their organs."

Dom leaned back in his chair with his hands behind his head. "So, how do I fit into this?"

Williams spoke up. "You'll be operating as a disgraced doctor, who lost his medical license for performing illegal euthanasia."

Burrows cleared his throat.

Dom spoke. "Why Canada?"

"You will be checked out. It means an extra step for them. The Cartels know that the U.S. is eager to squash the cross border trafficking. Canadians are seen as less of a threat. You haven't been licensed in seven years, and should fly under the radar. With the help of the Canadian government, we've created a new identity for you. Your team will be hired as roving transplant operatives for one of the local drug cartels, which operate near Acapulco."

Williams looked Dom straight in the eyes. "Major, you'll have to do things that may go against your morals."

Dom could see the implications clearly. "Extractions?"

"Yes. We need you to become dependable to the Pacifica Cartel. They have strong affiliations within Southern California and L.A's La Eme."

"I've heard of La Eme…a gang, right?" Dom inquired.

"We think they're one of the U.S. links to the cross border traffic, but can't prove it. What's more important, we find out where the organs are going within the U.S., and it will take some time. Your goal is to provide evidence, nothing more. We want to bust whoever is behind the American money. To solve a problem, you must get rid of it at its source…the money. We will need a paper trail…trails in blood for all I care, hard evidence from the source that will clearly implicate the U.S. perpetrators. Believe me, we know who they are, we just can't get anything on them; they're slippery,"

"Sounds like a tall order. Why me? Doesn't sound like the army's jurisdiction?"

"Find us a civilian doctor trained in combat and willing to put his life at risk for the money you make. The State Department came to us, not the other way around. You're smart, Dom, too smart for your own good. You were the only possible candidate who spoke Spanish as well as being a damned good field surgeon."

Dom smiled. "Was I the only one you could dangle a medical license in front of?"

Tom Williams grinned. "Take some time to mull it over."

Dom smiled. "General, what if I was to say no?"

Williams shrugged his shoulders. "I know you, Dom, you want back in the game. Your license is valuable and we'll reinstate it if you're successful. There are others, but no one with your credentials and ability."

Dom sat for a few moments. "General, I don't need the time."

"Somehow, I knew you wouldn't."

***

Dom passed the final checkpoint, leaving the Pentagon behind, his mind buzzing. The armed forces differed from civilian life, where you had choices. In the Army, you were ordered to do things, if you didn't, you were court marshaled, shot or in his case, put out to pasture, left to rot in some hole, waiting to be decommissioned. He could see the writing on the wall.

He'd been offered the chance to make a difference, a chance to do what he loved, and to get back into the action. What he would be asked to do might shake his beliefs to the core. He would have learn to live with what he would be required to do: to hurt people. He resolved himself to the fact that he'd need to find a higher moral ground. After all, it was for the greater good, and only for a time. He couldn't contain the grin that formed on his mouth.

CHAPTER FIVE

HERNANDO SUAREZ, NO taller than five-seven, was thin and wiry like his nickname, *The Cobra*, suggested. His hand combed a waft of his hair over his balding head. He leaned back in his favorite chair, said to have been owned by the great general, Pancho Villa, who fought in the Mexican Revolution. He glanced at the table filled with some of his favorite foods and wine, looking out over the edge of the patio to Acapulco Bay and the Pacific, which glistened in the distance. Picking up his fork, he delved into a spicy chicken casserole with egg and avocado on top.

His trusted 45 Magnum sat on the table beside his place setting. The weapon never left his side, one of life's necessities as a Cartel boss, especially for Hernando as he didn't trust anyone. He didn't eat unless his private chef Jesus or one of his bodyguards tried the food first. He liked to keep the process random.

Hernando looked across the table at his number one daughter, Carmen Suarez, and his number two, his youngest daughter Camille. They alone were the two people he trusted. When the girls were young, he'd found their mother in bed with his brother Edgar. He'd shot the two of them on the spot, the infidelity leaving a scar that would never heal, his perception of human nature forever jaded.

Hernando was the President of Pacifico Industries, which he'd formed in the sixties with his three brothers, none of whom were alive today. The drug wars would prove to be deadly, just as Edgar's infidelity. Since 9/11, due to increased scrutiny at the United States border, Pacifico did not exude the same influence as it did in the sixties, seventies, eighties and nineties. You could no longer fly into a remote landing strip and unload cargo. Now, the U.S. used advanced radar tracking and satellite surveillance, making the process of cross border trafficking much more complicated and expensive. Hernando, now eighty, and growing frail, didn't help either.

"Camille, are you feeling better? You look pale."

Camille picked at her food, dropping the fork onto her plate. "Papa, I am fine. I don't have an appetite lately." She looked down at her plate. "Don't worry about me."

"Jesus will make whatever you want."

"I know that, Papa. I'm fine. The specialist said that I have an irritable bowel. Some days, its better. Today's not a good day."

"Okay then, down to business. How are the shipments this week?"

Camille swallowed the food that was in her mouth and sat back in her chair, choosing her words carefully. "We have a plane leaving for Los Angeles twice this week."

Hernando smashed his hand down on the table; the cutlery rattled on the plates. Both Camille and Carmen sunk down slightly into their chairs. Their father's anger was quick and something to fear. "Ten years ago, we had a flight once…even twice a day?"

Camille spoke up timidly. "As you know Papa, we fight for our suppliers, and people have been distancing themselves from us…as we grow weaker. Many of our soldiers have been killed, and the Gulf Cartel infringes on our territory, threatening those that are loyal to us. Our truce with the Cineole Cartel is the only thing that's keeping the tenuous arrangement that exists." She looked her father in the eye. "We have to be very careful when we move cargo to the States. We are at the mercy of La Eme. They will only work for the highest bidder and choose when we can move. Our costs are going up. I have a meeting with Don Ricardo in Miami. I'm flying to Florida next week. He's indicated that he might be able to receive some product."

Hernando didn't acknowledge Camille's words. "We need more men."

Camille paused for a moment, picking at her food. "We are recruiting, but it's a slow process…well, since we started taking the kidneys. Those that survive bear the scar, which is now known as a branding mark of our Cartel. The men look at it shamefully."

"But it is lucrative, no?" He looked directly at his daughter.

She took a sip from her coffee. "Papa, it is. Each kidney grosses us more than $30,000 US. If the patient passes, we are able to harvest the more 'in-demand' organs. But still, I question whether this is the right direction?"

Her father cut her off. "It's not for you to question."

"Yes, Papa. We have another problem though. There's a shortage of trained medical practitioners, doctors in particular. We've been advertising through the usual channels. They don't last very long on the job. Some simply disappear. A few have been killed by the other Cartels, or they are taken into custody by the police, who we no longer have on the payroll."

Hernando frowned. "I'll speak to my friend Pablo and see if we can't fix things. He still pulls some weight."

Carmen jumped in. "Pablo is more corrupt than is even customary. You give him money, he'll be off to the Gulf Cartel asking for more in spite of you."

"You have little faith, Carmen" he smiled.

"I'm a medical doctor, I've learned not to rely upon faith. I believe in science and fact. When was the last time you gave Pablo money?"

"A month ago."

"And why?"

"It's customary."

"When is the last time you gave him money and threatened him? Have you asked him how much the Gulf Cartel is paying him?"

Carmen was the one person in Hernando's sphere of influence who would freely speak her mind. One day she would take over from him, but until then, she still needed to know her place. "Are you challenging me daughter? Don't think for a moment that I don't understand this." His face began to redden.

"I know that, Papa. I only want to reinforce the fact that we need to take matters into our own hands, more now than ever. If we show weakness, we will be eaten up. Pablo needs to know that there will be consequences for his cavalier attitude."

Hernando smiled. "You are your father's daughter."

The look of disappointment on Camille's face was not missed by Carmen. Nothing Camille could say or do could change the dominance that Hernando held over her younger sister. He was a bully and could not help but assert himself over her weaker personality. She tried to stand up for herself, but the dominance was far too engrained. It was a shame that she hadn't been married off to a Columbian Cartel, as was customary, but Hernando refused to give up his hold on the two young women. They were all he had.

CHAPTER SIX

CARLOS SLOWLY OPENED his eyes, afraid to move, the pain in his side unbearable. He let out a low moan. He laid on a small cot, which smelled of piss and sweat, still hooked up to an IV, the needle loosely stuck in his forearm. The tape, which should have held the tube tight to his arm, no longer possessed sufficient stickiness. He needed to stay very still for fear that it might fall out. It was his only lifeline to the morphine injection, which he received twice daily. The dark room held many cots similar to the one he rested on. They too, were filled with men like himself. An old sheet covered the only window and there was one light in the ceiling, a clear bulb that flickered periodically. The pain in his back was building, the nurse was due any time now; at least he hoped so.

He turned slightly to look at Hector, who lay in the cot beside him. He didn't look good and hadn't moved in over a day. His eyes were sunken, and ringed with black, his sheet pulled up to his throat. If it wasn't for the shallow rising and falling of his chest, Carlos would have thought him dead.

The door at the other side of the room opened abruptly. The male nurse Mendezes, who had aided the doctor during the procedure, entered the room. "Time for your medicine," he chortled. "If you are good, I will give you a little extra." He made his way through the room giving each patient a tablet, and some water, then an injection into the intravenous tubing.

When he arrived at Hector's cot, he shook his head. "This one no look good." He turned to Carlos. "The infection is bad, I can smell it." He flipped the sheet off Hector, revealing his side which was distended, purple, and black, with and angry incision stapled together, nearly 12 inches long. "We will know about your friend by tomorrow. If he makes it through the night…he might survive."

Mendezes took a syringe out of a plastic wrapper and filled it with a clear liquid. He then jabbed it into Hector's rump, pushing the liquid through the needle. He covered him back up.

"Some liquid gold, Carlos?" He didn't wait for an answer, adding the morphine to his drip. The relief was almost instant, his arm burning for the briefest of moments. He handed Carlos the little paper cup that held his antibiotic, and a plastic bottle of water. No words were needed. Carlos swallowed the large pill with a short sip of water.

With numb lips, Carlos asked the man, "What have you done to us? We were supposed to have checkups? Why did the doctor cut us?"

"You didn't think that your employment would be free, did you?" He chuckled. "You'll survive with one kidney, only one is needed. You are showing loyalty to your new boss, Don Hernando Suarez. Now, he will treat you with respect. Respect is important Carlos, and you have earned it."

The nurse rolled him over onto his side, and looked at his incision. "You'll be fine. The wound isn't petrifying, and the seeping has stopped. Two more days and you will be on your feet." He rolled him back over, replacing the sheet. "You're lucky this didn't happen in the street. Pacifico looks out for you; you owe the bosses."

Carlos was numb, and wanted the man to leave. *Kidney? Owe the bosses for what? Cutting him up?* He shivered as the man left the room.

Beside him, Hector stirred. Carlos said a prayer for his friend, performing a painful Hail Mary.

CHAPTER SEVEN

"DAMMIT ALAN, I'M sick of your bullshit!" Bonnie Chambers pushed her feet against the passenger side floorboard, tension creeping into the back of her scalp.

Her husband looked at her through the corner of his eye. He knew nothing he could say would make things right when she was in one of these moods. "Honey, you know I'm just as upset. Maddie's my little angel. We both love her. She's seen the best specialists that money can buy. We have to be patient." He shifted in his seat.

"Bullshit Alan. You make a lot of money, and I don't care if we end up in the poor house. If we lose her, I don't know if I can go on. I'm going to do whatever I can to help my little girl." Her eyes welled up. "You didn't have her in your stomach for nine months."

He couldn't argue that point, and it was senseless. "We've seen the best of the best. We need to wait for a donor heart, there's nothing else we can do at this point," he said calmly, trying to keep her from reaching a state of hysteria.

"That could take a year. Do we have that kind of time? I doubt it!"

He put his hand on her thigh. She brushed it off forcefully, folding her hands again on her lap. It had been two months since their only daughter Maddie, collapsed after a rowing practice. She studied at the University of Southern California, on a full rowing scholarship, on the short list for the U.S. Olympic Team. Both he and Bonnie had been living in a stress-filled, fearful hell since the incident.

Alan reflected on the first time they heard the diagnosis from Dr. Philip Klime, their family doctor. Klime, an extremely bright young doctor, in his mid-thirties, garnered their utmost respect, carefully on top of the issue from the beginning. Klime didn't enjoy having to say what needed to be said, his compassion evident in his voice and demeanor.

"Mr. and Mrs. Chambers…" He did his best to look them each in the eye, but his gaze bounced back and forth between them and his notes. "Maddie is the unfortunate owner of a congenital defect."

Bonnie sat up straight in her chair, her right knee crossed over her left leg. "Congenital, doesn't that mean we should have known about it? Isn't there something we could have done?"

Klime put up his hand. "I understand your distress. Let me explain. In some cases these defects can be detected in infancy, but the sad truth is, many are not discovered until the patients are young adults. I suspect that the stress she put on her heart rowing pushed things forward. I'll be frank, we're lucky that we still have Maddie."

Alan, in a semi trance, grabbed his wife's hand, her fingernails unconsciously digging into his palm. Tears began to trickle down her pale cheeks.

"Maddie has a ventricular septal defect, a hole in the septum, the inner wall which separates the left and the right ventricle of her heart. To make things worse, the walls of the septum are abnormally thin, and the hole cannot be closed, nor will it close on its own. Over time, the ventricle, which is made up of the heart muscle, has been stretched, not allowing the heart to pump properly, which ultimately leads to heart failure. I know that's a mouthful, but it's the reality of it. The defect is more common in females, no comfort to you I'm sure."

He hesitated, looking them both in the eyes. "I'm surprised, but sorry that the problem could not be picked up earlier. Nonetheless, we would still be at the same crossroad."

Alan spoke. "So what can we expect?"

Klime slumped into his chair slightly. "The problem is this. The extra work that's been placed on the right side of her heart has caused irreparable damage. The prognosis from Doctor Bright, her cardiologist, is that she'll be lucky to survive six to eight months, without a heart transplant."

The blood rushed from Alan's head, the room swirling as the news hit him. Bonnie became very quiet, her face devoid of any emotion.

"We've placed Maddie on the heart recipient list. Her rating is A-1, the most dire." He put his hand up before Alan could speak. "There is another complication. Her blood type is rare, and it'll make the process of finding a donor heart much more difficult. She's been placed on an intravenous drip of Dobutamine, and will be on the drug until we find a donor. She is in a private ward." He looked down at his desk briefly. "How's your medical insurance?"

Alan looked to the ceiling. "We're good."

"Great, we may be able to buy some time. There's a good team in place, and The Anderson Health Sciences Institute is the best private facility in southern California."

***

"I'm sorry Alan." Bonnie reached over and squeezed his hand as he navigated the Los Angeles rush hour. "I can't help but think back to her as a baby and a small child, the way she hums when she's happy."

Alan sighed, not knowing what else to say. "We're in this thing together, and we'll see it out together. We're lucky we still have her. We'll do whatever we can. I promise."

He reached for his wife's hand. He was doing his best to hold things together. It disturbed Alan to see his wife in such a frail emotional state, too used to her being the strong one in tough situations like this. Sure, he made a lot of money and was a tiger in the boardroom, but she was the glue of the family, whether it be for the three of them, or their extended family. Alan wasn't used her uncharacteristic vulnerability, especially when he felt he needed her strength more now than any other time in his adult life.

The drive to the Anderson Institute took roughly forty minutes from their rented apartment. Alan pulled the Bentley into the hospital parking lot. The facility was state of the art, clean lines, with ultra-modern decor. The Chambers were met in the entrance foyer by a young man dressed in a light gray business suit. "Good afternoon, Mr. and Mrs. Chambers. Welcome to the Anderson Institute. I trust that the drive was okay. The highways in L.A can be challenging, to say the least. I'm Glen Rogers and I will be your personal concierge while your daughter is with us. If I'm not here, Gwen Owens will be pleased to assist you."

Alan and Bonnie shook the young man's hand. Within ten minutes they found themselves in front of their daughter's private room. Glen placed Maddie's file folder into a holder at the side of the door. "There's a call button just inside. Press it when you're ready to leave. I'll meet you. We have a few billing options to discuss."

"No doubt," said Alan wryly.

They both looked at each other as Alan turned the door lever. Alan felt as if his own heart was in his throat.

The interior of the room was pleasantly bright and decorated to look like the bedroom of an upscale residence. All of the modern amenities were present, including a state of the art bathroom, equipped with lifts to assist patients to and from the toilet and bathtub. A 60-inch television hung in front of the plush and movable in every which way bed. The TV could be retracted into the ceiling of the room with the push of a button.

Madeline Chambers looked up at her parents, a weak smile forming on her lips. She slowly placed the Play Station controller on the side table. She looked bright, her long blond hair washed and styled. All that looked out of place was the oxygen tube under her nose, and the IV connected to her bruised right forearm.

"Mom, Dad," she said with some effort, having to catch her breath after the exertion.

Both Bonnie and Alan couldn't restrain themselves, and moved to the bedside, kissing her on the cheek, offering careful, heartfelt hugs.

Bonnie spoke first. "Maddie darling, you look good. Sorry we were a bit late. The traffic is dreadful this time of day."

"It's okay mom, they forced me to clean myself up. Don't let it fool you, I feel like shit." She cracked a quick smile. "My breathing is getting worse. The doctor says that my heart's floppy, and the muscle's no good. I guess I really did myself in."

Alan sat down in the chair next to the bed. "Maddie, it's a defect that you were born with. You didn't do yourself in. Let's look on the bright side, we're lucky you're still here, and you survived what was inevitably going to happen." He paused. "We're going to work through this."

"How the hell do we work through this?" she said. "I need a goddamned heart transplant, and the doctors say there's none available."

Bonnie interrupted. "Maddie!"

"Mom, I'll f'n swear if I want to. That's the one thing about dying, it brings things into perspective. Swearing is the only thing that makes me feel good, it's a release. Mom, everyone f'n swears."

Alan smiled, turning his face towards the window. She was his daughter.

"I'm really okay with everything. I feel worse for the two of you. Dying doesn't scare me. It is actually a very calm feeling. There is no pressure on me anymore. I don't have to get good grades. I don't need to keep up my ERG times. I can eat whatever I want, and I'm not worried about the weight. I don't want you to worry about me. Promise that you won't let my dying eat you alive." She turned her head towards Alan. "I know that you hide everything inside, I worry more about you Daddy."

"Look, you're not going to die." Alan stood up from the chair. 'We'll do whatever we can do to get you better. I won't leave one stone unturned" He wished that he believed the words as much as he was trying to sell them.

"What are you going to do, search for someone with my blood type and ask them for their heart? Come on, dad. Let's be real. I am gonna' die."

Bonnie couldn't hold it in any longer, and let out a stifled wail. Then there was silence for a minute. Their awkwardness was broken by the door opening. A man in his late fifties, with brushed back gray hair, and a hawk-like nose, entered.

Alan went to greet the man offering his hand. "Dr. Bright?"

"Mr. and Mrs. Chambers." He smiled and turned towards the bed. "Maddie, how are you feeling today?"

"Great, until mom started crying." She smiled, diffusing the tension.

"How's the breathing?"

"Not so good. I feel like I need to get just a little more with each breath, but can't. It's tiring."

He stepped up to the bed and had a look at her hand. "Are you cold?"

Maddie smiled, "If it wasn't so darned hot in here Doc, I might be."

He looked at the monitor. "Your pulse is low."

He turned back to face Alan and Bonnie. "You have a fantastically brave young lady here." He paused for a moment. "She's struggling."

Bonnie spoke. "Should we step outside?"

"I'll have none of that bullshit mom!" Maddie fought to sit up, but slumped back down into the covers. "I'm the one who's dying. If there's anything to be said. I want to be part of it.

Bright gestured towards Maddie, using her chart. "She's over 18- she has that right."

Alan nodded in agreement.

"Folks, if we don't find a heart soon, Maddie's will stop. The right side of the heart, unfortunately, lost most of its elasticity and strength. It worsens every day. I would hazard a guess that with the drugs she is receiving, and confined to bed, she might have three to five months on the outside. The chances of finding a heart with her blood type in our ward are slim. The United States is broken down into wards for donors. We might be lucky to find ten hearts with her blood type in the whole country over this time period, and they would have to be of compatible age. Unfortunately, and to make matters worse, Maddie is not the only patient in the state of California looking for such a heart."

He patted Maddie's arm. "I think we should let my patient rest for a bit. It's not good to get her heart rate up for any reason. We want her to be calm as a clam."

He turned to Bonnie and Alan. "Can I buy you a coffee?"

"Why not," Alan said, as he squeezed one of Maddie's feet.

Bonnie kissed her on the cheek. "We'll be back, sweetheart."

Maddie looked at her mother, a scowl forming. "Why did we have to go through that bullshit about me being able to hear what's going on, when you're just going to leave and talk about me anyway?"

Bright interjected. "This is a money issue, Maddie, I don't want you to stress yourself over it."

She nodded slightly. "Oh, okay, bring me a double-double."

Bright placed Maddie's chart on the end of the bed, and led them out into the hall. He looked like he was chewing something over in his mind. "Mr. Chambers." He looked Alan in the eye. "Can I talk off the record?"

"Certainly." Alan said nervously, his hands fidgeting with a pen he had picked up.

Bright paused to let a nurse pass by. "I know that you are a reasonably wealthy man or Maddie wouldn't be here. Can I call you Alan?"

Alan nodded. "Of course."

Bonnie put her arm through Alan's, grabbing his hand.

"There are other avenues."

Alan let the words hang in the air for several seconds. "What are you saying?"

"I'm saying…if you are willing to pay, there are other ways to attain what we're looking for." He put a card into Alan's free hand. "Call this man, but only if you're willing to think outside the box. He may be able to help you." He looked around the hallway. "Now…we didn't have this conversation, did we Alan?" He looked at Bonnie, her face white as a sheet. He turned and walked away from them.

Bonnie looked up into Alan's face. The expression told her all she needed to know. "Alan, you're not thinking seriously about this?"

"I'm not sure…Let's put it this way, I want to at least explore all of our options, and there aren't many. I don't want to diminish the seriousness of the situation, but I have to look at this pragmatically. Let's think of this as a business."

She frowned.

"I'd be on the phone with the man as soon as I could. It's another opportunity, that's all."

Bonnie didn't say a word. Letting go of his hand, she walked back towards Maddie's room.

Alan caught her arm. "Hey, earlier you said you'd do anything to save her. Now you're giving me a shit show over looking into some potential solutions. If you are truly willing to do anything, as you said earlier, we need to call this man."

She glared at him. "It's dirty, Alan."

"What?"

"You know. He wouldn't be dragging us out into the hall all hush-hush, if there wasn't something dirty about it."

"Okay, I see your point, and I was thinking the same thing. But

Bonnie, this kind of crap happens. People get donor organs from sources outside the U.S. all the time. Why should we be any better?" He grabbed her by the shoulders. "If I said to you, that there is a donor heart ready right now...we don't know where it's from." He paused, wanting to get the words right. "She's going to die tomorrow without it...what do you do? Let her go because of some higher moral ground? When she's dead, are you going to chastise yourself for not taking that next step?"

Bonnie grasped his hand, looking away from him. "Maybe you're right, perhaps I haven't been pushed far enough. I can't help but think that it's wrong."

"Of course, from a legal and moral perspective, it's damn wrong. Let's find out...okay? That's all."

Bonnie took a heavy breath. "I can agree to that." She turned and entered Maddie's room.

CHAPTER EIGHT

DOM LOOKED AT his lonely house. He was the quintessential bachelor. Some might call it minimalistic, he liked to think of it as practical. He'd been living the past seven years waiting for the call to duty. He hadn't for the life of him thought that it would take as long as it did. He wanted to be ready to leave on notice. The house was rented and his possessions would be stored by the military.

It hadn't been a happy home. He'd met a few nice women over the past few years, but for the most part, he'd not wanted any real relationships, for the same reasons he'd not wanted to be tied down to a home.

He'd learned enough from his first marriage, to his wife Gina. From the beginning, it hadn't been right. He'd gone ahead and married her, because it would have been too difficult to leave her at the altar. In hindsight, perhaps he should have. The unhappy union, fortunately, produced two children. For that he was forever grateful; he loved them dearly. Molly just recently turned fifteen and Richie would be eighteen in a month. The marriage ended messily, and Gina carted the children off to California, making it next to impossible to see them, once a year if he was lucky.

He wanted someone on the same page as him the next time. Could he settle if he'd met the right person? Dom sighed deeply. Would it bring him happiness? Sadly enough, he'd grown used to living alone. He rationalized his existence using the typical clichés. He didn't like shackles; he didn't want the pressure of having to worry about someone at home should something happen to him; bad enough having two children who lived on the other side of the country.

The mission ahead of him would be dangerous…and exciting. Yes, he would admit it. As much as he wanted his medical license reinstated, his adrenaline now flowed with the anticipation of the game, a game that could be a deadly diversion to what had become a boring existence.

He carefully laid out his clothes. He folded and stowed them into a large hard-shelled suitcase, tucking a picture of his kids on top.

Dom heard a knock on the front door. He looked out the front window and saw a black Tahoe sitting at the curb. A young officer saluted as Dom answered the knock.

"Major Tavano, I'm here to take you to the airport, sir."

Dom saluted the young man. "At ease, Lieutenant."

"Let me get your bag, sir."

***

The flight from Washington to Montreal passed by quickly. He sat in the squishy charter seat and leafed through the mission dossier, given to him earlier in the day at the Pentagon. He'd never been commissioned for a covert operation and wanted to be clear on all of the details.

Dom's new identity would be that of Dr. Dominic Chavez of Montreal, a doctor whose medical license was under suspension for malpractice, illegal euthanasia to be specific. General Williams indicated that Canadian Intelligence had been preparing an identity for several years for this purpose, including the implantation of fake backstory in the local papers, and their archives. The Canadian College of Physicians and Surgeons assisted in the process, and made the necessary changes to public records and documentation, making sure that Doctor Dominic Chavez existed, and was indeed under suspension, his records present in the Canadian Directory of Physicians. He would meet Captain Chantal Turcotte at the airport. She would be his wife and medical assistant. Dom raised his eyebrows. Captain Chantal Turcotte saw active combat duty in Afghanistan, with two citations, and was a trained operating room nurse.

He and Chantal would spend two weeks in Montreal getting to know each other. They would be briefed on current transplant protocol. Spending some time with the woman seemed like a wise idea; their relationship would need to appear flawless.

After two weeks, they were to take a direct flight to Guadalajara, where they would meet with Major Bachman, and the United Nations Liaison Dr. DeRosnay, who he'd met during his interview at the Pentagon. From there, they would travel to Acapulco – Game on.

***

As he came down the escalator into the vast reception lounge at Pierre-Elliot Trudeau International, he instantly recognized Chantal from her dossier photo. The military photo made her look rather punkish and butch. The woman who greeted him at the bottom of the escalator appeared to be neither. Though on the short side, Captain Turcotte, wearing a very fashionable dress, looked quite attractive in an athletic way, not your prototypical model. She was more…cute, with shoulder length brown hair. As he neared the bottom of the escalator, her dark brown, nearly black eyes pierced him as they met his, he felt his heart skip. *Really?* She quickly looked to the ground, avoiding his gaze. So this would be his wife for the foreseeable future? He suppressed the urge to grin.

As he stepped off the ramp, he put his arm around her waist lifting her slightly, and kissed her upon the lips. "Enchante Chantal." He could tell that she wanted to squirm away from his clutch, like a wiggly worm.

He let her escape. Though she didn't make her intentions look obvious it was made clear to him that he needed to let her escape his embrace. She put her hands behind his head and pulled her mouth up to his ear, speaking in French. "Try that again Mon Cher, I will cut your balls off." She kissed him on the cheek.

He smiled coyly, any flirtatious intentions instantly deflated. "I trust that you can remember where you parked the car honey. I'm tired, and need a drink."

Chantal ushered him through the throng of people that mobbed the reception area. They retrieved Dom's suitcase from the baggage claim, and in no time were traversing the aggressive Montreal traffic. Chantal appeared to be an excellent driver, which pleased Dom. He didn't particularly like driving.

"Major Tavano."

Dom corrected her. "Chavez. Dominic Chavez, though I think it would be appropriate to call me Dom."

"Of course," she said, her voice wavering slightly. "Dom." She let his name hang in the air for a second. Her French was abrupt, with some slang not familiar to him, but he understood her meaning well enough. "Dom, I don't want there to any confusion as to our roles in this. I pride myself on my professionalism. You are a Major, I'm a Captain. We need to maintain this relationship."

Dom smiled, a playful grin. "Captain Turcotte. That may be tough when we're in full cover. The moment I stepped off that plane, our mission began. Our names are being checked out by the Mexicans, and the medical conglomerates. I'd not be surprised that we're under surveillance. I've been told by my superiors that we're to meet with Pacifico Cartel when we arrive in Acapulco. There's no guarantee that we will be hired, but I'm told that medical practitioners, doctors in particular, are in demand. Once our interview was set up, you can take it to the bank that we were being watched and checked out. We're supposed to be married, and I think that the kiss was appropriate, if that is what you're getting at?"

"Dom…I–"

"Don't worry…Can I call you Chantal?"

"Oui."

"Now we're making some headway. We'll be spending a lot of time together over the next few months. In private, I expect nothing but professionalism. In public we're a well-oiled team. We've been married for ten years, so we don't need to appear lovey-dovey. There can be some tension. Money could be getting tight, with my license being suspended. On the other hand, I'd been away for a week, and I was happy to see you. This is normal. Are we on the same page?"

She swallowed hard. "Yes, Major."

Dom smiled. "When we get home, wherever that is, we'll need to work hard on brushing up our extraction and transplant procedures. General Williams assured me that we'll be getting expert instruction. A Dr. Greenman will be our liaison."

She gave him a quick look, running her hand along her thigh. "Have you done this before?"

"This?"

"This type of surgery?"

"As a combat surgeon, I've removed every part of the body that the body can sustain after its removal. I might say, with a high degree of success."

"High degree of success? You're not giving me a good feeling, Major. I was told you were an expert…tops in your field."

"We're talking combat, Chantal. Not everyone can be saved."

Her face turned ashen. "Have you ever performed a transplant?"

"He smiled again, "Absolutely! The lifestyle of a soldier is hard on the liver and kidneys. Many vets become raging alcoholics after their discharge – post trauma stress. At the Veterans Hospital, I oversaw dozens of kidney and partial liver procedures."

"Oversaw…?"

"Of course. I've only just reacquired my medical license this past week. I've been a teaching doctor for the past seven years at the Uniformed Services University."

"Tabernac. Why did you lose your license?" Her grip tightened on the wheel.

He turned to stare at her. His smile was now replaced with a more serious look. "I understand what you're thinking. I am a little out of practice, but I'm an excellent surgeon. I have fifteen years' worth of recommendations for exemplary work under fire. I can't remember how many lives of young soldiers I've saved. You've got to believe me when I tell you, I'm a damn good doctor!"

"Talk is cheap, you didn't answer my question." Her stare judging.

Dom paused. "Okay, it's a sore spot with me. I guess I'll tell you…I want you to trust me."

"You don't need to keep saying the word *trust*. This isn't about *trust*, it's about doing our goddamned jobs."

Dom frowned, unaccustomed to being interrogated, and he didn't know whether he liked it or not, but still he continued. "I was stationed with NATO, as commander of Medical Field Services in Iraq. We were traveling with the British 6th Regiment. There was a Left Tenant Colonel, named Fields, Gregory Fields….pompous asshole. I made no bones about letting him know of my dislike for him. Unfortunately, there were others who knew of the disdain I felt for the man. I'm one that likes to tell you what I'm thinking, and this guy got under my skin. Fields took it upon himself to make life miserable for me, as well as my staff. The tension was thick whenever the two of us were in the same room. He called me a maverick, I can hear his snooty up your ass British accent as if it were yesterday."

Dom did his best to replicate the man's accent, which finally brought a smile to the corner of Chantal's mouth. "The forces have no need for your type. Major. You are a rascal and a maverick. I shall see you out at the soonest convenience."

He let a smile return to his face. "The boys called me Maverick after that, which only fed the man's hard-on for me. Anyway, we're in the same Humvee one day, heading to a NATO briefing, when the truck hits a land mine. It blows the Hummer into rat shit, the place becomes ground zero. The driver is killed instantly, as well as one of the soldiers accompanying us. I'm not badly hurt except for a cracked rib, and the concussion from the bomb left me deafer than a doorknob. You'll appreciate this. I have no field kit…nothing. I'm an officer on the way to a meeting. The other vehicles in the convoy have also hit mines, and are under guerrilla fire.

"Fields and his attendant, a nice young man, are nowhere to be seen at first glance, but then my hearing starts kicking back in, and I can detect a deep moaning. The kind of moaning only a soldier would understand. I run around the other side of the Hummer, and there I see the two men. Fields is missing both his legs and is being burnt alive by the gasoline, which emptied in a steady stream from the vehicle's tank. His attendant is in no better shape.

"Chantal, they were screaming, bleeding…frying. I can vividly remember the look on Fields face, he was pleading with me through his eyes. I hate to see anyone suffer, and at that point, I could only think of one humane thing to do. I still wake up in the middle of the night, their faces etched in my dreams. True enough, I didn't like the guy, but no one should have to die like that. I couldn't put my hands on their bodies to save them, I would have burned myself… it was that bad. I took out my pistol and planted a bullet in each of their foreheads.

"Unfortunately, the act was seen by a returning British Hummer. I was put on trial, and if it wasn't for my good friend, General Tom Williams, I would have been court marshaled instead of being put out to pasture in Bethesda."

Dom met her eyes briefly as she turned to stare at him. "Good enough?"

"Okay, you have me leaning in your direction," she said, and her eyes softened. "Dom…that is terrible. I might have done the same."

***

Dom and Chantal spent the next few weeks in a flat just off St. Catharine's Street, Montreal's main thoroughfare. The Canadian Security Intelligence Service used the apartment as a special needs location, the deeds changed eight months prior to reflect that it was owned by Mrs. C. Chavez. Dom hadn't been assigned the mission at that time, but Chantal had been put in place some time ago, to help consolidate the paper trail with whoever her partner would be.

Dom woke the first morning on the chesterfield, the sun blaring through the floor to ceiling windows of the modern apartment. He'd finished off the better part of two bottles of fine red wine, which he and Chantal bought before arriving at the flat. His head ached, and he needed water badly. He heard the rapping on the door again. Yes, that was what woke him, the door. Chantal was upstairs in the lone bedroom and must not have been able to hear the banging.

He stumbled across the hardwood floor and unbolted the heavy oak portal. Standing in front of him were two men. One in a gray suit. He remembered Major Bachman from his initial meeting at the Pentagon. The other man appeared to be in his sixties, dressed in jeans and a tee shirt, his long gray hair pulled back into a ponytail.

Bachman spoke first. "Dr. Tavano."

Dom looked at his watch, *8 am*. "A bit early don't you think?" he said, scratching the back of his head, resisting the urge to do the same to his crotch.

"I'm Major Chris Bach–"

Dom couldn't help himself, cutting the man off. "Major Bachman. We spoke the other day at the Pentagon. My memory isn't that short."

Bachman frowned. "This is Dr. Harvey Greenman, from McGill University Health Center."

Dom extended his hand. "Dr. Greenman."

Bachman interjected. "I am here to brief you on your mission, and Dr. Greenman will be providing expert knowledge regarding organ transfer protocol."

Dom couldn't help but think that Bachman seemed to be trying too hard.

Greenman cut him off. "I can speak for myself Mr. Bachman." He extended his hand to Dom. "Pleasure to meet you Dr. Tavano. I'll tell you. I wish it was me going in your place. I have strong thoughts regarding the organ trade. But we can talk about that at another time. I am here to assess your knowledge, technical skill, and hopefully bring you up to date on the newest trends in organ transplantation. May I call you Dominic?"

"Dom, please…come in."

Chantal appeared at his side. She must have been there for some time without him realizing. The large loft apartment featured one very high ceilinged room, with second floor master and en-suite, open to below. The walls were whitewashed, and adorned with pieces of modern and early 20th century French Canadian artwork.

Greenman nodded, eyeing some of the pieces. "Dom, during your mission, I'll have a private phone set up for your calls and texts. If I am not available, my associate Dr. Stephen Heyes, who you will meet tomorrow, will be available to answer any of your technical questions 24/7. If you will excuse me, I have some literature and video to set up."

Bachman cleared his throat and Greenman nodded. "I think Mr. Bachman wants an hour of your time for briefing, and then you'll have the pleasure of having the remainder of the next few days with me." He shuffled off into the loft.

Dom couldn't help but like the man. He possessed an infectious twinkle in his eye.

Bachman gestured towards the dining room table. Once Dom, Chantal and he were seated, the dour man didn't waste any time. "I trust that you've reviewed your dossiers? They provide all of the basic information you'll require, and I'd recommend that you keep them in a safe place." He shuffled a few more papers around. "I'm here to provide you with the newest intel." He placed a number photographs in front of them.

Chantal interjected. "Is it safe for you to be here? Have you been followed?"

"Captain Turcotte, I assure you that this is less risky than taking you to another location. We're careful, and I'll leave it at that."

She looked at him skeptically.

He returned his attention to the dossier on the table. "Your objective is to provide proof of the link between the Pacifico Cartel and the U.S. medical system. Let me be clear." He placed both hands on the table. "Though the State Department would like to break the back of the Mexican Drug Cartels, this is not our intention at this point. We don't want you to engage the Mexicans in any way, other than to gather information. Our goal is to cut off the flow of money to the Cartels, by busting whoever is behind the U.S. domestic operation. That's it. Even if we can get something on one of them, it would be a win as far as the Department is concerned. We have our eyes on several of them; Sun Medical in particular is linked to The Pacifico Cartel."

Dom placed his hand on the table. "We're not to engage the Mexicans? May I ask why you've recruited two medical practitioners with military background?"

Bachman hesitated. "I'll be truthful. You're not the first team that we've sent in. You'll be entering a hostile environment. We want to ensure that the intel you do obtain gets out of Mexico. The last team, with nonmilitary backgrounds, were intercepted crossing the Mexican border. All that we found were their heads in a Tijuana garbage dumpster. We're sending the two of you in because we believe that you will have a better than good chance of returning."

Dom couldn't help but ask, "What do you classify as engagement?"

"When I say that we don't want you to engage, I don't want to infer that you shouldn't protect yourselves."

Chantal's cheeks began to redden. "Would you like some coffee?"

Both Dom and Bachman nodded in unison.

Before she left, she added, "Did the Cartel find out that the U.S. Government sponsored the last mission?"

"We're not sure. If you're concerned that we might be sending you into a blown cover, you can rest your fears. We've set up an interview for you, as you know, with an organization known as the Pacifico Cartel. We've had little contact with them over the years. They used to be bigger players, but their boss, Don Hernando Suarez, better known in Mexico as 'the Cobra,' is getting on in age, and delegates a lot of the responsibility to his daughter Carmen, who in fact is a doctor. Second to Carmen is his younger daughter Camille. The last incursion involved the Gulf Cartel, who are adversaries of the Pacifico Cartel. You'll be okay."

Chantal nodded and left the room to make the coffee. She didn't like how the man simply took things for granted. It seemed sloppy to her, like they were an afterthought. *You will be okay* wasn't good enough for her.

She returned a few minutes later with a tray filled with bagels and three steaming cups.

Bachman jumped right back in where he'd left off. "On your arrival, you're to confirm a meeting with Carmen Suarez. She'll be expecting it. I'll brief you on the correspondence we've experienced to date on your behalf. The organ trade is big business, but the medical practitioners that are required to perform the needed procedures are becoming difficult to find."

He shuffled some pictures around on the table. "The pay is extremely good, but the work is dangerous. The Mexican police will back whichever Cartel pays them the most. There's been increased raiding by the Federales, and if a medical practitioner is caught, imprisonment is guaranteed. A rival Cartel's doctor is fair game. Many have been killed in the crossfire."

Chantal took a sip from her mug, then pinned Bachman with her gaze. "I get the feeling that you're glossing things over, Major Bachman. Are you throwing us to the sharks?"

Bachman's expression didn't change. "The decision to send you in was made by our military superiors. It's not my concern; I'm here to make sure you have the required intelligence."

"Nice," quipped Chantal.

He stirred some milk into his coffee and continued. "Another consideration is the fact that the process is deemed immoral, and it is hard to find many medical practitioners that are willing to execute the work. You'll not be looked at in high esteem by your benefactors – Pacifico Cartel. They understand how you are viewed within the medical community, and they will play on this negativity, using it to their advantage. The system is filled with rogue physicians, most without a license; bad doctors doing what they have to do to earn a buck."

"You paint a grim picture." Dom took a sip from his coffee. "Will our cover hold water?"

"The backstory should be sufficient, but you'll have to sell yourself. They'll be suspicious, but they need people to do the job. If you don't create problems you'll get paid. If you do a good job for them, hopefully they'll pull you in closer. That's what we want. Look, you're a corrupt doctor that needs a buck, end of story. That's all they want, and they don't really care if you're lying. If you cross them though, they'll simply kill you, and move on to the next medical practitioner."

Dom raised his eyebrows. "I see."

"There's no better way to describe it than it's a tough posting. The players are corrupt, the public officials are corrupt. The system here in the states is corrupt." He pushed some photos in front of

Dom and Chantal. "These are the principals of the Pacifico Cartel," he indicated the members of the Suarez family. "We have a pretty good idea where the flow of cash is coming from, but we can't prove anything. We're hoping that you'll be able to get close enough to the Suarezs to verify who their U.S. connections are. It could take time, so be patient."

He pointed to another picture. "This is Doctor Richard Brice, head of Sun Medical. Sun Med runs seven major private hospitals in the States. If we can acquire evidence that they are performing transplants with illegal organs, we are one step closer to finding out who the players are, one more rung up on the ladder."

"Government officials?"

"Yes, we believe there is a hierarchy which finds its roots at the lowest levels; public officials like coroners and record keepers. The list goes on, all the way up to Washington."

"That's it?" asked Dom.

"Basically. You'll be renting a house on the outskirts of Acapulco. We've set up a Mexican bank account, and you will be provided with the medical equipment necessary to do your work. The Cartels vary in their handling of medical locations. Usually the operating rooms will be provided for you, but the conditions will be bad. You'll need your own scrubs, and operating tools, scalpels, and hemostats, etcetera. Like I said, we'll make sure that you have them."

He looked at Dom. "I hear you were chosen because you're good at thinking on your feet?"

Dom pondered the comment for a moment. "That's what they say. Is this the first time the military's been involved?"

"That's classified information."

"That's okay, you've answered my question. I'm becoming a little skeptical that we're not just a stop gap to keep someone up above us…happy."

Bachman's cheeks reddened. "The CIA has been trying to crack the Mexican mobs for years. They've never been successful at getting a qualified practitioner like yourself into position. This is why Central Intelligence contacted Military intelligence. The process needed a real doctor. For a number of reasons, your name came up top of the list."

"Yeah, I'm the only one you can dangle a license in front of." He paused, then continued. "What backup do we have? Let's say the shit hits the fan, and Chantal and I are in a bad spot?" He slapped his hand down on the table.

"The Mexican government is not willing to admit that the situation exists within its borders, and don't know anything about your mission. This of course doesn't give us the benefit of any real military backup. We do have operatives who will be following your moves, including myself. We can remove you from a hot spot, but we can't promise any direct intervention. The optics would be bad if a connection was made to the U.N. or the U.S. government. You'll be on your own once you're remote. We'll be installing a microchip under the surface of your skin. We'll know where you are at all times."

Dom smirked, sipping his coffee. "Well, that makes me feel a whole hell of a lot better. Glorified body tags."

Bachman didn't respond to the quip. "Here's your new passports, medical licenses, even though they have been revoked, they may still want to see them. We have plane tickets and banking particulars. In your case Major, your notice of revocation." He placed three smart phones on the table. "One is to be used for your affairs as Dr. Dominick Chavez. Mrs. Chavez, we have one for you as well. A third is to be used only in case of an emergency. Leave instructions as to where you will need a pickup, and an extraction will be ordered. All you need to do is turn on the phone and dial the only preprogrammed number on it. Then destroy the phone."

Bachman looked at each of them. "Questions?"

Chantal spoke. "Will we be equipped with side arms? No matter how docile you might want us to be, I for one will not feel comfortable going into this unprotected."

"You will find them in your residence. Their location will be sent to you by text."

Dom folded his hands on his lap. "This is all very ambiguous."

"You have a lot at stake Dr. Tavano, as do we, but it's the best we can do at this point. The Cartels don't try to make things easy for us. We have you covered, and as long as you do a good job for Pacifico, and don't make things any more complicated than need be, I think that you will be fine. We'll know where you are at all times. Use the third phone if you're in trouble."

Dom furrowed his brow. "What do you mean by keeping things less complicated?"

Bachman chose his words. "Do your job, and let the information come to you. Don't try to force anything. You must gain their trust, then hopefully you will become privy to more information. I know that you don't want to be there any longer than you have to, but you need to remain patient. This could take a year, or more."

Dom rolled his eyes. "Great." Patience wasn't one of Dom's better virtues.

Bachman stood to leave. "General Williams has great faith in you Major, otherwise, he wouldn't have chosen you for this mission. Dr. Greenman, I'll leave you to your work." Bachman let himself out through the flat's large wooden door, pulling it shut behind him with a slight click of the locking mechanism.

Once again, Dom wondered if his promotion had more to do with circumstance than his abilities. He intended to do a standup job. If he was to have to do things that would play havoc with his morals, he wanted to make sure that the mission was legitimate, not some dog and pony show. His hackles went off as Bachman left the flat. It was as if the man couldn't get out quickly enough.

***

Greenman made his way back into the dining area, carrying an armload of books, which he'd gone back outside to retrieve. "Dom, Chantal, I would like you to call me Harvey. I promise you that the next few days will be a hell of a lot less indicting than what you just experienced with Mr. Bachman. The suits must do their jobs."

"No doubt," said Dom.

"I'd like to begin with a review of the common organs you will be dealing with, their chemistry, and related functions. I hope this won't bore you Dom, but it is just as important that Chantal understands the process. Your obligation will be to help those whom you will be operating on to survive, and you will need her help to do so."

"On the contrary, I would've suggested this myself. We don't want any hesitancy with what we're getting ourselves into."

Over the remainder of the day, Harvey gave Dom and Chantal a crash course on organ extraction, conditions for transport, and a brief overview of transplantation practices. Harvey at one point noted, "Dom, we must be able to fix that which we undo, to better understand the process. Growing up in Montreal, I will use this analogy. A hockey player must learn to skate backwards, in order to skate better forwards."

Chantal smiled. "I'm starving. Anyone hungry?" Lunch earlier in the day consisted of half a small chicken, some semi stale bread, and Gouda cheese.

Harvey was first to answer. "Good call. I don't think I could take any more stale bread though. I think we've gone over enough for today. You seem to have a good grip on things Dom?"

"I do. I've watched the procedure a hundred times over the past few years. I wanted Chantal to get a better understanding. Perhaps we can concentrate on the pharmacology over the next couple of days. I'm sure that there's some cutting edge drugs that we don't get to see in the army."

"And you won't see them where you're going. I think you'll have to settle for low cost, low level drugs. Anti-inflammatory and antibiotics will be your mainstay. Aspirin to prevent clotting. You won't find Lovenox, or Xarelto in these ghettos, maybe Warfarin if you're lucky. I hear that there are a lot of rats in Acapulco."

He patted his tummy. "There's a really good gourmet pizza place just around the corner, not your typical pie. You'll love it. We'll grab a few bottles of red wine."

Chantal raised her eyebrows. "I know the place. You're right, it's good. I've eaten there quite a few times. I don't mind taking the walk to pick it up."

While Chantal was gone, Harvey encouraged Dom to sit down on the couch. "Can I ask a few difficult questions, Dom?"

Dom nodded, undoing the top button on his shirt. "Sure, why not."

"Why are you doing this?" His forehead scrunched up into a big wrinkle, his eyes probing him. "You're going to have to do things to innocent people for the benefit of others, things that will hurt them. Though you will be working for the greater good, you'll be put into situations that will shake your morals. To take one of two healthy kidneys from a donor, though it may be morally corrupt, the patient will live. What if you're asked to remove a heart, or liver? Will you be able to do this? What if the patient isn't dead?"

Dom pondered the question as he walked into the kitchen to get a bottle of wine. "I'm a soldier Harvey. I have to follow my orders. Maybe that's why they've commissioned me for the posting. As I see it, I really didn't have a choice in the matter. As an officer, we're conditioned to the fact that there will be collateral damage in war. I think that what we're going to be doing is fighting a war of sorts. We don't have to like what we do, but if we fail, the problem will still exist."

"I'll call you on that bullshit, doctor. What if one of your patients dies? You'll have in effect caused the termination of life. Life is what we've been trained to protect and nourish. You're just flashing the military M.O, I don't believe what you say for a moment."

Dom lowered his head. "Be thankful that you've never gone

to war. I've seen things that have made my skin crawl, things that have given me nightmares, and the sweats. I think that I've seen enough death to be able to deal with it at this level." He poured out three glasses.

"To use a psych term, you're compartmentalizing. You're using coping devices given to you by the military, so that they don't have to send you to therapy for the rest of your life. You military doctors are thrown into a lot of tricky situations."

"We are, but we don't have to deal with our patients, at least those that we treat on the battlefield for a prolonged period of time. I couldn't handle being a G.P. You get to know people after a time. You see some of the crap that happens to families, like young children dying of cancer. Couldn't handle that. Perhaps you're right. Maybe for those reasons that you speak, I might be the correct choice for the mission. I plan on writing it all off for the greater good." He lowered his head for a minute then raised his eyes to meet Harvey's. "I'm not happy about what I'm going to have to do."

"I think I believe you Dom. I hope you're the man for this job. I'm starting to feel that you might be."

"I've been in this gig long enough to know that you have to jump in feet first before you know what your reality will be. I might be alright, or it might mess with my head. I appreciate the concern, Harvey."

"Promise me that you'll get out if you feel the need. I think you'll know when that time arrives."

"We'll see. It'll have to get pretty bad before I'd bail. We're raised tough in Brooklyn. I've been fighting since kindergarten."

Harvey laughed. "Let's get you doing some cutting tomorrow. I want to see how you handle a scalpel."

"No worries there Doc."

Chantal returned with their food. "Bon appetite Mon chere's," she said, bustling through the door.

Once they were settled, having eaten a few slices, Harvey addressed

Chantal. "Dom and I have been talking. Some of the things you're going to have to do will not be easy, far from it. The two of you will have to lean on each other. There will be no support group…you will be on your own. I want you to keep an eye on Dom, and vice versa." He turned his gaze to Dom.

Chantal nodded. "I've been thinking the same thing. We'll manage." She looked at Dom. "I think the Doctor possesses what it will take, at least I'm starting to think so." She grinned.

Harvey left them after he'd eaten another piece of the fabulous pizza. "We'll see you at the University Hospital tomorrow at 8 o'clock. The pathology department."

***

Dom and Chantal sat in the living room finishing off the dregs of a bottle of red wine.

"So, Dr. Tav…Chavez. Are you going to be able to pull this off? If you screw up, I don't want to become shark food. I hear that's what Don Suarez prefers to do with his enemies."

Dom reclined on the couch, placing his hands behind his head. "I'm feeling reasonably confident. I'm more concerned with you. Will you be able to handle the workload of two nurses in a compromised environment?"

She didn't respond to the comment and there was an awkward silence for a few minutes.

"It's been a long day Mrs. Chavez, I think it's time for bed."

Chantal stood up. "I'll throw down a blanket and a pillow from the loft. The couch is comfortable." She became quite serious, her smile gone, her words sharp.

"But Mrs. Chavez, we must keep up appearances." He resisted the urge to smile.

"I draw the line at the bottom of those steps, you cross it, we'll be looking for a new Dr. Chavez."

He followed her eyes across the huge loft apartment, to the spiral staircase that led to the loft bedroom. "Have it your way...dear. I hear that our apartment in Mexico will not have the luxury of this much room."

She stuck her nose in the air in pretend indignation, and stomped up the steps.

***

Chantal and Dom met Harvey at the McGill University Health Center, a state of the art hospital, just before 8 am.

Harvey looked chipper, and he handed them each a Tim Horton's coffee. "I'm not sure what you take. There's cream and sugar in the bag. Did you sleep well?"

"Not bad, I woke up every hour on the hour though." Dom took a sip from his coffee. "Who's Tim Horton?"

Harvey chuckled. "A hockey player, started a doughnut and coffee franchise back in the seventies. It's a Canadian institution now."

Dom nodded, taking another sip. "It's really nothing special."

"It's convenient. You can't drive through any Canadian town or city without finding one." Harvey placed a hand on Dom's back and ushered them though a set of double doors. "Dom, we're fortunate, we have a live kidney donor this morning, a sister who is willing to give up one of hers for the benefit of her sibling who's in need. I've arranged for you to assist Dr. LaPierre in the extraction and transplant."

Chantal and Dom looked each other in the eye. "Excellent. I wasn't thrilled about having to practice on cadavers." He rubbed his hands together. "There is nothing like the flow of real blood to revive your instincts."

Harvey chuckled, "I'm glad you see it this way...I thought you would."

CHAPTER NINE

Acapulco, Mexico, 1953

HERNANDO SUAREZ SAT in the dusty coffee house with his two brothers, Franco and Davide. Acapulco in the fifties began to see the improvements that modern tourism would bring. The seaside town was blessed with a beautiful bay and rich tourists from places like Los Angeles, New York and Mexico City. It would be common to see the likes of John Wayne, Elizabeth Taylor, or Frank Sinatra walking the strip. Where there was money, there was business, sometimes dark business.

The Suarez brothers made a name for themselves as providers of things that you were not supposed to have, namely drugs and prostitutes. They rose to the top of the Acapulco crime scene, with a reputation for being ruthless. Hernando became known as "The Cobra," due to his reputation for quickly dealing vengeance upon an enemy.

It was particularly hot today, and the late day sea breeze that would blow in from the Pacific chose not bless the town's inhabitants with its presence yet. Hernando could feel the sweat rolling down his back. He turned to Davide, who was the enforcer. "The truck is late." They were waiting for a shipment of cocaine coming from Guatemala, via what was called the "South Road." The route was renowned as a location for conflict between rival drug lords, who strove to control the main route from South and Central America into Mexico.

Davide shrugged. He wasn't much for words, and when he spoke it was with a pronounced lisp, caused by a ten-inch scar that ran from his chin over his left eye socket and on into his forehead, the byproduct of a close call with a machete.

Franco, the smallest of the three men, took care of the numbers, the day to day accounting of their illicit businesses. He slowly sipped his coffee. "Our boys are watching the road. Julio is supposed to be following the truck up from the border. I'd give them another hour. There's always the chance they were delayed by Federales."

Hernando pinned Franco with his stare. "Did you pay them?"

"Of course. But you never know when you are…outbid. They will take from both, and never tell you who the winner is."

Hernando's feet shot out abruptly from under the small table in anger. "That truck is worth all the pesos we've earned in the past three months. There will be blood to pay if this is messed up." He downed his coffee in one long sip.

Davide and Franco were silent. They knew better than to feed their older brother's foul moods.

***

It was ten minutes later that one of their men, Renaldo, a thin older man in his mid-sixties, appeared through the throng of people that filled the market square. He was one of their most trusted soldiers. Davide offered him his seat. Renaldo took off his hat, and flopped into the chair. Hernando immediately noticed the gunshot wound to the man's shoulder, dark red blood stained his brown shirt. Hernando's face became pure fury, his mouth squishing into a tiny oval, his brow pulled tight into a knot, his face beet red. The Pacifico boss's voice was eerily calm as he spoke. "Federales?"

Renaldo looked afraid to answer, his eyes pasted to the dirt floor. "Non, Señor."

"Who then? The Gonzalez?"

"Non Señor…Mendoza."

"Hernando cursed lowly, just over his breath. "Fucking Mendoza. We should have dealt with them earlier. They have become brazen."

"I hide in a pile of rock after we were attacked. All our men are dead, except…me Señor. I'm so sorry. They don't know I live. They think their work has gone unseen Señor."

Hernando placed a hand on Renaldo's shoulder as he stood. "You are a loyal servant Renaldo, and it will not be forgotten. You've paid in blood."

The man smiled over the top of a pain-riddled grimace.

Hernando turned to Davide. "Assemble our men. We'll teach the Mendoza some manners." He turned back to Renaldo. "The Federales?"

"Only at the border, Señor. They took our pesos, and asked no questions."

***

With an hour of sunlight left, the Suarez family and its soldiers went to war.

The Mendoza hacienda lay 15 miles outside the northern edge of the town. The stronghold consisted of low squat central buildings, with clay tile roofs, surrounded by a tall wall made of red clay bricks. The inner courtyard took up roughly an acre of land, the ground composed mostly of dry and dusty dirt. In the middle stood a larger central building and courtyard with clay interlocking brick, and a well.

The Suarez soldiers crawled on their bellies to surround the

Hacienda's outer wall. They dragged crude ladders behind them. Hernando and Davide pulled up in front of the main gate, which was manned by two men, with bandoleers, large sombreros, and Winchester rifles. The Suarez brothers smoothly slid out of their newly purchased 1952 ford pickup, and walked up to the entrance, two pistols in the back of their belts each, so that they were not visible to the guards.

They stopped ten feet in front of the men. Hernando could see the large green Suarez produce truck just inside the gate, next to a small clay building. The two men leveled their rifles at them.

"Señor. I am Don Hernando Suarez of the Pacifico Cartel." The brothers had never officially used the Cartel's name before, but Hernando felt that it an appropriate time to introduce it.

One of the men replied, with a nervous look over at his come padre. "We know who you are Señor Suarez. It would be best that you left now." Sweat beaded down his face.

Hernando smiled broadly, his near perfect teeth filling the bottom of his face. "I've come to talk to Don Diego Mendoza. Please let him know that I'm here." He knew Mendoza, ten years his senior, and in the past, Hernando enjoyed his company in many of Acapulco's finest nightclubs. But, where there were drugs and lots of money, there would be no loyalty.

Diego Mendoza must have been aware of the pickup truck's approach, as he appeared from the front door of one of the closest buildings. Diego stood a head taller than Hernando, a handsome man, with sharp features, and salt and pepper colored hair. He spread his arms out wide. "Hernando, what gives us the pleasure of your visit? I hope you come in friendship?"

His eyes stared directly into Hernando's without the slightest blink, not registering the truck with Suarez boldly emblazoned on its side 20 feet to his right. He clasped his hands in front of his belt buckle, then offered one to Hernando.

Hernando stood his ground, looking at the reddening sky in

thought. *The fucker offers his hand to me with my stolen truck standing beside us.* "Why of course Diego. We've been good friends for some time now, what is it, ten years? But there is some business yet to be discussed."

The smile left Diego Mendoza's face.

Hernando moved forward to extend his hand as was customary, even between rivals.

"Diego met him halfway. Mi cassia esta…"

He didn't finish the sentence, caught off guard by Hernando, who intentionally missed the handshake and pressed the trigger of the hidden stiletto knife taped to his wrist. He jammed the seven-inch blade into Diego's belly. The man howled in shock, the knife coated in fresh garlic, which delayed the onset of pain. Hernando pulled the knife abruptly upwards, slicing Diego's insides, then let the man drop to the ground.

The two guards were stunned by the swiftness of the act and froze, mouths open in shock. The hesitation cost them their lives, as Davide blew a hole in each of their heads with two clean shots from his long barreled revolvers.

Within moments, a dozen men poured out into the courtyard from various buildings, but were cut down by the Suarez soldiers who had scaled the undefended walls. The gunfight lasted no more than a minute. Hernando ordered the houses to be quickly scoured. Several men were rounded up, as well as three women, one of whom Hernando recognized as Diego's wife. He assumed the other two were his daughters. All three were clutched together in real terror.

Hernando looked down at Mendoza's pain filled pitiful face, then at the women. He spoke to Davide. "Take them away. We can sell them in Bogota for a nice profit." He looked down at Diego. "Your women will become whores for your act of friendship today, Diego Mendoza."

The women screamed and clawed at the men, who took them away into the impending darkness of the evening.

"Your remaining time my friend, will be used to teach an important lesson to your men." He grabbed Mendoza by the hair, and dragged him to the pickup. He and the four remaining men were tied up and thrown indignantly into the back of the pickup.

Hernando motioned to his men to go ahead and loot the hacienda, and to retrieve the produce truck and its valuable goods.

***

Davide rowed the long fishing skiff out into the middle of Acapulco bay. Darkness hid the craft from the view of anyone who might be interested in looking. The bay was full of similar moored fishing boats, the long rowboat wasn't noticed.

Hernando looked down at the five men, who lay in the bottom of the craft, gagged and tied. He grabbed one of them by the shoulders, and with more strength than the wiry man looked to have, shoved the prisoner halfway over the gunnels. The man didn't have a chance to struggle as his throat was cut by Hernando from ear to ear, the lifeblood spouting out into the dark water. Once the flow of blood ended, and the man began to quiver, Hernando pushed the body over the side, retaining hold of the man's foot. Within a few minutes there was a great thrashing of water, and he let go of the body.

Hernando spoke with the eerie calmness that he would become known for. "Tiger Shark, by the looks of it. Good. Their hunger is insatiable."

He looked down at Diego Hernandez, and grabbed him by the hair, pulling him up to the edge of the boat. He looked over the side and smiled as he saw the large tiger, now joined by a few reef sharks. He looked at the three remaining men, enjoying the fear in their eyes. He smiled. Without any wasted motion, he grabbed the machete that lay on the wooden seat beside where he stood and hacked down on Mendoza's arm, lopping off the forearm, allowing it to drop into the water. The limb was gone within seconds, a black tip shark, grabbing it in the middle, quickly descended into darkness.

Diego Mendoza didn't have the strength left to struggle, his eyes glazed over in pain and terror. Hernando looked down at the three men. "Do you see what your leader's lack of respect has caused him on this night?" He grabbed Hernandez by the hair, and with three mighty hacks, chopped his head off. He held it up in front of the men, Diego's eyes still moving. The body fell to the bottom of the boat, a stream of blood covering the men and the dirty wood bottom. "Do you see?" The men in unison, shook their heads up and down vigorously.

Hernando tossed the head into the water, then proceeded to chop Diego Hernandez into several large chunks, taking his time to throw them over the side, with morose pleasure.

Hernando looked down at the men. "Who's next?" If the men could have sunk into the wood of the boat's bottom, they would have, shaking their heads in fear. "Well Señors. Tonight is your lucky night. You are now working for the Pacifico Cartel. Tell the rest of Don Mendoza's men that they can find employment with me."

They all shook their heads up and down vigorously.

"All this will cost you, is your little finger…for your insolence on this night." With this being said, he proceeded to chop of each man's pinky finger from their right hand, tossing them to the circling fish. "Now you have paid in blood."

CHAPTER TEN

DOM PAID THE young, dark skinned man. Indian food was one of his favorites. He rolled up the tops of the paper bags, so that they would be easier to carry, especially having to walk five blocks with the jam-packed parcels. The smell of the lamb vindaloo…intoxicating.

St. Catherine's Street buzzed with activity. Montreal though an old city, stood alone as a bastion of quasi-European culture amongst other big North American cities. Dom confided in himself that he could get used to the place, however, he heard that the winters were brutal. He wasn't a big fan of winter. Their two weeks in the city were nearly complete, and he began to pine about what lay ahead. What the State Department envisioned for him and Chantal differed from being placed on active duty. If he were to go back to the Middle East, he would have the comfort of working out of the base hospital. It would be clinical; patients would come in and he would react, fixing their gunshot wounds and prescribing antibiotics for those that couldn't stay away from the local girls. It was amazing how many of the men contracted STDs.

He started to get a bit panicky about the undercover aspect of the mission the last few days. In essence, he would be required to live in a big lie. He would have to lie to the cartel, he would have to lie to people he might meet as acquaintances. He considered himself a pretty straightforward guy…but not a very good liar. Could he do what his superiors asked of him? There were a lot of ifs. The biggest being the veracity of the mission itself. He and Chantal, after talking, believed they were not being given the straight bill of goods.

He was glad to nearly be home as his fingers were beginning to ache. As he turned the corner, Dom looked up at their loft apartment. The lights were on and he could see movement inside. It became evident to him very quickly that someone else was watching the same apartment. The watcher had tucked himself into a small alleyway thirty feet up ahead. Dom could see that the spy held a small telescope trained on the only lit apartment in the complex: Dom and Chantal's.

The man didn't look as if he'd noticed Dom's appraisal of him. Dom weighed his options: walk as if you didn't care, and bring up the food to Chantal, or confront the man. It wasn't in Dom's nature to back away from a confrontation. If he acknowledged the man, Dom would be admitting guilt or arousing suspicion. He decided to walk as if he'd not seen the hidden observer, though he would have loved to get a look at his face.

Crossing the side street, he opened the street level door leading to a well-appointed foyer. The elevator took a few minutes to arrive at their floor. When he got out and went to their door, knocking with the toe of his boot, Chantal expected him. She came to the door within seconds and peeked out the opening in the crack. Seeing it was Dom, she unlatched the chain.

"Why are you knocking, forget your key?"

Dom put a finger to his lips and ushered her out into the hallway. He spoke in a whisper. "There's a man on the street watching us through some sort of telescope. He may not be the only one and

I think we have to go on the assumption the apartment may be bugged. Bachman assured us it wouldn't be, but there are ways of eavesdropping that don't require a physical bug to be in the same room. We use them in the military, to advance scout buildings before infiltration." She nodded. "We leave for Mexico tomorrow, until then we need to be careful. Let's eat, the smell of this stuff is driving me crazy."

Dom and Chantal spent the rest of the evening preparing for the next day's flight. The stairs to the loft bedroom ran up beside the loft's floor to ceiling window. As they went upstairs, Dom patted her backside.

Without turning, Chantal scolded him. "Major!"

"I'm just hurrying you up to bed, darling, putting on a little show." Dom smirked, he didn't have to see the look on her face to know she did her absolute best not to turn around and slap him. "Don't worry," he whispered, I'll sleep on the floor."

CHAPTER ELEVEN

ALAN LOOKED AT the *unknown caller* displayed on his phone. It didn't register with him who the person might be, until he heard the accent. Over a week had passed since he'd called the number on the card given to them by Maddie's doctor. He'd left the message with an answering service. Ironically, he'd been at the point of calling again.

"Alan Chambers." There was a moment of silence.

"Mr. Chambers, this is Benyamin Leahner. You called last week and left a message, I am returning your call."

The man spoke with a pronounced Yiddish accent, with a hint of something Germanic, typical of the Orthodox Jews who lived in New York. Alan recognized the intonation, having grown up in Westchester County. "Mr. Leahner, thank you for calling back." Alan didn't know what to say, and stumbled on a long "ummmmm."

"Mr. Chambers, we must be careful not to talk on the phone. Can we meet next week? I'll be in LA, from Tuesday until Friday."

Alan felt uneasy about agreeing to a meeting, but didn't see that there would be any real choice. He needed to save Maddie. "Yes Mr. Leah."

"Leahner, Benny Leahner. In the future, please don't use my name over the phone."

"My wife and I can meet with you on Tuesday. The morning would be better."

"That's perfect Mr. Chambers. I know where you live."

Alan felt the hair on his head stand on end.

"I'll text you twenty minutes before we are to meet, let's say 10 AM, and I will give you a location. I am a busy man, Mr. Chambers, if you are one minute late you will not hear from me again." Click.

Alan stared at his phone, raising his brow, listening to dead air. What did they get themselves into? He felt a touch of remorse, bordering on panic, like when he'd been caught doing something bad as a child, and knew his mother was going to find out. Or when he got his first call from the IRS.

***

Bonnie and Alan sat in the front seats of their car, which Alan pulled out of the garage and into the driveway, just in case the cell phone reception in the garage was poor. They were both on edge, staring at Alan's iPhone, sitting on his lap. In unison they nearly jumped out of their skin when the phone rang. Alan answered. "Hello?"

"I will meet you in the 7-11 parking lot just around the corner from your house. I'm driving a dark blue Dodge Caravan. You can step into the back seat without knocking. I'm parked beside the ice cooler." Click.

***

Alan pulled the Bentley into the 7-11 parking lot and immediately spotted the blue minivan. He parked the car, and within a couple of minutes, he and Bonnie were sitting in the back of the Caravan. A short, slight man, possibly sixty years old, sat in the driver's seat. His hair was well kept and he wore a well-tailored gray business suit. His face was stern, with a prominent curved nose, as typically Jewish as it gets.

He offered his hand to both of them. "Benny Leahner. It's a pleasure to meet both of you." He looked down at a clipboard that sat on his lap. He placed a small recording device in the middle console. "I hope you don't mind if I record our conversation. It will help me to remember the details."

Alan felt a bit uneasy about the recording. *What if this was a police setup?* "I would prefer it if we didn't, Mr. Leahner. The whole situation makes me uncomfortable, and the secrecy behind our meeting sets my hackles off. The last thing I want is to end up in prison because of our association."

Bonnie squeezed his leg. Looking into her eyes, he could see the fear in them.

He knew that look. "Do go on Mr. Leahner, but no recording."

Benny shrugged his shoulders. "Mr. and Mrs. Chambers, we can end our association right now, and I can go to my 12 o'clock appointment. To be fair, I haven't eaten breakfast today, and would be happy to find a quick bite. The recorder stays on. I have five such meetings today, and it's very important that we keep the facts of our meeting straight. We wouldn't want your daughter to receive the wrong heart now, would we?"

The use of the word heart, and the realization of why they were here, calmed Alan a bit. "Okay, reluctantly I will agree."

"Thank you," he said indignantly. "Let's get down to business then." He flipped the page over on the clipboard. "Your daughter is Madeline, and I understand her blood type is very uncommon. Okay, I see it here. Hmm. This could be problematic."

He flipped open a laptop and tapped away at the keys for a few minutes. "I can help you, but it will be expensive."

Alan rolled his eyes. "Of course Mr. Leahner."

Benny smiled. "We are not dealing with computers or cars, Mr. Chambers. We're dealing in live organs. If your daughter doesn't receive the transplant within a reasonable time after harvesting, how shall we say…it's not a good thing? I like to think that I'm the best at what I do, and pride myself in the procuring a top quality product. If you're going to spend the money, let's get it right. Now, are we on the same page?"

Alan acknowledged the man's words with a nod of his head. Bonnie simply sat there, looking like she might break into tears at any moment. Alan was amazed at how the man managed to bridge the gap between introductions and talking about donor hearts in the matter of seconds.

"Let's see here. I've only three options for you. Now the first is always open to my clients, but it comes with no guarantees. The Republic of China offers a medical holiday for those who can pay. Their donor base is huge, but questionable. Rumor has it, they are killing political prisoners and harvesting their flesh. The lack of medical follow-up always makes me nervous."

"How many of your clients opt for this?"

"Most do sir, but most don't have your financial capability."

"How would you know what my ability is?"

"Come now Mr. Chambers, the first step I take is to hack into your bank accounts and financial portfolio. I am a busy man, I can't be wasting time. You can afford the best option, but I will explain the second. The Iranian government is the only political entity in the world to openly and legally offer organ transplantation. However, the cost is high, and truthfully, it's not a safe place for Americans. They cater mainly to other Arab states."

Alan found the little man irritating, and he didn't like the fact that he knew so much about his finances. But, no matter how much he didn't like the man's approach, he got the feeling that he knew what he was doing, and this wasn't his first time to the rodeo. Alan, over the years, earned a small fortune being able to read people, but he controlled the situation and the environment, much like Leahner managed to accomplish with them. "Okay, we're not going there.

Please hit me with it." Alan slumped down into his seat waiting for Benny's answer.

"Mr. Chambers, we can procure a donor heart with the same blood type as your daughter, but we may need to search abroad for some time. If you want the operation to take place outside the United States, the cost will be $600,000. If you want the transaction to be taken care of in the U.S., the cost will be $950,000. We can take care of the procedure right here in L.A. The price tag will include my fees and follow up medical help for as long as your daughter needs it. I think that this option would be best for…" he looked down at his board. "Best for Madeline."

Bonnie spoke for the first time. "Mr. Leahner. How long will we have to wait?"

"On the outside Mrs. Chambers, three to five months. There's a lot of paperwork to take care of. We need to falsify documents to guarantee that the donor is a blood relative of yours. Then there is the transportation of the living organ. You see, we will need to smuggle the heart into the country."

Bonnie felt her heart thump. "Where do the organs come from?"

"I can't be specific Mrs. Chambers, but I will tell you that the mortality rate in the third world is more than three times what ours is in the U.S. Most likely, though, it will come from central or south America. We can transport a kidney from say…Bangladesh, but hearts are a different animal. Like I intimated, the transplant must take place rather quickly after the death of the donor."

Benny turned to look at the both of them. His face was solemn, his dark brown eyes unwavering. "Mr. and Mrs. Chambers. I can give you one day to decide whether or not you require my services. I will text you tomorrow at noon. All I require is a simple yes or no in the text. If your answer is yes, my associate Yolanda will be in touch with you within the week. I will need $400,000 US, transferred to an account in the Cayman Islands. Once the money is secured, our search will begin. The deposit is nonrefundable."

He fumbled for a moment in his briefcase. "If your answer is yes, contact this number." He gave them a business card. "This is the number of the surgeon who will be performing your daughter's transplant. You will leave a number at which you can be reached and the doctor will contact you once the funds have been transferred. This is a routing number and is not traceable." He lowered his glasses and looked both Bonnie and Alan in the eye. "You understand that what we do is illegal? These precautionary measures are necessary. A blind eye is turned to most of what we do. We save lives, Mr. Chambers, and everyone gets well paid. I hate to cut this short, but it's time that I was moving."

Alan thought everything well scripted and cold, but then, what else had he expected? He shook their hands and then backed out of the parking spot as soon as Bonnie and Alan were clear of the vehicle. Alan could think of only one thing to say: "Christ almighty, what have gotten ourselves into?"

"The choice is clear to me Alan."

"I thought you were against the idea?"

"I was, but once he started talking…Maddie getting better became a reality. No matter how bad this might be, I'm going for it. If this kind of thing goes on all the time as you said the other day, why are we to be the martyrs?" She paused, gathering her thoughts. "Why should Maddie die, when we have the capability of saving her? I want to give her the chance at a normal life. I can live with the morality of it. When I was listening to him, it suddenly became clear. I won't be able to live with myself knowing that we have the ability to rectify the situation."

Alan put his arms around her, nesting his nose into the hair on the top of her head. "Darling, I couldn't have said it better."

"You've already said it. I wasn't ready to listen."

CHAPTER TWELVE

THERE WERE NO direct flights into Guadalajara from Montreal. Dom and Chantal had a long layover in Dallas. With hours to kill, Dom decided that he needed to eat. He eyed up a Longhorn Steakhouse, in the airport concourse. "You feel like getting something?"

Chantal nodded. "I don't know about steak. I'd like a salad though."

"I'm sure you could get a Caesar."

Within twenty minutes, Dom was cutting into twelve-ounce ribeye and Chantal into a fresh garden salad with chicken. She watched as Dom devoured his meal. "I don't think I've ever seen someone eat as much as you Dom. You just polished off that steak as if it was your last supper. You've polished off an incredible amount of food these past weeks. How do you stay trim?"

"Been that way since I was a kid. My ma said that I'm like a cow with a second stomach. We didn't have a lot of money in the early days, and I probably ate my folks out of house and home. I stay away from the carbs, and nightshades. You can eat as much as you want that way."

"Hmmm."

"So, you're ready, Mrs. Chavez?"

"Ready as I'll ever be. From my dossier, you know this isn't the first time I've done this."

He nodded. "When we touch down in Mexico, it's game on." He pushed the remaining food around on his plate with his fork, raising his eyes to meet hers. "Do you have my back, Chantal?"

"Of course."

He could tell by the way she dropped her eyes, that there was something else. "You've managed to be pleasant enough these past weeks, but I know you're just putting in time."

Her cheeks began to redden. "What do you expect of me? You said that we needed to keep up appearances, that's what I'm doing Dom. Nothing more, nothing less. Please don't read anything more into it, you'll only be disappointed."

Dom sighed. "I get the feeling you're here beyond the scope of being my medical assistant. I know how these things work. Military Intelligence wouldn't leave me alone to do this without contingencies. I'm not the bad guy you've seen written about in your dossier. I'm a straight forward person, who doesn't like any bullshit. I see it the way it is, and then I act upon it. I don't want you blowing the whistle on me, or putting a bullet in the back of my head the first time I steer off the rails."

She nodded slowly. "Let's put it this way…I have your back as long as we're on the same page. You're in charge, but if you want your ass covered, don't take me by surprise. Is that fair enough?"

He exhaled deeply. "All's fair in love and war, Chantal. Things don't always go as planned."

"I've told you, what I've told you, Major. That will have to be good enough.

Dom nodded slowly, he hadn't expected anything less.

***

There was a different smell in warmer climate countries. It filled Dom's nose the moment they stepped out of the cabin of the jet. First, you were hit by the extreme heat, then the scent of vegetation that never went dormant during winter, the scent of humanity with a lower expectation of cleanliness, whether it be garbage, or the odd unwashed airport worker. It wasn't a bad smell, just different, and it gave Dom an instant jolt of adrenalin. Excitement.

Dom took Chantal by the arm as they walked towards Immigration. They were faced with a massive line, which took the better part of an hour to navigate.

They were greeted by a middle aged man, with a sour look on his face; he spoke in English. "Señora, Señor, What is the purpose of your visit?"

Dom answered, laying down the visas and passports given to him by Bachman. He felt a nervous thump in his chest. "Business, Señor."

The man shuffled the paperwork around, scanning the passports. "You are Doctor?"

"Yes. And my wife Chantal is my medical assistant."

"Do you have employment Dr…Chavez?" His eyes flicked back and forth from the passports to their faces.

"Yes, I have a letter from Pacifico Medical. I'm to meet with them this week to confirm the terms of my employment. We've rented a villa in Acapulco."

The man raised his eyes to meet Dom's at the mention of Pacifico. He handed Dom a card with the number 23 written on it. "You will need to clarify this with an immigration officer, Dr. Chavez." He indicated a short line off to the right.

After another hour wait, they were ushered into a small windowless office, where they were greeted by a female immigration officer. She stood from behind the desk and motioned for them to sit. "Dr. Chavez, Mrs. Chavez," she said as she looked down at their papers, which were spread out on the desk. "What is the intention of your employment?"

"Intention?"

"Sí, this is a simple…standard question. We are careful who we let into our country. Jobs are hard to find, Doctor. I hope you appreciate that we don't like to displace qualified Mexican practitioners. I am also curious when professionals like yourself come to Mexico for work. Why do you leave Canada?"

Dom didn't hesitate to follow a script, which had been given to him by Bachman. "I met Dr. Suarez at a symposium in Brussels, roughly a year ago. Three months ago, I received a call from her asking if we would be interested in heading up a department within Pacifico Medical. She did a good sales job on us, and here we are. I'll be honest as well, I'm not a fan of the Canadian winters anymore. The term of our employment, as I understand it, is for one year, with an option to extend." He smiled. "The money was hard to turn down."

The woman frowned slightly. "Okay Dr. Chavez. I will grant you a temporary visa, which will supersede your original one. Within two weeks' time, we will need to see a copy of your employment contract. If this condition is not met, you will be deported."

"Then everything is in order?"

"Sí, Dr. Chavez, welcome to Mexico."

CHAPTER THIRTEEN

Acapulco Mexico

THE SOILED SHEET covering the window came down with one very angry yank. The woman holding it cursed, but it wasn't Spanish. French? Carlos understood the words *swine,* and *hell,* words in common with his native tongue. The men laying in their cots covered their eyes from blinding sunlight. Carlos surprised himself by being able to sit up for the first time in however many days he'd been there. The woman left, shaking her head, looking at the men one last time before she closed the door behind her.

Carlos looked over at Hector, his face extremely pale, and his breath shallow, almost non-existent. He carefully returned his head to his pillow. Carlos had always been a clever boy. He'd spent many hours of the day wandering through his hometown and immediate countryside – looking, questioning. He would bring insects and strange flowers to school wanting to know their names. He wasn't blind to his surroundings; inquisitive, but not a confrontationist.

He preferred to sit and think before reacting. These men had taken advantage of him. It angered him. He would make them pay for cutting him, cutting Hector. He would be smart about it, he would bide his time…Before long, he once again fell sleep, the morphine taking hold.

***

Loud yelling, a confrontation; Carlos woke with a start. The French woman verbally attacked the male nurse, Mendezes. She spoke in broken Spanish. "These men are dirty. You don't operate on a patient, and then leave them in their own filth. Were they bathed before the procedure?"

"Non!"

"I didn't think so. These men are dirty, living like swine. Where did you get your license?" Her cheeks were red, her eyes fiercely pinning the man to his spot.

"Señorita, can I call you Chantal? You walk in here, and you are not from here…I would watch yourself" he said, pointing his finger at her, his body stiff, but his eyes not able to hold hers.

"Is that a threat Señor Mendezes? And it's not Señorita or Chantal, its Señora Chavez. We were hired by Doctor Suarez, to do a job, Señor Menezes. I made an oath when I became a nurse, clearly you didn't, or have forgotten it. These men need to be bathed, their wounds properly tended to, not just a goddamned shot of morphine every twelve hours."

She lifted the sheet off one of the men. "Look at this…this poor man has been pissing himself for days. Do you not believe in the use of a catheter? We're going to spend the rest of the day making sure that the patients are clean, and have fresh dressings."

Chantal walked down the row of cots and stopped at Hector. She lifted the sheet and recoiled from the stench of the infection. "Mr. Menezes, this one will be dead within a day if he doesn't get medical attention in a hospital. He needs an intravenous drip, with a strong antibiotic, and that wound needs to be looked at by a doctor. My husband will not be able to get here for at least a day. He is busy elsewhere. Do we have access to a hospital?"

"Señora…Chavez…what we do here is…" he searched for the correct word. "Frowned upon."

Chantal squared up to the man. "Frowned upon?" She turned her head away and then returned her gaze to his. "Let's be realistic, this is goddamned illegal. I'm looking at the incisions on most of these men, they've had their kidneys removed, correct? This is a real hack job. Did a doctor perform the operation?"

He sighed. "Indeed…yes."

"Where's the doctor?" Chantal placed her hands on her hips, contorting her face into a fearsome scowl.

"He's not here…anymore."

"God dammit, I can see that. Where did he go? This man needs some help."

Menezes crossed his arms over his chest. "He's not…anywhere, if you get my meaning."

Chantal couldn't help but swallow hard. "Well, this is a shit show, and it's not right, it's inhumane."

"That is most observant of you Señora Chavez, and you would know that…it's illegal by the fact that you are here. My bosses have told you what we do, and you are being paid well to help. Don't play coy." He pondered his words for a few moments, then replied rationally, "I will help you see to the men." Mendezes wisely knew when to pick his battles.

His comment led her to another question. "Are there any women, Señor Mendezes?"

He nodded. "But not here. They are graded. The pretty ones go to the whore houses, the…not so pretty ones, lose a kidney before they are put to work."

"Tabernac!" Chantal exclaimed.

***

Carlos followed the conversation pretending that he was asleep. He smiled to himself. He liked the fiery woman, she possessed spirit.

CHAPTER FOURTEEN

DOM SAT BACK in the wooden lounge, the intense afternoon sun seared his bare chest. The house provided for Chantal and he suited their needs adequately. It was comfortable, well equipped and spacious. He'd been delighted to find the rooftop patio, filled with half kept scruffy palm trees and cacti. He took a long sip from one of the Corona bottles he'd purchased on the way back from his lunch meeting with Carmen Suarez. Dom wondered how Chantal would be making out as she inspected Pacifico's extraction clinics. He didn't envy her, but the inspections were necessary. If push came to shove, he had a feeling she could look after herself.

He peered out over a sea of rooftops. They were not in the best location in Acapulco. Many of the buildings were in a bad state of repair, but at least he could see the sparkling Pacific in the distance, between the tall hotels along the beach strip a few miles away.

They'd experienced a whirlwind of activity since arriving. Dom remembered the town from his university days, when he'd spent a booze filled vacation with friends during spring break. He was disappointed to see that the once beautiful resort town, now seemed an echo of its past self. The drug wars and the violence over the past several years, took its toll on foreign tourism. He halfheartedly laughed, as he'd googled Trip Advisor, looking for a decent restaurant. Acapulco found itself listed on the tourist advisory as being somewhere you went with the utmost caution. Further investigation revealed that it was in the top twenty most dangerous places in the world, and the second most dangerous municipality in Mexico. Several statements were made as to the untrustworthy nature of the police. He chuckled again to himself. Normally he wouldn't worry too much about this kind of thing, just here to party and catch a few rays. Chantal and he were here to find out what they could about the dark underbelly of the place. They were sure to uncover the bad element hinted at in the advisories sooner or later. He reflected back on the first two meetings with his new employers.

***

The first took place on the day of their arrival. Chantal and he were lucky to survive a harried taxi ride through the shanty, which circled the resort town. Ramshackle buildings, seemingly piled upon one another, continued as the miles went by. It was in the shanty that they saw the poverty that permeated the area away from the resorts, something you expected to see in the dirtiest streets of Bangladesh, not several hundred miles south of the U.S. border.

The two of them were on edge in anticipation of the meeting, and the white knuckled ride did nothing to lower their stress level. When the driver pulled up to a plain cement block wall with barbed wire on top, they both let out sighs of relief. A large metal studded door was pulled to the side by two men, both with semi-automatic rifles slung over their shoulders.

Once through the main gates, they were greeted by a sprawling estate, completely out of character with the surrounding neighborhood. The grounds were magnificent, with a spectacular view of the hillside, and the Pacific in the distance. The gardens and central plaza were something out of a *Christie's Real Estate* magazine. The cab driver drove down a cobblestone lane, shaded by overhanging tropical plants and trees. He pulled up to a magnificent whitewashed stone building.

Stepping out of the cab, Chantal and Dom were greeted by a woman in her mid-forties, dressed impeccably in a white business suit. A bodyguard, semi-automatic rifle slung over his shoulder, followed her every step. The woman's hair was jet black, her face stern but beautiful, like a Hispanic movie star. They both recognized her from their briefings as Dr. Carmen Suarez. What struck Dom most were her dark, almost black eyes. They were intelligent, but carried what looked like sorrow, or exhaustion. She waited for Dom to offer his hand before she reached out to accept his. Her handshake was firm, her thin bony hand possessed strength Dom hadn't anticipated. Dom's fears were realized when she greeted them in perfect Parisian French. Luckily, the weeks he'd spent in Montreal were spent talking to Chantal in her native tongue. He turned on the French Canadian slang, to make up for his imperfect dialect. "Whay" instead of "Oui."

"Welcome Dr. Chavez, Mrs. Chavez." She extended her hand to greet Chantal. "I'm pleased that you've contacted us and accepted our invitation to meet today. I'm Dr. Carmen Suarez. I trust that your travels have been safe." She let the words hang for a moment. "Let's sit down and talk."

Dom nodded. "Our flight wasn't the smoothest, but your beautiful weather makes up for the bumpy ride. I'm pleased to meet you."

Chantal and Dom followed her through a spectacular atrium, filled with multiple species of parrot, wild flower and exotic greenery. She gestured at the glass enclosure. "This is the third largest atrium in Mexico. My father is passionate about our domestic flora and fauna." The massive greenhouse was absolutely spectacular, but hot. They arrived at a glass table in the middle of a beautiful room surrounded by ponds filled with exotic fish.

A young girl dressed in black with a white apron approached, addressing them in Spanish. "Señora, Señor, can I offer you coffee?"

Chantal nodded, "Si."

Dom shook his head politely. "Bottled water for me thank you."

Carmen with a nod of her head, accepted a coffee. "Do you prefer French, or shall we speak in Spanish…or English?" She smiled slyly.

Dom felt a bead of sweat forming on his brow. He responded in Spanish, "I feel equally comfortable in both, all three actually, but since we're in Mexico, let's speak the native tongue."

Carmen nodded with a slight smile. "What is your heritage Dr. Chavez, your name hints that you are of Hispanic descent? You come from Montreal yet both your Spanish and especially your French are awkward…actually, pretty poor."

Dom pondered her comment for a moment, the hair standing up on the back of his neck. He decided to offer her a partial truth. "Dr. Suarez, I was born in Brooklyn, New York, the by-product of a Hispanic father and French mother. My mother grew up in Martinique. When I was young my parents spoke to me in both tongues, but as I grew older…not so much, and my friends spoke English. We moved to Canada in my teens, to West Mount, a part of Montreal, which is primarily an English speaking community." He'd been ready for the question. "I don't see why it should matter?"

"Curious," she said, raising her eyebrows. She took some papers out of a manila envelope, which were waiting for her on the table. She took a few minutes to review the document, letting Chantal and Dom wait in silence. "You've practiced in Toronto, and Montreal and I see that your license is under suspension…for a year now. Why do you come here, Dr. Chavez?"

Dom didn't hesitate, again prepared for the question. "The money."

Carmen nodded, as if she'd heard the answer a dozen times. "I understand the allure and motivation of money." She looked him in the eye. "You know why you are being hired, doctor. Will your conscience allow you to take from one to give to another? We get doctors that don't bat an eye. Are you one of those, or will you be gone within a week?"

Dom took a deep breath. "Dr. Suarez," he could feel his morals pulling heavily at him as he said the words. "This won't be an issue for me, as long as the payment is commensurate."

She nodded, flipping a strand of black hair behind her ear, she'd obviously wanted to hear what he'd said, but he couldn't help but detect a little bit of disdain in her eyes, disappointment. Perhaps the oath meant something to the woman, but he found that hard to believe.

"Why here? You could have chosen a dozen other locations."

Dom took a sip from the water bottle, his throat dry. "We came because it was easier. Bangladesh was always in the running, but Mexico is our first choice. You pay better, and it's more familiar, closer to home."

Chantal nodded in agreement with Dom's logic.

Carmen smiled. Dom perceived it to be a false smile. "Your license…You went to McGill University, then after your internship, you worked for several years in the far north."

"Moose Jaw, Saskatchewan, middle of nowhere."

"Doctor, your credentials do not fill me with optimism. There are many citations on your transcript, but we are in need of medical practitioners, whether you are telling us the truth or not." She looked at the dossier. She raised her eyes and met his. "Are you telling me the truth?"

The question caused a pang of uncertainty. "Dr. Suarez. I wish I didn't have to be here, but we have debts. Until I can get my license reinstated, I have to somehow keep the ball rolling at home. Without cash, the ball won't roll. My lawyer says that we can expect a hearing within a year's time. Until then, I'm all yours."

She nodded, seemingly satisfied with the answer. "What is your knowledge of urology?"

Dom crossed his left leg over the other. "I'm up to date on all of the latest procedures, I studied hard before coming. The anatomy hasn't changed since med school. It's just been some time."

"Your suspension?"

Dom drew his lips tightly over his teeth before speaking. "My suspension came from performing assisted deaths. I feel strongly about the issue."

Suarez tapped her pen on the table. "Ultimately, it matters not that you are who you say you are. Some are, some are not. If we find you to be a fraud, our business relationship will be…terminated." She glared at him. "We pay well Dr. Chavez, but we don't tolerate insolence, and we demand loyalty, whether you feel it or not. You can start by looking after some of our remote patients. Our post-op care is not what it should be. There are several patients that haven't seen a doctor in days."

Dom nodded. "I have some matters to take care of tomorrow, but Chantal can get a start on things. We need access to drugs, Dr. Suarez. I have a list. I need Insulin, Arginine, Vasopressin, Thyroxin, Triiodothyronine, Methyprednisolone, some heavy duty pain killers, antibiotics."

"Dom," said Chantal. "We will need disinfectant. Surface Clean if you have it, CaviCide will do. Comvita gel for wounds."

Carmen nodded. "I will requisition the materials, at least those that are available, but remember, we're not running a rehab clinic. We can only offer minimal help." She placed a document in front of Dom. "These are the terms of your employment. I suggest you read them over and return them signed. You understand that we cannot allow you to keep a copy, should something happen to you, there can be no record."

"Immigration requested a copy?"

"We'll take care of that for you, though we will require your signature."

Dom frowned, expecting no less. "And our pay?"

"It will be directed to the account you specified in the Cayman Islands." She tapped her pen on the table again. "You understand that what we do is…not legal? I'm sure you do, and I don't want to insult your intelligence, but it needs to be said. Currently the Federales are not on our pay docket." She looked him in the eyes. "We have been outbid by one of our rivals. You could be detained or shot on the spot depending on…" She eyed him for a long moment. "I think you understand?"

Dom sighed deeply. "I understand the risk, as I do the reward."

She offered her hand to Dom. "We need to keep our noses clean. I say this, so that you are aware."

"Noses clean in what way?"

"We prefer that you keep a low profile, Doctor. This is for your own good as well as our benefit. If you draw attention to yourself, you cannot guarantee whose eyes are upon you. We have rivals who would kill you on the spot. This is a war; you will be viewed as one of our soldiers." She smiled for the first time. Dom nodded. "Then we have an agreement. Please execute the document. You can bring it with you to our meeting tomorrow."

Dom nodded, looking over at Chantal. She returned his gaze, her mouth turned down. Dom accepted Carmen Suarez's handshake. "If it's possible, I would like Chantal to get a head start and see to these patients that you mentioned. I believe that you have me scheduled for a briefing tomorrow at noon?"

"That's correct Dr. Chavez, and yes, that would be fine." She gestured with her hand towards Chantal.

***

Dom looked over the contract that evening; the most one-sided document he'd ever seen. Part of him wanted to make a bunch of changes, just to keep up appearances. If it had been something that he'd been doing of his own accord, he would have taken it to his lawyer, telling him rip it apart. Basically, the paper indemnified Pacifico against any occurrence that would leave Suarez Medical Inc. liable for anything, including the deaths of both Dominick and Chantal Chavez and any of their patients. There were no guarantee as to the effectiveness or quality of the drugs and equipment. The bottom line, Dom would be paid $40,000 US Dollars per month, and would be responsible to Carmen Suarez at her discretion.

He looked up over the rim of his glasses as Chantal examined the handguns that, as promised, had been left for them. Bachman, true to his word, texted the location of the weapons early that morning. Chantal identified them as Glock 42mm pistols. Dom became intrigued by the efficiency with which she took both of the weapons apart, examining them for any deficiencies. There wasn't a moment of hesitation in her movements.

"You've done that before?"

She turned to face him, a scowl forming, her eyebrows drawn down. "Standard procedure Major Tavano. You've been at the teaching academy too long. It's a smaller make of the standard Glock 22 used by many police forces, including your FBI. Packs a pretty good punch, and easy to conceal. With these hollow point rounds," she indicated the boxes on the table, "you can pretty much stop anyone in their tracks."

Dom put the papers down on the table, nodding at the same time. "So what's your story Chantal? I know I've asked you this before."

"Then why you asking?" She snapped a fully loaded cartridge into the bottom of one of the handguns, then in one fluid motion took a two handed firing stance, pointing at a vase at the other side of the room. Nodding to herself, she put the weapon down on the table. "What did my dossier say?"

"Active duty with the Canadian forces, Afghanistan, the Middle East with The United Nations. You're an RN, trained by the Canadian Navy. Not much more."

She nodded, as she picked up the second gun, giving it a once over.

"That's it?"

"What more do you need to know Dom?"

"Okay." He rose from his chair. "Why did they choose you?"

She shrugged her shoulders. "It's all there in the folder, what more can I say besides you're starting to get on my nerves."

Dom smiled. "There's more to it than that. I know you're a good nurse, very knowledgeable. But why the military background?"

"You're military, what's the difference?"

"Big difference Chantal, I took basic training, you've been cited twice for bravery above and beyond the call of duty. Are you here to protect me?"

She raised her eyes to meet his. "I think you can look after yourself, Major. Like you said the other day, I'm here to pick up the pieces if you do something brash or inappropriate."

"Inappropriate? What the fuck is that supposed to mean? What exactly does it say in my file?"

Her cheeks began to redden. "If you screw up, I'm to make sure that there are no serious complications."

Dom started to laugh. "Okay, I'm starting to get this now. I'm expendable. All the great things that were said to me about being able to think outside the box etcetera. Fucking bananas, that's what this is." He went to the fridge and grabbed a beer. "You want one?"

Chantal sighed. "Sure, why not. Look, I didn't mean to make you feel badly, Dom."

He put his hand up, handing her a corona. "Not your fault. I'm just a little tight over their bullshit. No one likes to feel like they've been taken advantage of." He took a long sip from his drink. "Say, I'm mad hungry. Why don't Dr. and Mrs. Chavez go out for a nice dinner? There's dozens of decent looking restaurants pretty close to here. I've been checking them out on Trip Advisor."

"Trip Advisor?"

"Yes." He said, his brow rising.

"That's just paid advertising. Check out Urban Spoon on my iPhone." She handed it to him, after taking it out of her pocket.

"Does that mean you're coming with me?"

"Possibly."

"You're a cold fish, Mrs. Chavez."

"Just focused on the mission. Nothing more, nothing less." She picked up the sterile gray handguns and returned them to their carrying cases.

"Okay, here we go, Jose's Authentic Mexican. Says it looks a bit hokey, but the cuisine is one of the best in Acapulco. Mariachi players, the whole enchilada."

She canted her head slightly to the side, in a quasi-nod.

"I'll take that as a yes then. We may as well get the full Mexican effect and try this place."

***

Dom sat at the dining room table and went over the final details of the contract with Pacifico, shaking his head from time to time. He decided that he would have to negotiate with Carmen Suarez. He'd be looked at as a fool if he didn't at least make a few small changes for appearance sake.

Chantal walked into the kitchen. Dom did his best not to look shocked, keeping his eyes on the document. He raised his head, and smiled. "You look very nice Mrs. Chavez." She wore a simple short white dress, with a floral pattern on the hem. Her hair pulled back off her face in a barrette. With the addition of some makeup, Dom admitted that she looked quite stunning. Her cheeks reddened with the comment.

"Just trying to keep up appearances Major; I can clean up nicely when I want to."

Dom pursed his lips, letting out a long stream of air, then finished the last dregs of his Corona.

***

Typically Mexican, gaudy, like one would see in a movie – the only way to describe Jose's. The outside looked like a hacienda, but with bright neon signs denoting the name and boasting, "The Best Mexican Food in Acapulco." They were greeted by a host in a black suit with a sombrero on his head. A Mariachi band busily played for one of the many occupied tables. Despite the tackiness of the place there was a good vibe.

A waitress came to the table and addressed them in English. "Good evening Señor y Señora, welcome to Jose's. Something to drink?"

Dom responded in Spanish. "Tequila and some spicy tomato juice."

"Sangarita?"

"Si."

"Señora?"

"That sounds good."

Dom raised his eyebrows. "Mrs. Chavez…you like tequila?"

"From time to time. My roommate back in nursing school got me on it. It's been some time, I think she liked Patron."

"Then we finally have something in common, and there's better stuff down here than Patron. That stuff is all about the marketing." He raised his hand, waiting for a high five that she greeted with a sour stare. "Chantal look, I'm not out to try anything funny. I think that it would be important to appear somewhat normal. If we're going to be spending a lot of time together, we may as well be at ease with each other."

She choose her words carefully. "Dom…you don't have to keep saying this, I understand, truly I do. Like I said, this isn't the first covert mission I've been on. I've been through it before. The last time was not…pleasant. I'll leave it at that. I'll do my job as best I can. I can't promise to be your friend. I just won't." She breathed in deeply, looking off to the right.

"Though I would have liked to have been a psychiatrist, I don't need to be one to know what you are saying. I've experienced some bad deaths Chantal. Many friends. I won't ask you to be my friend, but let's at least be civil."

The waitress came back to the table with their drinks, and Dom asked her to bring the house specialties. She nodded. "Si Señor."

Chantal picked up the tequila and tapped her glass to Dom's, then drank half of it. "I think I might be able to agree to that Major."

Dom nodded with a wry smile, "Okay, at least we have some kind of treaty. Here's to civility." He drank half of the fiery liquid, then a tiny sip of the spicy tomato juice. "Takes the edge off."

"Yes, it's nice." She pondered her words for a moment. "So what now Dom? Can I trust you? I've been thinking about what you said about having your back. Do you have mine? I'm here, hanging on a string waiting to see if you screw up or not. Are you going to have the decency to let me know what you're thinking, or what you're planning do? The stuff that's written about you in the dossier could be true, maybe not. I figure mostly the latter based on what I've seen so far, but I'm sure that there is a thread of truth in the report. Where there's smoke, there's fire. Have you changed since you've been in Bethesda?"

Dom could feel his blood starting to boil. "I'd like to see this damned report. Really, when we get back to the villa, I want to see the goddamned thing. I'll tell you one thing. I can't promise that I won't be impulsive. I'll promise you that I won't do anything innately rash and stupid. I pride myself on being a quick thinker. I can't promise that I will give you the luxury of letting you know what I'm going to do in a tight spot. That's why I'm a damned good surgeon. I think quickly and I'm not afraid to react quickly."

Chantal shook her head. "You see, that's exactly what I took from the dossier. I don't feel any better after this conversation."

The Body of Thieves

Dom ran his hand through his hair, finishing his drink. "Wish I could make you feel better darlin'." Say, let's change the topic. I'd like to take a look at some of the local towns close to Acapulco. I feel like I'm in a cocoon."

Chantal took another sip from her drink. "Do you think that's a good idea? I hear that the banditos are a real problem around here. You'll get your chance when we go to one of the medical sites. Nuevo is pretty damned oppressive."

"I suppose."

The waitress delivered their food. Dom as normal, felt like he could eat a cow, and dug into the spicy fish tacos without hesitation. "How poor is the town?"

Chantal shook her head. "Worse than you could imagine. These poor people. When you have nothing, you will do anything to get something, including money for a spare body part, it's hard to imagine…but it damn well happens all the time."

Dom nodded. "I've read stories where the poor bastards sell one of their kidneys, and then get robbed coming home by the people who bought the organ, sickening. And there are those who have their bodies raped and pillaged and killed against their will. The value placed on a human life here is negligible."

Dom put his hand up to stop the conversation, as a man with a bushy mustache and a balding head, approached the table. He addressed Dom in Spanish, ignoring Chantal. "Dr. Chavez."

Dom was caught a little off guard…"Yes?"

"I have come to give you some professional courtesy. I represent the Gulf Cartel. I will let you know that we are watching you. I highly recommend that you enjoy the sun, and the finer things that Acapulco has to offer." He gestured to their dinner, placing his hand on their table. "Go back to Canada. You're not wanted here."

Dom smiled. "I will keep that in mind Señor."

The man nodded, frowning slightly. "We have experienced a lot of bad press in Acapulco. We don't need any more. You follow?"

Dom smiled, resisting the urge to stab the man in the hand with his steak knife. Surely Chantal would classify this as being brash. In his younger days, it would have happened in a heartbeat. He spoke calmly, in a subdued voice, pronouncing each and every syllable. "Please, Señor, tell your bosses to go and fuck themselves. And while you're at it, you can do the same."

The man's face began to turn red in fury, his voice attracting the attention of the nearby tables. "You can consider yourself a dead man walking, Dr. Chavez."

The couple at the table next to them looked as if they were going to run for the exit. The room became less loud.

"As I said, Dr. Chavez. We don't need any more bad press. However, I promise that you will regret this."

Dom lowered his voice almost to a whisper. "I don't know what your name is, but I will not be bullied…and I will give you some professional courtesy. If I were you I would go straight to a hospital and have your blood pressure checked, and you could stand to lose some weight."

The man turned and walked out of the restaurant. Dom could see the host on his cell phone looking directly at them.

"Dom, we need to get out of here. What the….F were you thinking?"

"In due time Mrs. Chavez."

Dom stood, and walked over to the host. He looked edgy, nervous, as could be expected. Dom took out his wallet and handed the man two one hundred dollar bills. "Señor, there will be no more trouble tonight. Put your phone away. You look after us, we look after you." The man smiled nervously, nodded his head, and quickly stuffed the money into his pant pocket.

Dom returned to the table and sat down. The couple next to them were clearly frightened. Dom turned to them. "You look like you're from the States?"

They both nodded. The wife spoke to her husband through her hand. "I told you we shouldn't have come here!"

Dom put his hand up. "Hold on, there will be no more trouble here tonight. Please relax and enjoy your dinner." He called the waitress over. "Let me buy my new friends a round of whatever it is they're drinking."

He turned to Chantal and said, low enough that the couple couldn't hear him. "We can show no fear, Mrs. Chavez."

"I just don't see the need to have done that?"

"What's the difference? That man is going to do what he's going to do anyway. If I get shot tomorrow, at least I will have had the pleasure of telling him to fuck off."

Chantal shook her head, not necessarily in agreement. "Is this what the dossier meant by brashness?"

"Possibly." He grinned.

"How would he have known about us, we've only been here a few days, I've talked to no one."

Dom raised one of his eyebrows. "You just don't know, do you? The whole system is corrupt. It could easily be the immigration officer we spoke to. I didn't like the way she looked at me when I mentioned Pacifico Medical, and she did ask us to produce our contract." He shook his head. "This place is bananas."

"We were told to expect this Doctor. If our job was an easy one, somebody before us would have done it. I think if we expect the worst, we will be better prepared for roadblocks and disappointment. It's not as sophisticated as the network in the U.S., but the Mexicans do have their intelligence, one that has been honed for hundreds of years." Chantal paused. "I think that we should operate under the assumption that we are known to many of the players involved. This caution will serve us well - keep us alive."

Dom took a deep breath. "Sounds like a plan, Mrs. Chavez."

***

The next day, Chantal and Dom took a taxi to the Pacific Medical Center, located just off the Hotel strip. It catered to the tourists who visited Acapulco. It offered cheap prescription drugs, medical assistance, and dental work. Patients, Americans mostly, could fly in for a couple of days, get some bridgework or a root canal, and then relax on the beach. It was cheaper than having it done at home.

They walked into a bright and airy waiting room. A young woman with a scowl on her face looked up as they approached the registration station. Dom addressed her. "Dr. Chavez. I have an appointment with Dr. Suarez."

The grumpy receptionist looked down the appointment register. "Please have a seat. Dr. Suarez will be with you shortly."

They waited for close to an hour before they were escorted to a small board room around which sat four people. They recognized Carmen Suarez, who stood to greet them.

"Dr. Chavez, Mrs. Chavez. You have signed the contract?" She looked at Dom.

He nodded. "With a few minor changes, nothing of the deal-breaking nature."

She nodded. 'Let me introduce you to our directors." Dom recognized the first without introduction. "Dr. Chavez, Hernando Suarez, my father and the President of Pacifico Enterprises." The man looked amazingly good for being eighty years old. He nodded his head.

The next was a man was in his mid-thirties. "Dr. Lee Stains, head of Dentistry."

The tall thin man stood and shook both their hands. He spoke with a London accent. "A pleasure, welcome aboard." His words were easy to read. He'd probably greeted several incoming doctors on a regular basis, the process becoming more of a custom than anything for the man, his tone lacking sincerity.

The last of the group, a small dark haired Hispanic man in a white lab coat. Carmen introduced him. "Alfonzo Benitez is our CFO and pharmacist at the clinic." The man nodded.

Carmen looked at the grumpy receptionist standing at the door. "Cecilia, Señora Chavez is to be taken to Nuevo, She will see to the patients there."

The woman acknowledged Carmen and gestured for Chantal to follow. She and Dom locked eyes for the slightest of moments as she left, a confident look. *Atta girl.*

Once Chantal was gone, Hernando Suarez spoke. "Dr. Chavez," his voice purposefully quiet. Dom needed to concentrate to hear the man, especially in Spanish. "I make a point of meeting all of our employees, be they shit diggers or doctors. Let me make things clear." He opened up both of his hands in a reconciliating gesture. "I value the shit diggers as much as I do the doctors. Don't take this in a bad way. You will get paid very well by me, and the shit shoveler lives a decent life because of Pacifico. He's not rich like you are, but he respects his job and in return, we offer him respect. Follow? I want to let you know that you gain no favor with me because of your education. If you cross me, I will cut your throat, just the same as the shit shoveler if he does the same. Understand?"

Dom nodded. "Si, Señor Suarez." He struggled to push the lump down that suddenly formed in his throat, a twinge of panic. Suarez wasn't a big man and he was old, but Dom didn't think for one minute that he wouldn't, or couldn't follow through on his words.

"Good."

Carmen interjected. "I trust you find our terms of employment satisfactory?" She smiled, holding his eyes.

He hesitated for a moment, then agreed. "They are not what I'm used to, but I will agree to them, except for a couple of minor issues, banking."

"Very well." Carmen looked over to her father.

The old man cleared his throat. "Dr. Chavez, as I intimated, we look after our employees. We normally ask for something of value in return for our trust. But medical practitioners are hard to come by these days. We do not offer second chances, Dr. Chavez."

Dom resisted the urge to smile, perhaps the stress of the situation perversely tickling his funny bone; he swallowed back the unwanted gesture, humor wouldn't be wise at this juncture. "I appreciate your attention to, and belief in your morals, Señor."

The old man frowned. "Though your Spanish is poor, I detect sarcasm." The other members of the board began to fidget in their seats. "I don't mind sarcasm, as long as there is an understanding that I am the boss. I appreciate strong-willed individuals, they make strong employees. Just remember that you will follow my daughter's orders implicitly, or you will answer to me."

The speech was forceful and very convincing. The man was perceptive and Dom would have to be very careful with him in the future. He could just imagine the impact it would have had upon him when the man was younger, less frail looking. As the dossier stated, the Pacifico Cartel showed evidence of decline, mostly because of the diminishing strength of the once great man. Yet there wasn't a doubt in Dom's mind that the man would kill him if he stepped over the line. He hoped that Suarez's presence was still strong enough to persuade his adversaries from taking any actions against the Cartel, which might affect him and Chantal. He remembered the man from dinner last night. He would have to be very careful from now on, perhaps even carry the gun he'd been provided.

Carmen spoke. "Dr. Chavez, before we let you know more about our business, I will ask you to perform a few rudimentary procedures. Let's look upon it as a test. It will give us security; we'll have enough evidence against you to be arrested and placed in prison for life. Mexican prisons are renowned for their despicable conditions. As Mrs. Chavez is busy in a remote area of Metlatonoc, south of Acapulco for a couple of days, I will be your assistant."

Dom squirmed in his seat. "Dr. Suarez, Chantal and I are a team." *Shit!*

"I understand. I want to see if you know what you are doing, Doctor. There is no hiding behind a scalpel. If things go well, Mrs. Chavez will return and our contract will then be honored."

Dom tried his best to show no emotion. *The bastards are holding her hostage.* "Can I ask what the procedure will be?"

"We will be harvesting a heart, and two kidneys, and I'll leave it up to you to decide what else. The patient was…in an accident. He's one of our employees."

Dom felt a bead of sweat roll down the small of his back. "May I ask what protocols will be in place for the procedure?"

"What protocols do you refer to? You take out the organs and my father is happy, what more could you want or need?"

Dom's head swirled. "When did the Donor die? How many will be on the transplant Team?"

"Transplant team?"

"At home we call the extraction team, a transplant team, or a crash team. You don't always know when a donor will present itself, and a team of medical practitioners is always on call in the major centers. Usually, it's made up of at least two doctors, an anesthesiologist and a minimum of two nurses."

"We don't use anesthetics, Doctor."

Dom stood up. "Is the donor dead?"

"Brain dead."

"Well, we will need an anesthesiologist. It's standard protocol throughout the modern world."

"This is not the modern world Dr. Chavez, and the man will be dead soon enough. We see it as a waste of time and money."

Dom nodded, his anger not very well masked. "You do know that it can lead to complications, morality set aside?"

"Where you are going, you will not have the luxury of a modern facility like we have here." She paused, "Nor any time for morality. We need to see that you can improvise. Let's not forget doctor…what we do is illegal." She banged her hand on the table for emphasis. "We are not worried about the morality of the goddamned procedure. Do you understand?"

Improvise? "Yes. What about the transport of the organs after extraction? Do you use any advanced transportation devices, like the Life Cradle Heart Perfusion System?"

"For cardiectomies yes, though you may not always have that luxury, especially with the extraction of the kidney. The distance that we have to transport the heart makes it an expensive necessity, we use a less expensive Russian model. Besides the heart, we prefer to chill the organs and infuse them with cold Collin's solution."

Dom nodded. "Cold infusion is an outdated procedure."

Hernando Suarez cleared his throat. The room went silent. Dom did his best to remain calm. "Dr. Chavez…You are missing the fucking point. You will perform the work or you will find yourself dead! Then we will be taking out your fucking heart. We tell you what to do…you do the work and you get paid. Comprende?"

Dom couldn't resist. "With a gun to my head."

"Yes Dr. Chavez, and I will be holding it."

CHAPTER FIFTEEN

"YES MR. LEAHNER. We can accommodate the procedure. As you've requested, Dr. Finlay will perform the transplant…He's scheduled to be in LA for the month following…

"Post op?"

Yes, he will be available for post op and follow up."

"And our understanding?"

"Yes Mr. Leahner, our association remains anonymous. The funds have been transferred?"

"Yes."

"Okay, good. I will let Dr. Finlay know that he will be contacted."

"A pleasure as always."

"Yes…it's a pleasure doing business with you as well Mr. Leahner."

Benny hung up the phone, sat back with a cigar and a glass of expensive cognac, which were his only two vices. The deal appeared to be coming together, but a niggling feeling persisted. This deal would not be as clear-cut as most. He'd learned to be patient, but only to a certain extent. If a transaction looked like it needed to be pushed along too hard, he would drop it. The Chambers transaction set off mental alarms, alarms that should be heeded. He couldn't tell exactly what the implications were, but that sixth sense feeling that he prided himself on persisted. He'd follow it through for one more step and see if he felt any better. Perhaps he would push Alan Chambers for more money soon, play him a bit; what did he have to lose? The man had it. He blew a thick cloud of smoke out, which rolled along the ceiling of his living room.

***

Alan sat back in his favorite reclining chair in the large living room of his well-appointed home. The windows of the room overlooked a very private, wooded back yard. A massive flat screen television in front of him showed only a dark blank screen, the room deathly quiet. Bonnie came and sat down on the couch next to him. She remained and didn't speak for a time, knowing the look on her husband's face, knowing enough to leave him alone until he chose to speak. Alan, not a mean spirited man in any way, needed his space from time to time. Bonnie would normally have left him alone, but she needed to know what ground away in his mind. She needed to know how his day had gone. She knew that the pensive mood revolved around their daughter.

Without prompting, Alan spoke. "I paid the money."

Bonnie sat for a few moments, slowly nodding her head.

"I would think that I might feel better about doing it…but I don't."

Bonnie frowned.

"Don't get me wrong, I'd give Maddie my heart if it were possible. I feel dirty for doing this. It's not easy to walk into the bank, and say that you need to transfer four hundred grand to a bank account in the Caymans. John Holmes, our bank manager, looked at me funny. I would too. I had to fill out a document stating the reason for the transfer."

"What did you say?"

"I don't think anything you could say in that situation makes you look like you're above board, especially if you're feeling sleazy in the first place, people pick up on that kind of thing. I could see it in his eyes. It's done though. I said we were buying property. I'm positive that he didn't believe me."

"I've had a hard day as well, but I do understand. I think that I would feel better if I knew that the person's heart we were buying… no, whose heart we are receiving was legit. You know, brain dead from a car accident. I'd like to know that our money was going to the family so that they might better their lives. I know this isn't what's going to happen. I've been reading about it Alan, innocent people are being killed for these organs."

"I can't put a stop order on the money, it's been e-transferred." He leaned back into the chair.

Bonnie crossed her legs, and turned to face him. "What about Maddie? We glossed over the concept with her. I don't think she understands the full meaning of what we're doing. Do we lie to her, knowing she's going to have to live with this too?"

Alan took a long sip from his drink. "I think that it would be best that she doesn't know. We can make up a story that will pacify her. I know what she's like. She won't let us do this if we don't."

Bonnie sighed, exhaling a long breath.

"Could you live with yourself knowing that she didn't have to die? I mean I know that I can't. I just couldn't. But we've talked that issue to death."

"Then we don't tell her?"

"Let's not make that decision right now. I think that it's enough of a moral dilemma, coming to grips with the nature of the whole process." Alan stood up and went to the couch and pulled his wife into his shoulder. "Life's not fair. I mean…it sucks that we're blessed with enough money to find ourselves in this…this horrible dilemma."

"This is a nightmare Alan, it's no dilemma. Remember how simple life used to be when we didn't have anything and we would cuddle like this on the couch that my parents gave us, that horrible multicolored thing."

"Yeah, those were the days. Unfortunately, life throws you some curve balls and this is a dandy, Roger Clemens."

Bonnie looked into his eyes. "We'll get through this. I can feel it in my gut."

"We can only pray that you're right." He kissed her on the mouth, then pulled her head to his chest.

CHAPTER SIXTEEN

CHIEF INSPECTOR PONCHO Aguilar, of the Regional Security Division, flicked his ash on the ground, then took a deep drag of the strong unfiltered cigarette. He looked over at his men, five in total, who stood at various spots around the street corner. Poncho sat in the small café, waiting for a man named Barbarossa. They'd met before on a few occasions, to discuss business. One of his men motioned that the target had arrived, and was moving towards them. The night was very warm; beads of sweat glistened on Poncho's forehead. The drug war, which raged for the past decade, made being a police officer a challenge. You needed to deal with more than what was right and wrong. If you made a mistake it could be costly, even deadly. Accepting pesos from one Cartel would always have repercussions. The other Cartels more often than not found out that you had been paid more from a rival. They all wanted you in their pocket, which of course was impossible, a tricky but lucrative balance to maintain.

Barbarossa needed to be respected, an enforcer of the Gulf Cartel, a relatively new upstart organization that threatened to overtake the other area Cartels, namely the Pacifico and Souza. Poncho was familiar with them all, and with their principals. The Federales, as the Mexican Police were called, existed on the periphery. A what have you done for me today attitude was prevalent with the policing hierarchy, everyone got paid off at some level, and Poncho was at the top of the food chain. The relationship had been ingrained in Mexican culture for hundreds of years, since the time of the Conquistadors. The Federales were not feared by the Cartels, they were looked upon as a useful tool, if you were willing to pay enough pesos. All parties involved walked a fine line. If you crossed that line, it was not uncommon to find the odd dead Federal officer or Cartel soldier floating in the harbor.

Barbarossa sat down at the table beside Poncho, looking out at the street. He shook his hand.

Poncho blew a thick cloud of smoke out over the sidewalk. "Barbarossa my friend, how can I help you this fine evening?"

The large man accepted a cigarette offered to him. "As I said on the phone earlier, I think you should watch a Canadian doctor. He's new to town; Chavez is his name. He's been hired by The Suarez."

Poncho lit Barbarossa's cigarette with a fancy looking zippo lighter, flicking the top open in one smooth motion, well-practiced. "Now, why should I do this Señor Barbarossa? Don Suarez is a friend of mine. You know that I look after the old man. It's a long standing relationship."

"I respect your loyalty Poncho. We both know what goes on. Pacifico moved into the flesh trade recently, they can't compete in the drug industry anymore. The old man's time has come, and gone. It's time to change. I ask you to do one thing for me." He handed a thick envelope to him. "Pacifico operates several remote clinics in the countryside, smaller towns. I will tell you where Dr. Chavez will be. Have some of the men from the south rough him up a bit. You won't be blamed. If you can find anything incriminating, please have the man arrested."

"I will see what I can do Señor."

"I don't like being disappointed Poncho."

"Like I said, I will do what I can do. It's not as easy as roughing someone up. Your soldiers can do that. We must walk a fine line. There is some serious government pressure being placed on us lately to make sure that this kind stuff doesn't make the news. Times are changing. We will have a word with the doctor."

Barbarossa frowned. "Hopefully words that bite, Señor. If you disappoint me, you disappoint my boss. You know how it works. I can't allow that to happen." Barbarossa stood, stomping on the half-finished cigarette. He gave Poncho one last sideways glance and disappeared into the evening crowd.

Poncho texted his men, letting them know that it was time to go. He liked Hernando Suarez. He'd always treated him respectfully. The new blood disrespected the old ways. He shook his head. He was smart enough to know that if you didn't change with the new ways, it would be bad for your health. With that thought, he flicked his cigarette onto the sidewalk and stood.

CHAPTER SEVENTEEN

"SEÑOR MENDEZES. YOU surprise me, your work is more than excellent today. I can see that somewhere in your past you have been trained."

Mendezes looked back at Chantal, as he finished replacing a dressing on the patient's side, a frown forming. "You mock me, Señora."

"On the contrary, I may seem like a bitch, and a hard taskmaster, but I will give a compliment where it's due."

Mendezes continued on with his work for a bit. Then out of the blue asked her, "Your husband, Doctor Chavez, what is he like?"

Chantal passed the other end of the sheet to him, and in unison they draped it over the patient, who looked at them nervously. They mindlessly tucked in the bottom and sides. "He's an excellent surgeon. We'll not have to deal with chop jobs like these."

The patient's head popped up over the sheet as they tucked him, and exclaimed: "Chop job, what do you mean Señora? We no come here for chop job!" He started to struggle.

Mendezes moved to restrain the man, but Chantal halted him,

putting her hand up between him and the patient. She then put her palm gently on the man's chest, applying very little pressure. She looked at the name on the chart. "Ronaldo, you can reassure yourself in knowing that you are one of the few who didn't get a chop job." She lied, the man's wound had been brutally closed and still seeped with yellow puss. "You'll live a normal life as soon as the swelling goes down. There's lots of work for you with Pacifico; your family will be provided for."

The man calmed. "Gracias, Señora."

Chantal pondered Mendezes comment. *Who was Dom Tavano?* "Dr. Chavez will take no bullshit Señor Mendezes." She tried to paint a picture as best she could. She didn't trust Mendezes. He would certainly inform Carmen Suarez of anything out of the ordinary. "He's a good husband. Like me, if you do your job well you will have no problems." She hoped her words were true, if even for her own selfish benefit. She didn't know the answer to the man's question, so she told him what she hoped Dom Tavano might be like.

She patted Ronaldo on the chest, and moved on to the second last man in the row. She looked at the chart. Hector Rivera. She could see the man on the far side of Hector looking at them, his bottom lip pushing up against the top one, his brows deeply sunken. He rested on his elbows. Chantal moved over to the foot of his bed.

"Carlos Rosales. What brings you here, Carlos?" she asked, smiling.

Carlos returned the slightest of smiles. "Medical exam, Señora, well, maybe some work."

"What's done is done, Carlos." She looked over at Mendezes who scowled back at her. "I promise that we will make you better. I can see by the way you're up on your elbows, you're already on the mend."

Carlos looked over at Hector, nodding his head towards him.

"He's your friend?"

"Sí Señora. We go back a long way. We grew up together in San Vincente, in the mountains. I can't see his chest rising anymore."

She pulled up the soiled sheet that covered Hector. The smell of the infection hit her quickly. She put her shirtsleeve up to cover her nose. The abdomen was grossly swollen and the wound had mortified. She reached down to check the man's pulse. She breathed in deeply, letting her breath out between tight lips. "Carlos, your friend Hector is no longer with us." She draped the cover over the corpse's head.

Carlos' bottom lip began to quiver, he let himself fall back into the bed. He looked at the ceiling, closing his eyes, his body shaking ever so slightly. Chantal put a hand on his arm. "I'm so sorry Carlos." She turned to Mendezes a look of fury in her eyes. "Señor, have the body removed to the morgue."

"Señora, we no have morgue."

"Well then find a cupboard or spare room. Do you take them back to their families?"

"We use a work shed out back." A wry smile formed on his mouth, "Take them back?"

"Why not?"

"Ask The Cobra."

Chantal rolled her eyes back and shook her head. She hadn't thought the idea that bad. "Do what you have to do Señor."

Mendezes pondered her words. "If we take dead men back to their families, it would make it hard to recruit these men, no?" he said sarcastically. "They will not be missed. No one comes back to poverty once they've left it."

Chantal nodded. "Get rid of the body."

CHAPTER EIGHTTEEN

DOM PRESSED THE end button on his phone. He'd felt the risk of calling Harvey Greenman to be worth it. The news that he was to be harvesting a heart put him on edge. For the first time in years he was doubting his ability to do the work. Harvey went over the key areas of concern with him, the ones that would be second nature to a pro.

Harvey's words remained etched in his brain. "Dominic, you need only appear competent, after all they think that you are trained in another field. These people are used to hacks. I am positive that your work will be a revelation to them. You have worked on a beating heart, in the worst conditions. Remember your patient doesn't have to survive, what you are doing is purely clinical. You'll be fine."

***

Dom held his hands up after washing them in disinfecting soap and hot water. The nurse assisting snapped the latex gloves onto his outstretched fingers, then pulled them down over his wrist. He looked over at Carmen Suarez as the nurse did the same for her. His heart began to pound heavily; he was distressed enough to have to navigate through a pang of anxiety. *Damn.* He forced it down.

He'd assisted Dr. LaPierre in Montreal with the kidney extraction and subsequent transplant, but this would be entirely different. He would be examined. He didn't know if it would be a good thing or not, that the impending procedure took place at the Pacifico Medical center. *If I fuck up it will be easier to get rid of me.*

"Something wrong Doctor?" Carmen asked.

He shook his head. "No, everything is fine." He followed her and the female nurse down a short hall, eventually entering a small room used for lesser emergencies. There were no windows and the room smelled of the foul human odor, the kind found around people who seldom bathed; the BO accompanied by the smell of strong disinfectant. True to his word, Hernando Suarez sat in a chair along the wall. He nodded to Dom, a slight smile on his thin cold looking lips. He tapped a ring on one of his thin fingers against what Dom figured to be a handgun, the clinking sound echoing through the procedure room.

Another man stood up as they entered. He wore a surgical gown and looked to have been scrubbed. Carmen introduced him. "Dr. Chavez, this is Paulo. He's our technician and runner. He'll be the one taking the organs for transport."

Dom nodded to the man.

Lying on an examining table appeared to be an adult male, prepped for surgery, his head bandaged, dried blood covering much of the binding. An IV tube ran taped along his arm, attached to a thin needle piercing a vein in his wrist. The patient's vitals were displayed behind the operating table. Dom tried his best to walk towards the donor without any hesitation.

He lowered his surgical mask. "Dr. Suarez, may I ask the cause of his injury?" Really, he wanted to make sure that the man was injured badly enough to warrant that his heart be removed, but sure that it wouldn't matter anyway. Really, he stalled for time, feeling terrible about performing the impending procedure. Sweat rolled down his back.

"Gunshot to the head. We're certain that the man is brain dead, a breathing, heart cadaver as you call them in the States."

"What tests have been performed to back up your assertion Dr. Suarez?"

Carmen hesitated, her eyes darting to her father's then back. "My word that he is will have to be good enough. If you are going to be asking me this every time we need you to perform an extraction, we may as well terminate our agreement. Is that what you want Dr. Chavez?"

Dom didn't answer. The look on Hernando's face was all he needed. He moved to examine the equipment and repositioned the overhead light. He put on the awkward looking headlamp, which sat beside the other surgical equipment. Finally, he moved to take a look at the man's head.

Carmen Suarez intervened. "No need for that Dr. Chavez, get on with your job."

Nodding, he raised his brows. "The man should be put under anesthetic, just in case he regains consciousness; it's not unheard of."

"Anesthetics decrease the value of the tissue, Dr. Chavez. Please get on with the procedure."

Dom continued to look around the room, feeling foolish for not asking more questions earlier in the day, but he'd been rushed…and literally under the gun. "What method will we be using to preserve and transport the Heart, Dr. Suarez?" Dom could feel his body temperature rising, his heart pounding even harder than before.

"We'll be using a hybrid of the device you mentioned, not as dependable, but the lower cost is worth it in our estimation. The Russian model we spoke of. It's smaller; smaller is better when it needs to be smuggled over the U.S. border."

"What happens to the cadaver after the extraction?"

Carmen raised her voice, clearly getting angry. "Doctor, this is none of your concern."

Hernando patted his breast with the ring, the clinking sound echoing once again throughout the room...as if Dom needed the reminder.

Turning to the nurse, Dom said, "Are you familiar with the procedure?"

"Yes, Doctor."

He looked at Carmen. "Yes, Dr. Chavez, I will be here to assist you. I am curious to see if we have ourselves a real doctor."

Dom shook his head, raising his brows again. "Do you have a stereo system in here?"

Carmen stared at him questioningly. "Stereo?"

"I work better with music."

"We have a central system that. I guess can be turned on." She moved to the intercom on the wall beside the door and pushed a few buttons. Some peppy Hispanic song began to play. "This is what we have, please get on with it."

Dom grimaced, "It will have to do, though I would prefer the Clash or some David Bowie."

Carmen frowned again.

He moved to the operating table. "I would like to use a quick extraction. Do we plan on taking the lungs?"

Carmen shook her head. "No, doctor."

"Good, that makes our task a bit easier, less prep. Heart, liver and both kidneys. Nurse, Take some blood samples please. Do you have a lab here?"

"Yes."

"Take the samples immediately and have the blood type documented and checked for everything. If we are treating this as a business, you will want to know that we aren't selling damaged goods, unless this is normal protocol?"

Carmen answered, "It is, but you won't have to worry about it in the country. We take tests after the organs are transported."

"Archaic."

"A matter of cost and time doctor."

"You'd make more money if you could do a better screening on site. A standard blood test checking for deficiencies. You can't do this accurately once the organs are infused."

"Doctor!" Carmen looked over to her father.

Hernando stood. "Take out the fucking heart. I'm getting impatient."

Dom nodded. "Dr. Suarez, may I call you Carmen during the procedure?"

"Yes, Doctor."

"Good. I don't want to have to mince words, as we're understaffed."

"That's okay."

"Good then, Carmen, I want 30,000 units of Heparin in the drip."

"Doctor?"

"We don't want any blood clots."

Dom took a sterilized surgical marker and drew a blue line from the patient's neck to the pubic area. Once the nurse returned, he put his hand out. "Scalpel." He took the tiny knife and made a quick, smooth incision along the etched line. The nurse didn't need instruction, quickly moving to manage the flow of blood.

"Carmen, saw. Nurse, have the sternal retractor ready."

Dom took the electric medical circular saw and quickly, but with precision cut through the sternum. As he finished the last inch, the body suddenly heaved up, the back arching off the table, knocking the saw out of his hand. It landed on the floor, spinning in circles. Dom shouted "Dammit!" and quickly grabbed the tool, shutting it off.

Everyone in the room were on their feet. Hernando, his handgun out, pointed it at Dom's head. The old man looked like he was going to burst a blood vessel on his forehead.

"Precisely why we use anesthetic! Everyone remain calm. This can be expected." *Holy Fuck! But why now!* "Spinal reflex is common without anesthetic. Hypertension, higher levels of catecholamine. Do we have a neuromuscular block?"

The patient continued to buck up and down. He yelled at Paulo. "Hold him down." Paulo moved quickly and held his shoulders down.

The nurse yelled: "Like we use in childbirth?"

"Yes, an epidural will work. Are you familiar?"

She nodded. It took her a couple minutes for her to return with the IV drip and related equipment.

Dom, turned the man's head and pointed to a spot at the base of the skull on the spine. "Insert the needle right here…Carmen, help Paulo and I hold him down."

The nurse without hesitation inserted the needle into the spine. Within seconds the man's back slumped down onto the table.

Sweat streaming down Dom's face, he turned to the nurse. "I need a cleanup." She immediately wiped the sweat with a gauze pad. Calm returned to the room. Hernando returned the gun to a holster under his jacket, and used a handkerchief to pat down the sweat on his own brow.

Dom finished the last of the cut. He turned to Carmen. "We'll discuss the benefits of being knocked out when we're finished." He retrieved the Sternal Retractor and placed the clamps of the device on either side of the cut. The retractor was old, but did the job. With her help, the chest cavity was opened, exposing the internal organs of the patient.

Dom put both of his hands into the cavity and gently examined the heart for any obvious defects. He pinched the coronary arteries checking for atherosclerosis.

"Tie."

The nurse responded. "Tie?"

"Silk tie. We need to shut off the superior vena cava. But it must be tied…I don't have time to explain." He looked around the room. "Señor Suarez, your tie please."

Hernando looked at him, his eyebrows raised his hands open in front of him questioningly. "But it's expensive tie."

"We will make an inventory later, but for now, the tie."

Hernando removed the multicolored necktie and handed it to the nurse. "Six inch section. Immerse it in disinfectant."

While he waited, he cut the ligament at the top of the liver, then held the esophagus to the side and made a cut in the chest wall, freeing the upper part of the heart, exposing the inferior vena cava. Carmen Suarez watched carefully, helping to stem the flow of blood. "I'm impressed, Dr. Chavez." Dom ignored her.

The nurse returned with the wet section of tie, holding it with a hemostat. Dom took the length of silk and tied off the blood vessel.

"Clamp." He then shut off the inferior vena cava. He needed to be quick but precise. "Clamp." He shut off the aorta.

"Paulo." He pointed at the transport device. Paulo brought the carrier, which looked like a bread machine, over to the operating table. He opened it up. "Full and functioning, Doctor."

Dom nodded. "Carmen, I'm going to hold the heart in my hands, I want you to carefully hemi-sect the inferior vena cava." Carmen performed the cut perfectly. "Cut the superior vena cava." Again, Carmen performed the task perfectly. "You've done this before?"

"Continue, Doctor."

"Nurse, infuse the heart with Collins solution."

"Carmen, cut the Aorta…. Now the inferior."

Dom pulled the heart free from the cavity, and quickly placed it into the Collins solution, which the nurse held out to him in a small bucket, cleaning the blood from the precious organ. He carefully placed it into the warm fluid of the transport container. The device would infuse the heart with warm vitamin enriched liquid, which would allow for approximately twelve hours of transport time before the heart would start to deteriorate. Paulo closed the device and left the room with it.

"Now for the liver." Dom inspected the liver. It was starting to blanch. He quickly cut it free. There was no longer any risk of damage as with the heart. The liver and the rest of the organs could be retrieved without blood flow. The liver and kidneys were extracted and placed in cold Collins Solution with ice. Generic coolers were sufficient to transport these less precarious organs. Dom took the time to harvest the eyes and pancreas.

Carmen looked him in the eye. "Not bad. You move through the body far too easily Doctor Chavez. Your work arouses new questions. However, I now know that you are able to do the work for which you were hired. Nurse, help us clean up."

The scrubs and gloves were removed and Carmen guided Dom out of the procedure room, followed by her father.

***

They returned to the boardroom and sat down. Carmen looked to her father. "Papa, Dr. Chavez is more than capable to do what we ask of him." Her eyes returned to Dom's. "There's no panic in you Dominic," she used his first name for effect.

Hernando spoke. "We have had good surgeons before. It's what we do which is more of the concern. Dr. Chavez…" He looked at him through squinting eyes. "Can we trust you? I mean, if you are interrogated by the Federales, will you give up my name?"

Dom sat for a few minutes, drinking from the bottled water that sat in front of him. From what he'd read, the Federales probably didn't care, but he wasn't going to make an issue of it. "You're not a stupid man, Señor Suarez. At this point in time, I don't know you very well. I know that you're a man that demands respect. Thus far I can offer you that. Loyalty should be earned. I know that you would not hesitate to put a bullet in my head if I crossed you. I get that.

Now you have some shit on me, shouldn't that be enough? If you were put in the same situation, what would you say?"

Suarez looked him in the eye. "There is more to you than I can read Dr. Chavez. I'm a man that found he could not trust his brother not to fuck his wife." Carmen turned her head away. "Let's make this easy. I don't trust you, but I will pay you. If you cross me, I will kill you, or I will hunt you down and kill you if necessary. If you end up in a Federales prison, I will make sure that you will pay for any insolence by never seeing the light of day again. Dr. Chavez, whether or not you want to respect me, you will. I own your skin. If you fuck with me, you will die a painful death, that's all there is to it." He smiled and stood up, extending his hand. "Welcome to Pacifico, Doctor."

CHAPTER NINETEEN

"MR. LEAHNER, I APPRECIATE your perspective and I understand the need for subterfuge, but I don't like being leveraged."

Benny stared at the large man, allowing a smile to creep into the corner of his mouth. Dr. Richard Brice was a powerful man in Benny's world, President of Suncoast Medical, one of the largest independent medical conglomerates in the Western United States. Suncoast controlled seven independent hospitals in California alone. Brice insisted on meeting privately with Benny and those like him who provided unscrupulous services. He didn't trust anyone below him, except Suncoast's CFO, Adrienne Thiessen, who sat at the other side of the table. Adrienne made the financial end of their clandestine operation work. There were accounts that needed to be manipulated and funds to be transferred to offshore accounts and made to disappear. Adrienne excelled at erasing trails.

"Richard." Benny said, his hands splayed in a conciliatory gesture.

"It's Dr. Brice."

"Okay, Dr. Brice. I am a busy man. I don't have time for niceties, nor do you evidently. I will give you the honest truth. What I do becomes more difficult with every passing day. I'm increasing my fee to 20 percent from 18. I justify the increase by what I will call danger pay. I can no longer rely upon my sub-agents to find the needed organs. They are all corrupt. The people we deal with can be bought by the highest bidder. Now, I find myself entering the arena personally. I must meet with the Cartels and the Chinese government. Travel is a tangible increase in my overhead." He folded his hands on the table. "You say leverage, but I say that it is a justifiable expense. My leverage is in your underestimation of my demand, Dr. Brice. If you do not agree to it, I will take my services to the next bidder, and believe me there are several."

Brice looked over at his controller. Adrienne raised her eyebrows.

"Dr. Brice, we have a seamless arrangement," he continued. "I do the dirty work and you reap the rewards. Your doctors are more than pleased with the extra money and your benefactors like what it does to the bottom line. I'm getting squeezed on one end and I'm passing the squeeze down the line. That's business." Benny stood, extending his hand to Brice.

Brice didn't stand. Instead he looked as if he might be contemplating the little man's offer.

Benny didn't waste any time and pressed. "From your response, it appears as if our business arrangement is terminated?"

Brice stood, his tall frame dwarfing the other man. "Mr. Leahner..." Brice looked him in the eye. Benny was unflappable. "We are in the business of saving lives, but it is a business. We will pay your two percent...and that's it. Don't come to us in the future expecting any more."

Brice extended his hand. Benny accepted it, nodding. "You'll not regret the extra cost." He sat down and opened his briefcase. "I think it would be prudent to go over your current needs." He sat down again, pulling out several dossiers.

CHAPTER TWENTY

"SHE WON'T TALK to us since we told her about Leahner."

Dr. Brian Finlay nodded to Bonnie, the corners of his mouth turned down with concern. He moved to Maddie's bedside, taking a quick glance at her vitals. "Maddie, my dear." He said in his Irish lilt. "It's understandable that you might be upset. We haven't ruled out a donor from a domestic source. They can become available at any time. We need you to keep up your spirits young lady, just in case this happens. Be strong. You'll need every ounce of resolve to make your procedure a success."

For the first time in two days, Maddie rolled over and looked at the doctor and her parents. Both Alan, and Bonnie's faces lit up in anticipation of what she was might to say. Her voice squeaked out of her dry throat, strained and soft. "I understand Dr. Finlay. I've been googling, and have seen where some of these hearts come from. Innocent people!" Her voice shook, slowly rising in volume. "What gives me the right to take someone else's heart? I don't want it. My cards have been dealt, and they suck. If some poor soul dies in a car crash, or what the fuck ever, I'll let you do it. Those are my terms. If I find out that I've got some poor bastard's heart beating in me, I swear to God I will jump off a bridge."

"Maddie!" said Alan.

"Dad, I swear to fuck I will. You and mom are doing this for yourselves. I get it. You have to respect my wishes. I'm 18, I have my rights."

Finlay ran his hands through his orange-red hair. "We've had this discussion, and yes, you have your rights. No one can take them away."

"I don't want you guys to start plotting anything else out. I can see the look in your eyes Daddy. I swear - I really mean it." She slammed her fists down beside her on the bed. "If you don't mind, I really don't want to talk about it and I can feel my chest getting a bit tight."

Bonnie's voice wavered. "It's okay sweetheart, we won't let that happen. Calm down, and ease your mind. The doctor's right. You need to save your energy."

Maddie turned away. Dr. Finlay gestured with a nod of his head that they should leave the room. He led them to a hospice suite where they sat down around a kitchen table. "Bonnie, Alan, your daughter is correct, we must abide by her wishes. The path that we have taken is dark. I don't want to put myself in the position of a future lawsuit filed against me. If your daughter finds out that she's carrying a heart from a secret source that she didn't approve, she could sue me. And believe me, it would be for a huge sum of money, unprecedented. We need to re-think the direction we've taken."

Alan twisted in his chair. "What about the money we gave to the agent?"

"I can't help you with that. It might have been better if you were in line with your daughter's wishes before you started the process."

Alan's voice rose, shocked with Finlay's words. "Listen Dr. Finlay.

We weren't the ones who suggested this path in the first place. What if I were to lodge a complaint with my lawyer?"

"Alan, my role in all of this is here-say. It was Dr. Bright, Maddie's cardiologist, who suggested the alternate solution. I'm simply the transplant specialist; you wouldn't be able to prove anything. Do you have a receipt? Let's not go down that path, I'm on your side. I'll talk to my superiors and see if there is anything that can be done. Maybe the agent can be asked to dig a little deeper. What if we could prove to Maddie that the donor heart came from a true beating heart cadaver?"

"I don't follow?" Said Bonnie.

"You may have to sweeten the pot. Our agent will have to work a little harder to find a donor that's suffered head trauma, but is still alive. We can have the heart flown in once the crash team, as we call them, removes the organ. Now of course, there is competition for such organs."

Alan cut in. "So we have to fork over some more money…?"

"Alan, believe me I understand, but I can't tell you what to do."

"The little bastard is playing us like a pro."

"I hear that he's the best."

Alan folded his hands behind his head. "Can you get word to him?"

"Of course."

CHAPTER TWENTY-ONE

MENDEZES PAUSED BEFORE entering the ward. He could hear Chantal speaking to her husband. He put his ear close to the door so that he could hear the dialogue between his new bosses before entering with the patient's food trays. He didn't like the Canadian nurse, and he knew that his work would soon become more unpleasant with the arrival of the doctor. He didn't like the change in his job description. He felt that the new bosses would have what it takes to stick it out at the clinic, not good for Mendezes. He liked the transient flow of medical practitioners that passed through the clinic. None lasted long. The odd doctor would stay a few months, then leave, their consciences getting the better of them, or they would be arrested by the Federales. The last doctor, Degas, was found washed up on the beach east of Acapulco Bay, half eaten by sharks. The kickbacks that he received from the men who delivered the donors would end. He decided that if he didn't take proactive steps to change things at the clinic, he might need to find employment elsewhere. Nurses were in demand, especially with the Cartels. But then again, there were alternatives, and he didn't feel like moving. He'd led a pretty cushy existence at the remote clinic.

***

"They burn the goddamned bodies Dom." Chantal placed her hands on her hips, a gesture that Dom looked at as the new normal, something that happened every few minutes. He refused to chuckle.

"The young man who passed, is he in the morgue?"

"No, they don't have a morgue either. There is an old tool shed behind the clinic, and as you can see, I use the word clinic loosely."

Dom walked down the row of cots, picking up the charts that were attached to the base of each bed, disgusted with the state of the place. He'd half expected it, but the reality exceeded his worst dreams.

"They didn't have charts before my arrival. No charts! These men are treated like animals."

Dom hesitated for a second, placing a hand on his chin, his index finger covering his lips. "Damned convenient. Steal their kidneys, then use them to work for the Cartel, hell knows doing what. They die in the drug war, the rest of their organs are conveniently recovered, like from the guy I worked on the other day. I think that we're only scratching the surface of what goes on here Mrs. Chavez. I've been reading about the chop houses. Pacifico isn't the only gang that makes a profit from the sale of organs. At least Pacifico performs the theft in closed confines. I hear that in some cases, the procedures are performed at the side of a road, or worse, if there could be such a thing as worse." He let out a deep breath, running his hands through his hair.

Chantal looked up at Dom's face. "You okay?"

Dom wiped a stream of sweat off his forehead. It was damned hot and the smell of dirty sheets, sweat and piss was suffocating. "I experienced a moment, I'll get over it. It's one thing to think about this shit, but when you actually get here and have to start doing things, it's a whole new can of worms. I'm trained to fix things, not break em'."

Chantal nodded. "Keep up your resolve Doctor, I don't think there will be a happy ending if we lose focus. Our mortality ranks just slightly above that of these men."

Dom's phone rang. "Dr. Chavez…Yes Dr. Suarez…I understand. Metlatonoc? Okay. A week ago? It's getting late…I'll make an assessment. To be honest, I haven't come to grips with what's going on here in Nuevo. Yes, I'm always game for more money. Yes…I would have no idea where I'm going. Mendezes? That will leave no one here. Okay, will do, text me. Goodbye."

Chantal looked him in the eye. "I could follow most of that."

"Apparently one of the doctors at a remote location disappeared a week ago. The attendants have contacted Carmen Suarez, and have indicated that two of the patients are in dire need of medical attention."

"They expect us to go today?" Chantal didn't appear the least bit happy. "I have worked nearly two days straight."

He nodded. "I don't really feel like it either, but it wouldn't hurt, it'll only take us a couple of hours, and besides, they're paying us a bonus of $3,000. You can have a nap in the car."

She nodded hesitantly. "Okay, I'll get finished up as quickly as I can."

Dom made a few notes after checking the wound on one of the men's sides. "What a mess. Whoever stitched this up should have their license revoked. You started him on an antibiotic yesterday? The bastards don't have any regard for antibiotic prophylaxis."

Chantal responded, "Yes, but a lot of this could be helped by keeping the environment sanitized. This wound hadn't been properly cleaned and dressed when I arrived. With your permission, I started him on a course of Cefazolin."

"Cefazolin?"

Besides amoxicillin, that's all we have."

"No… That's good. I'm surprised that we have Cefazolin. Keep an eye on him."

***

Mendezes could tell from their conversation that the two Canadians were more than they appeared to be sneaky and guarded. He smiled and pushed the trolley towards the entrance. There are those who would pay well for such information, and he'd made his mind up that he didn't want to see any more of Chantal Chavez.

***

The door on the far side of the room opened abruptly, the squeal of the rusty hinges resonating through the dormitory. Mendezes entered the room, pushing a trolley with water and some horrible looking gruel-like stew, to be doled out into wooden bowls for the patients. The tall thin man exuded a snide look about him that Chantal had warned Dom about. A word popped into his head with his first look at the man: *slimy*.

"Dr. Chavez, this is Señor Mendezes, the head nurse at the clinic."

Dom shook his hand. "Señor Mendezes."

"Pleased to meet you, Doctor. Your wife has sung your praises."

Really creepy. "Señor Mendezes. Mrs. Chavez has brought it to my attention that there isn't a proper morgue here." The man reminded him of Snidely Whiplash from the Rocky and Bullwinkle show.

"Si, there's no money for that. When I get to it, I dispose the bodies. The shed out back has to make do until I get enough to burn. Until then, the rats grow fat."

Dom wrinkled his nose, stepping back slightly. "How long do you leave the corpses in there?"

"Sometimes a week. It's not pleasant task."

"Rats spread disease. This is bananas! From this day forward, we dispose of the bodies on the same day that they pass, the second day at worst."

"It's late, Doctor. I burn bodies in the morning."

Chantal interrupted, her cheeks flushing slightly. "Bodies?"

"Si Señora Chavez, there are two others. Unfortunately they have been there longer than when you first arrived."

"Señor Mendezes, where do you burn them?"

"In the far corner of the yard. I burn the bodies in the garbage. I use gasoline, to make sure the job is finished."

"Señor Mendezes," said Dom, "you will burn them tonight."

"I leave for home soon. I do it in the morning. No need."

Dom came close to growling. "You leave these men unattended through the night?"

"Sí. There's not enough money to pay for two and I have a family. There is a girl, Angelina. She watches, but she no has medical license. She brings water, cleans their shit."

"I see…there is very little evidence that the shit gets cleaned. We'll see to the men, then I want the goddamned bodies taken care of."

"Have it your way, Doctor. Señora." He turned to Chantal. "You no want to bury the corpse like you ask?"

She pulled him to the side and whispered in his ear, not wanting the patients to hear. "Non. I've decided that it would be a bad precedent."

Mendezes returned his slippery sideways gaze to Dom, slowly nodding his head. "We have more men coming tomorrow. Should I prepare operating room?"

Mendezes caught Dom off guard. *Men?* "Which men?"

"More recruits, we must take their kidneys."

Dom hoped that he would have more time to build up his resolve before having to begin the business of extracting innocent people's organs. "Yes, prepare the room. When will they be arriving?"

"In the afternoon usually."

"I want the room sanitized properly. Mrs. Chavez will go over the procedures with you, once you've burned the bodies. I'll finish up with my assessment."

Mendezes raised his eyebrows. "Assessment? I need to get home, Señor."

"You damn well will go home when I tell you to go home. Señora Chavez and I have to look in at a remote clinic before we get to go home. Metlatonoc, where ever the heck that is. I've heard of the region, I didn't know there was a town. The last goddamned thing I feel like doing."

Mendezes looked at him as he changed one of the men's sheets. "It's in the mountains. Not much to see I'm afraid." He picked up a basket of soiled sheets. "I'm finished here, I will see to the bodies."

"The procedure room?"

"I clean that in the morning Dr. Chavez." He left the room.

Dom leaned over the young man Carlos, the friend of the deceased man Hector. He checked his pulse and took his blood pressure. "Carlos, you look as if you have made a full recovery. I'm going to discharge you tomorrow."

Carlos sat up in the bed, squeezing his eyes open then shut, his mouth hanging open. "Doctor?"

"Yes, Don Suarez asked me to expedite our discharges. You will report to work tomorrow."

"Dr. Chavez, you go to Metlatonoc?"

"Yes Carlos, you have big ears."

"Okay…?" He looked at Dom nervously. "You know where you are going?"

"No clue young man. I know we take the coastal road south, then cut in on a regional highway. My boss is texting me the directions."

"Yes, it's not much of a road. Doctor, I can show you how to get there, and I can help you find the clinic."

"Do you know about it?"

"No. But if you have the address, I can help you. The roads are tricky."

Dom had a niggling feeling that he might be making a mistake. "If I take you there, what guarantee do I have that you will not run once you're within spitting distance of home?"

Carlos pondered Dom's words for a few moments and looked him in the eye. "I give you my word. I'm not happy with what's happened to me, what happened to Hector."

"You're having second thoughts?"

"Sí."

Dom worried about travelling through the inner confines of the Mexican countryside. He'd been afraid of getting off the beaten track, lost and getting robbed, or worse. He turned to Carlos. "Okay, but you can consider yourself under house arrest. You bolt, we shoot you."

"Shoot me?"

"You heard me."

Carlos laughed. "Doctor shoot me?"

"Believe me, I know where to aim."

Chantal shook her head, frowning deeply. Dom was beginning to get used to the look. "You've got to be kidding?" she said in French.

"Why not? The kid wants to come; I see no downside. He runs, so what?"

***

The stench of decomposing bodies was awful, a smell one never forgot once hit the senses. Mendezes stood with the gasoline can in hand, a wry smile forming on his face. He dragged the body of Hector from the pile, then set the garbage on fire with the other two decomposing bodies.

He fetched some old sheets, duct tape and plastic garbage bags and proceeded to form a cocoon around Hector's corpse to keep the smell down. With a struggle, he stowed the body in the trunk of the Chavez's vehicle. Once finished, he pulled out his cell phone.

***

Chantal, Dom and Carlos slipped into an old Mercedes C Series that the State Department had provided. It was free of rust, but the interior had seen better days, the leather seats cracked and the dash faded to gray. Chantal liked to drive, which Dom preferred as he didn't mind the opportunity to check out their surroundings. They pulled out of the rear courtyard. Dom got out of the car and closed the sliding iron bar gate, which supposed protected the facility from intrusion. He made a mental note to buy a good padlock and chain. As he closed the gate behind them, he looked around, not knowing what he was searching for. He tried to ignore that spooked feeling that he got every now and again - a shiver up his spine.

Dom's intuition proved to be correct. As they pulled away from the gate, a black car pulled out of the shadows of a side alley and followed at a distance.

They left Nuevo and then soon passed through Copala, picking up route 200 heading east. Carlos sat silently in the back seat, as quiet as a church mouse.

***

It would be another two hours before dark and Chantal followed Carlos's directions. They headed north once they passed the small town of Marquelia. Dom couldn't believe the state of the town, appalled by the extreme poverty. His assessment worsened as they left the medium sized town and began passing through the small villages, which made up one of the poorest regions in Mexico, possibly the world: the Metlatonoc. The town of Metlatonoc lay just east of Cochoapa el Grande and twenty miles west of Carlos's hometown of San Vincente.

Dom turned around to talk to Carlos. "There's nothing here. Every town we pass through is a dusty street. There's no industry, besides the odd little farm where there's a crack of a stream coming out of the hills?"

"Sí Dr. Chavez. We eat after the harvest, but the food we grow only lasts a few months. We raise animals, but they require food. My sisters and I help our mother. We work doing whatever we can. My eldest sister is a prostitute in Puerto Vallarta; she sends some money back. We are lucky if we make 100 U.S. dollars a month."

Dom turned forward for a few minutes, watching the desolate countryside pass by. "So you went to work for the Cartel?"

"Sí, Dr. Chavez."

"Where's your father?"

"He left us years ago. I think he gave up; it's a hard life. We hear about how good it is to work in the tourist towns. There is nothing here, Doctor; we have no future. If my mother's family hadn't lived here for many generations, we would have left sooner. I am young and strong. I don't want to grow old by the time I'm 40. But look what happens, look at Hector. We were promised work, but we have to give up our kidneys."

Dom felt for the young man. "Mexico isn't the only country where this happens. Where there is intense poverty, there's extortion. I've read stories of men promised money for their kidneys. The organs were taken and the men were paid. When returning home, they were robbed of their money."

"That's happened in Metlatonoc. We've grown wise to the practice, but now it seems the same, except we do it…expecting to get paid."

"You're promised pay?"

Carlos nodded slightly.

Chantal interrupted. "Dom, we've been followed for some time now. There's a black sedan behind us, and it appears to have an agenda. I speed up, it speeds up, I slow down, and it keeps its distance."

Dom pulled out his Glock handgun, checking to make sure it was loaded and that the lock was off. He placed it on the seat beside him. "I see it. How much further, Carlos?"

The young Mexican looked uneasily at the weapon. "10 kilometers. Doctors carry guns in the Canada?"

Dom pondered the question. "I'm a military Doctor, Carlos."

Carlos nodded, the answer logical enough for the young Mexican, but it did nothing to wipe the concerned look from his face.

Dom switched to French. "Chantal, I want you to pull in to the side of the road, down one of these little dirt paths that lead into the hills. The next opportunity you have."

Chantal looked nervously at the rear view mirror. "What do you have in mind?"

"If we're going to have a confrontation, I'd like to have it on our own terms."

Chantal shook her head. "What if they're Federales?"

"We'll have to shoot them."

Chantal ran her fingers through her hair. "Have you always done things this way, shoot first and face the consequences later?" She scrunched her nose up. "It smells like a dead rat in this car…no, it's worse than a dead rat."

"What do you mean by that?"

"About the rat?"

"No, I've smelled it as well. What do you mean about shooting first?"

"You know what I mean."

"I didn't sign up for this…brashness. Did you have ADD when you were younger?"

Dom smiled. "I still have it, Mrs. Chavez."

The road continued to pass by without any of the side roads they'd seen, before they had entered the hills. Dom pointed to the right, a small road headed up into the hills after a long gradual corner. Dom switched to Spanish, "Go in there."

Chantal shook her head. "No, we need something more discreet."

"That spot would have been damned perfect!"

Carlos spoke, "Wait for the town, Señora. I know the streets well. I know where we can hide the car, my sister's place." Dom could see Carlos staring at the gun, clearly unappeased by his words.

Chantal looked at Dom, a smile forming on the corner of her lip. "We would have been trapped on one of those roads. We have two handguns, the Federales and the Cartels carry assault rifles and Uzi's. You are a good doctor…stick to what you know."

Dom frowned. "What the hell's that supposed to mean?"

"Exactly what is sounds like…dear. That's the second time you've asked the same question in the past five minutes. I don't think this is the best time for an argument, but if you want me to delve into the details I will."

Dom turned to the back seat. "Tell us where to go Carlos."

***

The sun was getting low as they entered the dusty hill town. Chantal needed to dodge a bunch of chickens as she passed the first group of buildings. The town seemed larger than Dom had anticipated. "What keeps these people here?" He said more to himself than anything.

"Silver, but there are only so many jobs and the bosses are more corrupt than the Cartel." Carlos pointed to a road on the right. "Go there."

Chantal turned sharply and the Mercedes disappeared into a narrow street. Dom looked behind as they passed the corner of a building, he couldn't see their tail any longer. The alley was filled with debris and Chantal alertly avoided the bigger obstacles.

"Once we come out of here, turn right, then we'll follow that street for a minute."

Chantal followed his directions. The town was filled with squat buildings, made of rough block and mortar, as well as piece meal wood-frame shanties. The place looked like it had been built in a bowl, surrounded by the hills that rose above the crude structures in the distance. The streets except for the town square, which they skirted briefly, were mostly dirt, filled with potholes big enough to swallow a small animal. The odd building of substance sprung up amongst the hovels, mostly churches and government buildings. Old mangy dogs, cats, pigs and chickens roamed the streets. The inhabitants of the place were poorer than poor. The children wore old clothing and no shoes, the adults, not much better. Their faces looked at the Mercedes and its inhabitants with a mixture of wonder and foreboding.

Carlos cleared his throat. "See Doctor, there's nothing here. My people, we struggle just to survive."

"What did you say the men from the Cartel offered you?"

"I could tell you many things, but the only one that matters is pesos. They told us that we a needed medical exam. The bosses wouldn't let us work for them if we were weak. Look what they did to me." He rubbed his side gently. "I fear that if they knew that you brought me here, they would kill me. You know they would kill you as well. If they are Federales, you will end up in prison, where you would wish they killed you." He looked at Chantal. "Especially you, Señora. Prison no place for American woman."

"I'm Canadian, Carlos and we were asked to do this, and are being paid extra to see to some patients at the Metlatonoc clinic… The doctor there disappeared. Don't play coy, you heard Dr. Chavez's conversation back in Nuevo."

"No matter, the car no longer follows us. I shouldn't have come." He pointed to the left. "Turn into this alley…that's it, now into the backyard on the right. They won't will find you here very easily. This is my sister's home."

Chantal pulled the car into the yard. Unless someone drove down the narrow alleyway, the vehicle would not be found, especially at night. As she turned off the headlights, the lights snapped on within the crude dwelling.

***

A short bald headed man walked out of the back door, with a machete in his hand. Carlos opened the door and slid out of the back seat and walked to meet him, his hands up in the air. "Marcos, it's Carlos." He moved forward slowly, his hands still in the air until the man recognized him. Marcos lowered the machete, and the two men embraced. Dom could see Marcos gesturing towards the car and as they moved towards the house, the exchange of words grew louder. Finally, Carlos returned to the car. "Doctor, we go inside."

The bald headed man stood back from the car, his arms crossed, and the blade still held in one hand. Dom and Chantal stepped out of the vehicle. Carlos gestured towards the man. "This is my brother-in-law, Marcos." He flourished his hand towards Dom and Chantal: "Doctor and Mrs. Chavez, from Canada."

"Pleased to meet you Marcos." Dom extended his hand. Marcos returned the gesture without any words, a slight nod of his head, his mouth sternly set, and clearly not happy.

Chantal spoke. "I want to have a look through the car, I think something died in it, probably a mouse, maybe a whole family. I'll be right in."

Marcos gestured that they should go into the house. Inside they were met by Carlos's sister Alejandra, heavy with child. The resemblance between the two siblings was uncanny. Alejandra and Marcos went off to the corner of the room and entered into a whispered, but heated discussion. When they returned, Alejandra briefly hugged her brother, a look of fear on her face. "Carlos, why do you come back and bring these strangers to our house?"

Carlos put his hands on her shoulders to calm her. "Let me tell you my story, it will explain much. I wouldn't knowingly do anything to hurt you or Marcos. We're in a tight spot, and we can trust Doctor Dom."

They sat around a small wooden table, Marcos poured out small glasses of what Dom assumed to be tequila; a small sip verified his assumption. It took Carlos minutes to recount the tale of how his kidney had been taken and how he'd ended up back in Metlatonoc.

Marcos and Alejandra nodded here and there, and acknowledged Dom, when he entered the story. When he was finished, Carlos drank his tequila in one fluid quaff.

Dom began to worry about Chantal. Just as he stood to go check on her, she entered the room through the rickety back door. Dom didn't like her body language, her movements jumpy, and her face drawn tight.

Marcos re-filled Carlos's glass and offered one to Chantal, which she accepted and downed in one swallow. Marcos filled it again; this time Chantal let the fiery drink sit for a few minutes. "Doctor Chavez, Señora Chavez, we thank you for looking after Carlos, but you cannot stay here, we will all be killed if the men following you find you here. As you can see, there is very little value placed on human lives where the Cartels are concerned, even a Canadian Doctor and his wife. You can't be seen here." He looked down at his wife's belly.

Chantal moved to speak, but Dom put his hand up, looking her in the eye. "Your advice is good, and I value it. We wouldn't be here if it wasn't for the fact that we're being followed." He placed his hand on Chantal's knee once again to silence her protest. "We'll leave right away, and thank you. Hopefully, we will have shaken our tail and not brought you any trouble."

Marcos nodded, an uneasy look directed at his wife, their eyes flickering back and forth between them. Marcos placed his hands on his thighs. "Dr. Chavez, let me explain what will–"

Dom started to speak.

Marcos cut him off. "What will happen if they find you here," he continued. "They will kill Carlos and they will kill his family Dr. Chavez. They will kill you and your wife. This is how we live. Carlos asked Alejandra if he can stay…He can't, you must take him with you. We can't support ourselves on the land anymore and we are forced to work for the drug lords, or we have to travel to find piecework, or die in the silver mines. We exist peacefully alongside the Banditos, until they are pissed off at you, and they will be pissed if they find Carlos. We don't want that, Doctor. So please take him back to Acapulco."

Dom looked the man in the eye. "Marcos, I'm sorry to have put you in this situation." He could see the pained looks on their faces. Carlos held his head down nearly between his knees.

Marcos continued. "If his mother sees him, she will never let him out of her sight again. She will talk, and she will be killed. The young men, some women, leave the small towns and never return. Young children disappear. If Carlos reappears, he will be taken and killed. Don't put Carlos through this, or his mother…or my small family." He pointed at Alejandra's swollen belly again.

Carlos nodded in agreement.

Chantal could contain herself no longer. "I need a moment Dom." She took him out the back door, guiding him by the arm.

"What is it?"

"The smell…is from a human corpse. Hector's." Anger filled her face suddenly, as a light went on in her head. "Mendezes."

"Christ. We need to get out of here." He shook his head, "Hmmm, nice little trap, I'm glad you had a look. It smelled like a body, but I didn't want to say anything, figured it could be a dead cat. Come on." He went back into the house.

***

Dom didn't take the time to sit down. "Marcos, thank you for your hospitality, but it's time we left."

Marcos stood up. "You're welcome. You were followed and they will find you soon, if they already haven't. They have eyes everywhere. These people who followed you are not Federales, the police would have stopped you on the highway. They wouldn't wait for you to get to the town. It is one of the Cartels."

***

"Where do we get rid of it?" exclaimed Chantal.

Carlos looked at her from the back seat. "It?"

Chantal spoke over her shoulder. "A body Carlos – Hector's"

"Mother Mary! How?" His eyes narrowed.

Dom answered. "Mendezes, it could only be."

Chantal put her hand on Dom's leg. "The clinic?"

Dom hesitated for a few moments. "Well…we're here." He looked at his phone and the address sent by Carmen Suarez. He read it to Carlos. "Are we close?"

"Pretty."

He switched to French. "We're here to build a trust with Suarez. Our followers have the same chance of finding us at the clinic, as anywhere we might go. Maybe we can hide the car once we get there. We can get rid of the body."

"Okay," Chantal reluctantly agreed.

***

They made their way through the side streets as the sun came down, dropping below the hills that surrounded Metlatonoc. They were fearful at every intersection that their pursuers might appear at any moment. The directions given by Carmen Suarez led them to what looked like an old warehouse.

Dom got out of the car and knocked on a small door located beside a large closed overhead sliding delivery entrance. Chantal and Carlos waited in the car. After what seemed an age, a slot opened in the middle of the portal. A pair of female eyes met his.

"Sí?"

"I'm Doctor Chavez."

He heard several bolts sliding and then the door opened. A woman who looked to be in her fifties, slightly plump and matronly looking, greeted him. "Doctor, I'm glad that you came. I'm Jenna."

"Are you a nurse?"

"No, but I may as well be with what they make me do."

"Can we hide our car?" He looked at the large warehouse to his left.

"Sí, we can open this door."

Within minutes, the old Mercedes sat, stowed away inside the large storage room. Chantal and Carlos, were introduced as his assistants.

Jenna led them through a door at the back of the large empty storage area. The scent of disinfectant hit their noses instantly.

Chantal commented. "This is a good sign."

Jenna smiled. "I know well enough to keep the place clean."

They went through what looked to be a kitchen area and then through another doorway into a large ward. The smell of infection hit Dom like a slap in the face.

He guessed that there were at least 40 beds, most of them filled by women in varying degrees of recovery. "Their kidneys were taken?"

"Sí, doctor," she said with a look of shame on her face. "I was only hired to look after their needs."

"I'm not here to judge, Jenna. The doctor?"

"He left over 4 days ago, said he could no longer do this."

Dom looked at Chantal. "Can you grab my field kit and bring the meds we packed. I'll start at this end and work my way through. I'm only concerned with the critical cases. Jenna, Carlos you can help me. I want sterile bandages, wipes and disinfectant. Jena, you called Pacifico?"

"Sí, doctor."

"Show me the patients that you are most concerned with. That's all the time we'll have. I want to get back to Acapulco at a decent hour, I have a busy day tomorrow.

***

It took the better part of two hours for them to treat those women who were in the worst danger. Two of them Dom figured, would not see the light of day tomorrow. In the end, Chantal insisted that all of the wound sites be looked at and cleaned. Instructions were given to Jenna for the dispensing of medications. None of the women after the extraction, received a course of antibiotic, which appalled both Chantal and Dom.

As they prepared to leave, packing up the car, Dom spoke. "Jenna. The two women that are in critical condition; move them away from the others."

"Sí, Doctor."

"What do you do with the dead? Do you have a morgue?"

"In a way…we use a room at the back of the warehouse. It's an awful place, filled with rats. The doctors that have been here insist that we bury the bodies in the hills, when there's time."

Dom's eyes flashed over the trunk of their car. Chantal put her hand on his arm, shaking her head ever so slightly. Dom nodded. "I'm sure that we'll be back soon, unless Pacifico can find another doctor. Here's my cell number." He wrote it on a piece of paper. "Call me if you have any questions. You have enough meds to get you through the week. Do you have help?"

"Sí, doctor. There are two others. Here's the phone number." She wrote it down, motioning towards an ancient phone that hung on the wall of the kitchen.

"Okay then. It's time we left."

"Thank you, Doctor. I was worried that I might make a mistake."

"No doubt. You shouldn't have been left here on your own. I will say though, you are doing a fine job. We'll be in touch unless Pacifico says otherwise tomorrow."

Jenna let them out of the warehouse, pulling the door across behind them with a loud slam.

***

Chantal pulled the car out into one of the side streets. "Okay Carlos, how do we get home?"

He thought for a moment. "We'll need to use one of the main streets soon. I'm not so sure of where I am if we stay on these small streets." He motioned to the narrow pothole filled road they were on.

"Do your best."

They bounced their way through side streets for five or so minutes, before Carlos indicated that they needed to take a right, onto the first decent road they'd encountered. "This road will take us to the highway."

"Dammit!" exclaimed Chantal.

Dom turned and looked out the back window. The dark car that had followed them earlier came racing towards them from behind. It had been sitting in a side street. "Carlos, we need to lose them!"

"I'm not so sure! Turn left onto the next street, it will take us…"

Before he could get the words out, Chantal swerved into the corner. The street was only wide enough for one car. They followed it, Chantal's foot to the floor for a minute until she cursed again in French. Ahead of them was a parked truck and no room to get around it. Chantal slammed on the brakes and turned to look out the back window. Their assailants unfortunately had followed them into the lane and came to a skidding stop behind them. "Keep your heads down," she yelled. She wasted no time and in one fluid motion opened the car door and dropped to her knee, retrieving her Glock handgun that sat in the side door pocket. She leveled it on the car behind them as four men got out.

Their assailants began walking towards them, one held a pump action shotgun, the other three carried handguns, pointed straight ahead. An older, paunched man with a cowboy hat and pointy black shoes took the lead. He spoke in a loud, confident voice. "Get out of the fucking car. Put your hands on your heads."

Dom shook his head. "If we do what they say, I've got a bad feeling."

Carlos spoke, his voice wavering. "Doctor, they will kill us. I've seen these men before. Really bad men."

Without any more hesitation, Chantal began firing. Her first shot took the lead in the forehead, the exiting bullet blowing the back of his head off, the cowboy hat with it. Before the body hit the ground, her next shot hit the shotgun-wielding man square in the chest, knocking him back five feet to the ground. Chantal caught them off guard. The other two managed to fire shots that were more defensive than well aimed. One hit the back of the Mercedes, the other hit the truck parked in front of them. The two men scrambled back towards their car.

Dom grabbed Carlos's head and pushed him down below the level of the back window. Keeping low, he grabbed his gun, which sat where he'd left it, in the pocket in the door. He stumbled out of the car.

Chantal didn't waste any time. She stood up and moved towards the retreating men and fired, this time hitting one of the men in the back, he flew face first into the dirt roadway. The last man let go of his gun and dropped to his knees, putting his hands up in the air. Chantal moved in on him and kicked away the weapon.

Dom appeared beside her, his gun in hand. He looked inside their assailant's car to make sure there were no more surprises. He turned back to Chantal, who held her gun to the man's head. "Nice work, Mrs. Chavez," he said, raising his eyebrows. She didn't flinch. Dom looked down at the young Mexican man. "Who sent you?" He said sharply in Spanish.

The man looked plenty afraid, but didn't look about to divulge anything.

Dom pointed his weapon at the man's thigh and squeezed the trigger. The bullet ripped a bloody hole in the man's leg, shattering his femur. He fell to the ground, screaming in agony. Dom dropped to a knee and put his hand over the man's mouth, placing the gun on his other leg. "Who sent you, who are your bosses?"

The man bit his hand.

"Fucking fuck…!" Dom pulled the trigger, ripping a hole in his other leg.

The man was in shock and started to hyperventilate.

"Who is it, you fucker!"

He muttered softly through his agony. "Gulf. Gulfa Car…" One of the bullets must have hit an artery and bled him out. He lost consciousness before he could say anything else.

Chantal looked at Dom, her eyebrows lowered, her lips tight. "Excessive…no?"

Dom shrugged his shoulders. "Necessary and no more excessive that what you just did."

Chantal began to walk towards their adversary's car. "I'll move the car, we have to get out of here." Lights along the alley began to flicker on from within the buildings.

Dom put his hand up. "No, not yet. Help me with the body."

Chantal looked up at him, a smile forming on her lips. "Yes."

Within a couple of minutes, with the help of Carlos, they stowed Hector's body in the other car, moved it from blocking the alley and were on their way.

***

Dom moved to slip into the passenger's seat, but noticed Chantal sitting there. He ran to the driver's side, slamming the door shut. He looked over at Chantal, before backing the car out of the narrow street. On the surface she was calm, but he could see her hands beginning to shake. He yelled back at Carlos, who looked like he could be suffering from a panic attack. "Which way?"

He pointed to the left.

They drove for a few minutes. Dom felt like he'd navigated a big circle, probably missing one of the turns because of Carlos's sudden inability to function and concentrate on where they were. They ended up in some sort of main square, which he couldn't remember passing through. He could hear sirens from behind them. He slammed on the brakes and looked into the back of the car where Carlos sat slightly hunched over, fear in his eyes.

"Carlos. I know you're upset, but let me make a few points clear. We need to get out of this town…NOW! I need to know how to get back onto the road to the coast. So sit up and tell me where we're going. If we get caught, we're done for…all of us!"

Carlos sat up and pointed to the far side of the square.

"Gracias."

Dom slammed his foot down on the gas pedal and released the clutch. The Mercedes surged forward and entered a fairly central and large roadway.

"Keep following this road and keep to the right at the 'T' and we should be on the coast road after that."

Dom put his foot down on the gas, pushing the vehicle forward, racing through the town's trash littered streets. He put his hand on Chantal's knee. "You alright?"

She pushed his hand off her leg without saying a word.

"There's the road ahead, you no can miss." Carlos shouted.

Dom didn't waste any time, and pushed the car hard towards the exit. Soon, they were on the road that originally brought them to Metlatonoc, threading their way through the hills towards the coast. Dom didn't remember it being this twisty, but then again, he'd been too preoccupied arguing with Chantal to remember.

Chantal finally spoke, but in French so that Carlos wouldn't understand. "Not good Dom. What the hell do we do now? Do we tell Pacifico?"

He thought for a moment. "Nothing…we get back to Acapulco and go to work tomorrow. If we're asked, we did our job and came home. Are you suggesting that we let them know that we are armed and were able to take out four gunmen? We may as well head for the Mexican border right now if we're going to do that."

"Oui, and now we're messed up in a Cartel war, drug war, whatever you want to call it."

"I'll admit that it didn't go as planned." He slammed his hands on the steering wheel. "This wouldn't have happened if Mendezes hadn't put the body in the god damned trunk. This is a setup. You can't plan for a fucking setup!" He paused for a minute trying to think of a way to phrase his next question. "You look as if you've done that before. You probably saved our lives."

"Nothing that I'm proud of." She sat quietly for a time. "I don't know what we're going to do with him." She gestured towards the back seat.

"He's seen too much, but we…I, can't kill him…No, really Chantal, that was special ops stuff, I've seen it before…enough to know it."

"Let's just say that I'm qualified to look out for your sorry ass. Kill him?"

"You know I couldn't do that." Dom turned to Carlos in the back seat. "Where does Marcos work?" He said, switching back to Spanish.

He seemed to have calmed down a bit now that they were no longer in the town. "Marcos works for the Banditos."

"The Cartel?"

"I think so. I've never asked, but he hangs around some bad people. He won't talk to me about it, not in front of my sister, and she's always around."

"They're not the men who recruited you to work on the coast?"

"No doctor, different men. The men who hired me are not from around here. I asked Marcos if I could work with him a few months ago, but he said my mother would kill him if she knew he'd gotten me the job."

"Did Marcos know that you were going to work with Pacifico?"

"No, I told him about the men who were talking to us and he said that they were bad men. I didn't tell him that I would be going with them. He would have told my mother not to let me go. It's common for the young men to leave Metlatonoc looking for work."

He turned back to Chantal, speaking in French. "Carmen Suarez mentioned that the Gulf Cartel were their biggest competitors."

"Yes."

"Carlos, does the Gulf Cartel recruit young men to work in the cities?"

"Yes, they and Pacifico, Cineole too; I think Marcos works for the Cineole."

"Chantal, the man at the restaurant the other day, he indicated that he worked for the Gulf Cartel. You never know what will shake loose when you kick a hornet nest. The man I shot said Gulf. I don't know if what we've done will turn out to be a good or a bad thing. But perhaps we might have started the proverbial ball rolling."

"Nice Dom, and this fucking ball might just roll right over top of us. We were told not to start any f'n balls rolling. Don't you remember?"

He smiled. "Look, I don't want to be here any longer than I have to. I'm just saying, and there's not much else we could have done about it…we may have expedited things a little."

"We were told to stay out of trouble. I've heard that you are a bit of a maverick. It's like you are getting some sort of perverted pleasure from stirring the pot."

"I will admit, I've been pretty good at getting myself into trouble since I was a little kid. My mother used to beat me black and blue." He sat quietly for a moment, his eyes intent upon the road. "You never did tell me about your training."

She sighed. "I can't tell you."

"Look, I can see that your brain is wired for that kind of thing, you don't just take four armed men out like that, unless you've been trained, and I mean you have to have some real life experience, and not just a little to operate like that."

She continued to look out the window. "Just let it go Dom."

"Why else are you here?"

"Let it go Dom. We've been through this before…how many times?"

"I'm not going to drop it. I'm not going to continue on this mission unless I know the real reason you're here. No one does that shit that you just did. If I'd jumped out, I might have hit the first guy somewhere and then after that, I would have been a dead man. You were way too calm. You were…deadly."

She turned to look at him. "I will give you this much. I am here to watch you, to make sure that you don't fuck up."

"So, have I fucked up?"

"That's an affirmative Major and technically, I've breached my orders."

"How so?"

"That last bullet should have been for you. I'm ordered to take you out if you do anything out of line. We may have started something here tonight…outside of our mandate."

"What! I didn't do anything, you're the one who started shooting. Are you losing your mind?"

She went silent.

"You're not making sense. So why didn't you shoot me then?"

She took a deep breath…"I don't know why." She turned to look out the window. "Well, I know that you are too smart for your own good. I can't get inside of your head, but somehow I feel that you might just be able to pull this off. If I shot you, I'd be going against my better judgment. If anything like this happened, I'm to put a bullet in your head and call for an extraction."

Dom didn't know whether to smile or frown. "Fucking nice."

"What do we do with him?" She gestured towards Carlos.

"I'm thinking we may need a temporary replacement for Mendezes."

***

As they descended out of the hills, the road straightened out somewhat, and Dom carried a bit more speed, accelerating as he came out of a bend, and instantly wished he hadn't. Ahead, 400 yards or so, a roadblock was set up. Three police cars, with their blue lights flashing, parked across the road.

Dom cursed, "Dammit!" He slowly eased on the brakes. "What now?"

Chantal slept, but jerked upright in her seat when Dom applied the brakes. She rubbed her hands on her face to clear her head, and turned to Carlos. "You don't say a word." Then she turned to Dom. "We've no choice. There's no way to evade them in the dark, especially in these hills. They would have us tracked down in no time."

Carlos spoke, "Señora Chavez, can I say one thing?"

"One thing."

"It is not strange for them to do this, they may be looking for banditos."

Dom hiked himself up so that he could pull his wallet out of his jeans. "Chantal…here. Look in the inside flap and pull out my real driver's license." He turned to Carlos, "If you say anything to mess this up, I will shoot you."

Dom slowed down the car as one of the Federales put his hand up, motioning them to stop. The officer flipped his fingers together, motioning for some ID. Dom passed him his true ID. He squinted to read the name on the card. He held it up to a piece of paper, his eyes moving from the ID and back to the information.

"You are touristo?" The officer said in English.

"Yes, sir."

"Is this your car?"

"No sir, it's borrowed from a friend." Dom couldn't help but notice the other officers and their assault rifles glaring at him from behind the man.

"It is late, Dr. Tavano and these roads are not safe. Please open the trunk."

Dom felt the hair stand up on his head. "Yes, we were worried, we took too much time at the ruins and we made a bad turn. We're heading straight back to Acapulco and our hotel now." Dom found the trunk catch and pulled it.

The Federal officer slowly walked behind the car, made a cursory inspection of the trunk, then slammed it shut. He handed him back his ID and tapped the roof, motioning him to continue.

Once they were back on the road, Dom let out a deep breath.

Chantal shook her head. "You're a pretty good liar, Dr. Chavez, would you lie to me so easily?"

Dom rolled his eyes. "Chantal, why would you say that? I just got us out of a mess. I'm not your goddamned…"

Chantal put up her hand.

Carlos could not contain himself. "Doctor…are you real doctor? Who is…Dr. Tavano?"

"Carlos." Dom took a moment to choose his words. "Carlos, how would you like to make more money in the next month than you could hope to earn in the next two years?"

CHAPTER TWENTY TWO

"OUR SOURCES INDICATE that four Gulf Cartel soldiers were killed in the mountains last night." Carmen Suarez tapped her pen on the table, waiting for her father's response. Her sister Camille and one of their strong men, Pablo Sanchez, also sat at the table. No one moved while the Patriarch let things churn around in his head.

Hernando smiled. Everyone sitting in the room felt their stress levels rise, sweat forming on their brows. Smiling is not necessarily the response you wanted from the Cartel boss; they were all relieved once the words began to flow. "Pablo, what can you tell me about this? The shootings are not necessarily a bad thing, no?"

Pablo had learned to choose his words wisely over the years and besides his ability to kill people, his caution served him well in his rise to the top of the organization.

"Boss." Pablo not the most eloquent of speakers, referred to Hernando simply as boss, since being hired by the Cartel in his teens. "I no order shooting. We spoke to the Cineole Cartel early this morning and they know nothing. The four men were taken out by pros.

One, shot in the forehead, two hit in the middle of the chest and back, not to the side, the middle. The last had his legs blown off, point blank. Federales would not do this."

"They asked him questions no doubt."

"I would do the same thing." The big man smirked.

Hernando canted his head to the side, nodding slightly. "They will think we did it."

"Yes Boss."

"Make sure that we have some muscle around our facilities. Keep looking, I want to know who did this."

Camille spoke. "It could be an agency or group from outside the country. The Venezuelans, Columbians…the American FBI. It would not be unprecedented."

Hernando nodded. "Our doctor Chavez, you sent him to Metlatonoc last night, no?"

Carmen answered, "Yes, but there couldn't possibly be a connection."

Hernando smiled again. "I have learned to take nothing for granted. Keep an eye on him." He turned his head. "Camille, you are looking frail."

"I'm fine, Papa."

"How did your meeting go with the Cuban last week?"

"Good. He's agreed to buy a shipment, which will be transported by freighter. We have made a deal with a car parts distributor for General Motors in Monterey close to Mexico City. The shipment is going to the Port of Tampa tomorrow."

"Excellent. Carmen, how is our new doctor doing?"

"He's been reliable so far. He'll be performing his first extractions today."

CHAPTER TWENTY-THREE

CHANTAL AND DOM sat in front of the laptop. Joanna DeRosnay appeared on the screen after Dom accepted the Skype invitation.

Dom spoke first, "Good morning, Dr. ReRosnay."

DeRosnay glanced at the bottom of the screen. "Yes, it is 8:20 a.m. Dr. Tavano, we were expecting your call at 8 p.m. last night." The irritation was evident in her South African accent.

"We experienced an eventful day, which I will recount in a few moments."

A man's face appeared next to DeRosnay. "Chris Bachman here, Major. We were able to track you through your implant. You were in the hills last night, Metlatonoc. Intel picked up a remote police report about a gunfight. You wouldn't happen to know anything about that would you?"

Dom spoke, "Major Bachman, Dr. DeRosnay, this is Chantal Turcotte next to me, my medical assistant and keeper after what I saw last night."

"Bachman nodded, "Captain Turcotte."

Dom continued. "Yes, we were involved." Dom proceeded to recount the events that occurred since arriving in Mexico, finishing up with what happened last night.

As Dom finished his update, Bachman responded. "Major, you have clearly crossed the mission's boundaries. You were ordered not to engage the Cartels. It seems as if you've stirred up a lot of shit. The airwaves are very active today, our taps have been picking up a lot of talk. The good thing is, no one seems to know who took out the Gulf Cartel's men. The blame is being directed towards Pacifico. Captain Turcotte, you have breached your orders."

Chantal's cheeks began to turn red. "We were asked by our boss, Carmen Suarez, to go to the hillside town and assess the remote clinic. A direct request. Agent Bachman, there wasn't any alternative. Our cover would have been blown and I don't doubt we would have been killed if we hadn't taken the four men out. I take full responsibility for my actions."

DeRosnay interjected. "Doctor, you must be more careful. You need only become reliable to the Suarez."

Dom pursed his lips. "I think I was being pretty damned reliable. I learned a lot last night, and I think that stirring the pot might bring things to a head quicker. We're going to learn who all the players are, if we haven't already."

Bachman spoke, "I don't like what happened. Though it would appear that the events were out of your control, you just used your get out of jail free card. If something like this happens again, were pulling the plug. You may have made things too hot. Suarez is a cagy old man. Don't think for a moment that he hasn't considered you as a possible source for the violence."

"I'm not so sure that the altercation wouldn't have happened regardless of where we were last night. Mendezes stuck that body in the trunk, and we were followed straight from the clinic…I'm sure that the Federales were tipped off."

Bachman nodded. "You were followed. One of the players knows that you were in Metlatonoc last night, the man you questioned and shot mentioned the Gulf Cartel. We have to assume that they were in contact with their superiors. You may not have blown your cover with the Pacifico, but you have created an enemy. You will be lumped in with Pacifico and I would watch your back. You're a rival doctor who just overstepped his bounds. If things get any hotter, we are going to have to pull you out for your own safety. Stay in your residence. Go to work, come straight home at night. Is that too difficult of an order to follow?"

Dom let out a deep breath. "Now, what about Mendezes? The young man Carlos?"

"I doubt that you will see Mendezes again, unless it's in a dark alley. Carlos…you will either have to dispose of, or keep a close eye on. Do you trust him?"

"He seems like a decent young man, I'd hate to see him…I thought bribery might work and then hopefully in time we could build some trust in him. You never know, he could have bolted as we speak. We took him back to the infirmary. I have offered him two years pay over the next four months to keep his mouth shut, $2400 US, I'll pay it myself. He'll be put to work with us, and we'll need him without Mendezes. He seemed quite happy. I'll make up some excuse to Carmen Suarez, saying that we need more muscle to move the patients around. It's in my contract with them that any extra resources will be at my discretion and expense."

"How will you explain Mendezes to Carmen Suarez?"

"I'll say that he became abusive with Chantal, and I kicked his ass out of the place. I didn't like the look of his face."

Bachman nodded. "Captain Turcotte, I'm ordering you to terminate Carlos if he blinks. Offering him lots of money is no guarantee that he'll keep his mouth shut. If he says one word to anyone, your cover will be blown. This is messy Major. You're on a short rope. Captain Turcotte, I mean what I said about Carlos Rosales, and that rope extends to you as well."

Chantal sat for a moment. "He knows that something is out of place. Dom handed the Federales his real license. Carlos heard the officer call him Tavano."

Bachman was silent for a moment. "All I can say, is that you are on the thinnest of ropes. In four days you've managed to kill four men, nearly blowing your cover, and now you have a young man, who if he blows his horn for any reason, could jeopardize the operation and your personal safety."

Dom spoke. "I have a strong feeling about the young man."

"Let's hope it's correct, Major."

CHAPTER TWENTY-FOUR

The Prior Year

RICHARD BRICE SAT at the head of a long and ornate mahogany table. The twelve people who formed the board of Sun Medical Corp filled the rest of the chairs. One entire windowed wall of the room looked out over the Pacific Ocean, unobstructed by the cliff face below the vista. The view was magnificent.

Brice stood, his hands clasped behind his back. "I would like to thank you for coming today, I know that you have busy schedules. Sun Medical, as you all know from your monthly statements, enjoyed an unprecedented period of growth over the past few years, our stock rising to the point where were are now anticipating a split. We've opened two new hospitals this year: Cleveland and Nashville."

He pressed a button on the desk and the window that looked out over the water became a video screen. "In front of you are charts that show our current financial position. The first," he walked over to the screen and pulled the edge of the chart down and to the right, making it bigger, "indicates the growth in gross revenue from domestic sources. The second, the growth from non-domestic sources. Our cross border business grew exponentially. We are attracting clientele from around the globe."

He looked each of them in the eye. "You have signed our strict nondisclosure statement and I'm sure that I don't have to reiterate the importance of your compliance."

He pressed a button and another graph appeared. "First, let me point out that our commonplace procedures such as births, open heart surgery, oncology, broken bones, etcetera, have been holding their own as far as anticipated growth is concerned. I think we can all be pleased with these numbers. Here are the figures relating to normal profit from domestic transplant procedures compared to profit from non-domestic sources. What it indicates is that there is a demand for our services from wealthy non-Americans who seek anonymity and exceptional health care and most importantly, are willing to pay for it. Domestic transplants have been on the upswing as well. Our outsourcing for donor organs being the driving force."

He stepped around the table towards the screen again. A map of the world came up, indicating the poorer regions on the globe. "The patient lists in the U.S. are far greater than donor lists domestically. Through our agents abroad, we've developed several sources for the organs in demand. We are, for a price, able to procure kidneys, hearts, livers and other important soft tissue organs. I look around the table and there are not many of you that I have not been in direct contact with to discuss this issue. Some of you may have moral issues and at this time I would ask you to stand down from the board if you have any discomfort."

No one moved, their eyes fixed upon Brice.

"The Chinese have been offering heart and kidney transplant vacations for years. What I am proposing is offering the Chinese some competition and at the same time, deflecting some of the heat away from our domestic hospitals. Our management team is proposing the building of two new facilities; one in Mumbai, the second in Mexico City, Monterey."

There was a low rumbling from around the table.

"I know there were concerns when we first started taking our search abroad for the needed organs, ethical issues. What I am proposing is setting up a few clinics in these third world centers, where we could ensure the quality of the harvested organs and tissue, as well as cutting down our costs by eliminating the middle men. As an added bonus, we get rid of the illegality of transporting the organs across the U.S. border. It's a win-win situation."

He pointed his finger at a middle-aged woman with blond hair. "Yes, Heidi."

"What is the exposure to the board?"

"Less than what we are receiving now. As I stated, the cross border trafficking is the difficult issue. It's where our process will ultimately fall down. Right now there is no cohesive set of international laws that explicitly prohibit the cross border transportation of human organs. The directive is geared more towards human slavery and the sex trade. A set of protocols were adopted by the United Nations in 2000, which clearly defined coercive organ sales, but a mandate for the creation of laws pertaining to cross border organ sales is not agreed upon. Mark my words, first world governments are making it a priority, and within two to three years, we'll see a set of laws put into place that will have some teeth, which of course will lead to diminished profits and potential liability."

He walked to the map, tapping on the poorer regions of the world. "The beauty of dealing with third world countries is that there is an accepted level of corruption that can be relied upon. Sun Medical could buy an existing resort in, let's say Acapulco or Puerto Vallarta, where a recipient could receive the best of care during their transplant, recoup in the sun and at a reduced price from what we charge here. Our profits are greater, the organs are fresher and our exposure negligible. I envision taking on partners in the countries that we set up in. Perhaps even with the government."

Brice smiled coyly, then pushed a button on the table and the window re-appeared. He sat down in his chair at the head of the table. "On your way out, my assistants will furnish you with a brochure explaining the process and fiscal projections. What I propose is that we see a show of hands and decide whether or not we shall proceed in our investigations. All in favor?"

The vote was unanimous.

CHAPTER TWENTY-FIVE

WHAT LITTLE SLEEP Dom did manage to get was fitful, and full of bad dreams. The only pleasant part of the night was when he woke with Chantal snuggled in beside him. To this point, they stayed to their individual sides of the king sized bed, a wall of pillows between them. She must have been having a difficult time with the previous night's events as well. They were afforded the luxury of being able to take their time this morning, not having to be at the clinic in Nuevo until 11 am. Dom enjoyed the cuddle for what it was worth, the smell of her, pleasant to say the least, and the feel of a soft feminine body next to him, priceless.

Chantal woke with a start and bolted to the far side of the bed. Dom couldn't help but chuckle. "All of your own doing Mrs. Chavez. I could hear you talking to yourself in your sleep and somewhere around 4 am you were like a heat seeking missile, finding your target at my side. I'll have to say, I didn't mind it one bit."

"Tabernac, you would take advantage of me Dom."

"Not in your wildest dreams Mrs. Chavez. I've seen what you're capable of last night and didn't want to move, afraid to startle you. Next time I'll wake you up, how's that?" He smiled, raising his left eyebrow.

"There won't be a next time." She twirled the sheet around her torso and moved briskly to the bathroom.

***

Dom took a stroll down to the outdoor market four blocks from their residence to pick up some bread and fresh eggs. He loved the smell in the air. It was a mixture of salt, spices, wild flowers and humanity. Normally these smells, including garbage and sweat, would be taken as being a bad thing, but to Dom, it was the smell of the place, part of which made up the whole. It wasn't going to change. The vibrant Mexican town teemed with life. Like many Latin American cities, Acapulco was young and full of energy. There were the sounds of ghetto boxes playing the latest Hispanic hits, children scrambling after a soccer ball, old men sitting in doorways smoking, talking about days gone by. It took his mind off of what he would have to do later in the day, a sick feeling in the pit of his stomach that wouldn't go away.

The place reminded him a little bit of the neighborhood he grew up in back in Brooklyn. He remembered being the kid chasing the soccer ball. There were the same old men, the same groove, except the different climate. "How the hell did I end up here?" he said quietly to himself. He was supposed to be a doctor, someone revered within the community. What he would have to do today shook him to the core of his morality. He didn't know if he would be able to do it. He took the Hippocratic Oath when he started MED school and he took the oath seriously, as should any doctor. "First, do no harm." Would he be able to rationalize the fact that what he would be doing would be for the greater good? He would have to hurt people today. He shook his head as if to clear the demons.

He picked up a nice round loaf of dense ciabatta bread, six fresh eggs and a slab of thick smoked bacon, then walked back towards their villa. He said out loud, "Some fucking doctor you've become Dom Tavano." He began going over the checklists in his head, which allowed a patient donor to be eligible for a nephrectomy. No hypertension, obesity, diabetes, kidney disease, both kidneys needed to be in good working order, low creatine clearance, no disease or transmissible infections, and the list went on. There was no way he and Chantal would be able to check for any of it, but it didn't matter anyway. "Welcome to the fucking chop houses, Tavano."

***

When he walked into the kitchen, Chantal, dressed in her medical scrubs, stood by the coffee machine making herself an espresso. She looked up at Dom as he entered, concern written on her face. She walked up to him and felt his forehead. "You don't have a fever. But there's something wrong. I can see it in your face."

Dom put the groceries down on the counter and sat in a chair, resting his elbow on the kitchen table. "Chantal, I know that you're supposed to put a bullet in me if I waver…I don't know if I can do this. I feel like I could throw up. Perhaps you should use the bullet you saved the other night. Let's get this over with."

She rolled her eyes up into her head. "Would you like a coffee? It might settle you."

"Yes please…and thank you."

Chantal filled the espresso bowl on the end of the handle with dark fine coffee grounds and placed it into the machine with a twist, then pressed the brew button. Within moments she began foaming up some hot milk to pour on top. "Here you go Dom…I understand what you're saying, I'm struggling with it as well. I'll be straight with you. If you were not feeling the way that you are, I would have serious questions about your soul. We're here because what these people do is evil. We're here to help fix what's happening. If you don't do what needs to be done, countless more will suffer. By doing what you deplore, you will do more than any other man could possibly do to help."

She placed a hand on the back of his head and put her forehead against his, looking him in the eye. "We will do this together. We'll be fine and I guarantee you that the people who we operate on today will at least be in the best hands possible. I am starting to believe in you, Dr. Chavez." She turned away and looked into the satchel that Dom returned with. "Well, it's not Canadian bacon, but it looks amazing. I'll cook. Sit down and relax, we'll have a nice breakfast and then we'll head to the coast."

Dom looked up at Chantal, smiling. "Thank you…Mrs. Chavez."

***

Chantal drove. It took a little over an hour to reach the small town. He'd become more accustomed to the destitution and poverty. Once you got away from the tourist areas, southeast Mexico was extremely poor. One thing he did note, however, was that the people seemed happy enough. They bore their poverty as if they didn't know any better. It wasn't like Bangladesh, where the intense poverty was accompanied by overpopulation and misery, though he'd heard that parts of the populous Mexico City were pretty crammed together and destitute.

Dom spoke as he looked out the window. "Mendezes?"

"He won't show up. If he does, I'll shoot him. He played his hand and lost."

Dom resisted the urge to smile at her comment, he knew she was serious and didn't want to risk mocking her.

***

Chantal stopped in front of the metal gate that blocked the back lot of the secret clinic. Two men stood on either side of the entrance, which Dom was pleased to see. Carmen Suarez indicated in a phone call this morning that there would be some additional security. He stepped out of the car, his heart skipping a beat in anticipation of what was ahead of him. One of the men held out his hand. "Dr. Chavez?"

Dom took out the ID card, given to him by Pacifico. The man looked at it quickly and motioned for him to go ahead. Dom, in the back of his mind, wished that the man would have been more thorough. The gate opened and closed as Chantal drove the car through. Dom retrieved his field bag, which held his personal medical instruments, scalpels, stethoscope, various bandages, compression packs and his trusted field manual. He'd also decided that he would pack one of the Glock handguns in it from now on, the weapon a sharp contrast to the medical instruments used to save lives.

They stepped through the back door after entering the code on the keypad. The door led to a small kitchen area. Carlos sat at a large round table in the middle of the room, drinking a coffee. Dom slammed his bag down. "I trust that the operating room is scrubbed and sanitized?"

Carlos jumped to his feet. "It is, Doctor. I scrub all night."

Dom could see that the young man's eyes were glazed over with fatigue. "Good job, sit down." Chantal nodded. Dom sat down in one of the empty chairs. "Carlos, there are a few things that we need to discuss."

A panicked look swept across the young man's face, he reached for the table to stand again. "You no more want the deal?"

Dom pushed him down by the shoulder. "On the contrary Carlos, we want the deal now more than ever, but there will need to be an understanding, a life and death understanding."

Carlos nodded meekly in the chair, not knowing what to think.

"What we are going to tell you, must stay with you. If you tell a soul, we have been given orders to shoot you on the spot. We don't want to, but when I tell you what I'm about to say, you will understand. I will give you one last chance to leave." He looked him in the eye.

"Doctor Dom, I don't want to go back and I don't want to work for Cartel. I'm very happy here."

"Carlos, you will be working for Chantal and myself. You can never question what we ask you to do. There will be things that will not be pleasant." He looked over to Chantal. "Both of us are not happy with what we are here to do." Chantal nodded. "We intend to treat you very well and for your loyalty, we will give you the opportunity to come to Canada or the United States with us when we leave."

Carlos's face lit up.

Dom looked at Chantal. She gave him an approving nod. "I lied to your brother-in-law Marcos and your sister. I didn't feel that Marcos could be trusted. Chantal and I are on a United Nations sanctioned fact-finding mission. I am a military doctor. Chantal is special ops and a certified operating room nurse. You saw her in action last night."

Carlos nodded emphatically.

"We're here to discover the link between the Cartel's organ collecting and the source of funding from U.S. medical institutions. To do so, we are posing as rogue practitioners down on their luck, needing the money."

Chantal spoke, "Now that Mendezes is gone, we will need your help. You will become my assistant. We will follow the Cartel's orders and remove organs as is required. The doctor glazed over the point about me shooting you, I have been given orders to do so. It is on our good graces that you live today. Understood?"

"Sí, Señora, you don't have to shoot me." He smiled for the first time, effectively disarming Chantal's hard stance.

"The doctor is not feeling good about what he needs to do today. So you and I will have to cooperate and help him out. We will meet with the new men. We will greet them and make them feel comfortable. We will assist Dom and you will listen to me very carefully. We will take the patients to the infirmary once we are finished."

"Sí, Señora."

"I gathered enough from Mendezes, that we need to discharge the men that are in ward one, before the new ones come in. The clinic's two wards function like this, one for the incoming and one for the outgoing. In many cases the outgoing were released too soon. It's my goal to expedite the healing process, cutting down on the mortality rate, which as Mendezes pointed out to me, to be one in ten."

Carlos nodded, slightly confused, but willing to move forwards, eagerly willing to help right the wrong which had been done to him.

Dom clapped his hands. "Let's get to it."

***

Chantal and Dom made their way down the row of cots, fifteen of the twenty men who remained were cleared to leave. They moved the five remaining patients to the other ward. They found three extra cots in a storage room and set them up in the receiving ward.

Part way through the process, Dom looked up at Carlos and Chantal. "I don't think I can take much more of this."

Carlos chuckled. "You no like hard work, Doctor Dom? Where I come from, we pray for such work. I thank the Lord for every moment that I'm here."

Dom nodded, grimacing, and continued.

***

When the rounds were completed, they sat around the kitchen table. Chantal put her hand on Carlos's shoulder. "You take on this work naturally. You have a good way with the men, you put them at ease."

Carlos nodded, copying Dom's mannerism.

***

As they were finishing up their lunch, one of the guards knocked and entered the kitchen. "Doctor, men are here. What would should we do?"

Chantal stood. "Carlos and I will meet them at the clinic entrance." She made a mental note to spruce up the dingy foyer. Some flowers would do wonders.

"Sí Señora."

"How many are here?"

"The men bring two."

"Okay, let us know when more arrive. We appreciate your help." She handed him a U.S. $20 bill. His eyes lit up.

"What's your name?"

"Enrique."

"Enrique, Carlos will bring out the men who are ready to work for Pacifico. Make sure they don't leave before the men take them away. Two come in, two go out."

"Sí Señora."

Chantal walked out the front door of the clinic, which opened onto a dirt road. There were no signs advertising its existence. Only Pacifico employees knew of the place…Her thoughts went to Mendezes. He seemed the type of man that could not be trusted and she was sure that they hadn't seen the last of him. When the right time presented itself, she would have to speak to Carmen about the man. Carlos appeared at the door. She turned to look at him sternly. "Carlos!"

He waved her back. "These men, they're the ones who brought me here."

Chantal stood for a moment in thought. "Wait in the foyer."

He nodded and retreated into the building.

Chantal went to greet the men who stood in front of an old rusty jeep. They stood with their hands on their hips, two young men stood behind them.

One of the men stepped forward, his breath stunk of stale booze and cigarettes. "Where is Mendezes?"

"He's not here anymore. I'm the head nurse now. I'm the new doctor's wife, Chantal Chavez." She extended her hand to him.

He accepted it, pulling her close without releasing the embrace.

He pushed his face into hers, his corrupt breath nearly knocking her down. He spoke quietly so that no one else could hear. "I no like Americanos."

Chantal backed him up, pressing her index finger into his chest, "What's your name?"

"Abel," he said, not as sure of himself as a minute ago.

"Abel," she let his name hang in the air for a moment. "I suggest you take these men elsewhere if you don't like – Americanos. I'm sure that Hernando Suarez will be happy to hear of your change of heart."

Abel pondered her words. "That's not what I meant."

"Bullshit Abel, you meant to bully me. You can leave now," she said, her voice rising.

"Señora, it's just–"

"How much does Mendezes pay you?"

His eyes rose to meet hers. "$30 US."

"You don't like Americans, but you like the money."

"I'm just being–"

"A bullying asshole. I will pay you $20 today. The next time it will be more, depending on your attitude. I will make Señor Suarez aware of your insolence."

"No, Señora, no need. $20 today is okay."

***

Chantal escorted the first patient into the operating room. Carlos remained in the waiting area with the other patient. He felt that it might help if he kept the young man company. He remembered how he felt being left alone in the empty dark room.

Doctor, this is Ramone Martinez. He's from Metlatonoc."

Dom looked down, tapping his foot. "Ramone, when's the last time you were sick?" His stomach started to turn over and he felt as if he might need the toilet. He used his stethoscope to check his heartbeat and lungs.

Dom's stomach turned over again, this time rushing towards the finish line. "Chantal, I'll be right back, I may have shat myself." He turned to leave.

"Christ, Dom!…hurry."

"Chantal, I'll be as long as it takes and no longer. Start by taking his pulse, blood pressure, check his heartbeat, standard stuff. I'll be right back."

Chantal looked him in the eye. "You better be telling me the truth. If you're not back in five minutes, I'll come looking for you. And it won't be in a nice way."

Dom forced a smile. "I'm telling you the truth, and it's not pretty. I promise, right back."

***

Chantal guessed Ramone to be in his mid-twenties, thin and tall. He wore nothing but his briefs. Chantal smiled, looking at the blank chart, she started filling in pertinent information. After finishing the notes, she looked the young man in the eye. "Ramone, we will be giving you a cursory examination before we can send you to your new work. It's company policy. Please have a seat on the table."

The man sat as he was told, Chantal could see the unease in his eyes. She checked his blood pressure, heartbeat and reflexes. "We will require some bloodwork." Ramone nodded. Chantal set him up for a drip, inserting a long hollow needle into a vein in his arm, taping it in place. "Lay back onto the table." Ramone reluctantly complied. She added the anesthetic to the drip. She hadn't conferred with Dom on the dosage, but gave Ramone what she remembered to be normal. Within moments Ramone slept like a baby on the table.

***

Dom cleaned himself up and was lucky enough to find a new pair of scrubs sitting on a shelf in the lunchroom. He looked at his bag. *I could be out of here in minutes.* Dom thought to himself. He washed his face with some cold water and stared at himself in the mirror. *I would become even more disgraced and…I can't leave Chantal on her own.* The thought surprised him. Did he have feelings for her or just professional courtesy? It really didn't matter, no time to think about such things. He sat down one more time on the toilet to make sure. He didn't know why he did it, but he grabbed his duffel bag, which held his Glock, and returned to the examination room. *I can do this.* He scrubbed his hands with soap and hot water.

***

As he entered, he could see that Chantal managed to set up an IV and the patient had been anesthetized, lying nicely on his stomach, out like a light, his vitals displayed on the monitor behind his head. "Chantal, can you prepare the ice and Collins liquid? We'll need separate coolers for each organ."

"I did that an hour ago."

"Okay. Let's get this over with, wait! Music." Dom rummaged through his duffle bag for his Bluetooth speaker. He fiddled around with his iPhone. The opening riff of *Hey Joe* echoed through the room. Dom nodded. "Nothing like a little Jimmy to ease the nerves."

Dom finished scrubbing again, holding his hands up for Chantal to snap the surgical gloves over them. He moved towards the table, his feet like lead. "I've come to shoot my old lady, caught her messin' round' with another man." He softly sang softly to himself.

"Doctor?" Chantal said, more to urge him on than anything. "Scalpel?"

"There will be no formalities once we begin, understood?"

"This isn't my first time in an operating room." Chantal said, with a degree of sarcasm. "I've cleaned and prepped the site."

Dom, his hand shaking ever so slightly, drew a line six inches long from the tip of the man's tenth rib on a diagonal, slightly downwards and towards his back. He handed the marker back to Chantal. She handed the scalpel to him, not having to ask. "It's too bad we couldn't do this laproscopically, it would be a lot easier on these men. The proced–"

Chantal grabbed his wrist and guided it towards the man's side. "You're stalling."

Dom deftly made the first incision, cutting along the marked line, opening up the epidermis. Chantal used a gauze pad to staunch the bleeding. He then cut through the muscle lining in the direction of their fibers, hopefully minimizing postoperative pain. "Retractors and once we're finished opening the peritoneum, I want you to prepare 25 g's of Mannitol and 5000 u's of Heparin."

He stretched the muscle with the retractor and voila, the kidney lay exposed. Dom moved to the ureter, dissected it and clamped it with a hemostat, which Chantal handed him. Dom made a few cuts in the perinephric fascia, mobilizing the kidney.

"You are doing well, doctor."

Dom raised his eyes to meet Chantal's, his expression deadpan.

"How are your bowels, Doctor?"

"Clamps ready." The slightest of grins formed on the sides of his mouth. Dom moved to the left and cut the adrenal and gonadal veins. Chantal quickly applied the clamps. "Staple those right away."

Once Chantal finished, Dom dissected the renal vein to its junction with the inferior vena cava. "Staple." He did the same where the vein attached to the aorta. Before she could put the stapler down, he pointed to a spot on the ureter. Chantal applied another staple.

"Inject the Mannitol and Heparin to the IV."

Chantal followed his orders. "What's this for?"

"It will reduce the trauma to the site, minimizing ischemia-reperfusion injury to be specific."

"Oh. I must say…you have the hands of an artist. I've never seen a surgeon move with such quick precision."

"I began to worry when my hand started to shake drawing the line. Something about the heat of battle I suppose brings out the best in me. Being an army doctor is different from being a civilian doctor. We tend to be more under the gun, no time to think about things."

Chantal cocked her head to the side, the sides of her mouth dropping, acknowledging the comment. "You could have been a bit shaky from the bowel evac."

Dom raised his eyebrows, shaking his head. "I'm going to take the kidney out now and prep it. You can begin with the sutures. Start with the fascia and muscle, then close up the epidermis with staples. Do a nice job. The bastards closed up poor Hector with one set of staples, no wonder he died."

Dom left Chantal to close up the wound. He washed the kidney in Collins solution, then checked it for any abnormalities. He placed it in the Collins ice slush. He returned and helped Chantal finish up. He looked at his watch. "35 minutes. Not bad."

Chantal nodded.

"Help me roll him onto the gurney."

Ten minutes later, patient number one rested soundly in the infirmary.

***

Dom and Chantal performed seven more nephrectomies over the next six hours. As they returned to the operating room from settling the last patient, Dom put a hand on Chantal's shoulder. "I need to rest and so do you. My feet are beyond sore and my shoulders are bloody aching from the tension."

As they both slumped down in the only two chairs in the room, Carlos entered with a boy no older than eleven or twelve. They were accompanied by a balding man in his mid-thirties.

Dom looked up at the man, his face drawn into a scowl. "Chantal. Please see to the boy." He stood and took the man by the arm into the hallway outside the room. Once out of earshot he laid in. "Look, I draw the line here. We will not be taking that boy's kidney. He's not fully developed. The standard cut off age for the harvesting of organs is 18 years old. There's a good reason for this."

The man splayed his hands out in a reconciliatory fashion. " Señora Suarez told me to make sure that the operation is performed. The son of a wealthy business acquaintance needs the organ."

"I see…."

"Señora Suarez says that you are to be shot if you are unwilling," the man said, smirking.

Dom stared at him until his eyes dropped. He didn't say a word and returned to the operating room. Chantal looked up at him, detecting the angst on his face. He spoke to her in French. The young boy stared at them, the corners of his mouth turned down, apprehension in his eyes. "I draw the line here."

"What are we going to do? What did the man say to you?"

"Said they would have us shot if we didn't do the operation."

"Tabernac! The bastards."

Dom, Chantal and the boy turned their heads as one as the door of the infirmary flew open, banging against the wall. Carlos ran through the door. "There is shooting outside."

Dom shook his head. "Can this get any worse?" He looked at Carlos. "Take the boy." He grabbed his bag and pulled out his handgun.

Chantal's eyes widened. "Mine is in the car. What made you think to bring it with you?"

"Premonition, I don't trust Mendezes to not sell us out." He looked back and forth between the gun and Chantal. "Here, you're a lot better with one of these than I am."

Chantal took the gun, nodding. "My thoughts as well. Extra rounds?"

"Two clips in the bag."

"Give them to me."

Dom dug them out and Chantal promptly stuffed them into her pockets and made for the infirmary. The others followed. Dom grabbed the two coolers with the kidneys. He'd taken the time to tag and take blood samples for all eight.

They made their way through the cots and stopped at the door to the kitchen. Dom made a pretend kicking motion, indicating that Chantal should be ready with the gun.

Dom kicked the door open. Mendezes stood in the middle of the room arguing with a man neither Chantal, or Dom had seen before. They both held guns. Mendezes turned as they entered, his eyes immediately focusing on the coolers. He quickly stuffed what appeared to be some American dollars into his pocket, and pointed the gun at Dom. "Give me the coolers!"

It was at this point that he noticed Chantal's gun. His eyes reverted to Dom and he pulled the trigger. The bullet hit Dom in the upper chest, throwing him backwards to the ground.

Before he could move, Chantal shot, hitting Mendezes square in the middle of the chest, ripping a hole through the man. The other man, shocked by the exchange, didn't move for a moment, giving Carlos enough time to charge, throwing him off balance. He swung his arm and fired. The bullet caught Carlos in the earlobe, narrowly missing his head. Chantal couldn't shoot as Carlos blocked her target.

Carlos put his weight into the man and the two of them toppled over the kitchen table, landing in a pile of broken wood and flailing limbs. Chantal seized her opportunity and jumped on the man's wrist, which held the gun. She stamped with her other foot, dislodging the weapon. Within a second she had her gun under the man's chin. He raised his hands in submission.

"Get up…NOW!"

The man slowly rose to his feet. Chantal moved behind him, the gun's muzzle touching the back of his skull. She quickly drew her hand back and hit him in the back of the head with the butt of the gun, knocking him cold. He fell to the ground in a heap.

She turned to Carlos. "Pick up the gun. If anyone comes through that door, you shoot him. Okay? I'll be right back."

Carlos nodded.

She bent down and felt Dom's pulse, it was still pretty strong, but his eyes were glazed over with pain. "You hang on! I'll be right back."

Dom blinked a couple of times and let out a muffled groan.

Chantal ran as fast as her feet would carry her to the operating room. She spied Dom's bag and started throwing things into it: Gauze pressure pads, gauze rolls, tape, a hemostat, needles, morphine, antibiotics, and sutures. She flung the bag over her shoulder and ran back to the kitchen.

She bent down over Dom and ripped what was left of his shirt open. He was lucky that the bullet wasn't hollow pointed like the one she'd shot Mendezes with. She put her hand down his back. She couldn't find an exit wound. *Not good.* She quickly opened up several gauze pressure pads and applied them to the wound. She motioned for the boy to kneel down beside her. "Hold these here and don't take the pressure off." The boy was too scared to do anything but. She injected Dom with a low dose of morphine.

She stood looking down at the boy. "What is your name?"

"Pedro."

"Okay Pedro, you stay here until I come back to get you, and keep pressure on that wound."

"Carlos," she waved him to follow her. She opened the back door to the facility a few inches and peaked out. She could see that the back gate standing open and that the two guards appeared to be dead beside the entrance, a black Denali blocking it, still running. Two men stood outside the vehicle. She turned to Carlos and whispered. Can you carry the doctor?"

"Sí."

"Okay, I want you to go back and get him. Have Pedro pick up the two coolers. Go!"

Chantal used the frame of the door to brace her aim. The men were no more than twenty yards away. Her first shot took the man facing away from her square in the shoulders, dropping him instantly. The second man turned to face her, an M16 in his hands. He didn't have a chance. Chantal squeezed off two shots, one hitting him in the shoulder, the second one in the throat, nearly ripping his head off. He dropped in a bloody heap.

Chantal turned and saw that Carlos and Pedro were able to follow orders. Chantal retrieved Dom's bag, and then escorted the two young men to the Denali. There wasn't time to move the SUV and take the Mercedes, so she instructed Pedro to get into the back of the vehicle, where Carlos carefully laid Dom down on his back. "You know the drill Pedro, constant pressure." Chantal and Carlos jumped into the front. Chantal backed out of the entrance in the nick of time, as two more men appeared out of the kitchen door, both wielding assault rifles. Bullets rained off the hood of the truck, one taking out the top left hand corner of the windshield. Chantal slammed the SUV into forward, the wheels screeching as the vehicle straightened out. A similar SUV appeared 30 yards behind her, the lights flicking on. "Tabernac. Carlos, do you know how to fire one of these?" She handed him her Glock.

"I think so."

"I want you to get into the back with Pedro and Dom, don't disturb him if you can help it. I'm going to hit the rear window release, push it open and I want you to empty the gun. Fire at the windshield of the truck following us. Take your time and aim."

"Si Señora." He climbed over the seat and braced himself against the bottom panel of the back door.

Chantal navigated the narrow streets, pushing the Denali to its limits. It didn't take long to reach the coastal road. The SUV following quickly gained ground on them. "Okay, ready Carlos?" She pushed the rear window release. Carlos pushed the window open and took aim, hesitating. "Carlos, we don't have all night."

One of their assailants leaned out the side window, holding an M16. Before he could fire, Carlos pulled the trigger and hit the SUV's window…it swerved from side to side. The glass was punched out by one of the truck's inhabitants. The man with the M16 pulled the gun into the car and rested it on the dash, taking aim.

"Carlos, fire!"

He did, this time ripping off three quick shots. One must have hit the driver, as the Denali swerved to the left and then to the right and off the road, slamming into an abutment.

"Get back up here, but first look for a cell phone in the doctor's bag."

He tussled around with the bag and pulled out a phone. "Got it, Señora."

"Bring it up." She pressed her foot down on the accelerator.

Carlos slid into the passenger's seat and handed the phone to Chantal. The coastal road was fairly straight and she didn't have a problem accessing the phone directory without taking her eyes from the road. She quickly found Carmen Suarez's number, there weren't many numbers. The phone rang five times and then clicked into Carmen's message.

"Dr. Suarez, this is Chantal…Chavez. We were attacked in Copola-Nuevo. I am on the coastal road towards Acapulco. Dr. Chavez has been shot and we need medical attention. Call me back on this number."

She exhaled deeply through her lips. She glanced at the phone's screen. She yelled. "Is the doctor still breathing?"

" Sí," said Pedro, his voice shaky.

"Is he bleeding badly?"

"No, Señora. He seems settled."

Chantal worried about the bullet, a good news, bad news thing. If it would have been a hollow nosed round, he would be dead. She could easily tell by the small entry point. If the bullet would have passed through his body, he would be fine. When a bullet hits a rib or some other structure, it could be deflected into a critical organ. She hoped for the best. When she'd first met the man, she'd formed preconceived notions about his character. His dossier indicated that he was brash, self-motivated. It indicated many relationships and the rep of being a womanizer. No doubt a good doctor, but often refused to follow directives. She smiled. The words in the dossier described the man, but another quality existed in him that couldn't be placed into words. She could see how he might be a woman's man; devilishly handsome, but he'd been nothing but courteous since their first encounter at the airport in Montreal. There were good things hidden behind all of his bravado. She hesitated for a moment…she felt him to be honest, a trait she'd not anticipated.

The road took a sharp turn and Pedro called out. "Señora, the doctor whispers to me. He wants agua."

She looked around the front seats and saw a half finished bottle of water. "Carlos, pass this back."

It made her happy that he was cognizant enough to ask for the liquid. Her thoughts returned to Dom. Why did she put up the wall? She felt an attraction to him physically, he kept himself very nicely. He could be funny. She went back to the look on his face when she ushered the first young man into the operating room by. He'd been torn, he cared enough to be sick to his stomach at the prospect of having to do the extraction, his soul laid open to her. She smiled. *Now how do I save him?*

When the cell rang, she put it to her ear. "Oui?"

"Chantal. It's Carmen Suarez. Is the doctor okay?"

"Yes…but I am worried about where the bullet went in. He was hit in the chest by a standard round, five inches below the collarbone, four inches from the center line. If it deflected off a rib and went down, who knows what it might have hit."

"What have you done to stabilize him?"

"Morphine, compression on the wound. I don't know who is

behind the attack, but I can tell you that Mendezes was involved. We were able to bring the kidneys that were extracted. We don't know about the patients."

"So you have them?"

"Mmm…yes."

"Chantal, I'm going to have you leave the coastal road just as you enter the city. Do you have internet on your phone?"

"I think so."

"Good. I want you to drive to Hospital del Pacifico. Take the exit on, you won't believe it, Dr. Ignacio Chavez Blvd. Follow it to the hospital. I will meet you there. Just pull up to the front, they will be expecting you. We do have some pull here."

***

"The Doctor is not conscious," Pedro yelled from the back of the SUV.

"Christ!" Chantal said more to herself than anything. She laid her hand on the horn to speed up the car in front of them, the driver in no hurry to accelerate on a green light. She followed the hospital signs that were now quite frequent. Her heart skipped a beat as she saw the Hospital del Pacifico sign. She swerved into the emergency parking and slammed on the brakes.

Carmen Suarez, true to her word, met Chantal at the rear of the vehicle. Chantal lifted the rear hatch and pulled down the tailgate. Pedro's hand was still on the wound. Blood seeped through the compression pad, covering his arm. Carmen's eyes panned between the boy and Chantal. Chantal ignored the subtle question.

Orderlies lifted Dom onto a gurney and rushed through the automatic doors to the hospital emergency ward, his eyes closed, head rolling to the side. Chantal tried to follow, but Carmen held her back. "He's in good hands…you look exhausted and would be no help."

***

Carmen escorted Chantal to a private room on the second floor of the building. Outside the room stood two men, both holding Uzi machine guns. The room inside, set up for family members of patients to the hospital drew Chantal in. She fell into an armchair, exhausted.

"Can I get you a coffee? or tea? I'd offer you something a little stronger if we could get access to it."

Chantal wiggled in the overstuffed chair, making herself more comfortable and nodded. "Tea would be fine."

Carmen plugged in a kettle that sat on a counter in the room's efficiency kitchen. As she put a tea bag into a small porcelain cup she asked, "What happened?"

Chantal scratched her scalp and ran both of her hands down her face thinking about what to say. She didn't dare hesitate. "I think we were sold out by Mendezes. We'd just finished the last of the extractions when one of the patients, Carlos is his name, entered the operating room, telling us he'd heard gunfire. We were engaged by Mendezes in the kitchen where he shot Dom."

"What of Mendezes."

Chantal chose her words carefully. She pulled out the Glock from her jacket pocket. "Dom and I acquired this shortly after we arrived. He didn't feel safe. You can't expect us to do what we've been asked to do and feel any differently." She put the gun back in her pocket. "I don't think Mendezes expected us to be armed. I caught him off guard and shot him. I think he's dead. We grabbed the two coolers that held the kidneys. They're in the SUV."

Carmen held a finger up and pulled out her phone and made a call. "Roberto…yes. There will be a couple of coolers in the vehicle that the doctor arrived in. Please take them to the clinic. Yes, right away. Yes, give them to him." She hung up. "There were other men? If a rival Cartel is involved, they would not leave things to chance. I know that we wouldn't. I would expect there to have been at least ten."

"Yes, but I don't know how many. The SUV blocked the driveway and fortunately was left running, so we did what we could and took the vehicle."

"You are very resourceful Chantal. Very lucky to have escaped with your lives." She handed Chantal the tea. "Are you okay? Have you ever shot anyone before?"

Chantal tried her best to look defiant, her face twisting in mock anger. "What do you mean by that Dr. Suarez. No…I haven't and I'm sure it will sink in soon enough. Even though I did not like the man, and he shot my husband. I've never taken anyone's life, and I will say that I'm a little distressed by it."

Carmen nodded, taking a sip of her own tea. "Where did you buy the gun?"

"Does it matter?"

"I'm curious."

Chantal could feel her cheeks go warm. She needed to be careful. "Dom bought it down at the market. It took a few days, but we were introduced to a man and we paid quite a bit for it. He promised that it was clean and could not be traced."

"I would doubt that. You should be careful, the streets have ears and it's not commonplace for a doctor to carry a gun, especially one like that. You might have drawn some unwanted attention to yourselves. Information travels in this country faster than you might imagine. Word of mouth is powerful and dangerous."

"Like I said, Dom didn't feel safe, and if we hadn't owned the weapon, I'm sure we would both be dead." She couldn't help herself, wanting to change the topic. "So what is it like to be the daughter of a Cartel Boss? Every time we've met, there have been bodyguards with guns, and you blame us for buying this." She tapped the gun in her pocket.

Carmen frowned, pinching her bottom lip between two fingers. "I don't blame you, I just hope that you were inconspicuous, but I doubt it would matter. Anyone not Mexican asking to buy a gun will have attracted attention." She sighed. "As far as being the daughter of Hernando Suarez, I've known nothing else. There are those in Mexico born into poverty. I was born onto the family of a drug lord. I have power and money, more than I could spend."

She stared down at her hands. "It's been a lonely life, Chantal." She suddenly puffed herself up. "But this is no concern of yours.'

Carmen's phone rang. "Yes…that is good news. I'll tell his wife." She hung up.

"Your husband is stable. His right lung was pierced and the bullet did not travel. The Doctor pulled it out just below the surface of his skin on his upper back. He's lucky, but lost a lot of blood. The doctor said that once he's stitched and cleaned up, he should make a full recovery. Dominic will need to stay in the hospital for a few days. They worry about pneumonia when there is trauma to the lung."

Chantal breathed a deep sigh of relief, which was heartfelt. "Of course." She surprised herself by how much concern she felt for the man.

CHAPTER TWENTY-SIX

ALAN WAITED FOR over an hour for the call. When it finally came, he resisted the urge to voice his displeasure with the caller. He pressed the answer button. "Alan Chambers."

"Yes Alan, I'm sorry that my call is so late, but some things cannot be helped."

"Mr. L…"

"Alan, I thought we discussed this issue."

"Yes, my apologies," he said as he remembered the man didn't like having his name used over the airwaves. "I would like to up the ante, my daughter is failing. The doctors feel that if something doesn't present itself within the next month or so, she may not have the strength to accept any heart."

"Alan, this is the world in which you and I now live, but on opposite ends of the spectrum. I will have my girl contact you as before. I'll warn you though, my time is very expensive. I will be dividing it between you and my other clients, though you will be given preference. I do promise to keep a close accounting of my costs. There will be travel involved."

"Don't patronize me while you extract your pound of flesh. I understand the implications and cost of what I am asking."

"Now Alan, I am no shylock," quickly discounting the Shakespearian reference to his religion. "I am a simple businessman, who operates in a very high risk-reward environment. The cost to you is purely money, my risk is more than money."

"And my daughter if you don't do your job."

"Fair enough. As I said, my girl will contact you. Good night."

Alan felt like chucking the phone across the room as he hung up. He didn't believe that the man would have to do any more work than he'd already been doing. Maybe…he would make a few more calls. He would most likely move him up on the priority list, nothing more. At this point, though, he didn't care about the money. It was all about Maddie at this point. He'd made a promise to Bonnie that he would make the call. What's done is done. He poured himself a bourbon, then sunk down into his favorite plump armchair.

CHAPTER TWENTY SEVEN

TWO WEEKS TO the day since he'd been shot and Dom felt worse now than when he'd been in the hospital. The heavy-duty pain killers were taken away by Chantal and the best he could get his hands on were regular Tylenol. She feared he would become dependent on the stronger narcotics. The slightest movement caused intense pain. "You are lucky to be alive," the Mexican doctor who'd performed the operation told him. The bullet made a mess of his upper chest, but missed all major blood vessels, including his heart. He sat in the shade of the roof top garden at their rented house. It was quite pleasant, especially now with an attendant to look after him.

Pedro had been placed under house arrest by Chantal, under pain of death, until they could figure out what to do with him. Pacifico wanted Pedro's kidney and Dom didn't want to show any weakness. As far as the Cartel knew, he'd escaped to the hills after helping Chantal deliver him to the hospital. Pedro brought Dom the Corona he'd asked for with a smile. His life was a hell of a lot better in the Chavez household than in the remote destitute town in the hills from which he'd come, and as a bonus, he retained both kidneys. "Thank you, Pedro."

The young boy nodded. "You're welcome, Señor Doctor."

Dom gestured for him to sit. "Tell me, how did you end up with the men from the Cartel?" Dom smiled at the innocence of the boy.

"The men took my Papa over a year ago…to work. Mama died a few months ago. She fought the fever and never got better. I miss both of them. My father is a good man, I know he would have come back for me if something hadn't happened to him." A tear began to well up in the corner of his right eye. "My older brothers have moved away, but they beat me anyway. I'm glad they left. The men who brought me to see you knew my parents and said they would look after me."

"Pedro. I will tell you something. These men are not your friends. I am like your father. I have no choice but to work for them. Tell me. Would you like to go to the USA?"

His eyes lit up. "If you keep low and help out around here, do as we say, I will help you." Chantal and Dom talked about sponsoring the boy. They couldn't see letting him loose on the streets. Dom would find him a foster home back in the States, he'd sponsor him. "If the men knew that you were here, they would kill you."

He nodded.

"Another beer, por favor, in an hour."

"Sí, Señor Doctor."

***

Three hours and three Coronas later, Dom woke from a mid-afternoon siesta. He dreamt that someone was poking him. He rubbed his eyes, clearing the fog. Chantal sat on the end of his reclining chair and strangely enough, was rubbing his leg.

"Glad you're awake. You're not in the shade anymore, you silly man. You'll survive a gunshot wound and succumb to melanoma if you're not careful." Her hand remained on his leg.

Dom rubbed his face with his hands again, more out of nervousness than anything, not used to the sudden attention from the woman. "How did you make out today?"

Her closeness making him uncomfortable. Normally he wouldn't shy away from a pretty woman, but their relationship since they'd met in Montreal could be classified as being cold and distanced. They shared a bed, but that only for appearance' sake. Chantal made a ritual of building up a fortress of pillows between them, each staying to their own side of the bed, sometimes the wall was reinforced by a stern look. He detected something different since he'd been released from the hospital. He tried his best to appear relaxed; it wasn't easy.

She stood finally, and moved to sit in a chair beside him. He hoped that she didn't detect his slight sigh of relief. Pedro appeared on the hour with his Corona. "Corona, Señora Chavez?"

"Sí, Pedro."

He gave the bottle to Chantal. "I get you another one, Señor Doctor?"

The empty bottles building up beside his chair were gone, Pedro thankfully saving him from Chantal's scorn with his diligence. "Sure, I could go for a cold beer."

The boy winked and hurried off down the stairs.

"We finished the move to the new site. The last of the patients have been released, and Carmen Suarez sang your praises. Your work is excellent, Dom."

"Our work," he corrected her.

She smiled. "The eight men that you operated on are now working for Pacifico. The new site is a bit more remote, but will not be known to the Gulf Cartel. Carmen explained to me that raiding is a common practice among the Cartels and that she wasn't surprised that the incident occurred, especially after hearing about Mendezes.

She confided in me, stating that she'd never fully trusted the man. He must have sold us out for cash."

"This is good…well, sorta. Did she ask about Carlos?"

"I told her that we enlisted a helper now that Mendezes is gone. The fact that the man is no longer on the payroll kept her quiet. Carmen also told me that there are two more remote sites, and that we will be required to assist at them when required." Dom nodded. "Back to Carlos, he's been a great help over the past couple of weeks and takes to the work with ease and enthusiasm."

"Can we trust him to keep his mouth shut?"

"He appears to like the pay and I think that he knows on which side his bread is buttered. I think that he's in line for the time being. He seems like a well-balanced, nice person, very clever."

"Good."

"Pedro?"

"I can't see sending him back into the hills. He's a good little worker and I like his spirit."

Chantal took a small sip. "Dom, if we were here for a year, I somehow feel that we would have a house full of these orphans." She paused for a moment, her eyes dropping to the floor. "I thought you were some Rambo type American military guy, a loose cannon, a womanizer."

Dom was caught off guard. "Whoa now! Who told you all that, and why this all of the sudden?"

"No one in particular really. I read your dossier, I heard a few things from my briefing officer. She told me to stay away from you and be careful not to start any relations. In fact, it was mandatory."

"Mandatory?"

She looked up and ran her finger along the bottom of her left eyelid. "Dom, my first job is to assist you in all medical endeavors. The second was to take you out if you wavered from the mission plan."

"You mentioned that the other night. I figured as much; it's pretty much standard protocol to put a failsafe in place. The way you took out those men up in the hills confirmed my suspicion. I don't know where the womanizing thing came from, except the fact that I did have an affair four years ago with a naval officer's wife. It caused a pretty big stink. I swear that I didn't start it. She was lonely and we lived next door to each other. One thing led to another and that's it, other than the fact that we got caught red-handed. I hadn't been with a woman for three years prior to that, and really, a lot longer. The last few years of my marriage were not happy times, if you get my point."

"I read that you were married for ten years, and that you have kids."

"Yep, the marriage was a mistake from the beginning. The kids, bless their hearts are wonderful. They live in L.A. I see them every year, when I can. I don't really think they know me and it seems like it's a chore for them every time we get together. My wife Gina fooled around on me for years while I was away. I came home one time and found the house packed up, a Dear John letter on the counter. Real fucking nice." He took a long swig of his beer.

"This isn't my first mission."

"So you said."

"I'll stop right now if you're going to be sarcastic."

Dom grinned. "Sorry."

"I became close with a French Colonel a few years ago. I can't go into the details, but he died in the line of duty. I swore that I would never become…entangled again."

Dom tried not to smile, doing his best to keep a straight face. "What are you trying to say Chantal?"

She looked him in the eyes. "I don't really know Dom. I built myself up that you were going to be some monster. It was easy at first, especially the way you greeted me in Montreal."

"Yeah, that wasn't so good. I've never been undercover before and I thought that it fit within the role."

"A hug and a kiss on the cheek might have sufficed."

He cocked his head to the side, raising his eyebrows, slowly nodding.

"I guess what I'm saying is that…I've seen a caring, sincere man these last few months. You don't let it out and I have to look for it, but I like the man that I see. I know that it's just killing you, doing what we have been commissioned to do. I can see it in your eyes. I can see that it's breaking your heart. I don't want to see that. Dom Tavano, I've seen into your soul through your eyes. You're a smart man, but I think that your greatest weakness is your inability to keep your thoughts and feelings close to the vest. This can be a bad thing in the business that we're in, but when it comes to matters of the heart, a woman needs to see these things in a man."

"You didn't answer my question."

She stood, finishing the last of her beer. "I think I did. I told you that you are a kind man and I will do my best to protect you. You make my job more difficult." As she passed him on the way to the stairs, she kissed him on the forehead.

Dom watched as she descended. "What the hell," he whispered.

***

That night she helped him into bed. As she pulled the sheet over him after changing his bandages, he gently reached for her hand. She squeezed her thumb into his palm. Her eyes met his. "I can't." She tried to pull away. "Dom, please."

He let go.

Before he could say anything, she cut him off. "I will not break my orders, Dom. Please respect me for this. I hope that we can live through this mission with mutual respect. If we were in another place and time, things might be different. This is the way it needs to be."

Dom took a deep breath, which nearly killed him, the pain stabbing him in the middle of his chest. *This woman is damn confusing.*

The Body of Thieves

***

"You are doing a remarkable job, Dr. Chavez."

Dom didn't see Carmen Suarez as she entered through the door behind him. He'd been focused, intent on assisting Chantal, as she closed up the wound on a donor patient. He nodded. "Dr. Suarez. I will admit that after performing nearly 90 nephrectomies in the past month or so, not to mention a good number of heart and liver extractions, one tends to get the hang of it."

"If this isn't your specialty, what is?" She didn't phrase it as a question, but more a matter of fact, possibly trying to catch Dom with his guard down. He frowned. Maybe being too sensitive.

He canted his head to the side, holding one side of the sutures with a hemostat, as Chantal finished up. "I'm a surgeon. In a way… what I did before losing my license, is somewhat similar Doctor, but the patients tended to have some say in the matter."

"One day I will figure you out, Dominic." Suarez smiled, but it wasn't necessarily a happy smile. "Your mortality rate is perfect since you've been here. Your output is not that of some of our practitioners, but we can accept this as a suitable compromise."

"I will take that as a compliment. I won't take all of the credit though. Chantal is equally instrumental in our success. She cleaned up the environment and as a doctor, you know how important cleanliness and proper sterilization is in the process."

"Yes, I would agree."

Chantal didn't say a word, intent on her work. She didn't ask, but took it upon herself to inject the patient with a strong dose of antibiotic, once done with the sutures.

"I have heard good reports about you as well, Chantal. I'm passing though and I wanted to see how we were doing. It looks as if you are well under control."

Dom nodded.

"There's another reason I came. We're having a cocktail party at

Pacifico Clinic tonight. We'll be entertaining some important business associates and I thought it would be good if the two of you could make it?"

Dom caught a sharp glare from Chantal.

"Yes, of course. At what time?"

"Nine. That should give you time to finish up here and time to get home and clean yourselves up."

"Thank you. We'll be there, Dr. Suarez."

***

By the time Chantal and Dom cleaned up the clinic, with Carlos's help, it was nearly 7 pm, which left them an hour drive home and an hour to shower and make it to the reception. Chantal navigated the Mexican traffic expertly and they made it home in good time.

Showering was still not an easy task for Dom, he found it hard to raise his hands above shoulder height. His wound had cleaned up nicely, but the trauma within his chest was still very painful, probably something that would bother him for the rest of his days.

The past several months had flown by and he somehow, somewhere found a place to hide and reconcile the tasks they performed on a daily basis in the back of his mind. He remembered Harvey calling it *compartmentalization*, a big word for what his mother would have simply called sweeping problems under the mat. Call it what you will, it seemed to be working in the present.

Chantal and he usually took turns getting ready in the master bath, but today, time did not allow for it. Dom dried himself off, wrapping the towel around his waist. He quickly brushed his teeth and applied a shot of Axe under each arm. Chantal impatiently rapped on the bathroom door. "Almost done Mrs. Chavez." He opened the door, the steam pouring out into the bedroom. Chantal stood impatiently in her mauve bathrobe.

"You would leave no time for me, Dom. Hurry, get out."

In his haste, he rubbed up against the door latch, catching his towel, which promptly fell to the ground. He momentarily stood naked, inches away from Chantal. She reflexively took in the length of him, her eyes pausing on his large and rapidly engorging penis. He stooped down and picked up the towel, covering himself, then scooted into the bedroom. Chantal pulled the door shut behind her.

***

As quickly as his sore body would allow, Dom dressed himself in a light summer suit, white pants, light tan blazer and a floral tie. He retired downstairs and joined Pedro watching television, a luxury he'd never enjoyed before moving into Chez Chavez. He smiled up at Dom from the white leather couch. "Chores all done, Señor Doctor. Corona?"

"You read my mind Pedro." Dom plunked himself down on the other smaller couch. Pedro liked watching mixed martial arts. The Mexican version seemed a bit more brutal than what he'd seen from time to time in the States, but then again, he'd never paid it much attention. Pedro returned with the bottle, which Dom accepted with a nod.

The two of them proceeded to watch the fight as he waited for Chantal. She usually took little time getting ready, he would have to give her that, and it was a trait that he admired in a woman. She bore a natural prettiness that didn't require a lot of fuss and wasn't one for much makeup, she didn't need it. Five minutes later, she sauntered down the stairs. Both Pedro and Dom stared at her, momentarily at a loss for words. She wore a pant suit, with a low cut top, which showed off her medium-sized perky breasts to their fullest. Her hair was pulled back off her face and held together at the back with a Japanese style comb, with a long pin holding things in place. She didn't have a stick of makeup on besides some red lipstick, which somehow accentuated her sexiness. She looked at the two of them. "Is there something wrong?"

Dom stood up from the couch. "Au contrair."

***

They were fashionably late for the reception. It differed from the typical American style function, mainly due to the heavily armed guards who stood at attention wherever you looked. Dom didn't need any explanation, In fact, he found some comfort in their presence.

He put his arm around Chantal's shoulders as they walked in the main door. She didn't shy away, pulling herself closer for a moment, looking up at his face. They looked the perfect couple as they made their entrance. They were greeted by Camille Suarez, who conversed with an Arabic man in a white suit with a gold tie. "Doctor and Mrs. Chavez, I'm so glad that you could make it. Let me introduce you to Dr. Mohammad Agazedah."

The thin, good-looking man extended his hand to Dom. "Dr. Chavez, I've heard good things about your work."

Dom accepted his hand. "Thank you Dr. Agazedah. We only do as we were trained. This is my wife Chantal and my medical assistant."

He extended his hand to Chantal. "Please…" He stared at Chantal for the briefest of moments, perhaps just a touch too long, which surprisingly irked Dom. "Please call me Moh."

Chantal released his hand. "Pleased to meet you, Moh."

Moh escorted them towards the bar. "I don't drink alcohol, but I am told that the Suarez pride themselves in their vast selection of rare tequilas."

Dom nodded. "Sounds good."

Moh ordered two small glasses of what might be the best and smoothest tequila Dom had ever tasted, with a chaser of spicy tomato juice.

Chantal shot hers back in one go. "Mmm, that is delicious. I promise I'll sip on the next one."

Moh chuckled. "A hard day, Mrs. Chavez?"

"It was long."

"It's okay to speak. I am in the same field as you are. I operate the extraction clinic in Oaxaca."

Both Dom and Chantal were visibly relieved to finally meet another professional in their station.

"I hear that you were shot, Dr. Chavez."

"Please call me Dom. Yes, it wasn't one of my finer moments."

Moh laughed. "I should say. I've had my close calls. What we do, I am afraid, sooner or later can be perilous."

Dom took a sip from his tequila. "If you don't mind me asking, what brings you here Moh?"

"I don't mind at all. I am a persecuted man. I'm from Jordan. My medical papers were removed for helping wounded foreign soldiers. In fact, I barely escaped with my life." He gestured to Chantal. "My wife was killed when we fled. Allah praises her soul."

Dom could see the sorrow in his eyes. "I'm so sorry to hear that." Dom looked around the room as they talked. There were probably forty people. He could see Carmen and Hernando, talking to a small skinny man in a well-tailored suit on the other side of the room, just in front of the doors to the outside patio. "It seems that you're out of the frying pan and into the fire, Moh?"

"Not really. Mexico is an impoverished country, where the wealthy survive at the top and the poor are miles away at the bottom. This breeds the opportunity for the organ and human trade to flourish. There are some bad people and the odd doctor or Cartel soldier gets killed. Jordan is in a state of civil war. No one is safe. It is not a good place to live whatever your social ranking. Here is my card with my cell on it. Give me a call if you are in any trouble or need any advice. I've managed to survive for three years. Those years have provided a lifetime's worth of experience. I will help you as best I can." He bowed slightly and moved on to a small group of people.

From the other side of the room, Carmen tried to catch Dom's eye. When they made contact, she waved them over. They wove their way through the mingling people. When they reached the small group of three, Carmen greeted them. "Dr. Chavez, Mrs. Chavez. I'd like to introduce you to Benny Leahner."

Both Chantal and Dom shook the man's hand. Dom quickly turned to Hernando Suarez. "Don Suarez." He shook the man's extended hand.

Hernando's eyes squinted slightly and a trace of a smile formed at the side of his lips. "Dr. Chavez. You are a true member of Pacifico now. You have paid in blood and you are still living. You now have my respect."

Dom released his hand and smiled. "Thank you. I take your compliment as an honor. I can't say that I wish it to happen again, but what's done is done."

He reverted his attention back to the weasel-looking man, who impatiently awaited Dom's attention. His words were slow and very deliberate. "Dr. Chavez. I have taken the liberty of asking your employers if it's okay to talk to you and the other Pacifico practitioners."

Carmen cut in, to Benny's irritation. "Benny is our agent in the States."

Dom tried not to look too shocked. "I see."

"Dr. Chavez, I prefer to be called a medical facilitator. I help people."

Hernando laughed. "And you get paid well to do what you do, probably too well."

"I like to say that I get paid commensurate to the risks that I take." He turned back to Dom. "I have a few A-list clients back in the United States and Israel who…" He smiled, his eyes flicking to Hernando. "Who are paying me an extra stipend, to find various organs for transplant. The organs are typically for patients with irregular blood types, the ones that don't stand a good chance of finding donor parts before they would pass. These clients are typically very wealthy. Señor Suarez agreed to let me offer to you a $60,000 bonus, which of course he so graciously offered to split with you, for the delivery of any of these A-list organs."

He pulled out a piece of paper and handed it to Dom. "Here are our requirements. My number is on the bottom. You won't get me immediately, I usually return my calls once I've listened to your message. I throw the phone out after one month. In one month's time, I will text you a new number. I hope that you will give consideration to my client's needs, Dr. Chavez. Now, if you will excuse me, I have a few more people to talk to. I hope that you will understand that in my field of work, it's not wise to linger in one place for too long."

Dom shook the man's hand again. "Of course I will." He handed the man his cell number, written on a cocktail napkin. He looked to Hernando for approval; he nodded his head.

Dom turned to Hernando after the organ agent was out of earshot. "Is this man to be trusted?"

Hernando laughed. "What the hell does it matter, Doctor? No one in this business is to be trusted. As long as you accept this fact, you no have problems. Any problem you have, you shoot them before they shoot you. It's simple."

Dom raised his eyebrows.

***

Dom waited until they stepped out of the taxi in front of their place before he said anything. He checked his pockets to make sure that no bugs were planted on him. "Pay dirt Chantal."

She looked up at him smiling. "So, I was wise not to shoot you when we were in the hills?"

"I've always said, there's no use in shooting a perfectly good husband."

"Are you good, Dom?"

He felt his face flush. *Christ! Was this an invitation?* "There's only one way to find out." He looked into her eyes searching for hesitance, or a stop sign. *All good...* he confidently put his hand on the back of her head, leaned down and kissed her deeply. She reciprocated, pulling herself into him. He guided her towards the door as they held onto the kiss. He fumbled with the keys, finally getting the door open. He held her hand and ushered her through the main floor. Pedro slept on the couch. Dom turned off the TV and followed Chantal up the stairs, the smell of her as he followed in her wake making him crazy with want. His throat went dry.

She stopped and turned to him. "Are we making a mistake?"

"Possibly, but I'm past the point of worrying." Before she could say another word, he kissed her again. He could sense her succumbing to the heat of the moment. He slipped the top of her blouse off her shoulders, revealing her perfect breasts. He'd been staring at them for months now and it was like unwrapping a present that sat for too long under the Christmas tree. He gently kissed both of them, taking her nipples into his mouth, twirling his tongue around them. She moaned.

She helped him pull down her pants and petite thong underwear, pleased to see that she preferred to shave herself completely. He lifted her onto the bed and gently ran his tongue down her belly and nibbled on the inside of her thighs. She squirmed slightly. Her ticklishness stopped however as his tongue found her sweet spot.

She exhaled deeply. "Mon Deu!" After a few minutes of his ministrations, she abruptly sat up and kissed his mouth as his head popped up. "Your clothes, husband."

He fumbled at his belt, careful with his zipper as his erection raged to get out of its forced confinement. It sprang to attention as he dropped his briefs. She slid down off the bed and took him in her mouth. His knees nearly buckled. He could only bear a minute or so of her attention before he lifted her onto the bed and in one smooth motion guided himself into her. She moaned. "Treat me like your wife."

"With pleasure, Mrs. Chavez." He leaned into her deeply and passionately kissed her mouth. She responded, pulling his head down into her, her tongue fiercely probing his mouth. The months of pent up sexual tension between the two erupted. They both enjoyed the pleasures of each other's bodies deep into the night, in the way that first time lovers would.

***

When Dom woke in the morning, the wall of pillows didn't exist, instead, Chantal cuddled into him in a spoon position, still fast asleep. He normally found a way to feel bad about similar situations in the past. He'd never felt comfortable with Jasmine from the beginning. She'd been nothing more than a sexy lay, one that went on longer than it should have. But he somehow felt with Chantal that he would be the one that could possibly outstay the welcome. She seemed very hard and set in her ways, which would probably be a good thing for him. He'd been the controller in all of his past relations. He'd longed for a relationship in with some equality.

His leg began to get uncomfortable and he moved it from under her, causing her to stir. She awoke abruptly. It took her a few moments to get her bearings. He feared that she would be upset for some reason and move away from him. Instead, she turned towards him and ran her hand up his chest. She could see the look of concern on his face. "Don't worry Dom, once I make my mind up on something, it takes me a long time, if ever, to change it."

"Why did you change your mind?" He stroked her hair.

"I told you. I saw your soul through your eyes. When I could see that you were a good man it was easy. I just needed enough resolve to say fuck it and blow my orders, really that's it."

"In what ways do you think I'm a good man?"

"Okay, don't let this go to your big head. When I first saw you in Montreal, my heart skipped."

"So you've been playing hard to get all this time?"

"Mon Dieu, non. I told you of my previous relationship on a similar case. We were in love and he was killed. It ripped my heart out. I tell you the truth when I say…no. I can show you the mandate in my dossier. If you were to get out of line in any way, I am to take you out. By doing what we have just done, I have disobeyed orders on three levels. I'm not to enter into a relationship with you. I should have killed you back in the hills and now I might just find myself incapable of following any directive. I'm all in with you, husband."

It was strange that her words didn't bother him. In the past they would have with any other woman he'd been with, including Gina. Even when they were first married, and things were relatively okay, he never felt warm and fuzzy when she'd told him that she loved him, and vice versa. *Could he truly love this woman?*

She turned to lay on her back for a few long moments. "Tell me Dom, you behaved yourself after our first meeting. I began to think that I was ugly to you or something."

He brushed a stray wisp of hair behind her ear. "I would say that that statement is far from the truth. You put up such a good wall that I was afraid to try anything. And the way that you handle yourself in combat situations left me a little nervous. I have experienced more combat than I choose to remember, but I have never seen…"

"A woman?"

"Well…yes, a woman who handles herself like you did. It was a turn-on in one hand and a stop sign in the other."

"Glad you went through the stop sign, Dom, and I'm giving you permission to do it again."

"Mrs. Chavez! Can I tell you something?"

"Of course."

"You may think I'm being mushy, but…"

"Dom?"

"When I first saw you in Montreal, my heart skipped as well."

"Mon Dieu, kiss me."

***

As they sat around the breakfast table drinking their coffee, Dom asked Chantal the question that both of them had been pondering. "Okay, we now know that Benny Leahner is the link that we've been looking for. What now?"

"I think we need to contact the state department and let them know."

"Agreed. But his words are not an indictment on their own. They don't prove anything." Dom sat for a moment in thought. "Can we get a mini lab at the clinic? One where we can check blood type?"

"You know as well as I do that the technology is there. It's commonplace but expensive. I'm sure that Pacifico will spring for the bill, they will be in on half the cut if we find a compatible donor. It would be taking organ trafficking to the next level."

"We need to catch Leahner red-handed."

"Would 60K, plus the usual fee for an organ be enough to warrant the use of a private jet?"

"What are you getting at, Dom?"

"I would want to ensure I received my bonus. The total cost for say…a normal heart on the black market, from what I have read, is 60 to 80k. What I'm saying is that I would want to deliver the heart personally to Leahner, and receive all of the payment. He's one nervous dude, it would have to be plausible to personally deliver the goods. Money is always a good reason. I would assume that the recipients reside in Southern California, possibly Texas. The shelf life of these organs is short. We put a homing device on the Organ carrier. Badda boom…we've done our job and then we're outa here. I have my medical license and life returns to some normalcy."

"Does your normal life include Chantal Turcotte?"

He reached across the table and held her hand, grinning. "It does, unless you shoot me or something."

***

Three days later, Dom took a taxi north to Toluca. The day happened to be a national holiday and the roads were packed with cars, Dom likened to it being a free-for-all for terrible drivers in Mexico. He would have preferred Chantal to drive, but she needed to stay back to look after some patients at the remote clinic. The cab driver seemed intent on setting the world record between Acapulco and Toluca, whatever the consequences.

They arrived at the address given to him and Dom sighed in relief when he put his feet on the ground outside the car. If he were religious, he'd have made a Hail Mary. He asked the cabbie to wait for him while he went into a multi-story apartment building. The neighborhood looked very rough, the street full of garbage and the buildings in dire need of some serious concrete restoration. A group of men stood on the street corner, eyeing him as he stood talking to the cabbie. The driver expressed his misgivings about hanging around. Dom gave the driver an extra $20, which seemed to solve the issue. It usually did.

The apartment was on the second level of the dilapidated building. The hallway smelled of damp and moldy carpeting. He went to room 204 and knocked. The door opened and a Caucasian man holding a gray short-muzzled handgun greeted him. Dom handed him his credentials as he'd been instructed to do. He followed the man into a large living room decorated with the bare necessities. He recognized two of the three people who sat around the dining table. Joanna DeRosnay and Chris Bachman. The third was a Mexican man dressed in a suit and tie.

DeRosnay stood to greet Dom, offering him her hand. "Dr. Tavano, it looks as if you've made some progress?"

Dom shook her hand. "It would seem so."

Bachman stood, as did the man in the light green suit. "This Roberto Pingue, one of our men in the field in southern Mexico. He's been watching over you since your arrival."

He shook Dom's hand. "Big brother right?" Dom smiled. *How much has he been watching?*

"Something like that."

DeRosnay spoke. "Your contact with the organ agent is a major breakthrough Dom. We both flew in when we heard the news."

Bachman cut her off. "Yes, we've been in touch with the FBI and they've been watching Leahner for a several years. We've made some assumptions, but he is a slippery target, extremely careful. He won't stay put anywhere long enough for us to get a tail on him, and we haven't been able to gather any concrete evidence."

DeRosnay frowned at Bachman for interrupting. "The fact that he's been to Mexico is strange. He's opened himself up a bit. There must be some real money involved."

Dom handed Bachman a copy of the requisition Leahner gave him. "There are no names, just the tissues that are required and the blood type."

"We'll cross reference the intel with all known donor waiting lists."

Dom nodded. "I'd concentrate on the two donor wards that abut Mexico: California and Texas. The Cartels, I've discovered, don't like to spend much on medical transport apparatus and thus the time allowed to safely get the organs to the States is relatively short."

"We'll take that into consideration Major. I think that your plan to personally escort the organ to the site of the operation in the U.S. is a good one. He won't like it, but you'll argue that you want to guarantee that you get paid and that you don't necessarily trust Pacifico, or him for that matter…you are cutting ties with them."

Pingue spoke. "We can have a jet ready for you on one hour's notice. You'll have to coordinate with Leahner and get us a destination if possible, ahead of time would be ideal, but unlikely. We have your tracking implant, but it will take time to get to you once we see where you've touched down. The tracking device doesn't work very well when you're in the air."

Bachman spoke. "We'd love to nail him, but it won't be easy."

Dom looked at Bachman skeptically. "How are you intending to do this, once I've done my part?"

"We look at getting Leahner as a bonus. The big target in all of this is one of the U.S. medical companies. There will be a transfer of funds to one of his accounts. If we're lucky, it will be the same one that he uses to transfer funds to you, but I doubt it." Bachman smiled.

"Seems too easy." Dom said. "Who gets paid by the person needing the transplant?"

Bachman paused for a moment. "There are several ways it can happen, but we are assuming that the original funds, probably a deposit, pending delivery of the tissue, are paid to an off shore account. The FBI has been monitoring all accounts associated with Mr. Leahner and the medical conglomerates for a few years now. We assume that there will be funds paid by Leahner to one of the hospitals, or vice-versa. There will be a secondary payment upon delivery of the organ by the recipient. I don't want to belittle your involvement Major, but we are crossing our fingers that the payment gets caught somewhere within the web of electronic money transfer protocol, and hopefully the transaction occurs at the same time the tissue is delivered. But Mr. Leahner is a master at manipulating the underground banking structure. We're counting on the medical conglomerates not being quite as savvy."

"Isn't it enough that we will have the organ? Won't we have them red handed?"

"There will be a chain of cover. Documents will be procured, falsifying the source of the organ. The tissue will be tied to a death somewhere, and there will be a familial tie made to the recipient. We'll be hoping to make some headway to break down the source of the falsification. Morgues, public officials. We need to see how far up the kickbacks go. "

DeRosnay spoke. "They go to the top, Mr. Bachman. I can assure you of this." She changed tack. "There are a lot of ifs. I think the plan is a long shot at best. I don't think Leahner will trust Dom to transport the tissue."

"Do you have a better plan Dr. DeRosnay? The mission will have been a success in my eyes if we only manage to find one small piece in the puzzle." Bachman said curtly. "Dom, use the phone that we gave you for emergencies if you are able to acquire any of the organs. Tell Leahner that you are fed up with the Cartel and the illegality of the process, and you want to have one last payday before you leave Mexico. I'd ask for more money. You'd be speaking his language."

Dom smirked. "That seems logical. You talk like all of this is a matter of fact. I'll be taking my life in my hands. When I get on that jet, the whole thing is over down here…right? What about Chantal?"

Bachman looked him in the eye. "Yes, it'll be over. But do I detect some untoward concern, Dr. Tavano? We'll look after Captain Turcotte."

Dom resisted the urge to retort, catching a knowing look between Bachman and Pingue. "Where's the airfield?"

"We'll let you know."

"Not good enough Bachman." Dom said irritably. "I want to know by tomorrow at the latest. I want to take a drive and find out where it is. I've been in the forces long enough to know that the best laid plans never turn out the way they're supposed to. I don't want to be searching for the goddamned place in the middle of the night, with the Mexican Mob chasing me."

"We'll get you the location as soon as we've nailed it down."

"Do we have a backup plan?"

"We could pull you out by chopper, but that would risk Leahner finding out something is not right. It has to look legitimate. On top of what we just talked about, I'd tell him that you don't trust him. This might give the lie some teeth."

Dom stood. "What happens if he disagrees with me bringing the donor organ? If he's as savvy as you state, he's going to smell something here."

"We have to count on the fact that for some reason, he's got a lot more invested in this project than normal. It's not like these guys to stick their necks out this far. Maybe he's getting too old for the game and is cashing in on a few big deals. There is a lot of money at stake, even for him, and he's got his reputation on the line. He needs to produce, or he loses credibility. This is the opportunity that we've been looking for. All criminals eventually slip up and we have to be ready to catch them when it happens."

"Okay, I have this sneaking feeling that we will need some more bait. I met the man and looked him in the eye. He is a wary predator. We risk everything if he gets spooked in the slightest. I'm sure that he's made contingency on top of contingency. I guess that's why I'm a bit concerned, that we have only one."

"Leahner's contingencies have been created over years. We have had months. This is why these bastards are so hard to catch. We have little choice."

Dom didn't feel good about the operation. Could there be more to the whole thing than nailing Leahner and one of the medical conglomerates? The thought continued to percolate in his mind during his drive back to the Acapulco residence. Could he simply be a pawn? He sighed. It was a long shot anyway. The chance of finding the donor with the correct blood type would be next to impossible. He felt a small pang of anxiety as a thought popped into his head. Finding the missing organs might be the only way he'd get out of Mexico. How long would he have to work for Pacifico? A year, more…? The thought of what he would have to do and any trepidation was suddenly superseded by the horrible thought of being stuck in the job from Hell.

CHAPTER TWENTY-EIGHT

IN THE 1970S, Acapulco expanded dramatically. New hotels were built, bigger and better than the fifties standbys. With the tourist trade came the heyday of the drug trade, and Hernando Suarez and Pacifico Cartel were right at the heart of it.

Pacifico owned a small fleet of cigarette boats, aircraft and trucks that carried illegal contraband along the coast, over the hills to and from Central America and the United States, and to small airstrips anywhere within a fuel tank's range. The Cartel became rich and attracted the poor to act as its workers and soldiers. Labor was cheap, and the borders porous.

Acapulco became a hedonistic destination, where anything could be found at any time of the day, including drugs, liquor and whatever one was looking for as far as sexual preference might be, male, female, young and old.

During this time, Hernando Suarez built his grand fortified compound in the hills that overlooked Acapulco Bay and the Pacific Ocean. The Federales and the local Police were firmly in his pocket and all that he feared were the hit men from the competing drug lords. Hernando's policy was simple: "Hit them before they hit you."

Camille and Carmen played with their dolls around the pool as Hernando received a briefing from his second in command, Juan Hechievary. Hernando took on the responsibility of raising his two girls after shooting his brother and wife, whom he'd found in bed together more than a year ago. He tried his best to spend as much time with them as he could. He couldn't take them with him on Cartel business. Hernando did not like to leave the safety of the compound walls if he could help it, let alone take them with him. He paid a household full of attendants, chefs and nannies, all at his beck and call. He lived like a King in his castle overlooking the peasants in the city below. His daughters never left the walls of the hillside fortress until they went overseas for their education. Carmen went to the University of Dublin to earn her Doctorate. A good friend and business associate in Ireland watched over her during this time. He too, was a man to be feared. Camille went to Venezuela, where she received a degree in business, she too watched over by close friends.

Hernando motioned for Juan to help himself to the food and wine that were delivered by one of the male servants. Juan knew that it was a double-edged invitation. The Boss never ate first. He used to be bothered by the custom, but after some time, shrugged it off as an opportunity to be first to the wonderful food served in the Suarez household. Juan helped himself to deviled eggs, roast chicken and a fresh mango salad. He poured a glass of wine for Hernando and himself. He didn't hesitate to sip first.

"Boss. The Hondurans are up to no good again. They're moving in on the nightclubs."

Hernando smiled, that smile never a good thing to see forming on the man's face. "You see Juan. I took your advice last time and we gave them a warning, now look what happens."

Juan felt a bead of sweat forming on his brow. "Boss, I suggested that we don't kill them, that's all. For a time they have paid us for their spot on the strip."

Hernando cut him off with a waved index finger. "Warnings are for children." He motioned to his girls. "Camille likes to play at the pool's edge. I warned her that she could drown if she fell in. The warning lasted for a couple of days. You see, she needed to fall into the pool to learn her lesson. We cannot treat these fuckers the same way. They need to see the consequences. Juan, we will pay them a visit and show them consequences."

Juan didn't like the look on his boss's face. Hernando, calm as a cucumber, dug into his food and sipped from his wine. Juan excused himself after lunch as Hernando took some time to be with his daughters; the calm before the storm.

***

The Hondurans were notorious for bringing in fabricated narcotics, Speed, LSD, MDA. They would sell their goods to the younger vacationers, the party seekers. This in itself wasn't what angered Hernando, but rather the side effects of the drugs. He didn't like to deal with non-organic drugs. He thought they were dangerous. No one knew what was in them, and sometimes the concoctions were deadly. He worried that Pacifico might be blamed.

The drugs would sooner or later get back his girls in the Pacifico brothels. Their heads would become messed up. The young men who took the drugs would often become violent. MDA, a notorious sex enhancer, made people crazy. The police didn't like crazy. It was customary to pay the police to look the other way, part of Mexican culture, but the police didn't like to look foolish. Pacifico ran a tight ship, the police turned a blind eye, the tourists paid for their prostitutes and everyone remained happy. The Hondurans were putting a monkey wrench into the well-oiled machine. It would be expected of him to clean up his own mess and the Federales would back him up. It would be no secret that Pacifico had received payment for the Hondurans spot on the strip. Hernando cursed the fact that he'd allowed himself to be swayed by Juan's words in the first place.

***

Hernando turned to Juan, who sat beside him in the back of the Mercedes. "You know where they operate from? You have the men in position?"

"Sí Boss. They've been partying at The Tropical for the past few weeks. They have become brazen and careless. The Federales are ready. Those that we don't deal with will be arrested and deported. They are happy that we are cleaning up our own backyard."

Hernando tapped his ring on the side window. "It should never have come to this Juan; have you learned your lesson?"

Juan didn't say anything, instead he took a deep breath.

"You will see. We need to send a message to these fucking punks, so that they never come to Mexico again." Hernando seldom swore, though he'd recently taken to the "F" bomb. It made Juan nervous.

The Tropical, a fairly new nightclub, one street back from the bay, ran a terrific poolside bar that stayed active until four in the morning. The sun had just set and the place appeared reasonably quiet. Hernando's men moved in, just as he arrived out front. Half came in from the back, half from the front ahead of him. The staff were alerted and many of the patrons told to leave, their tabs covered and VIP lounge tickets issued. Before they realized it, the Hondurans were surrounded by twenty Pacifico men, sidearms brandished as they opened up their coats. Three men pulled out Uzi sub machine guns. The place would have been dead quiet but for the Bee Gees 'Night Fever' that blared through the poolside speakers.

The Hondurans eyed their adversaries as the Pacifico soldiers eyed them back. All heads turned as Hernando Suarez calmly entered the pool area from the front lobby, accompanied by Juan and two

Pacifico soldiers. He preferred to dress in a white suit on such occasions, his hair slicked back with Brill cream and his mustache oiled and turned up to perfect thin points. He walked directly toward the man he remembered to be their boss. His name if he remembered correctly, Sandor Alvarez.

He walked up to the chunky man, who remained seated at the bar. "Señor Alvarez. You were given the benefit of the doubt a few years back and were politely told to leave Mexico and never return. Juan convinced me that you were a man of your word. I treated you with courtesy." He let the words hang in the air, his eyes not leaving Alvarez's.

Hernando could see Alvarez's Adams apple contracting in his throat, his eyes not able to hold his. "You come to Mexico and you bring drugs made with chemicals. You have the nerve to sell it to my girls and to the Americans who come here. You will give our town a bad name."

Alvarez tilted his head to the side and smiled, though his lip quivered slightly. "Señor Suarez. I have not been given the honor of meeting you. I have only talked to your men." He looked at Juan, his eyebrows narrowing. The look was not missed by Hernando.

Hernando reached under his coat and hauled out his silver-plated 44 magnum, its barrel extended by the manufacturer to meet Hernando's specifications. The gun was more of a cannon than a pistol. Alvarez squirmed in his seat. Hernando lifted the gun and turned to Juan, pressing the barrel of the gun into his chest. "Where there is garbage, there is a rat. How much are they paying you Juan? Not enough." He pulled the trigger and blew Juan's chest apart. As the bullet passed through his torso, it hit one of Alvarez's men in the leg. Juan's body hit the ground with a heavy thud. The man who'd been hit howled in pain, dropping to his knees. The Hondurans to a man looked like they wanted to go for their weapons, but the sheer number of Pacifico men acted as a deterrent, their weapons cocked and aimed.

Hernando could see fear in Alvarez's eyes, the tendons standing out on his neck. Hernando turned and placed the barrel of the gun up against his groin. "Señor Alvarez, there is always one who makes the decisions for the followers. My men follow me. It is a shame that Juan betrayed me. I liked him. My faith in mankind shrinks as the days pass. How much were you paying him?"

Hernando waited for the man to speak. The silence was heavy. He eventually croaked, "200,000 U.S."

Hernando shook his head in agreement. "That is a fair price and worth the risk." He looked at all of his own men. "Is it worth the risk?" All of his men to the last one shook their heads. He walked over to one of the younger men and placed his gun against his head. "Is it worth the risk?" The young man pissed himself. "No Señor Suarez."

"Good, then we understand each other." He turned to Chico, a chubby man from the hills. "You have been with me for twenty years. Is there any amount of money that is worth it?"

Chico stared Hernando in the eyes and said matter of factly, "No, Señor Suarez. I will make sure that the men know. I will remind them that you are to be obeyed above all cost."

"Gracias." He turned to Alvarez. "Señor, you cannot be allowed to live. Will you die with honor or as a coward?" Hernando watched his eyes carefully, his gun cradled in his arms.

Alvarez dropped his head, slowly shaking it from side to side. "I will not die a coward."

Hernando patted him on the cheek. "Then I will honor my word. Chico, take him to the hills, let him die like a man."

Chico patted Alvarez down and removed a bevy of weapons that were concealed on him, then escorted Alvarez from the bar.

All but two of Alvarez's men showed fear looks upon their faces. Hernando pointed his gun at them, the barrel moving back and forth between them. He liked men who showed no fear. "Kneel down in front of me." Both men followed the order, looks of concern slowly forming on their faces. "One of you will live. I give you the option of working for Pacifico. Who will be the first to take my offer?"

The taller man on the right looked Hernando in the eye, the

other man was still defiant and wouldn't raise his eyes. The tall man said, "I will take your offer, Don Suarez."

Hernando in one swift motion put the Magnum's barrel between his eyes and fired. His brains splattered in an arc ten feet behind him, his body falling to the ground. He put the barrel of the gun under the other man's chin and raised his head. "I appreciate a man with some conviction. What is your name?"

"Jesus, Señor."

"You have conviction, Jesus." He turned to one of his men. "Have the rest of these men turned over to the Federales." He spoke to all of them, meeting each one's eye. "You will spend some time in jail, but you will be released. Let me promise you one thing. I have looked all of you in the eye and I never forget the look of a man's soul. If I see you in Acapulco, or Mexico again, you will not be given an honorable death." He motioned to the dead men with the barrel of his shiny pistol.

He lifted Jesus by the chin to his feet. "Jesus, you come with me."

CHAPTER TWENTY-NINE

AS DOM WOKE, he sensed Chantal's eyes on him. He turned to see Chantal lying on her stomach, her chin resting on the palms of her hands, observing him. He frowned. "Chantal darling, what are you doing?"

"Just looking at you."

"I can see that. You're making me nervous, you're gonna' give me bad dreams."

Chantal giggled. "Bad in what way? Bad can be good depending on how you look at it."

"Suppose so. Anyway, why you staring?"

"I'm just trying to take you in. It's taken me so long to accept that I truly want to be with you. I'm just afraid that it'll all be taken away."

"Come here." He pulled her up onto his chest, wrapping his arms around her. "I believe in fate. We were meant to meet. We cannot determine when that time will be. Here we are. Let's make the most of what we have. I hate like hell what we're doing, but we're on the doorstep of a tropical paradise, what better place to have a love affair? Let's treat it like that. We'll make the most of the days that we have, not looking to the future; we can't. We both signed up for this mission, fully knowing the dangers. If we get out of it alive and we're still willing, we'll take it from there. If we have one more day together, it will be the best day of my life to that point, okay? I am then going to hope that the next is the same if not better."

"That's a lot of puffy words from someone who's supposed to be a hard ass?"

"I don't get all of this hard ass shit." He wrestled her over onto her back, pinning her arms over her head. "I just do my job without letting assholes get in the way."

"So I'm not an asshole?"

"Damn, I love the way you say asshole, with that accent."

"Dom!" She laughed, trying to free herself.

He bent down and kissed her. She accepted more than willingly.

***

As they were getting ready to leave for the hour drive to the clinic, Dom's phone rang. "Chavez."

"Dominic, this is Carmen Suarez. I wanted to catch you before you left. Do you have a minute?"

"I'm on your dime, Doctor."

"I have a favor to ask of you."

"Okay...?"

"It's my sister, Camille. She's been not well for a couple of years now. She's been on dialysis, as her only good kidney is failing. It is a congenital defect."

"I'm listening."

"We both share a rare blood type. Please keep an eye out for a donor kidney. I have asked the other doctors to start taking blood tests from all donor recipients. We will be installing the same equipment that you have used at their clinics."

"We can do that." He didn't see that he had much choice. "Text me the details."

"I would also ask that you perform the transplant when the time comes."

Silence…"Okay, I don't get that. You have plenty of good doctors here in Mexico. Your top tier medical knowledge is first class. Surely you can find someone else to do this?"

"What you say is true Dominic, but there are not many that have performed hundreds of extractions, without one incident in the time you've been here. I will also be truthful in saying that it is my father's wish. He says that you have spilled blood for Pacifico, where the other doctors haven't. And, in our local hospital, he will be able to be present. Papa likes to think that by putting a gun to your head, you will perform with our best interests in mind."

"Charming. Do I have a choice?"

"Not unless you wish to terminate our professional relationship."

Dom thought through his options and he didn't see many. "Okay Dr. Suarez, I will keep an eye out for your kidney." He prayed that he wouldn't find one, but fate always seemed to find a way of making his life more difficult.

"Thank you, Doctor."

***

As Chantal drove into the hills north of Acapulco, Dom sat pondering the strange phone call. He briefed Chantal. She looked upset, pushing the hair away from her face.

"I think that we should take what money we have and run. We can go live in Bali. You have your license, we can set up a clinic that does something positive. We could go to Africa and help the poor.

We could survive. As long as I have you, I would be happy. I'm sure that our governments would set us up in witness protection."

"Perhaps we can make some contingencies. I've always wanted to go to Bali." He smiled at the thought.

"Like?"

"We can check into some other places needing medical help, somewhere far from Mexico. We can start to stash some money."

Chantal nodded. "I would like to do that, but I don't have a good feeling. See, now that we have started…what we've started, I'm becoming defensive, not good." She frowned.

Dom grabbed his shoulder bag, opened it and pulled out a file folder and read the short list on the piece of paper that Benny Leahner gave him. "You realize that the blood type that both Camille and Carmen share is the same as that of three of the donor recipients on Leahner's list."

"What organs?"

"Four kidneys, a pancreas and two hearts."

"No matter how you look at it, we'll have to kill the donor in order to get the required organ for Leahner. One kidney will have to be for Camille."

Dom paused for a moment. "I envisioned taking one of the kidneys that we were to harvest, if it matched the blood type, and smuggle it out of the country. No harm done…really."

"The trouble is, it could be our only chance."

"Yes, but I don't know that I could do it. I can't kill some innocent soul in order to save the life of another. Remember, we took an oath. What we are doing is bad enough."

"You said that you believed in fate, Dom. Let's leave it to fate. We'll work on our contingencies and put one foot in front of the other. Deal?"

"Deal." He reached over and held her hand.

CHAPTER THIRTY

RICHARD BRICE SAT in the back seat of the limo, his eyes intent on the scenery as the car flew along the busy highway that led from Mexico City to the small suburb of Monterey. His personal assistant, Candice Blake, sat across from him, a troubled look on her face, pressing her lips into a fine line. Richard spoke, having detected her angst. "Yes, the poverty is bad. But they don't know any better and that's why we're here. I look at it this way. Sun Medical will be bringing jobs to these people. Good paying jobs."

"Yes Richard, I understand, but it's somehow all about the numbers when we were preparing the business plan. Now that we are here, I can see what we are really doing. When we passed the General Motors plant a couple of miles back, I couldn't help but think that maybe we are better off just keeping our business in America. Why do we have to make American cars in Mexico? It's all about money, Richard. You can't tell me that we would be better off if that massive plant was in L.A."

"The big car companies build what they call loss leaders down here. They build smaller cheaper cars…entry level. They get the first time buyers hooked on their brand so that when they are making more money, they can sell them something more profitable, something made in the States. This is America…the new America. Within twenty years there will be one currency. If we sit and wait, we'll miss the boat. What we're planning is different from manufacturing engine blocks."

Candice looked him in the eye. "True, but at least there are no moral questions to be asked."

"Medical holidays Candice. It's happening all over the world. The Chinese have been doing it for a decade, the Iranians. It's a free economy. If we don't do it, someone else will."

"What is it that we're doing, sir?"

"Providing a service with the utmost professional medical care. The U.S. government is going to buckle due to pressure from the bleeding hearts. There's new legislation being bandied about. We have been able to succeed because the powers that be have turned a blind eye…because we're saving lives. We're opening up the first resort of its kind and we're not going to have to be covert anymore. The Mexicans have said that they will turn their backs to the process, as long as we grease their wheels. It's an accepted practice here."

"But for how long? I hear that the Mexican Cartels are behind most of what goes on. Do we have to grease their wheels?"

"Probably, but it would have to be a hell of a lot cheaper than paying the middle men we have been dealing with. We've been greasing the wheels for years now. We've been in contact with an organization called the Gulf Cartel. They have become the big honchos here over the past number of years. Some smaller Cartels have been in the mix, but I've been given intelligence that states that they are soon to be out of it. I think that we'll be able to deal with them directly. We have set up contacts in Central and South America. The Venezuelans will do anything for a buck. If it wasn't such a damned dangerous place, I'd have setup down there as well."

Candice shrugged her shoulders. "We are to meet with the Mayor of Monterey at noon, then we visit the site. The contractors would like you to review the plans. They've been having some problems sourcing out trades and materials."

"That's to be expected. Ron isn't Mexican. Maybe we need to have him source out a local contractor to help. As you can see, I just created a new job." He smiled.

Candice shook her head.

CHAPTER THIRTY-ONE

DOM LOOKED AT the piece of paper that Chantal held under his nose as he finished the last of the sutures on a young girl's side. He raised his eyes to meet hers, sure that the look on his face under the surgical mask matched the stunned look that adorned her face. "Did you double check?"

"Triple, that's what took me so long. What now?"

Three months passed since the phone call from Carmen Suarez, and Dom, to be truthful, nearly forgot about it. "Get on the phone with Carmen Suarez while I finish up. Have Carlos get the patient's bed ready. I'll wait for him to help me carry her in." He paused, looking down at the young Mexican woman's face as she slept, a look of contentment upon it that would turn to scorn once she woke. "We could be finished here, if we took the other kidney."

Chantal put her hands on her knees and looked down at the floor, her mind churning. "Mon Dieu Dom. If you called your friend the General, you know what he would say. It's a General's prerogative to spend people's lives for the greater good. Do you hear what I'm saying?"

"I do, but my prerogative is different than that of a General's. I'm only a Major and the rank is more to do with my pay scale than anything, not my moral assessment of things. I'll not do it. Have Carlos come with the gurney once he's finished, as I requested."

Chantal walked slowly at first, irritated by Dom's shortness, then quickened her step realizing that it was not directed at her. Once again, she found herself countermanding a direct order by not forcing Dom to do what really needed to be done. She was too far into it at this point; she took a deep breath.

He fired off another order as she reached for the door. "Pack the kidney for transport while we get her settled in."

Carlos came in a couple of minutes later. The young man looked a lot different from when he'd first met him a few months ago. He'd taken naturally to the job been given to him. His strength was deceiving, useful when moving patients, and his bedside manner, second to none. Perhaps his ordeal allowed him the benefit of empathy.

"Carlos, we won't be back for at least a day. Make sure that they all get their meds on time. We'll leave Chantal's cell with you in case you have any problems."

The frown on his face indicated that he felt a little uncomfortable. "You'll be fine Carlos. We're an hour away."

***

Chantal drove in silence towards Acapulco, not saying a word for at least the first twenty minutes. Dom couldn't take it any longer. "Look…I understand that you were supposed to step in today. I appreciate what you did, or rather didn't do. Being shot once in a year is one too many times as far as I'm concerned." He grinned.

"Dom, don't try to find humor in this. It's about more than just my directives. How much longer will we have to wait? I want to be finished with this. I want to move on with our lives."

"So do I, but I have to get through this by doing the right thing. If it takes us longer, then so be it."

"What about the two British officers you told me about, the ones that you shot?"

"Come on Chantal, you know that there is no comparison. I put them out of their misery. They were frying to death in a gasoline fire."

Chantal nodded. "No comparison? Let's pray that things work out…Carmen said that we are to go directly to Hospital del Pacifico. I remember the way. She's cordoned off one of the operating rooms."

"Good, I wasn't looking forward to doing this at the clinic."

"The attending surgeon will be present during the procedure."

"Okay, things are looking up. I don't want to be the only doctor besides Carmen Suarez present if something goes wrong. I'm getting pretty damned good at taking the organs out. Putting them back in is another skill set altogether."

"You'll do just fine." She smiled for the first time.

"I can see Camille's father with the big bulge under his jacket and that look on his face."

"You will be fine."

***

Chantal pulled into the Hospital's general parking lot, her nerves on edge as she guided the car into a vacant parking space. She looked at Dom; his face looked dreadfully pale. He slipped out of the car and went to the back door, opening it like a robot. He'd wedged the cooler between the front and back seat. He hadn't taken the chance of allowing it to spill over. He pulled it out with a little extra force, slammed the door and started walking towards the hospital entrance. Chantal hurried to catch up. Dom suddenly stopped dead in his tracks. He turned to Chantal. "Suarez said that her sister Camille only has one functioning kidney. When I assisted the Doctor in Montreal, that patient had two."

Chantal's eyes widened. "Mon Deu!"

"This is a cluster fuck, Chantal. No self-respecting surgeon would go into this without a full pre-op plan. I hope to hell that Dr. Suarez is ready with a dialysis machine. I need to call

Greenberg, I'm not sure of the implications."

"You're a field surgeon. This is why they chose you. You need to be able to function when things are not at optimum levels."

Dom nodded and turned back towards the hospital entrance. "I guess that's what the problem is. In the field you get something horrific thrown at you and you have to react as best that you can. I've got too much goddamned time to think here. Too much goddamned time to think through this whole fucking mission!" He began to hyperventilate.

Chantal grabbed his shoulders roughly with both of her hands and looked him in the eye. "Okay, stop thinking, Major. I want you to remove everything from your mind. I want you to walk into that damned hospital and don't think about anything until the patient is prepped and ready. I'll be with you."

When his cocky smile returned, she lowered her head.

Thankful for her little speech, he began to calm down.

They both turned and walked slowly towards the hospital entrance where they were greeted by two armed guards, m16s cradled in their arms. "ID," said one.

As Dom fumbled for who-knows-what card, Carmen Suarez came out of the building through the automatic door and flashed her credentials to the guard. "They are fine."

The guard nodded and stepped aside to let them through.

***

Carmen led them through the maze of corridors, which ended in a large waiting room. A set of double sliding glass doors led to three operating rooms, the waiting room packed full of people. Some appeared anxious to hear news about loved ones that were in the O.R. The rest, Dom figured, were connected with Pacifico. Several men stood around the room, dead obvious that they carried weapons; their hands under their coats, or resting on top as if the guns were going to run away on their own. Dom, Chantal and Carmen passed through to the OR.

Carmen guided them through the glass doors that opened after she flashed her ID card in front of a door's sensor. She took Dom by the elbow and ushered him into a prep room.

A very young looking man in scrubs sat at one of the tables, flipping through what looked to be a medical journal. His head bobbed up, a questioning look upon his face.

Carmen introduced him. "Dr. Dominic Chavez, Dr. Ramon Vargas."

Vargas stood and shook Dom's hand. "Dr. Chavez."

"Dr. Vargas. This is my wife and nurse assistant Chantal Chavez."

"Mrs. Chavez, please call me Ramon."

Chantal nodded.

Dom placed the cooler on the table and sat down. "Ramon, have you performed a kidney transplant recently?"

Ramon deadpanned, "No, I did assist twice during my residency."

Dom looked at Carmen. "Dr. Suarez…this is not a good idea."

Her face transformed into a scowl. "Dominic. We have little choice. You know as well as I do that my sister's blood type is rare and by the time we find another donor, her time might be up. Since the last time you saw her, she's failed."

"Surely to God there's another surgeon in southern Mexico who's performed a kidney transplant?"

"Mexico City. I have tried, but Dr. Reyes is not available."

"The States?"

"The border logistics make it next to impossible in the time that we have, 24 hours, correct?"

Dom's eyes wandered for a moment. "We have more time than that, but the chances of a successful graft become less likely."

Carmen slammed her fist on the table. "I am not asking you Dr. Chavez. I am telling you that you will perform the operation. GET SCRUBBED!"

Dom let the tirade blow over his head. "Do you have a dialysis machine prepared?"

"Yes, we are prepared."

"The patient?"

"She's in the O.R."

"Ramon, you will assist Chantal and I. We will sedate the patient, then we will hook her up for dialysis. We will perform the kidney removal, which I'm not worried about, I can do that with one hand tied behind my back. Ramon, I take it that's a medical journal and you were looking up kidney transplantation?"

Ramon nodded.

His eyes moved to Carmen's as he spoke. "Ramon, you will guide us through the procedure. Let's pray that we don't run into any complications."

***

Dom followed Carmen into the O.R, Chantal and Ramon close on their tail. The entourage in the OR didn't surprise him, pretty much what Dom anticipated, more like a posse. Hernando Suarez stood along the back wall dressed in a white suit, adorned with red needlework designs, his face devoid of any emotion. His eyes found Dom's within seconds, telling him with a glance that he'd better not fuck up. There were three men, bodyguards. They made no attempt to conceal their guns.

"Dr. Suarez." Dom stated curtly, lowering his surgical mask. "Will you risk the chance of infection from these men who've not been scrubbed and who are not wearing sanitized clothing? It's one thing to be present when we made the extraction months ago. In order for the transplant to take, there can be no risk of infection, it's essential. Once we take the old and poorly functioning kidney out, your sister will be reliant on the new one. If something goes wrong, you can call them in to shoot me. And if I'm going to have a gun to my head, be it in this room or just outside the door, I want a fighting chance to succeed."

Carmen turned to her father. "He's correct Papa. You can't be in here."

Hernando's face started to turn red. "I'll fucking stay…"

"No, Papa." She cut him off. "I know you want to, but the doctor is right. I'll come and get you if something goes wrong. Infection is our enemy and if you want to take this risk…" She turned to Dom, her eyes narrowed. "We don't anticipate anything going wrong, do we Doctor?"

Dom nodded as both Hernando and Carmen stared him down. "Señor Suarez, you've asked me to perform this operation against my better judgment. I'm going to do my best. Holding a gun to my head isn't gonna' help, it'll only add to the stress. It'll be a long procedure. Please, go sit down. Carmen can give you updates as we proceed. If something goes wrong, I give you permission to come in and shoot me."

Hernando stared down Carmen as he walked from the room, venom in his eyes. Once gone, she turned to Dom. "He's a proud man. In any other situation you would have been shot on the spot. Fortunately for you, he will do anything for his daughters."

"Regardless, it's the correct thing to do." Dom could feel the adrenalin coursing through his veins. The whole mission could be looked at as a war, not conventional, there could be no doubt of that. Dom felt that he'd been winning his fair share of the battles thus far, and he'd just won another foray. He smiled under the surgical mask. If anything did go wrong, they didn't stand a chance at surviving with Hernando and his thugs in the room.

***

Chantal and Ramon prepped Camille and set up the dialysis. A ventilator was in place, tubes being pushed through her nostrils and into to her lungs, and her life blood circulated through the device. Dom spoke, "Music?"

Chantal glared at him. "Not now!"

Dom looked up at the vital signs. *Normal.* "Okay gang, let's get the kidney out." Chantal and he were now a well-oiled team. Dom made the first incision with the certainty of an expert. Chantal inserted the retractors to open the wound site. The ureter and the blood vessels were dissected and the kidney removed carefully. He placed the defective organ into a small metal bowl and handed it to Carmen. "She has only one kidney?"

"Yes, Doctor, but not quite, I'm the same. We both have two, but the second is the size of a grape and useless. Otherwise, I would have gladly donated mine to her."

"Dr. Vargas, you can begin reading aloud." Dom looked Carmen in the eye. "Immunosuppressants?" She raised her shoulders, not being able to answer the question.

"I'm not sure."

"We have Rapamune." Ramon interjected.

"Please prepare the drug, Doctor and inject through the IV. What's the suggested dosage, Dr. Vargas?"

He fumbled through the papers and finally tossed them on a table. "Hang on." He pulled his iPhone out of his pocket. He tapped away for a minute or two. "It doesn't make any suggestions, other than to say that 1-2 Mg's is a normal dosage once a day."

"Hmm." Dom knuckled his eyes, starting to feel a bit punchy. It had been a long day and it wasn't getting any shorter. "Let's be safe. Start her on 3mg's then we'll decrease it tomorrow to 2 mg's."

Carmen nodded as she prepared the injection.

Dom muttered under his breath. "We're running blind here."

Vargas picked up the papers again. "Kidney should be allowed to warm to room temperature."

Dom looked around, shaking his head. "Place the donor kidney in a bowl and let it warm up. Carmen, why don't you give your pappy an update."

"Good idea, he'll be pulling out whatever hair is left on his head by now."

Dom gestured to Ramon as she left the O.R. "I'd like to confer with Chantal privately for a moment."

He shrugged his shoulders as if to say okay.

Dom pulled Chantal to the corner of the room and spoke to her in his broken French. "I don't like this. I want you to prepare two needles with a heavy dose of anesthetic, enough to knock out a large man. Leave them both within easy reach. I will distract him," he said, not wanting to say Ramon's name. "If I say 'Jack Daniels,' I want you to inject Carmen. I'll do the same with…No harm done, but they need to be right out of the picture. I want an escape route for us in case something happens." She nodded. "Do you have your gun?"

"Yes, in my bag."

Dom nodded.

Carmen returned a few minutes later.

Dom raised his eyebrows at her.

"Not happy, but fine for now."

Ramon returned his gaze to the manual and began reading.

Dom gently laid the kidney into position and then, with Chantal's assistance, proceeded to attach the blood vessels and then the ureter to the donor kidney. Dom let his head drop in fatigue, his neck stiff with tension. It was intense work making the small sutures. One mistake could be costly. "Chantal, please remove the clamps. Let's see if this puppy works." He felt a bit like someone who'd just hooked up a stereo system, about to throw the power button. Would there be music?

Dom focused on the vital signs. A slight drop in blood pressure, but the kidney accepted the flow of blood. Only time would tell if it would reject the organ. "Dr. Vargas, Chantal, if you wouldn't mind buttoning up the patient." Chantal looked exhausted. With his eyes on the monitor, he moved to stand beside Carmen, who'd been nothing more than a bystander during the operation.

"It's one thing to participate in a procedure, but I will admit watching my sister being opened up took me to a different place, un-nerving."

"She's in God's hands now. Please give the family an update."

She nodded. "Thank you."

"You can tell Hernando to take his hand off the gun and go home now."

He returned to Chantal's side once Carmen left, watching Vargas as he finished up the sutures and staples. "Chantal, please administer Heparin."

Suddenly the alarm went off, Camille was flat lining. Dom cursed, "Son of a bitch! Ramon, turn her onto her back and prepare the paddles." He turned to Chantal. "Jack Daniels at the door."

Ramon looked at him questioningly, the beginnings of panic showing on his face. "Dr. Chavez, her blood pressure has dropped off the board, she's in arrest."

"Where is the goddamned defibrillator? Get some paddles on her." Dom began performing CPR while Ramon retrieved the machine.

Within moments, Ramon returned. "Doctor, shouldn't we call for assistance?"

Dom looked him straight in the eye. "Do you know who that man is outside the door?"

"I think so."

"Whomever you think he might be, multiply that by ten on the badness scale. If he finds his daughter died in here tonight, you and I are not seeing the light of day tomorrow. Got it?"

"Yes, Doctor."

"No, I mean it. Do you get it?" Dom turned and put his hands on Ramon's shoulders. "If she dies, you and I are dead men walking. There will be no protection for us. You will not be able to rely upon the hospital and whatever you call your professional medical association here in Mexico to protect you. Do you understand?"

Ramon looked pale as a sheet. "I think so."

"Okay, so that we are clear. If Hernando Suarez doesn't kill you, I will, if you don't follow my lead." Their eyes met for the briefest of moments. Ramone nodded.

Ramon hooked up the defibrillator and greased the paddles, placing them on Camille's chest. "Clear!"

The electrical jolt bounced Camille's body as her lips began to turn blue.

Dom looked at the monitor. *Nothing*. "Again!"

The electrical blast jolted her again bouncing her lifeless body on the table.

Dom began CPR, his hands pumping her chest, clamping his mouth down on hers, giving her his life-saving breath. He kept breathing into her until he looked up after twenty pushes. "What the fuck, Ramon, did we forget something?"

"No, Doctor. Why would her body reject the kidney so quickly? She's still hooked up to dialysis. Could the Heparin be reacting with the Rapamune?"

"Christ, I don't know. Still no vitals…too much Rapamune?"

The door buzzer to the operating room went off, indicating someone wanted to come in. Chantal, listening closely to the dialogue between both doctors, moved to the side of the door. With the syringe in her left hand, she pressed the locking mechanism with her right hand. Her face looked haunted, praying it would not be Carmen Suarez accompanied by her father.

As the door opened, Chantal saw the Doctor's jet black hair, she firmly grabbed Carmen's arm and injected her backside with the syringe containing the anesthetic. Carmen looked at her in shock before she stumbled. Chantal eased her to the ground, making sure her head didn't bounce off the floor. Looking back at the closed door, she engaged the security lock. She moved across the floor quickly to assist the two doctors. Chantal looked Dom in the eye, not saying a word.

Ramone exclaimed, seeing Carmen lying on the floor. "What the Hell!"

Dom stared down at Chantal's bag that now lay against the wall. She nodded back to him.

Dom put his hands on his hips, and stared down at his failing patient before turning quickly to Chantal. He lowered his surgical mask as a smile slowly formed.

"Dominic. I find no f'ing humor in the situation."

Ramon's head bounced back and forth between the two of them and the body of Carmen Suarez on the floor.

"Ramon." Dom said and paused. "I'll give you one chance to find absolution. I can inject you with anesthetic and you will be the innocent victim."

"And if I disagree?"

"I'll inject you anyway."

Chantal produced her handgun without threatening him, but the intent was clear.

Dom felt for a pulse on Camille. *Nothing.* "Ramon, I will make this short. I am a U.S. Military surgeon here on a NATO sponsored mission to find a link between those that procure illegal organs to sell to the States and the medical institution there that buys them. I have been working undercover for the Pacifico Cartel for the past five months. The reason we are here right now is because of Camille's blood type. We've been waiting for a donor with the same, but with no luck. We've established contact with an organ agent from the U.S. who offered a large monetary reward for a heart or kidney with the same blood type. We will be able to break the link if we can make the transfer to the States. I don't want to take the risk of trying to resuscitate the kidney. We need to extract Camille's heart."

Chantal couldn't contain herself. "Mon Dieu!" She placed her hand on her head, trying to calm herself.

Dom turned to Ramon, who didn't look terribly calm either, his chest heaving to catch his breath. "I don't see that we have many choices. If we succeed, you could return to Mexico a hero. We can sedate you now…Hurry."

Ramon took a deep breath. "This is not the way I foresaw the night enfolding, Dr. Chavez."

"I guess not. Are you with us?"

"You leave me little choice. My family will never forgive me for doing this, but I will not respect myself in the future. I will not be a coward."

Dom clasped his arm. "I need your help doctor. If we don't pull this off, we're dead."

He nodded. "You have it."

Dom turned to Chantal. "Call Carlos, I left your phone with him. Have Carlos get a taxi and bring a life cradle to the hospital. No…close to the hospital, give him your credit card number for the cab."

"Wouldn't they have one here?"

"Come on, Chantal. What are they gonna say when we ask for one?"

"Sorry, I wasn't thinking."

Dom looked around. "Do they have an electric surgical saw in the O.R?"

***

Within half an hour, Dom and Ramon removed Camille Suarez's heart. It lay on a cold metal plate beside her more than dead body. Dom glanced at Ramon and Chantal. Both looked as if they'd gone through a war. "How do we deal with Hernando Suarez? He's just outside that door with enough firepower to kill us all within seconds?"

Chantal's head shot up, a wry smile forming on her lips. "Carmen and Camille have a strong resemblance. If we dressed Carmen up with a hospital cap and a gown, covers up to her chin, she might pass a less than close inspection. Their biggest difference is in hair color. I could wheel her up to her room and keep a watch on Hernando."

"I don't mind doing that." Said Ramon.

Dom smiled. "Sorry, Doctor, but you're not leaving my sight until we get out of this hospital."

***

Ramon and Dom placed Carmen on a gurney. Chantal dressed her in a patient's gown, her head covered by a surgical cap, and a ventilator and vital signs monitor hooked up. Dom escorted Chantal out the O.R. Doorway. Hernando Suarez and his posse stood up from a table at which they sat playing cards. Dom intercepted the Cartel Boss before he could get close to the gurney.

"How's my daughter?"

"She is fine Señor Suarez. There were a few moments of concern, but I will assure you that Carmen helped save the day. If it wasn't for her, we might still be in there with your daughter Camille."

"I would like a word with her."

"She's still scrubbing up. Why don't you follow Chantal up with Camille and I'll send Carmen right away once she's finished."

Hernando didn't answer verbally, giving a cross little nod instead.

Dom took his hands in his and shook them slightly. "Your daughters are brave girls."

A slight smile formed on his tight lips.

Chantal began wheeling the gurney towards the nurse's station to find the location of Camille's room. Hernando followed like a sad puppy dog.

***

Dom picked up his phone as soon as he returned to the OR and dialed Carlos. He answered on the second ring. "Sí."

"Carlos, are you close?"

"Just entering the city, maybe 15 minutes."

Dom paused to think. "If I remember correctly, there is an OXXO convenience a quarter of a mile down the street from the hospital. We'll meet you there. Did the taxi take the credit card?"

"Sí Doctor."

"We'll see you there. Is the carrier charged?"

"Sí Doctor."

***

Chantal tried to keep herself between Hernando and his daughter, so that he wouldn't be able to observe her closely. Her heart rate accelerated when they entered the elevator. Hernando ended up beside and slightly behind Carmen's head and luckily not in a position to get a good look. He moved as if to put his hand on her head, nothing more than a show of concern and affection. Chantal gently put her hand on his wrist before he could complete the motion. Their eyes locked, his instantly became pure fury. "No one tells me what to do." He began reaching under his jacket for his gun.

Chantal calmly put her hand on top of his, which now gripped his gun under the lapel of the jacket, her loo matching his fury. "Señor, if you move the ventilator, you could cause her harm. She's suffered a trauma and needs the oxygen." She took a deep breath. "If you plan to shoot me, I'd advise that you wait until we are out of the elevator. These walls are made of metal, your bullet could ricochet." She nodded towards Carmen. "My concern is for your daughter… that's all."

He nodded, his anger abated for the time being.

Chantal followed the orderly who guided them to their private ward. She helped him wheel Carmen's bed into position. The orderly assisted Chantal in securing the IV and that the ventilator functioned properly. She checked Carmen's vital signs and made sure that the surgical cap on her head concealed her jet black hair. She quickly pulled it down over her eyebrows when Suarez wasn't looking.

"Señor Suarez. It's best that you leave her alone until she wakes up. I'm sure that she will be happy to see you. It usually takes an hour or so. I'll come back and check, though I'm sure that Carmen will be up soon."

Hernando moved towards Carmen.

Chantal stepped in front of him. "I understand your desire to be close to your daughter…let me see, how about you sit here in this chair beside her. You can hold her hand if you wish. I don't want you disturbing the tubes in her nose, or the intravenous. When she begins to awaken, ring for a nurse."

"I will do that." He sat down below the level of his daughter's face, content for the moment to hold her hand.

***

Dom removed the ice from the cooler, which originally carried the kidney, then immersed Camille's heart into the cool Collins solution - water mix. "This will have to do until we can get it into the warm nutrient enriched fluids of the Life Cradle. Our assistant Carlos is bringing it."

"Dr. Chavez," Ramon interjected. He motioned to the disaster that lay on the operating table.

"We don't have time to button her up. Help me at least clean it up a little."

They removed the Retractors and allowed the chest cavity to close as far as it would, without surgical aid. Dom looked around the room. "Let's wheel the table over to the corner of the room. Pile all of the dirty linens as well as the clean ones on top of the body. We may be able to disguise it for what it is temporarily…" He stood in thought for a moment. "We need enough time to get out of the hospital. The orderlies will be in right away to clean up, so we are going to have to bully our way out if necessary, we'll only have minutes. Where's Chantal?"

***

She didn't believe for one moment that Hernando was going to sit nicely by Carmen's side for long. She smiled at him as she left the room and tried her best to walk calmly back to the O.R. She drew a sigh of relief as she saw the large double doors ahead of her. Three men stood outside, Pacifico soldiers. Two orderlies waited impatiently beside their cleaning cart. At the end of the hallway were two hospital security guards, both holding sub machine guns. She slowed to a walk as she approached the door. The guards recognized her and nodded to her. Chantal knocked on the O.R. door. There was no answer. She shrugged her shoulders, looking for one of the guards.

"They have not left yet, Señora."

She knocked harder. The lock chunked and one of the two doors opened. Dom looked her in the eye. She could see the panic evident on his face, his eyes darting side to side. He held her bag to her. She took it. Dom motioned towards the hall exit and moved towards it, the cooler in his other hand. Ramon followed. Dom did his best to sound jovial. "That went well Mrs. Chavez. How's the patient?"

"She's still asleep, but stable."

"Fantastic, I need some fresh air, been a long night." Dom ushered Ramon ahead of him. He didn't trust him to remain silent for long. Once out of the E.R. Hallway, they entered an elevator that would take them to the ground floor. Dom put his hand on his pants pocket, making sure that he'd remembered the syringe with the sedative in it.

As the elevator made its slow decent through the bowels of the

Hospital, an amber light came on over top of the door, signaling a hospital wide alarm.

Ramon began to panic. "Doctor, I can't do this!"

Dom took out the syringe, flipped the stopper off and stabbed it into Ramon's backside. He turned, looking at Dom in shock. The anesthetic worked quickly. As the door opened, Dom ushered Ramon to a chair in the hospital waiting room, sitting him down. A lady in the next chair looked up at Dom questioningly?

"The Doctor is dead tired."

Chantal remained calm and picked up the cooler, following Dom towards the hospital exit. They could see the front door security guards on their walkie-talkies. Dom ushered Chantal past them and walked in the direction of the hospital parking lot as calmly as he could without running. They both drew heavy breaths as they reached the Mercedes. Chantal fumbled for the keys. "Are you okay to drive Chantal?"

"Get in the other side," she said irritably.

As Dom stowed the cooler in the back seat floor, he could see a commotion going on at the front door of the hospital. "Let's get out of here Chantal."

She fired up the engine and headed towards the exit. "Do you have change?"

Dom fumbled through his pants. "No, dammit."

"Neither do I. Hang on." Instead of slowing, she accelerated and ran through the yellow security arm, busting it in half, the jagged edge scraping down the side of the car as they passed through into the busy main street ahead of them. Chantal barely missed an oncoming car as she swerved into the far lane.

"Carlos will meet us at the OXXO up ahead on the right."

"There's going to be police all over the place in minutes. We need to get as far away as we can, and fast!"

"Look, there he is standing out front. Atta' boy."

Chantal pulled the car up in front of the convenience store. Dom yelled out the open window. "Get in!"

Carlos pulled the door open, placing the transport device onto the seat across from him. He slammed the door behind him.

Chantal pulled out of the parking lot and continued south. "Now what?"

Dom let his head fall back against the rest. "I'm not sure. We need to get the heart into the Life Cradle, that's for damn sure, but we need to be stopped. Keep driving."

Two police cars passed them going the opposite direction, their lights flashing, sirens blaring.

Dom pulled his phone out of his pocket and dialed their residence number. It rang a few times before Pedro picked up. "Si?"

"Pedro, its Doctor Dom."

"Buenos noches, Señor Doctor."

"Listen to me carefully. There is a loose floor tile under our bed. Inside it is a locked metal box. I need you to get the box and bring it with you down to the market. Chantal and I will meet you in front of the entrance. We'll be there in twenty minutes. You need to do this quickly and get out of the house. Dangerous people may be watching the place. I need you to lose yourself in the crowd before you get to the market. Remember the men who brought you to us."

"Sí, Señor Doctor."

"They will kill you if they catch you. Get going now!" Dom hung up.

Chantal looked over at him. "You're taking a big risk asking him to do that."

"If he stays in the house, he's as good as dead and we have no choice. If we go back there, we'll be caught. Pacifico will be all over the place, so will the police. I'd give the edge to the gangsters arriving first though."

She nodded.

***

Chantal pulled into a tight parking space a few hundred yards from the market entrance, as close as she could get due to the mass of people. Dom looked over at her. "Could you and Carlos transfer the heart into the carrier, I'll go get Pedro?"

Chantal shook her head. "Negative Dom, I'll get the boy, you make sure that our cargo is properly stowed."

Dom didn't argue.

***

Chantal took the safety off the Glock, sticking it in the back of her belt under her jacket. She weaved her way through the crowd, hoping to sight the teenage boy. She doubted he would show up, the lure of what might be in the metal box, too much temptation. It contained their real passports and well over $30,000 U.S. Most importantly though, the secure cell phone they would need to contact Military Intelligence.

As she neared the entrance, she heard some shouting. She stopped for a moment, standing on a crate to get a better look over the crowd. It took her a few moments to find the source of the commotion; her heart sunk as she saw Pedro running towards her, three men with handguns in close pursuit, the metal box in his hands. She watched as if in slow motion, as one of the pursuers raised his gun and fired. Pedro flew forwards, face first into the ground. She saw the box go flying into the throng of people. A woman wearing decorative Mexican attire bent down and picked up the box, which landed at her feet. She looked like she'd been working in one of the tourist booths. The lady didn't waste a second of her good fortune and dashed into the crowd.

"Mon Dieu!" Chantal made a split second decision. She couldn't help the boy at this point, so she jumped down off the crate and headed towards where she'd last seen the woman, making the assumption that the she would head towards the side alley at the far end of the square, there didn't look like anyplace else to go. She shouldered her way through the crowd, trying to get a look ahead of her, but at 5'4" her height gave her no advantage. Chantal reached the entrance to the market square, her head swiveling from side to side, pleasantly surprised to see that she'd reached the narrow alley just after the woman, her white ornately decorated costume hard to miss. Chantal followed into the tight corridor, jam-packed with people. Out of the corner of her eye, she saw her dash into a doorway. Chantal ran to the storefront, looking in. Through the front window, she could see the woman enter a doorway at the back of the store, which sold coffee and tea for export. She entered and headed towards the doorway. A large man, in his forties shouted at her. She wasn't sure what he said, hyper-focused on the quarry, her combat instincts taking over.

The door led to a large storeroom. Sitting at the table the woman, a knife in her hand, prepared to pry the lid off the box. Chantal yelled at her in Spanish. "That's my box!"

The woman's eyes flashed up at her in shock. She jumped to her feet, brandishing the knife at her. "Why is it your box? I found it fair and square!" She yelled: "Thief!"

Chantal motioned for the woman to hand over the box. "Please, just give it to me and no one gets hurt!"

The woman leapt at her with the knife. Chantal used her martial arts training to deflect the attack. She dodged sideways, letting the woman's momentum carry her past Chantal's side. She grabbed her wrist, slamming her elbow down on the woman's elbow. Her assailant screamed in agony as the joint supporting ligaments tore, the knife clattering to the floor. Chantal took the opportunity to pull the handgun out of her belt and took aim at the middle of the woman's chest. "The box Señora…" She motioned for her to move away from the table. The woman slowly edged away, clutching her wounded arm to her chest.

Chantal stepped to the table and retrieved the box. As she

turned towards the door, the man from the front of the store stepped through it with a sawed off shotgun pointing it at her face. Chantal didn't waste a second leveling the gun at his face, walking directly at him. "Move or you are dead."

The man stepped aside, his appetite for the fight short lived.

"Slide the gun along the floor to me."

He followed orders.

She picked up the weapon and calmly walked into the front room, then exited out into the crowd. As she waded through the herd of humanity, she could see one of the thugs that shot Pedro walking through the crowd towards her. She stepped into the next shop as he passed. A hullabaloo erupted at the coffee shop, she could hear the woman yelling, "We've been robbed!" Fortunately, the thug seemed intent on getting to the source of the disturbance. She slid the shotgun behind a crate, then slipped back into the steadily moving flow of people as he passed.

As she returned to the main square, Chantal could see the flashing lights of a police car moving slowly through the middle of the crowd. She skirted the square, making her way back to the Mercedes, which waited in the nearby parking lot. She opened the driver's door and handed the box to Dom.

"I heard the gunshot Chantal, where the hell's Pedro?"

"He's been hit. It's a bit of a story. Someone picked up the box after he'd been shot and I had to retrieve it."

Dom shook his head. "Did he get away?"

"No Dom. I think he may have been killed."

"Christ!" Dom hung his head, running his hands through his hair. "Carlos and I have stowed the heart."

"Good, let's get out of here." She glanced over at Dom, the sudden heaving in his chest catching her eye. She could see a tear slowly roll down his cheek as he turned away, feeling her eyes upon him.

CHAPTER THIRTY-TWO

DR. BRIGHT CHECKED Maddie's pulse and blood pressure. He liked to do it the old fashioned way, watch in hand, counting the beats. He felt that it strengthened the bond between the doctor and patient. Maddie didn't open her eyes. He knew that she feigned sleep, fighting a losing battle with her will to survive, a commonality. He shook his head. Sooner than later she would ask for a way to expedite the process. It was hard for the layman to understand, but he experienced it all too frequently. The fight to survive, when it became difficult to breath, was exhausting. The battle was relentless, there were no breaks.

Allan and Bonnie Chambers looked on as he made his cursory examination. Once finished, he motioned towards the door and the hallway. The Chambers nodded.

Outside the room, he paused for a moment before speaking. The Chambers stood, knowing what he would likely to say, they were not blind. "There isn't much time left."

Bonnie nodded, taking a deep breath. "Is she in discomfort?"

"She's having a hard time catching her breath. It can be a tiring and extremely demoralizing. My guess is that if we could offer her a comfortable way out, she would take it, though I am by no means suggesting it. When the time comes, we can introduce a strong pain killer like morphine, reduce her oxygen. It won't take long."

Alan pursed his lips. "The agent…Is it too late, if we were to get a donor heart in the next week or so?"

Bright took a quick survey of Alan, he'd lost weight and he could smell cigarette smoke, not uncommon during a stressful time. "It's never too late, though her reserves of energy and will are almost as important as her body's resiliency. I question her resolve, Alan."

"She's a fighter. The agent mentioned taking her to China."

"Do you honestly think that she would make it? If you were going to take that route, you should have done it when she first suffered the infarction."

Alan began to pace. "I'm going to call that little prick one more time and offer him a reward that will make his greedy little hands rub together. The money isn't the issue anymore, I have more of it than I need. I only have one daughter."

"I cannot advise you sir."

CHAPTER THIRTY-THREE

DOM HUNG HIS HEAD, staring out the window as Chantal drove away from the square. He'd grown fond of Pedro. He'd planned on setting up a trust for the young man once they reached the U.S.

Chantal knocked him out of his stupor, slapping him on the leg. "Come on Dom…we need to think here."

"Sorry, just feeling really bad for the boy, he had spirit. I liked him."

"I did too, but we're here to do a tough job. We're dealing with tough people."

Dom opened the metal box as Chantal drove away from the center of town. He picked up the cell phone and pressed the "on" button. Surprisingly, it sprang to life. He'd wondered about the battery after all this time. Once the phone fired up, he dialed the only preprogrammed number in the directory. He let it ring several times.

"Bachman?"

"Major Bachman, this is Dr. Tavano."

"Are you in trouble?"

"We have a donor heart."

Silence…

"Bachman?"

"I'm here. Where are you now?"

"In the car, heading out of Acapulco along the coast road…west."

"You made a recon after our last meeting of the airstrip I'd mentioned?"

"Affirmative."

"We'll have a plane ready in less than an hour."

"There could be some heat." He explained the situation.

"Christ doctor, that's quite the story. You mean to tell me…you took out Camille Suarez's heart and you're still alive?…Christ…We'll be ready. "

Dom put the phone back into his jacket pocket and pulled out his personal one. He turned to Chantal. "We need to call Leahner."

"How much do we tell him?"

"Don't think we have much choice, I'll have to follow his lead. He'll have to tell us where to go." Dom looked up the most recent number given to him by the organ agent and dialed. As was expected, he heard a female voice telling him to leave a message.

"This is Dominic Chavez. We have found the gift that you've been seeking." He hung up.

Within a minute, the phone rang.

CHAPTER THIRTY-FOUR

BENYAMIN JACOB LEAHNER began his nefarious career entirely by accident. His father worked as a Swiss banker, with connection to the Rothschild banking empire, but primarily with the Swiss National Bank. Benny followed in his father's footsteps after graduating from ETH Zurich - Swiss Federal Institute of Technology. Jacob Leahner died before he could show his son the ropes; a congenital heart defect, which plagued him for much of his life, took him suddenly. Benny too, suffered from the defect.

After being hired by the Swiss National Bank, Benny was transferred to India for his internship. In India, he made his first contacts in the world organ trade. Life is cheap in poorer countries, such as India and Pakistan, and lots money to be made from the harvesting of usable organs for transplant. Benny also learned that there could be a future for an unscrupulous banker. Large fees could be charged for moving the money necessary to facilitate the trades, a lot of it under the table. His superior at the time, a man named, Tarim Rasheed, watched Benny with cautious fascination.

"Mr. Leahner," said Rasheed, calling Benny into his office after his first four months on the job. "You are taking to the business rather quickly. Our clients are pleased with your excellent high level of service. Are you enjoying India? Do you have any questions?"

"Yes and no, Mr. Rasheed." Benny made several contacts in the months he'd been in the Third World country and didn't want to let on to his boss that there were a few trades made that didn't fit within the guidelines laid out by the Swiss National Bank. Rasheed knew what went on, but the fees generated by the young banker were making him look good. Nevertheless, it was time to move him. He didn't want the business to come to light under his watch.

"You'll be getting a promotion next week Mr. Leahner."

Benny raised his eyebrows.

"I don't look at it as a promotion, but for you, it will present an opportunity for upward mobility. You're being transferred to Bangladesh, the city of Dhaka. A real shit hole." His Indian accent emphasizing the last two words. "If you thought Mumbai was dirty, you will just love Dhaka."

Benny didn't want to smile. He'd heard about the poverty that existed in the derelict nation and could see the numerous possibilities that existed there. "Thank you, Mr. Rasheed. You will be pleased that you placed your faith in my abilities."

Rasheed nodded, not wanting to seem too exuberant in his desire to offload the corrupt little man.

***

Benny stayed in Dhaka for five years and during that time set up a large network for the transfer of human organs to the Far East and Europe. In time, the bank was no longer needed and he started to freelance, using a wide list of private lenders and money movers. Benny learned to use the underworld of private banking that included the benefactors of the Swiss National Bank, the Rothschild's. As long as he paid his debts, there would always be a flow of capital. If money needed to be transferred through "non-mainstream means," he could accommodate his clientele.

***

Present Day

Benny, now in his early sixties, wondered how much more money he truly needed. He'd amassed a small fortune, in excess of $40 million U.S. worldwide, plus real estate holdings in ten countries.

He sat in his comfortable Malibu home, overlooking the Pacific, taking a puff from his Cigar, swirling Cognac in a glass snifter. The U.S. government and his Mexican benefactors were making him nervous. He needed to consider Dr. Richard Brice…Benny shook his head. There used to be some honor among thieves. Today, everyone was a mercenary. The money flowed wonderfully, but did he really need it? The Cartels were becoming more difficult to manage. Pacifico, with its aging patriarch, seemed to be slowly losing its once superior influence within the Mexican Mob hierarchy. He didn't trust Hernando Suarez anymore and the old man in turn became less trusting of him. He could sense it, which didn't bode well for a man in his profession. He'd done well by trusting these senses over the years and they were telling him that control of the present environment seemed to be sliding away.

Later that day, he received the call from the Canadian doctor. He'd hesitated, weighing the pros and cons of the deal. He decided that it would be his last one in Mexico. He'd pack up after this and shift his focus to South Africa. He loved Cape Town. Benny decided to follow normal protocol and returned the message on a clean line.

***

"Chavez?"

"Doctor Chavez." The voice was unmistakably that of the organ merchant. "What do you have for me?"

"A heart, as requested for recipient "C", the blood type triple tested. Not necessary, but I assure you that it is verified."

"Excellent news, doctor," Benny truly grateful. Alan Chambers was becoming a thorn in his side, no matter how much money the man offered to him. "Will the cargo be shipped by Pacifico?"

"We arranged for a plane. It's being readied and we're on rout, I'm going to deliver the merchandise personally."

"This isn't what we agreed upon," Leahner's voice rose sharply.

"On the contrary. I don't think we ever clearly spelled it out. I'll be up front. I terminated my association with Pacifico, and I will not be returning to Acapulco. I would prefer to deliver the organ personally and receive payment. I need the money, all of the money, not half of it. The situation is becoming unstable and I'm no longer comfortable working with Hernando Suarez."

There were a few moments of silence. Benny could find little fault in the man's reasoning, though it made him nervous for some reason. "Doctor, I don't like it."

"Okay then, I'll toss the organ into the Pacific and I'll bid you a good day!" Dom meant it, there was absolutely no benefit to him if the man didn't want to play ball.

Benny detected the sincerity in the threat. "I'll text you where I would like the organ delivered. I will need the routing and account number of your financial institution. I gather it's in a sheltered country."

"The Caymans."

"Good. How will you manage customs and immigration?"

"Our pilot promised us that it would not be an issue. His fee is eating up a good deal of my profit Mr…"

"Doctor, please!" Leahner interjected.

"Of course."

CHAPTER THIRTY-FIVE

IT TOOK THIRTY MINUTES to reach the airstrip located northeast of Acapulco. As Chantal turned onto the dirt road that led to the small airport, two black sedans pulled out of the bush and came charging up behind the little Mercedes. "These guys mean business, Dom."

He pulled out his cell and called Bachman. The FBI operative answered. "Bachman."

"It's Dom, we're on the road to the airstrip, but we've picked up a couple of aggressive pursuers. I'm thinking Pacifico, two cars."

"Roger that, Major. We have cordoned off the entrance and have a trace on you, we can see you on satellite. Head straight through the gate and our operatives will take out the trailers. The jet is 1,000 yards ahead…ready for takeoff."

Dom stuck the phone back into his pocket and looked behind at the fast approaching vehicles. He could see a figure lean out of the passenger window of the closest vehicle. "DUCK DOWN!" No sooner were the words out of his mouth, the back window was shattered from the fire from an Uzi submachine gun. Chantal hunkered down so she could just see over the dash.

Chantal nudged Dom in the ribs with her elbow. "My Glock – in the gym bag."

Dom nodded and wrestled the bag up off the passenger side floor. He pulled the heavy weapon out and looked over the seat and through the now glassless rear window. He nodded to Carlos to stay low. He could see the man snap another clip into the Uzi, leaning out of the passenger window. Dom focused on the driver and fired off the entire magazine. The front windshield of the sedan shattered, then the vehicle abruptly swerved off the road and slammed into a palm tree. "Ammo?"

"In the bag!" Chantal responded. "Good shooting, Dom!"

Dom nodded, the fight taking his thoughts away from Pedro. He fumbled through the bag and found another clip, and snapped it into the empty gun.

"There's the gate up ahead!" Chantal shouted.

"Bachman said to run right through it."

Chantal nodded and stomped down on the accelerator, putting a little distance between them and the remaining pursuer.

Dom looked to the side as they passed through the gatehouses. He could see several men with machine guns, standing behind huts that stood on either side of the road. As the car followed them through the entrance the hidden attackers stepped out and riddled it with gunfire. The car swerved into the compound ahead, turning left and right randomly, eventually doubling back towards the fencing. Dom focused his vision back towards where they were going.

Chantal stopped the car beside the small prop Jet that stood waiting for them. Two men carrying assault rifles, panned their guns on them as they got out of the car. "Major Tavano?" asked one as they approached the plane.

Carlos looked at him in question. "Tavano?"

"Yes, I'm Dom Tavano, this is Captain Turcotte, Canadian forces, and our assistant Carlos Rosales." He introduced them to the men who seemed less than thrilled to be here.

"Major, come aboard, no telling when we might have more unwanted guests. Please hand over your firearms."

"Really?"

The man didn't as much as smile as he placed a black duffel bag on the tarmac.

Dom put the Glock into the bag, forgetting that he still held the weapon in his right hand.

***

Dom at the best of times did not like to fly. He held down the vestiges of panic as the tiny craft soared what seemed like straight upwards, after a quick taxi. He found it curious that the two men didn't put their weapons away, both remained seated across from where Dom and Chantal sat…on guard. "Do you have names? This is the army and I'm a Major."

The man on the left responded. "Lieutenant Matthews, sir."

"Okay, Matthews, we're not the enemy. You're making me nervous with those guns. I don't see the necessity." Dom's hackles were raised.

The other man didn't respond, but remained intent on keeping a close eye on them.

Dom pulled his lips into his mouth, biting down on them. He detected a strange look upon Chantal's face, not concern, more a look of expectancy, like she knew why this would happen. Dom's sixth sense, which he'd learned not to ignore over the years, buzzed like a fire alarm in his head. He could see that Carlos was picking up on her vibe, his eyes intent upon her.

Mathews spoke, "Major, we need the coordinates to our destination."

Dom read them out from the text from Leahner, which arrived five minutes prior to takeoff.

***

Once they'd settled into the flight, Carlos tapped him on the arm. "Doctor...The man called you Major Tavano, and you just told him you were a Major."

Dom didn't feel much like talking. He glanced over at Chantal, whose eyes were pasted to the window, her head turned away. He owed the young man some kind of explanation. "The man's correct, Carlos. My name is Dominic Tavano. I'm a military doctor with the rank of Major. Like we told you back at the clinic, and maybe not in so much detail; we've been on a mission to find the connection between the Mexican drug cartels, illegal harvesting of body parts and the U.S. Medical institutions that use and purchase these parts. I'm sorry to have dragged you into this mess, and I may have made a mistake trying to shelter you from the Cartel. I should have let you run back to San Vincente."

Carlos put his hand up. "I understand. I knew that there was something different, little looks and conversations between you and Chantal have not always been as quiet as you might have wanted."

Dom nodded. "I'm sorry."

"It's okay, doctor Dom. I wouldn't be here if I hadn't searched your eyes to see that you are a good man." Chantal glanced over for a moment.

Dom couldn't resist. "What the fuck's up, Chantal?"

She traded a quick glance with the armed agents on board. "That's classified, Dom."

Dom moved as if he was going to undo his seat belt. The other agent, who remained nameless to Dom, raised his weapon and leveled it at him. Dom sat back. "Classified my ass. I'm getting the distinct feeling you're holding something back and I'm about to get the shaft."

"Dom!"

He stared down the other operative. "You better hit me if you pull the trigger." He put the gun down. "Come on Chantal. You told me you were supposed to shoot me if it looked like I was going to mess up. Is that the whole truth? Maybe I wasn't supposed to succeed? Is that it?"

The unnamed agent interjected. "Captain Turcotte made it clear that she cannot divulge classified information." Her gaze returned to the cabin window.

"Classified my fucking Brooklyn ASS!" He took one last go at Chantal. "Was having sex with me part of the initiative? You are good, Captain Turcotte, too fucking good! You're nothing but a fucking cheap French Canadian WHORE!"

CHAPTER THIRTY-SIX

HERNANDO BECAME FURY INCARNATE. He entered the operating room, looking aghast at the two orderlies, who, with fearful looks on their faces, tried to dissect the mess of sheet, gauze and mutilated body which lay on the gurney in the far side of the room. He could see Camille's face, there could be no mistake. A low growl emanated from deep in his throat. He slowly moved towards the gurney.

One of the orderlies moved to block him. " Señor, you don't want to see this."

Hernando pulled out one of the revolvers that were strapped across his chest under his white suit jacket, pointed it at the man's forehead and fired. The man's head snapped back, the other orderly splattered with blood and brain matter. The body fell to the floor with a sickly wet thud. "No one tells me what to do! Never again."

The other orderly scrambled out of the way and ran for the exit, intercepted by two Pacifico soldiers, who followed Hernando into the room.

Hernando yelled at the men, "Let him go." He began stomping towards the exit, his revolver in hand.

"Señor Suarez…" The man said with trepidation. "With all respect, there are men in the hallway with machine guns. They will have heard the shot. Please put the gun away."

Hernando had to try his hardest not to shoot the man. He was seething with anger and despair. He wanted to shoot everyone. His hand trembled as he slid it back into the holster. He pressed his index finger into the man's chest. "This Doc Dom, he's a dead man. Do you hear me? He's fucking dead. I put $5 million U.S. on his head. Someone brings me his fucking head in a bag, I give $5 million cash."

CHAPTER THIRTY-SEVEN

BENNY WATCHED HIS laptop intently, a deep frown slowly forming on his face. The computer was linked to a state of the art surveillance system, which monitored every property owned by him throughout the world. The heat sensitive cameras in the past few minutes had detected multiple intrusions. One at his LA office, his California residence and another at his home in Zürich Switzerland. All three break-ins happened shortly after he'd been contacted by Doctor Chavez.

Who the heck is Dr. Chavez? No question he's a doctor, Pacifico wouldn't have put up with him for nearly half a year if he'd been a fraud. American for certain, his Spanish poor, the American English inflection easy to pick up, New York, his first guess. His wife was French, but not from France, Canadian most likely. Benny prided himself at being good with accents in several languages, he was completely fluent in eight, including Mandarin. He'd survived knowing how to read innuendos and detect lies, no matter what language was being spoken. Chavez seemed out of his element. Benny didn't know why, but it would come to him.

His eyes flicked back to the screen, where he could see four men walking through his Swiss home, armed with silenced pistols. He'd seen enough to know that there would be much the same on each screen at the other locations. Benny planned for this day, he'd been through it once in the mid 90s, where the losses were massive. This time around, he'd lose some real estate, which would be painful, but his net worth was great enough to withstand the hit. He looked at his many residences as being part of the business plan, acceptable losses.

Benny didn't like to think of himself as a vindictive man, but he did feel that if he should suffer financial pain, the others who profited should feel some loss. It was only reasonable. There were two contacts in the Mexican operation, Richard Brice and The Suarez Family.

Benny tried to contact Camille Suarez after Chavez's call. Her voicemail was full. He called Carmen, only to get her voicemail. They always took his call? Without him, their enterprise would be dead in the water. He sat for a few minutes going over the possible motivations the Suarezs would have to screw him. He shook his head. Pacifico did not organize the systematic scouring of his personal residences, they didn't have the ability to ferret out his secret domiciles, and he couldn't see the motive. The estates were too well hidden behind false names and fake trusts. He watched as the alarms went off in his New York and Miami addresses. He still had Hong Kong, Rio and Dhaka. It could be the FBI, maybe CIA. But why?

The only reason for such a complete and quick breakdown in the hierarchy of the operation was that his identity had been leaked. No doubt, he'd been watched over the years, but he'd always been two steps ahead. The authorities must feel that they had a strong case against him, but it still didn't make sense. Organ trafficking was the perfect crime in which to make money. There were few laws at the federal level of any government on the planet and the cross pollination of protocol between countries very poor. The rich countries turned a blind eye on it, because it solved a problem. The wealthy did not die because they could find donor organs. Poor countries turned a blind eye because they couldn't enforce the crime prevention, and government officials receive kickbacks from the mobsters and cartels that ran the rackets. The plum in all of this, the fact that governments, even as big as the United States, were loath to spend the resources needed to crack down on the problem. But recently, pressure had been applied from the United Nations and Interpol. So they made mock efforts to appease these influential international bodies. These efforts were often just whitewash to make it look like something was being done to solve the problem.

Benny went to the cupboard over the refrigerator of his new apartment, located in East LA. The location would be perfectly safe, he'd purchased it only a week prior, using false documents from a long deceased woman. It would take months for the FBI, or whoever, to source this location. He pulled out a bottle of Stoli Vodka, his ritual when he needed to think. He poured out one shot and promptly knocked it back. His mind twirled in circles and he needed to figure out the riddle that sat in front of him. Why would the FBI want to burn him? Why was easy, but why now? The alcohol began to numb him nicely.

A light went on in his mind. Someone at the government level was on the take. Chavez, either directly, or indirectly, linked Benny, who was already on their radar. You couldn't move as much money around as he'd been able to do and not catch someone's attention. The breakdown could be as simple as a tapped cell phone line. Benny was a threat to whoever was on the take at the government level and to Richard Brice…Sun Medical was the culprit! Someone within the intelligence network, possibly the U.S. government was on their payroll…Benny smiled. Undoubtedly, his bank accounts would be under scrutiny, but not for a few hours, they would wait for the transaction to take place.

The medical conglomerate was powerful enough to find other sources of donor organs, there were other agents throughout the world. The shelf life of an organ trader was short. Benny had been feeling that he'd overstayed his welcome, he should have moved on sooner. Perhaps he shouldn't have demanded the fee increase months ago? Sun Med burned him using their under the table government source or sources to facilitate the "wet work." Fair enough, he'd made contingencies, but he would get his pound of flesh, whether it was wise, or not.

Chavez? Was he a mover, or was he a pawn, earmarked to take the fall? Did Chavez work for the US government? It would make sense…but at what level? He'd been useful to them in the linking of Benny to Pacifico. Benny did mention Sun Medical in his phone conversation with the doctor. The phone call must have set off the beehive, and the Queen Bee, Brice, was feeling very uncomfortable. Dom Chavez was in grave danger, they wouldn't waste time. He would be shot and his body incinerated in some dark and clandestine blast furnace. Benny could not make out the whole Chavez connection and it bothered him, but he'd been a productive pawn of the government thus far. Why not feed him some useful intel, and make Brice's life a little more uncomfortable. Benny would be able find some solace and pleasure at the man's losses, or perhaps his demise, but he would have to be careful, very careful. He would take one parting shot at the man, hopefully it would be a hit.

He switched out of the surveillance package and began drafting several encrypted email messages to his banking connections. Time to leave Mexico and the States. It had been extremely profitable, but he needed to cut loose and mitigate his recent losses. But not before he burned Brice.

CHAPTER THIRTY-EIGHT

DOM EXHALED AS the small jet touched down. He hated flying, especially the landing. The sun set an hour ago, but he could still tell that the runway wasn't attached to a major airport, most likely a private strip. The flight was deathly quiet after the brief altercation between him and Chantal. Dom didn't want to admit it to himself, but he felt that his heart was breaking every minute that she'd ignored him during the flight. Could she be this callous?

The side hatch and stairs were lowered to the ground outside; Carlos, Chantal and Dom were ushered out by Matthews. Dom picked up the Life Cradle containing Camille Suarez's heart as he exited the jet. A gray Suburban was waiting for them.

Before Dom slid into the car, Matthews asked him. "What's our destination?" He gestured towards the carrying device. "We'll be taking that, Major."

"Like fuck you will!"

Matthews raised his gun and pointed it at Dom's chest. "Orders Major, I'll shoot you if I have to, we're no longer on the plane."

He got the feeling that Matthew's threat was not idle. Dom pulled up the text he'd received from Leahner. He wanted to fabricate a location, but in the end, someone waited for, and needed the heart. He hated being at the mercy of the military operative. He would bide his time until forced to make a move. He chuckled inwardly, *like you have a fucking move*. "The Anderson Health Sciences Institute."

The other agent relayed the information to the driver. "That's not too far from here, your source knows what he's doing. I'll take that." He took the case from Dom.

Dom raised his eyebrows, uneasily letting go of the transport device. "It would appear so." Dom followed Carlos, then Chantal into the SUV. *Why was she doing this? Was it a front to throw off Matthews, or was this it? Did she play him for the past few months?* He frowned as he sat in the plush leather seat beside Chantal, her hands folded neatly on her lap. Matthews slipped into the passenger's seat, the Life Cradle on the floor between his feet. The other operative sat in the bench seat in the back, which made Dom very uncomfortable. He didn't like people at his back.

Dom couldn't help but wonder what role General Williams had in all of this? There was definitely a play on here. Did the General simply recommend him for the mission, or was he in on the deal? Dom didn't trust Bachman from the beginning. This wouldn't be happening without the call to him hours ago. He prided himself in being a good judge of character. Something didn't add up with Bachman. There seemed to be an unease about him from the beginning. Dom admitted to himself that he'd put the blinders on, the carrot hung out in front of him, his medical license. It all became somewhat clear, though he didn't know how far up the ladder the responsibility went. Could Williams have burned him? He was no more than a year off retirement, supposedly his friend, *the fucker*. Why not pad his pension? The mission seemed like a bit of a fairy tale from the beginning. His mind flipped back to the dinner, which Jasmine and he had been invited to at William's house a few months prior to the assignment. Generals don't invite Majors off the cuff for dinner at their home. It just didn't happen. He'd been flattered and at that point considered him a friend. There were many prodding questions that night. It all started to fall into place. *This mission from the beginning was supposed to fail.* Perhaps his superiors counted on his brashness, his perceived lack of diplomacy to aid in the mission's demise. It clicked into place: someone was getting paid off. The mission would prove once again that it was impossible to infiltrate the Mexican mob. Organs would continue to cross the border, unmolested.

His hackles suddenly went off, his hair standing on end. Matthews would have to kill him. Would he kill Chantal…Carlos? The young Mexican was good as dead. Chantal…maybe. This had to be an act to throw Matthews off? It would make sense…he prayed that it made sense. He wasn't a neophyte when it came to reading women. Could Chantal be an expert manipulator, did she play him like a puppet? He didn't rule this possibility out. He shook his head. What they'd lived over the past few months could only be real. You would have to be a real pro to pull that off. There was no bullshit with Chantal. Dom could damn well tell she was in love with him. In the end, love is what matters. He decided to put his fate in what his heart told him, it being the only thing he could grab onto. He prayed she was bluffing, waiting for the right moment, giving them a chance. Otherwise, they were dead.

Williams is involved, as is Bachman. DeRosnay, maybe not. Prendergast from the Department of State…Who the fuck knows? He wanted to put his hand on Chantal's leg. Instead, he smiled to himself. *Good girl!*

The large SUV lurched forward, leaving the small airstrip. Dom could see that they were probably in the hills to the east of Los Angeles, which he soon verified by a roadside sign. The city appeared in front of them as they rounded a corner, and started descending the escarpment. Dom couldn't help but look in awe at the massive sea of lights that spread out in front of them in the clear moonlit night. The driver leaned over and said something to Matthews, who nodded in response. He turned and looked out the back window. Dom could see a car following very close off the Suburban's bumper.

"Kids," said Matthews. He turned to Dom, "Who's the contact at the Hospital?"

Dom paused before answering as he looked down at his phone. "Shouldn't it be good enough that you get us to the hospital? Where's Bachman?"

"He's in LA, he'll be meeting us at the Anderson institute…Your contact?"

He lied and gave the name of the doctor, not Leahner. "Dr. Finlay."

Williams nodded, then turned to face the back seat pointing a Glock 26 in 9mm with a silencer at them. "That's about all that's required of you, Dr. Tavano." Dom felt the cold steel of a gun barrel against the back of his neck. "Apparently you did your job too well. Normally the military rewards its operatives for their success, but evidently you've been made redundant. I'll let you know though, I've been instructed to deliver the cargo as directed. It seems that my superiors do have a *heart* after all." He chuckled.

Suddenly, the world turned upside down. Glass shattering, steel bending, the Suburban jumped to the right several feet from the impact. A large Humvee had planted its reinforced front bumper into the side of the SUV. The driver and Carlos, who'd been on that side of the vehicle, took the brunt of the impact. Carlos's head lolled from side to side, blood running out of his nostrils. The driver it would seem, took worse.

Chantal reacted with precision, grabbing the gun from the stunned agent in the back seat as his arm hung loosely in his stunned condition. Matthews fumbled on the passenger's side floor trying to retrieve his gun. Chantal put a bullet in the back of his head, covering the front dash with vitreous. She then turned and put a bullet in the second man in the back. "Get out and grab the damned container, Dom."

Dom didn't argue. He quickly opened up the front door, and squeezed out of the vehicle, taking hold of the Life Cradle. The collision had occurred on an overpass that ran over a railway main line. "Carlos?" Dom yelled. The Mexican seemed either unconscious, or dead.

"No time, Dom!"

Dom instantly understood what Chantal meant. Through the window of the Suburban, he could see four men jump out of the Hummer. Behind them, the car that was following them minutes ago pulled up nearly touching the bumper. The doors flung open, and three more men, Mexicans if he was a good judge of ethnicity, jumped out, all carrying guns of various sizes and description.

"Dom." Chantal yelled. "Jump!"

He didn't hesitate and followed Chantal over the edge of the overpass railing, holding the organ transport device. They landed on a slow moving freight train rolling under the bridge. He fell awkwardly on the roof of a rust-colored car, barely maintaining a grip on the container. Chantal reached down to steady him.

"Dom, down the ladder." She stared into his eyes. "I'm sorry I had to do that."

He smiled. "And I love you all the more for it!"

She grabbed him by the scruff of his collar, and pulled him to his feet, kissing him on the mouth briefly. "Love?"

He shrugged, smiling, "It just might be." He hesitated for a moment, then kissed her again. "Yes, love."

"You silly man."

They rushed to the end of the car. As they reached the edge, the bullets started to fly. Dom went down the ladder first between two cars. Between Chantal's legs, he took a quick look and could see the Mexicans following them over the edge of the overpass, and landing on the roof of a car three back from theirs. Dom heard the thump of bullet meeting flesh. He knew the sound well. Chantal toppled down on top of him, as he did his best to retain his grip on the container and the metal ladder. She bounced off his shoulder and landed on the metal housing for the hitch, which attached the two cars. Dom hustled down the ladder and tried his best to see if she lived. Her eyes flickered open. She smiled slightly. "I had to do it…I didn't want to hurt you."

Dom could barely hear her her faint voice over the clatter of the noisy train. "I know."

She mouthed the words "I love you." Dom could do nothing but hang off the ladder, his mouth agape as she fell into the gap between the two cars.

"NOOOO!" He stared in shock, waiting to hear the sounds of her body being torn apart by the metal wheels. Thankfully, he was spared the horror due to the noise of the train. Then the first Mexican looked over the edge of the car. "Fuck!" He swung to the right of the ladder and caught the back edge of the car, his foot finding a tiny lip of metal. He jumped. The train moved slowly, but he managed to hurt himself pretty badly, mostly because he was doing his best to protect the container. He fell hard on his shoulder and then slid on his back through rough gravel for twenty feet, finally coming to a stop, the metal carrying device resting on his belly, wrapped in his arms. "I hope you're going to someone special." He said half in anguish, half in self-deprecation.

Dom didn't have time to mourn Chantal just yet. He could see the Mexicans a hundred yards past him scrambling to get down off the rail cars. He quietly cursed himself for not having a gun. He got up, and did his best to run towards a siding where another freight train sat idle. He scrambled between two cars. In front of him was a 10-foot tall chain link fence, with barb wire on top. "Christ…what now?" He looked both ways. The fence ran for as far as he could see in both directions. He could hear the Mexicans yelling, not too far away.

He decided to run in the opposite direction the train travelled, hoping his pursuers would anticipate him going forward. He guessed correctly. Turning, he saw the men coming through the train a few hundred yards away. Looking up, Dom cursed the moonlight as they spotted him easily. He heard the sound of gunfire, then the whistling of bullets hitting the train beside him and the chain fence.

Fortune shone down upon him along with the moonlight as he ran past a hole in the fence, probably made by kids or homeless people. He bent down and slipped through the gap. After trudging through a dry drainage ditch, there was a stand of trees on the far side that ran the length of the ditch for as far as he could see. On the other side of the trees, he found a massive parking lot, empty at this time of night, but lit by massive streetlights that stood every hundred feet. Moving as fast as his legs would carry him, Dom felt lucky that he'd kept himself in reasonable condition. Still, he would need to rest soon as he was running out of breath. Feeling the need to keep going, he heard his pursuers again. As they caught sight of him Dom cursed, "Bastards don't give up!"

His spirits lifted when he reached a main road. On the other side was a very rough, dilapidated looking housing development. Any other place or time, he would not have wanted to drive a car through the area, let alone walk. He had no choice and decided to head into the middle of it, carrying the shiny metal case and hoping the Mexicans would not be as daring. Windows were boarded up, but there were signs of life within, light creeping around the edges of boarded up windows. He rounded a corner and came face to face with what looked to be twenty black men, standing around talking. No use turning around, the Mexicans would shoot him if he did. He decided to take his chances there, and his chances didn't look good.

The men differed in age as they began to ring around him as he walked up to them. Dom noticed several carrying a book in one hand. One of them laughed. "What the fuck are you doing here? You got brass balls…homey."

Dom looked up at the moon and smiled before bending over

and placing his hands on his knees to catch his breath. He nodded. "Damn straight. I'll tell you the truth and you'll only have moments to decide. I'm a medical doctor and I'm being chased by a bunch of crazy fucking Mexicans with guns." He pulled out his wallet. "Here's five or six thousand dollars cash. All I have." He lied. "Here's my business card. Any of you ever need anything, just call this number and I'll look after you. I need to get this heart," He stopped to pat the carrier, "to a dying young woman at the Anderson Institute. I'd be grateful if you could slow down the bastards chasing me."

The man who laughed spoke up. "Put your money away, Doctor. That's one crazy assed story, too good not to believe. Come with me." The other men filed into the other buildings, leaving the courtyard empty.

At that point, Dom didn't have a choice. He followed him through what he assumed to be his house, a lot nicer than he would have believed.

The man saw the look on his face and laughed. "Pretty nice! We're like the Italians. Piece of shit outside and a palace inside, helps with the taxes." They kept walking until they went through the back door where the man indicated that Dom should get in the passenger-side door of a hopped up Honda Civic.

When Dom got in the car, the man slipped behind the wheel and offered his hand. "LeShawn."

"Dr. Dom Tavano. I owe you my gratitude."

"As the Bible says, doctor, do unto others. Anderson Institute?"

"That's it." Dom made a mental note to start praying more regularly.

It took ten minutes to get to the private hospital. LeShawn smiled. "I ain't never gonna see the insides of a place like this. It's too high end, Doctor."

"Hey, I come from the ass end of Brooklyn on the other side of the tracks, I know what it's all about. If it wasn't for Uncle Sam and the armed forces, I'd be in the same place as you, except my mom was Cuban."

"I get it, Doc. You want to be left off up front?"

"No. Let me off down the street a bit. There may be people watching for me."

LeShawn stopped two blocks to the south. Dom forced him to take a hundred dollar bill.

***

It's hard to tell if you are being watched, and Dom knew for sure that there would be multiple sources of eyes looking for him if he decided to enter the hospital. His phone rang as he contemplated his options. He didn't recognize the number. He pressed the answer button and put the phone to his ear. "Chavez?"

"Is that really your name, Doctor?"

Dom recognized Leahner's voice. "You could be onto something."

"I've been trying to reach you all night, Doctor."

"I've been in a few tight spots."

"I can appreciate that. We need to talk, face to face."

"You have to be out of your fucking tree."

"Have people tried to kill you tonight?"

Leahner had his attention. "No use beating around the bush…yes."

"Do you still have the heart?"

"Affirmative."

"You're military?"

"Go on…"

"I thought so."

"Are you wearing blue jeans and a green scrub shirt?"

"Go on…"

"I want you to go back in the direction you just came from and go to the gas station, a block and a half away. Quickly, this line is not safe." Leahner hung up.

Dom could feel the stress creeping up the back of his neck; he shrugged his shoulders up, trying to relieve the tension. As he walked, he reflected on the situation. He found it strange to be thinking this, but he felt relieved that Leahner called. He could possibly be the only person left that could help him. *What happens after I manage to deliver the donor heart? And that's a big if.* How would he get the heart to the hospital? He tried to remember the name of the Doctor. Bright? No, Dr. Finlay. He couldn't walk into the front door of the Anderson Institute carrying the silver carrier; he'd get snapped up before he even got close. He felt punchy. Tension in his neck worked its way up to the back of his head, his back a raw mess from sliding through the course gravel beside the train tracks. He'd been on point all day and it didn't look like the ride would be ending anytime soon.

He continued to walk briskly back towards the gas station. He could see it a block ahead. A blue Dodge caravan pulled up to the side of the road beside him. He kept walking. He half expected a gun to emerge as the window came down. He prepared himself to run. But then, he heard a familiar voice. "Doctor, I would advise you to get into the passenger side quickly." Benny Leahner's face appeared in the open window. Dom, thankful, slid into the empty seat, closing the door behind him. "Good." Leahner pulled the minivan away from the curb. "It's a miracle that someone didn't pick you up. Are you crazy? We have to go somewhere so that we can talk. Near the Hospital is no good. The place is crawling with the authorities and it looks like Mexican New Year's being celebrated early. I don't know what you've done, but the bee's nest has been shaken…and then kicked for good measure. I gather it's Suarez that's after you?"

Dom laid his head back into the seat, closing his eyes for a few moments slowly shaking his head from side to side.

"Doctor, you look terrible."

"I feel terrible, Mr. Leahner."

"Please, call me Benny. I know that your name isn't Chavez. Perhaps we can start there."

Dom turned towards him, frowning. "Perhaps we can start with…how did you know where to find me? And why the hell I should tell you?

"As I said, let's start with your real name."

"Dominic Tavano."

"Okay, that's a start. Dominic, I am the only friend that you have at this point in time. The airwaves are going crazy. What in heavens have you done? There is word of a $5 million dollar bounty on your head. There are Mexicans everywhere, not necessarily from Pacifico. It's open game, and I hear that Hernando Suarez wants it in a bag."

Dom took a deep breath. "The heart that's in here." He patted the carrier," is Camille Suarez's."

The minivan swerved, as Benny's head turned towards Dom. "Dear God! What were you thinking? "

Dom took a deep breath. "It wasn't a matter of thinking, I really had no choice. She died on the table, during a kidney transplant. Suarez, I'm sure would have killed me for letting his daughter die, well at least as soon as he found out. I'll be honest, the operation went like clockwork. She suddenly flat lined, I don't know what happened. So…we took out the heart."

"Who's we?"

"Is it that important?"

"I need to know the whole story if I'm to help you?"

"My wife, Chantal and one of the resident Doctors."

"Is she really your wife?"

"How the fuck do you know all of this?"

"The resident Doctor is as good as dead." Benny continued driving, his eyes focused forwards on the road. "Then you called me? The bloodwork matches up?"

"Yes."

"You have made an enemy that I would not wish on anyone. Hernando Suarez does not think logically, he's an emotional being. He will hunt you down."

"Better to be hunted, than shot there on the spot."

"Did your superiors implant a tracking device on you?"

"Fuck…yeah, right on my left shoulder."

Benny pulled the car over to the side of the road. "Bend forward."

"What the heck!"

"Doctor bend forward." Once Dom followed his command, Leahner pulled out a pocket knife and felt around on his shoulder. "There it is. Hold your breath, Doctor." He slid the sharp edge of the knife under the small bulge and pulled out the small capsule. "We need to take advantage of this." Benny pulled into a convenience store and got out of the van. He placed the homing device under the bumper of a parked car.

"Hopefully those people are going in the opposite direction." He chuckled. "Even so, they won't get very far. I can't believe you made it to this point without being picked up." He turned a corner. "Suarez will be after you 'til the end of his days Doctor, and I'm sure that Carmen Suarez will accept the baton eagerly. I hear the old man enjoys feeding people to the sharks, bit by bit. Now, let's stop messing around. I give you my word that I will tell you why I am dependent upon you."

"Why the fuck are you dependent upon me?" Dom squirmed in his seat in agitation.

"If you will tell me the truth about why you were in Mexico. You wouldn't be transporting that goddamned heart into the States if there wasn't a reason other than money. It would simply not be worth it."

"Benny, that information is classified."

"Just as I thought. You're military, you're not FBI. Have you been burned?"

Dom's head dropped. "Yes, I think so." He made a determined effort to say no more.

"I'm going to make a deal with you Dom Tavano. As much as I don't want to show my hand, I need you as much as you need me. I don't think you trust me, I wouldn't either." He paused as he turned to the right. "I'm a survivor. I live on the edge, picking up the crumbs left over from the big boys. But you see…I'm needed, but yet, I'm the first one to have the rug pulled out from under me. Tell me Dom, you brought that heart here to nail me, right?"

Dom remained silent, thinking.

"It will do you no good to try nailing me. I'll admit my role is of an unsavory nature, but I'm not the one that's driving this bus. There are many like me around the world. The FBI, I can assure you, know about me. Who you want to get back at are the people who contract me and pay the money, the ones who are paying off the government officials to turn a blind eye, the ones that have screwed you!"

Dom felt himself sliding further down into the seat. He felt like the world crashing down on him, the little Jew reading him like a damned open book.

Benny pulled off the main road onto a subdivision street. "I'm taking you to my apartment. You can have a shower and a change of clothes, then we can talk. I'll set up an exchange with the Chambers, the heart is earmarked for their daughter. There's no way you can take the heart into that hospital. You may make it in, but you won't make a hundred yards once you walk out the door. I like my money, doctor, but I'm also sensitive to my client's needs. The young woman waiting for this," he motioned to the transport device, "is very unwell."

***

Benny's apartment was in a three-story building in an unsavory part of East LA, but the decor was fashionable and Benny made him feel comfortable. "Take your time in the shower, there's a change of clothes in the spare bedroom. If you don't mind, I'll check on the state of the cargo. The carrier looks like it's had a rough ride." Dom nodded, too tired to argue.

The shower felt good. He turned the water up until he could barely stand it. His back raw, he used a shower sponge to clean it as best he could. Once finished, he toweled off and put on the clothes that were left out for him in the spare room. The legs of the pants were a little short, but they were better than the hospital scrubs he'd been wearing for the last twenty hours.

Dom walked into the living room, where Benny was finishing up with a telephone conversation. "Yes, Alan, you can complete the payment…You will have to bring the cargo into the hospital. It's been a struggle getting it here…Yes, it was from a female. Yes…drive to where I've told you to go, then text me. I'll text you back at that point, and tell you where you can pick it up." He hung up.

"The clients will be at the drop off in less than an hour. I think that it would be a good thing for you to talk with them. Their daughter is idealistic, not wanting to accept a heart from anyone who didn't give it freely in death. She swore that she would not accept… the gift. I think if you told Mr. Chambers the story, it would go a long way towards appeasing Madeline Chambers. You see, I do have a heart, Doctor." He smiled. "We will meet them on the street. I've frightened them enough to keep their mouths shut. Who knows now, though? The FBI, Military Intelligence are on this, as well as god knows who else. He will be followed, so you will need all of your cunning. You've made it this far, I don't see why you can't make it this last step of the way."

Benny poured two shots of vodka and handed one to Dom. "I think you might need this. Would you like some water?"

"Yes…thank you." He sipped half, placing it on the table.

Benny looked Dom in the eye. "I can't help you until you tell me who you are working for and why? I think that we might be after the same person or persons. I will tell you. I wasn't after them, at least until they tried to kill me tonight."

"Really?"

Yes, Dominic, we are tied together in this. I do have a bone to pick with you though. Your phone call precipitated the process." He reclined into the couch. "What if I told you that I could give you the name and the tools to nail the head of Sun Medical, the entity which is responsible for bringing in nearly ten percent of the illegal organs into the United States? Dominic, I'm small potatoes, and so are you. Unfortunately, you are a dead man without my help."

Dom finished the vodka. "Okay, I'm listening."

"That's better. Help me, help you." Benny crossed his legs waiting for Dom to speak.

"My name is Major Dominic Tavano, I am a military doctor, on a UN, U.S. State Department sanctioned mission, sent to gather any information I could which might be used against those that traffic organs from Mexico over the United States border."

Benny chuckled. "It's all whitewash, Dominic. The United Nations have been pushing the State Department for years to do something about illegal organ sales…since The Vienna Forum and Bill HR-3649 that the U.S. government recently passed. But they have not been given the funds to back up the mandate. The government turns a blind eye on the process, and some people are getting big kickbacks. The proof in the pudding is the fact that they tried to kill you tonight. You were supposed to go to Mexico, the optics are good, and within a month or so they find you washed up on some beach or in a dumpster. If the Mexicans don't do it, your compatriots do it themselves. Don't fool yourself. Whoever set you up for this mission harbored no regard for your well-being." He took a sip from his drink. "You did what you were supposed to do, but they didn't expect you to do it. To top all of that, you've killed the daughter of one of the most notorious gangsters in all of Mexico." He sat in thought for a time, shaking his head. "Is there someone safe that you can contact within the Government?"

"Possible…General Williams at the Pentagon."

"Are you positive? I've heard a saying that it's not wise to trust a General."

"No. He's a friend." He knew the words were not true, but wanted to save some face.

"Pretending to be your friend Dominic. No doubt he's getting a kickback. This is how it all works. Anyone else?"

Dom thought for a few minutes. "Joanna DeRosnay, she's an anthropologist from Duke University, working with the U.N. She's been crusading against the trade for decades."

"I've heard her name. A bleeding heart. You might contact her, but with caution and only one on one. She will find it hard to help you. She, no doubt is boxed into a corner."

"I can't trust my military contacts, that's for sure." He envisioned placing a bullet in the back of Bachman's skull.

"The organ trade solves a lot of problems. The doctors get paid, lives are saved."

"Yeah, but to the detriment and lives of innocent poor people."

"I don't get paid to make moral judgments, Doctor Tavano."

"You're just as bad as the rest of them."

"Sadly, yes." He crossed his right leg over his left knee. "I will tell you though, if it makes you feel any better. I've decided to call it a day and disappear. I'm giving you the opportunity to take down one of the real bad guys in all of this: Dr. Richard Brice. He's burned me. I'll not make a moral song and dance about it, but I want the man to go down. I'm not doing this to be nice to you, I'll be using you to help me make retribution against someone who caused me considerable financial loss. It gives you your opportunity to be the hero, isn't that what you want?"

"I have no desire to be a fucking hero. Maybe in my youth."

"Doctor, we're going to finish this transaction and the money will be sent to your account of choice, along with a sizable stipend, a bonus shall we say, if being a hero is not enough. I have little doubt that becoming wealthy will suffice. I am going to give you receipts and electronic paper trails for the past two years to my accounts.

With some digging, the FBI will be able to trace many of the transactions to Sun Medical."

"What will happen to you?"

"Don't worry about me, Doctor. I've been making contingencies for such an occasion for years. You see, I never start an operation without an exit plan in place, sometimes two, even three." He handed Dom a USB data stick. "There is enough evidence to cause Sun Medical some real harm, but the real culprit is Dr. Richard Brice, President of Sun Med. I'll give you his personal email and cell number. Once you've made contact with a sympathetic ear, hang tight, I'll be in touch and will tell you what to do. I'll leave you one of my phones. I'll be able to track you through it, on my laptop. I just might be able to help you if you get into a tight spot."

"That's comforting. An eye in the sky."

"Something like that. As far as Pacifico is concerned, I think you have done enough harm and hopefully some good will come of this, but you have made a lifelong enemy." He patted the silver carrier. I will admit, you have real balls to have thought of and pulled this off. Even I couldn't have fashioned a way to get Camille Suarez's heart over the U.S. border. Well done."

CHAPTER THIRTY-NINE

DR. FINLAY HAD called the Chambers nearly six hours ago with the news that a donor heart had been found. Bonnie and Alan were understandably ecstatic with the news. Bonnie looked like an expectant grandmother during the drive to the Anderson Institute. She couldn't sit still, a nervous smile upon her lips; cautious anticipation. The months of waiting and watching Maddie slowly slip away were agonizing. The sudden dangling of a carrot in front of their noses lifted them out of their stupor.

Five hours passed and Alan could tell from the faces of the hospital staff, who also waited patiently, that they were becoming concerned with the delivery, or lack of it. Dr. Finlay took Alan aside an hour ago to voice his concerns.

"Alan, remember what we're dealing with, and where the donor organs are coming from. From time to time, the cargo doesn't make it into the country for a myriad of reasons. Moreover, the longer we wait, the chances are greater that the heart, if it does arrive…may not be usable. I've been through this before. I'm so sorry to have to put you through the pain."

Alan could feel the anger building within him. He tried to remain as calm as was possible under the circumstances. He didn't mean to take it out on the Finlay, but he'd been pushed to his limits. "I get that Doctor. This family is maxed out. If this procedure doesn't happen tonight, I don't think that there will be any coming back. I've spent a shitload of money chasing a mystery cadaver in some poor ass country. I'm starting to feel as if I've been played. But it's not the money at this point. I don't care if I end up in the goddamned poor house."

Finlay put a hand on his shoulder to calm him.

"Get your damn hand off my shoulder." Alan said as he shrugged away from him. "I don't need your damn sympathy."

"Alan, I don't mean to patronize you…I can see that you don't need that. Your nerves are frayed. Getting angry and causing a scene will not help."

"Don't you pretend to…"

Finlay cut him off. "Alan, I will have to call security. I will tell you only once." His head dropped for a moment.

Alan put his hand up. "I'm sorry…I'm trying to be the strong guy here. This waiting and the possibility that it could be all for nothing has pushed me to my limit."

"Yes, I know. Look, I've grown fond of Maddie over the past months. I want nothing more than to see the three of you walk into my office months from now…smiles on your faces. I wish that we might have been able to find a donor through more conventional means, but as my father used to say, 'We have to deal with the fish that we have in the boat.' I am a God-fearing man, Alan. When all else fails, I pray. God has his reasons, but he doesn't like to be ignored." Finlay put his hand on Alan's shoulder again. This time the gesture was accepted. "Ask of God and he will provide an answer. That is all we can do at times."

"I'm not a religious man, but I'll take your prayers, doc. I'll take anything I can get."

Before any prayers could be spoken, Alan's cell phone rang. He picked it out of his pocket and answered. "Hello?…Yes…I can do that." Alan began to pace as he listened to the man on the other end. "Why does this have to be so damned clandestine Mr.…Yes of course. I'll do that."

Alan slid the phone back into his pocket. A wry smile formed on his lips. Bonnie and Brian Finlay looked at him expectantly. "That was Leahner."

Bonnie urged him on. "And?"

Alan hugged her. "He has the heart! I have to meet him and the doctor who delivered it to us."

Finlay frowned. "Doctor?"

"Evidently. I am supposed to meet him at a location. He will be texting me in ten minutes."

Finlay smiled. "That sounds like him. He's like a ghost, but I suppose one would have to be in his line of work."

***

Alan left the hospital in a hurry, so preoccupied with the events at hand, he didn't notice the swirl of activity caused by his departure. There were more than one set of interested eyes watching him leave.

***

Leahner pulled the minivan into a parking space at a convenience store, not too far from the hospital. He sighed and reached across his chest under his jacket and pulled out a small black snub-nosed hand gun. Dom, ready for anything at this point, moved to grab his arm. Leahner calmly, put the weapon on the middle console. "Don't worry Dom, if I'd wanted to shoot you, it would have happened already. The father of the young lady waiting on the heart will be pulling into this parking lot in ten minutes. He drives a black Bentley, you won't miss him. Help deliver the heart and then I will advise you on how to get lost and turn your attentions to Dr. Richard Brice. I would like to say it's been a pleasure doing business with you, but it hasn't, no fault of yours of course. Good evening Dr. Tavano." He patted the gun. "You may need this." Benny stepped out of the car and disappeared into the night.

Dom knew that he wouldn't see the man again. In the back of his mind, he'd wanted to expose Leahner, but he was a pro and used to surviving in this arena. He looked down and saw the memory stick sitting beside the gun. He shook his head. Everything seemed turned upside down in the past twelve hours. He'd lost Chantal, gotten both Pedro and Carlos killed, and now he'd been betrayed by his superiors. He slammed his hands on the wheel. "Dammit!"

He sat and stared at the gun that lay by his left hand. It would be easy to give up and just shoot himself. He really didn't want to go any further, but he would not die a coward, he'd never pull the trigger. There were enough people looking for him right now that would do it for him. He pictured his head being presented to Hernando Suarez, the look on his face. He shook his head. No, he wouldn't roll over. Deep down, he felt that there still existed a chance at retribution. He was a warrior, a soldier, and he needed to move forward.

In the past few months, he'd developed an intense dislike for the illegal organ trade and the body thieves that perpetrated the illicit industry. The whole process was flat out wrong. Even if he made a small difference, whatever it might be, it would be worth it. The whole mission had been a bit fantastical, surreal. It all made sense now. In the beginning he'd been asked to do the impossible. Now, on the precipice of achieving that goal, it was being dashed away. His superiors sent him on a wild goose chase, one where the result could have ended in death, death by achieving, or underachieving. He laughed out loud to himself. No way of winning.

An anger began to brew in him that he hadn't felt in a long time.

The bastards who'd sent him on this mission expected him to perform hundreds of extractions, with the goal of nabbing the perpetrators who were responsible for the killing and brutalization of thousands upon thousands of innocent and impoverished people throughout the world. In essence, they'd made him sacrifice and put his morals to the side, for nothing but his eventual assassination by either the Cartel or a military thug like Matthews or Bachman. "The bastards."

No, he wouldn't give up, he would vindicate the atrocities he'd been forced to perform, the deaths of Chantal, Carlos and Pedro, and the deaths of the innocents in the third world. He laughed at himself. "That's a tall order Tavano, let's just take one step at a time."

He took the snub nosed pistol and fit it in the back of his belt. He looked at his watch. Five minutes remained before he could expect Alan Chambers to arrive. He pulled out his cell phone and looked up Joanna DeRosnay's number and punched it with his index finger. It rang several times before he heard her sleepy South African accent. "Yes?"

"Dr. DeRosnay. It's Dominic Tavano."

There was a pause. "Dear God. You're alive."

"In the flesh."

"You've created quite the stir."

Dom probed her. "Does Bachman know what's going on?"

"Funny you should ask." She said sarcastically. "I spoke to him a few hours ago. Of course he does."

"General Williams?"

"Months since we've talked."

"Please tell me what you know."

"That's easy. You're wanted for murder in Mexico. The FBI has an all-points bulletin out for you. Interpol is involved."

"Do you believe that I am a murderer?"

There was a long pause. "Let me hear what you have to say for yourself, then I will answer."

Dom quickly relayed the events of the day back to her. "The

military and the State Department burned me, Joanna. I'm following orders. Camille Suarez died on the operating table. I was as good as dead and she possessed the heart that would help link Leahner to his source in the States."

DeRosnay went quiet for a time. "Where are you now?"

"Southern California."

"I don't know what to say. I'll assure you though that I am in no way involved in the conspiracy. I wouldn't jeopardize nearly thirty years of work, to fall prey to an illegal payoff. Tell me about the organ agent, Leahner."

"I think he was burned as well. He left me all of his banking data. Said there is enough evidence to link a man named Brice, head of Sun Medical, one of the big American players in the organ trade. I just have to figure out what to do with the intel. It would be easy if I knew who I could trust. You are the only one that I can see who would have a hard time finding any benefit from the fiasco."

"Doctor, I can assure you of that. Let me make some calls and I need to think. Can you ring me back in the morning?"

"I will...if I'm still alive."

A black Bentley pulled into the parking lot one space over from the minivan. He was pretty sure that there were at least three more cars that followed in behind it.

"Got to go. I'll call you."

"Be careful."

"Sigh."

***

Dom wasn't quite sure what to do. If he got out of the car, it might not be good for his health. He noticed the Samsung smart phone sitting in the middle of the driver's seat, Leahner's phone. He picked it up and looked at the last numbers called. One was an hour ago. He punched the dial button. It rang, instantly picked up.

"Leahner?"

"No, this is Dr. Dominic Tavano. Is this Mr. Chambers?"

"Why…yes?"

"Mr. Chambers, I have the heart."

"I'm listening."

"I'm two spots over to your right." Dom slipped into the driver's seat as he talked. "You have been followed by people. There are three cars that pulled in with you, that I can count, and both of us are in serious danger. I want you to calmly step out of your car, lock it and then step into the passenger's side of the gray Dodge." Chambers looked at him. Dom nodded his head. "Do it now."

Alan Chambers got out of his car and went over to the minivan, opened the passenger door and sat in the seat.

"Close the door!" Dom jammed the car into reverse and peeled backwards out the entrance, then slammed the brakes on as he reached the middle of the road. Alan held on for dear life. As Dom stomped on the gas pedal, he looked over at his passenger's face. Tense, fearful. Both of Dom's hands were glued to the steering wheel. "Mr. Chambers, I'd shake your hand if I could."

Alan made a gesture as if to say, "Keep doing what you are doing."

"I'm Doctor Dominic Tavano, US Military. I take it you're looking for your daughter's heart?" For the strangest reason the song, "I left my heart in Iran" by Forgotten Rebels, popped into his head. He grinned.

Alan frowned. "I find no humor in the situation, Doctor."

"Neither do I, but you have to excuse me, it's been a long day and I'm getting punchy. It's in that metal case in the back seat. It's been through a bit of a rough ride. If your daughter survives the transplant, one day I'm going to visit her and tell her the story. Please put it on your lap…Damn." He looked in the rear view mirror, and saw two cars pulling out after them. Then, the flash of gunfire from both cars.

Alan turned his head back to Dom. "They're shooting at each other!"

Dom nodded. "That would make sense." He looked back again

as he sped along the side road. One of the cars veered sharply into a ditch. The other slowly gained ground on them. Dom turned abruptly to the right, running through a red light to gain the main roadway, cutting off two cars in the process. The car continued to follow.

"Where did the heart come from?"

Dom pondered whether or not he should tell him. *What the hell.* "It's a bit of a story, but I'll try to squeeze it in before we get to the Anderson Institute."

"I'm all ears."

"Your daughter's blood type is rare. I was on an undercover mission to break down the source of money flowing into Mexico from U.S. medical institution. Your file was given to me by an organ agent."

"Mr. Leahner."

"Yes, this is his car. I would imagine he's on his way to South America or Africa by now, never to be heard from again. Anyway, we find a kidney with the same blood type; strangely enough, the daughter of the drug lord we were working for is the same type and needs a kidney transplant. I perform the surgery and she dies on the table."

"This is her heart?" Alan patted the top of the case.

"Yep."

"So these guys chasing us are Mexicans, who work for the drug lord?"

"Yep, and possibly the FBI or the Military police."

"What?"

"I've been burned. I wasn't supposed to get this far. Someone in the U.S. government hierarchy didn't want me to succeed."

Alan shook his head. "Most of them are corrupt bastards. I deal with the government all the time in my business. Money keeps the wheels of government well-greased."

"Yep, exactly. So…I will find some vindication to know that this heart will have been put to good use. It came from a beautiful woman and her father is a very bad man. Do you follow?"

"I do."

"Do you have a business card?"

"I do, strangely enough." He reached into his wallet and placed it on the console.

"If I make it out of this mess, I'd like to contact you and visit your daughter."

"I think that she'd like that, Doctor. Your story gives me hope. You see, Maddie when she found out the route we were taking to acquire the heart, put up the stop signs. She wasn't going to take the heart from some poor person in the third world. She just wasn't. She said she would jump off a bridge at the first opportunity. Her mother and I were going to have to make up some plausible lie to appease her."

"If she doesn't believe my tale, promise her that I will contact you as soon as I can. I'll tell her anything she needs to know."

"I appreciate that. Is there anything I can do? Do you need cash?"

"No, just get this to your transplant doctor. We're almost there." He looked at the front of the hospital. "This could get hairy, Alan. I'm going to pull into the emergency entrance and I'm not stopping. Can you manage to jump out?"

"I'll do whatever it takes." He placed his hand on Dom's. "Thank you."

"That's payment enough, Mr. Chambers. Best of luck!"

A long sweeping ramp led to the emergency entrance. He turned hard without slowing and sped up towards the busy area. People jumped out of the way as he laid on the horn. He spied two police officers talking to each other at the curb. "Okay Alan, ready? Gonna' drop you at their feet."

"Yes!" He opened the door, nearly knocking one cop down. He stepped out and rolled, protecting the precious cargo he held in his arms.

Dom hit the accelerator. As he did, the passenger door slammed shut. He barreled down the other side of the ramp. As he assumed, he'd not lost his pursuers, they were directly on his bumper. He didn't look back to see how Alan Chambers had made out. That part of the story was now out of his hands.

CHAPTER FORTY

CARLOS PUT HIS HANDS TO HIS HEAD. The blow from the crash knocked him out cold. As he came to, he saw Doctor Dom and Chantal jump over the side of the bridge. There were several men swarming past the SUV, his countrymen by the looks of it. Out of the corner of his eye, he saw Matthew's gun on the floor. His head hurt, as did his left leg, but he managed to reach through the gap in the front of the SUV and grab the weapon.

He peeked over the edge of the dash and saw six of the men hop over the side of the bridge, following Chantal and Dom. One remained, leaning against the guardrail. Carlos looked around to make sure there would be no surprises when he got out of the vehicle. A line of cars formed behind the collision. He wasn't sure, but he thought he could hear a siren in the distance. He put his hand to his mouth, the bleeding pretty heavy, he'd bitten through his lower lip.

The distance between the SUV and the lone man at the edge of the bridge was about twenty feet. Carlos wasn't sure he could look a man in the face and pull the trigger, but if it meant saving Chantal and Dom, he resolved himself to doing it. He stepped out of the already open door and slowly moved towards the man, gun in both hands. Someone from one of the cars in line yelled meaningless words in English. The man at the edge of the bridge turned quickly to face him, surprised to see the Berretta in his hand. Carlos squeezed the trigger, the man remained standing. Carlos cursed, surprised to see that he'd missed, he raised his hand up again, squeezing the trigger again. This time hitting his adversary in the leg. The man howled in pain, dropping to the ground, the gun sliding along the ground way from him. Carlos ran towards the gun and picked it up. It seemed much heavier than the one in his other hand.

"You fuckeen bastard." The wounded man yelled.

Carlos ignored him and ran to the railing, looking down to see the train moving away from him. He could see Dom and Chantal's pursuers running along the tops of the rail cars, jumping the gap between the next. He stuck both guns into his pant pockets and jumped, landing awkwardly. He heard gunfire and then he saw Chantal fall, his heart rose into his throat. "No!" Carlos didn't feel good about jumping the gap between this car and the next. He climbed down the ladder and stepped on the linkage between this car and the next. As he looked down to get his footing, he saw Chantal pass beneath him between the rails.

He needed to save her. He'd forged a strong bond with the woman over the past several months. He didn't hesitate to jump off the train. It wasn't going too fast that he couldn't make it without killing himself. He landed on his feet, but was forced to roll as he lost his balance. He got up quickly and ran back towards where he guessed Chantal might be, his guess perfect. He saw her form in the moonlight as the cars passed over. He yelled, "CHANTAL!" A jolt of electricity shot through him when he saw her head roll to the side, alive, the axles of the wheels just missing her as they passed over.

It seemed an eternity before the last car of the train passed. He jumped to her side the second the last car cleared. He quickly assessed her wounds. They were pretty nasty; a gash on her forehead and her left leg seemed bent at an awkward angle. He rolled her slightly, examining her for more trauma. There was a bullet wound in her upper back and one in the back of her thigh, which he guessed caused the leg to cant at a strange angle.

From a distance he could see flashing lights from the overpass. The people who'd been blocked by the collision would have seen him jump over the rail, they would have seen the shooting. There would be police. Carlos panicked in his confusion, it didn't help to be in a strange country. He looked down at Chantal. He knew that if she didn't get help, she would die. He took his shirt off and applied pressure to the wounds. He lifted her gently off the tracks and started walking back to the overpass. He would have to take his chances with the American authorities if he was going to save her.

CHAPTER FORTY-ONE

DOM ACCELERATED AS the minivan bounced over the corner of a curb and hit the main road. The damned car was still following him, glued to his bumper. He could see red and blue flashing lights in the distance behind. To make matters worse, he could see more flashing lights up ahead.

Part of him wanted to pull over and let the Police take him, but he feared that whoever drove the car behind him might have different ideas, like shooting him. Moreover, the police could simply hand him back to the Military. He didn't trust that option at the present time either. He needed to give DeRosnay some time. He needed to get the banking information into the right hands. But how? The current state of affairs didn't look good at all and grew worse by the minute. Another car pulled out from a side street, a Mustang with enough power to catch up and overtake the minivan in seconds. The car ran up beside him. A man in the passenger seat pointed a silver handgun at him through the open window. Dom slammed on the breaks. The shooter missed, Dom catching the flash of the gunfire out of the corner of his eye. The pursuers were Hispanic. *Fuck!*

If the chase went on any longer, the odds of him escaping would diminish. The Police would start to cordon off any possible escape routes. As the Mustang maneuvered to get another shot at him, Dom turned sharply onto a narrow side street. Both cars followed, but were now not able to pull up beside him. He swerved from side to side, blocking them from passing.

Leahner's phone rang. *Christ! Not now Benny!* Dom could see that device paired with the cars hands free. He hit the talk button.

"Doctor?"

"Benny?"

"I've been watching your journey on my laptop. I gather that you're being followed."

"You could say that." He swerved sharply to block the Mustang.

"Police?"

"They're a ways back, but the immediate problem appears to be two cars full of angry Mexicans. As much as I'd like to say that I admire your minivan, I don't. This piece of crap has ZERO F'N GUTS!"

"Calm down Dominic. You need to get out of the vehicle somehow and become invisible. I can help you do that."

"Great fucking idea Benny." He started to laugh maniacally. "Where did you think that one up? I'm not a fucking djinn!" Dom shook his head.

"Doctor, I've spent a lifetime becoming invisible. If you use your head, it's always possible. Right now you are panicking, calm yourself."

Dom shook his head again.

"There's a subway station coming up in a quarter of a mile, a parking garage next to it. I want you to pull into the garage. You're going to stop immediately and block the entrance. Get out of the car and run straight ahead to the other side of the garage. There will be a stairwell that will take you down to the public transit. If I calculate things correctly, there is a train due in four minutes. If you run, you might just make it. If you are lucky you might be able to slip your Mexican friends. Do you still have the gun?"

"Yes."

"Use it."

"Why are you helping me Leahner?"

"I need you alive to help me nail Richard Brice. I thought we understood this?"

"Right. Too much going on. Sorry." Dom could see the garage up ahead on his right.

"Keep the phone with you. I can track you with it and it's the only way that I can help you."

"Help me, help you, you mean. Jerry McGuire. You've used that line already."

"Huh?"

"A line from a movie."

"You have a strange sense of priority Doctor."

Dom didn't bother hanging up and stuffed the phone and memory stick into his pocket. The Green "P" came up quickly, indicating the Parking Garage. He braced himself for the collision and as directed, he swerved hard into the entrance. A curving ramp headed upwards. He grabbed the opportunity, ramming the front right side of the van into the wall, effectively blocking the passage. He jumped out of the car and ran up the ramp. He could hear the Mexicans cursing from behind. They would have to climb over the hood of the van to make chase. He'd gained a hundred yard advantage.

He spotted the stairway Leahner had mentioned. As he pulled the door open, the bullets began flying. He didn't bother looking behind him, but instead kept focused on the stairs. A bullet hit the safety glass in the door, shattering it. Dom took the stairs five at a time and soon spied the door indicating the subway. He pulled it open and ran for the turnstiles. He fumbled for his wallet as he ran. He yanked out a twenty and stuffed it into the cashier's wicket, jumping over the turnstile. Leahner was correct. A train waited, letting passengers on and off. He ran for the open door and found a spot amongst other travelers. He could see two of the Mexicans running full tilt to catch the train. They just made it, squeezing into the car ahead of his.

Dom slowly walked towards the rear of the train, slipping through the doorway to the next car. He hoped that his pursuers would go towards the front first. Over the shoulder of another passenger he could see one of the Mexicans heading towards where he stood in the rearmost car. Dom moved beside the doorway and picked up a newspaper, conveniently sitting on the bench seat. He sat down, holding the gazette up to cover his face, pretending to be reading. He pulled out the pistol from his jacket pocket. His assailant entered the car, looking ahead, scanning. Dom waited to see if the man might back out of the car. There was an awkward moment where the two men were no further than two feet away from each other. There would be a 50/50 chance that the man would turn the other way to leave the car. The odds were against Dom and the Mexican turned his way, hesitating as his eyes glanced over him and the paper. Their eyes met. Dom didn't hesitate and fired two shots through the paper, both hit his assailant in the side of his chest. He went down like a sack of potatoes. It took a few moments for communal shock to set into the car, a moment of disbelief before primal reactions took over. A woman screamed, others hit the floor, covering their heads. Within seconds chaos ruled.

Dom moved back into the other car, elated when he felt the train start to slow down. As it pulled into the next station, he heard screams of terror coming from the end car, where he'd shot the man. The train came to a halt. He calmly stepped out and made his way briskly to the exit. He didn't look back until he made the stairwell, checking to see if the other Mexican followed. He couldn't identify him in the mass of bodies.

Dom jumped onto the escalator, taking him to street level. He calmly walked to the taxi stand and slipped into the back seat of a yellow cab at the front of the line.

CHAPTER FORTY-TWO

RICHARD BRICE HELD the phone to his ear, trying his best not lose his cool with the person on the other end of the line. "How the hell does this happen?"

"We're in damage control now, Dr. Brice"

"I thought you said that this U.N. sanctioned mission was supposed to be smoke and mirrors?"

"No choice but to run it sir, and yes, it was intended to fail. The operative sent to oversee its lack of success…became successful. That's the best way to put it."

"Wonderful. Leahner?"

"AWOL. We have our eyes out for him, but he's slippery. He'll be on a private jet to the other side of the planet by now."

"He possesses the wherewithal to cause Sun Med some serious problems."

"I think he will disappear. That's what these guys do."

Brice was smart enough to not accept the comment at face value. "I hope that you're right, but it's against my better instincts to leave things to chance. I want to be able to sleep at night. You're in a position of power, find the Jew. What about the doctor?"

"He escaped after delivering the heart."

"He delivered the goddamned heart? Is there anything else that you need to tell me?"

"Yes, sir, the heart belonged to Camille Suarez. Pacifico is incommunicado. Hernando Suarez is out for blood at any cost. He's blaming everyone and anyone including Sun Med."

"I'm paying you a lot of fucking money to control this. Is our friend at the State Department up to date?"

"As soon as I'm off the phone."

"Then I trust you to fix this fuck up?"

"…Of course. This is minor and just a matter of time."

"I don't share your optimism and this isn't fucking minor. I can't think how it could be much worse."

Brice hung up. The timing was awful. With Sun Med about to break ground in Mexico, he'd have to put a hold on the dig. What would he tell the shareholders?

CHAPTER FORTY THREE

CARLOS STUMBLED ON the heavy gravel leading up the slope of the overpass. Above him, he could see flashing lights and he could hear yelling. A flashlight hit him. "Hey, who are you?"

Carlos could hardly speak, even if he understood English.

The beam of light caught Chantal's form in his arms.

Immediately, a group of cops began sliding down the gravel slope towards Carlos. The officer that held the flashlight slid to a stop at Carlos's feet. The blood-soaked form of Chantal attracted his attention. "What the heck do we have here? Christ!"

Carlos shook his head, not understanding.

CHAPTER FORTY-FOUR

THE CABBIE TURNED around and asked, "Where to?"

Dom wasn't familiar with LA, and didn't really know what to say. He needed a few hours of sleep and a hot shower…time to clear his head and think. "North. Please just drive."

"Okay, mister."

The driver headed north as directed, which gave Dom time to look at his phone and figure out where he wanted to go. "Hollywood," the only place he could think of that would get him away from immediate danger.

"You got enough to pay? That's a ways."

Irritated with the man he said, "Just goddamn drive!" Dom handed him a hundred-dollar bill. "This'll keep you going for a bit."

"You're the boss." The driver grabbed the bill, which pacified him for the time being.

***

It took an hour to reach the movie-making capital where Dom spotted a Best Western coming up on the right. "The motel up ahead will be fine."

Pulling in, he handed over another hundred-dollar bill. The driver offered no change; Dom too tired to argue, slipped out of the vehicle.

He walked into the lobby, knowing he wouldn't be able to use a credit card. A chubby woman in her mid-forties greeted him with little enthusiasm. At two in the morning, he didn't blame her. She looked as if she'd been dozing. "Can I help you?"

"Been a long night."

She looked him up and down. "So…?"

"I need a room for the night. Can I pay cash?"

"Need a credit card, sir."

He pulled his wallet out and handed her a VISA card, with Dr. Dominic Chavez on it. "Can you take an imprint and not run it through?"

She looked at the card. "Is there something wrong…Dr. Chavez?"

"Look…ma'am, It's been a really hard night…Here." He dug into the wad of cash stuck in his pocket. "Here's $300."

"Sir?…I mean, Doctor?"

"When's your shift done? I'll give you a hundred more at the end of it. Just stick it in your pocket…I don't care."

"I'm done at 7 am…?" The girl wrinkled up her face. "What's with all the secrecy, I'm feeling a bit uncomfortable?"

Dom looked up at the ceiling, then leveled his eyes with hers. "You can make four hundred bucks if you just take the cash. I'm sure you know how to manipulate things. I've been caught having an affair by my wife. She's not very stable and has some people looking for me…Her brother's a cop. You ring my card in, they'll trace it and blow up your hotel trying to find me. I need to get some sleep." He huffed, looking down at his hands on the counter.

The girl looked around. "Okay, I'm not gonna' run your card

through, but put the cash back in your wallet. There's security cameras in here. I'll come by your room. I want $500?"

Fucking bitch! "Yes…" He looked at her nametag. "Yes Rita, easiest money you'll ever make. I really need some sleep, so make sure there's no problems, and you get your money."

"Okay. I don't feel good about it, but I need it."

"That's a good girl."

Rita programmed the card and handed it to Dom. "Room 205, up the stairs to your left."

"I'll leave the first four in an envelope sticking under the door. Another hun, just before six."

Rita shook her head. "Whatever you say, Dr. Chavez. Have a good sleep."

Dom smiled and took the card. "Thank you!"

***

Dom didn't feel good about the woman being able to keep her mouth shut, even with the bribe. He could only rely upon the fact that the woman needed the money. He would need his wits about him if he was going to accomplish what he intended to do. He found an envelope in the drawer of the hotel room and put the money in it, slipping it just under the bottom edge of the door.

He set his iPhone for 5:45 am. After having a hot shower, he laid down on the bed without pulling the covers down. He fell asleep within minutes.

CHAPTER FORTY-FIVE

ALAN CHAMBERS PUT his hand on top of his wife's. Bonnie looked at him with nervous eyes. "We've done all we can. Thank the Lord that the doctor, Tavano is his name; risked his life to deliver the heart. It's like some story out of a movie. Unbelievable."

Bonnie sighed deeply. The operation had been in progress for roughly three hours, each minute excruciating. Bonnie's brother John and his wife Mary arrived half an hour earlier. They'd driven down from San Francisco when news of the donor heart first arrived. They didn't know the process, but understood that Bonnie and Alan seemingly went through hell over the past few months and came to give their support.

There existed an edge to Mary, which Bonnie never managed to warm up to, an 'I know more than you do' attitude, no matter what the topic. Mary watched Alan and Bonnie with skepticism written all over her face, her body language that of a preying lion, ready to pounce on a weak moment. John put his hand on her leg as she spoke, a subtle warning to be tactful. "John and I know that you have been living through hell the past months." She said it more to the room rather than at either Bonnie or Alan, looking for an audience.

Bonnie's head bobbed up, as if she'd been waiting for the comment. She raised her eyebrows. "It's been a long haul," she said irritably.

"Need it have been?"

Bonnie could feel the heat rising in her forehead. Alan stood up. Bonnie pushed him back into his seat. "I think that we understand the situation."

"Bonnie darling, don't get me wrong, I know that you have the means, we've been reading about these things...you know."

Bonnie paused for a moment. "No, what precisely do you mean?"

There were many uncomfortable moments over the years. Card parties ruined by a snide comment. Bonnie and Mary never warmed to each other, yet Mary felt, mistakenly, close enough to say things that she probably shouldn't. "You have money, a hell of a lot more than we do...you know what I mean."

John spoke up. "None of our business."

"Like hell it isn't. Maddie's our niece, we've suffered silently through this."

Alan looked to the ceiling, then put his hands up. "John, Mary...Let me tell you that I know what you are saying, and...I can't say anymore, except to say that we have exhausted every opportunity available."

Mary shook her head. "You can get organs on the black market."

Alan smiled. "What are you saying?"

"Exactly that. There are people out there that can get these things."

Alan lowered his hands nearly to the ground. "I've read about these options, I'm not stupid. I looked into it, believe me." He glanced over to Bonnie. "We have weighed the options and Maddie would not agree to come on board with that." He didn't lie. "We've stayed the course, and frankly, I don't think that it's worth talking about. I don't think that we're accomplishing anything."

Bonnie rubbed his shoulder. She looked at Mary with some sympathy. "I hope you understand?"

"We were concerned, I hope it will work out for the best… God forbid."

***

Another hour passed without much conversation, anticipation thick in the air. The doors to the O.R. opened and Dr. Finlay walked into the waiting room. He looked tired. He raised his eyebrows as he addressed the Chambers in his Irish lilt. "There were a few complications."

Bonnie raised her clasped hands to her mouth.

"But I have good news. Maddie is closed up and her new heart is beating. We'll have to wait and see if the transplant takes. She's on the best drugs money can buy." He gestured to Alan. "I think she will be fine."

Bonnie nearly swooned with happiness. "Thank you, Doctor."

"After what we've all been through, if it's possible, I'm as pleased as you are. It's been difficult watching Maddie fail over the past few months. These are the times that it's a blessing to be a doctor. We see enough despair. But we are not out of the woods yet. God willing, the transplant will take. Please say a prayer for the lass."

Alan stepped across the room and grasped Brian Finlay's hand in his. No words were spoken. Alan slowly nodded his head, his eyes welling up with tears. He released the doctor's hands and hugged Bonnie deeply. John and Mary looked on, visibly relieved.

CHAPTER FORTY-SIX

"SECURITY IS TO YOUR LEFT, the first hallway, Mr. Cohen."

Benny nodded, taking the boarding passes, slipping his false passport into his pocket. As he neared the entrance to TSA security, he paused. By dinnertime tomorrow, he would be in Cape Town, a connecting flight in Miami the only wrinkle. Why did he pause? He certainly didn't feel any loyalty or compassion for the American doctor. He knew better than to get emotionally attached to a situation. He'd made the correct decision to abandon the California operation. He would be sitting in a prison cell within weeks if he stayed. But… he didn't think that Dom Tavano would succeed in getting to Brice without his aid. That's it, but did he really care? He must if he contemplated doing what he pondered. The bastard Brice didn't think twice about dealing Benny to the Feds.

Benny took one step towards the TSA lineup…then stopped. He believed in fate. There was a reason he hesitated getting on the plane. "Dammit." He said to himself softly. "Get on the plane, Benny." However, the devil on his right shoulder carried more sway over him than the angel on the left at this moment. "Two days, that's it." He would invest two days in Tavano. He would make sure that Brice suffered for his betrayal, both physically and monetarily. He went back to rearrange his flight. The change fee, he hoped, would be well worth it.

CHAPTER FORTY-SEVEN

DOM WOKE UP just before the alarm went off. He possessed an uncanny ability to wake himself up when it was needed. He put on his shoes, placed $100 on top of the bed covers and slipped out onto the balcony, overlooking the parking lot a story below. He didn't want to risk leaving the motel by the front door. He could see paying the cash to the woman and then walking into a police ambush. He would have been suspicious of his own story. Dom hoped the lure of the money would be strong enough for the woman to set reason aside.

Climbing over the railing, Dom eased himself over the edge and then hung down by his arms. It was a five or six foot drop from that point to the concrete, which proved to be no difficulty. He poked his head around the building, to have a look out front. As he did, he saw two police cruisers pull into the front of the entrance. *You little bitch.* For a second, he contemplated going back for the hundred bucks, but thought better of it.

He didn't stop until he put several blocks between him and the motel. He did a Google search on his phone, looking for a local taxi company. Within five minutes, Dom sat in the back of another cab with the hopeful driver waiting for an answer.

"San Bernardino," he responded. The driver looked pleased, it would be a good fare.

Dom figured he needed to be away from the heart of the city. He'd been to San Bernardino a few years ago. Conveniently it was where his ex wife, Gina, and his two children lived. He didn't know how far the search for him had spread, and he hesitated bringing Gina into the puzzle. Still, he needed some help.

The sun rose as the car passed into the San Bernardino Valley, its starkness a sharp contrast to the busy city streets of Los Angeles. The naked mountains and hills loomed in the distance while the San Diego River ran beside the left of the highway. As the miles ticked away, he thought about Chantal and felt a pang of guilt…No, it wasn't guilt. He felt extreme loss. Her death, along with Carlos and Pedro, would leave deep scars. He had to admit he felt love for the woman. Love could be such a nebulous word. Their relationship went past attraction and sex. He'd enjoyed her company, seeing her in the morning when he woke up. Perhaps it was love, but it didn't matter now. It only made the pangs of grief all the more difficult the more he thought about her. He sighed deeply. At that moment, Dom felt destined to lead a lonely life in the end, that is, if he didn't find himself dead in the present.

He pulled out his personal phone, and looked up his son Richie's cell. He asked the cabbie to pull over at a pay phone and wait. He dialed his son's number with nervous trepidation. They hadn't spoken in nearly a year. He'd probably still been asleep.

"Yello! who's this?"

"Richie, it's your dad…Dom."

"Whaaaat? Why you calling me now?" Dom could hear the resentment through the sleepiness in his son's voice.

"I need your help and I don't have a lot of time."

"Typical. Where were you when we needed you, are you for real?"

The comment stung. "Hey, I didn't choose to have you move all the way across the country. Your mother did that, she decided to leave."

"Hang on…It's dad."

Dom could tell Ritchie was probably speaking with his mother. "No, he's calling me…" There were some sounds of shuffling, then a new voice came on the phone.

"Dominic?" Gina's voice.

"Hi Gina, yes its Dom…Look, I'm in a really tight spot and I need your help."

"What kind of a tight spot, you need money? Doesn't the army pay you enough, and what the hell kind of trouble can a teaching doctor get into? It's early, Dom."

"I'm in San Bernardino, I'll explain when I meet you."

"Meet me? You're here?"

"Christ Gina, I'll take an hour of your time. Where can we meet? I can't go to your house."

"Dom Tavano, what the hell's going on?"

"Look! I said I'd explain. I'm starving. I'll buy breakfast."

"Okay, there's a little place at 9th and Waterman."

"Fifteen minutes," he said, as he hung up and started looking the place up on his cell.

CHAPTER FORTY-EIGHT

CHRIS BACHMAN STARED at the road ahead as he drove. He cursed himself for not handling the situation personally, but the events transpired far too quickly to have been there. He found it hard to fathom how things become unglued in such a short period of time. Tavano and the Canadian Captain should have been detained and quietly dispatched. But now the doctor was loose and Tavano undoubtedly knew the truth by now. If he didn't, he soon would. He needed to get to him before the rogue doctor disclosed what he knew. Then the difficult part, he would have to cover everything up. The longer Tavano remained on the loose, the bigger the mess would be. He sighed. He would be the one that would have to do it. He didn't have any choice. His superiors would not take the fall or the blame, which would be placed squarely on his shoulders. He screwed the silencer onto his handgun as he drove, placing it on the passenger's seat.

He'd done a good job at hiding the payment trail from Sun Medical, but he knew that if the whole operation somehow leaked, the

FBI possessed the resources to easily unravel the scheme. He walked on very thin ice.

Christine Prendergast, from the Department of State, had been careful. All communication with her had been verbal. It would be his word against hers. There were no records as to how she'd been remunerated. The same with General Williams.

For the time being, an all-points bulletin on Tavano and Turcotte was the best he could do. Tavano proved to be very elusive. He'd evaded them again at the Anderson Institute. To make things worse, a donor heart had been delivered, believed to be that of Camille Suarez. The Mexicans were mad as hatters. The large bounty on Tavano's head by Pacifico put the Mexicans between Intelligence and their quarry.

Tavano would need help. Bachman's research team worked on any possible contingencies. They'd come up with a gold nugget. His ex and kids lived in San Bernardino. Bachman would pay them a visit.

CHAPTER FORTY-NINE

DOM WASN'T SURPRISED to see Richie and Molly accompanying Gina, as she walked into the Mexican-esque family-style restaurant. He stood up to greet them with a pang of guilt welling in his throat. He hadn't seen his kids in over two years. He could see varying levels of distain written on their faces, Molly was the only one to smile briefly. He embraced her first, then shook Richie's hand, as he didn't appear forthcoming with a hug. He finally looked Gina in the eyes.

"Dom, you look like hell! What's going on?"

He didn't want to raise any attention and ushered them to sit down in the booth where he'd been waiting. Finally they were seated and the waitress left after pouring coffee.

Dom started. "I can't tell a lot of the details as I suppose they're still classified…and I don't want to involve you or alarm you."

Gina put her hand down on the table, rattling the cutlery. "You've just surprised the hell out of me and the kids, dragging us to breakfast when they should be in bloody school. Out with it. You're worrying me."

Gina hadn't changed. She possessed the innate ability to start a fight out of the simplest of conversations. The brief exchange reminding him of why they were no longer together. "I've been on a United Nations sanctioned mission. I've been living undercover in Mexico for the past half year…" He then went on to tell a shortened version of what happened, leaving out names and most of the gory details.

When he finished, the three stared at him with stunned expressions on their faces, showing trepidation and varying degrees of fear.

Richie put his hand on top of Dom's. "Geez Dad! What the fuck?"

Gina shot a stern look at him. "Are we in any danger?"

"The fact that I am in LA and being hunted would bring you into this. Yes, I know, it's messed up and I'm sorry. I have one chance though, which might possibly help us all. I need to find someone within the military who I can trust. Joanna De Rosnay, the researcher from the UN, I think can be trusted, but I need more." The light went on and Dom blurted out by accident. "JOHN BURROWS!"

Gina turned towards him, her eyes widening. "I know that name. The two of you didn't get along, right?"

"Yep, he wanted me court marshaled, but for all the right reasons. He is the only committee member who didn't want me involved in this mission. I've thought about General Williams, but now that it's happened, I can see the reasons why he could be part of the betrayal. Generals think that way…I'm expendable in his eyes."

Gina fidgeted. "Okay Dominic, you have my temporary empathy. How can I help?"

"I need a cell phone. I'll give you the cash."

Gina nodded. "We can go to the mall just down the street and buy a pay as you play."

Dom smiled at her. "We need to make a copy of what's on this memory stick." He pulled it out of his pocket. "Then, I need you to send the files to Burrows. I'll text you the email address when I get it."

Molly spoke, "I can do that!"

"No honey, your last name's Tavano." He turned to Gina. "Can you send it from work?"

"Don't worry, I'll find a way to do it anonymously."

Dom sighed and looked at all of them. "I know I've been a shitty dad. I'll make a pact with you." He looked at both Richie and Molly. "If I get myself out of this, we'll spend serious time together."

Both looked at Dom skeptically, they'd heard that song before.

Dom sighed again. "No…really, we will. I promise!"

Gina pursed her lips. "Don't make promises you can't keep. It's all fine and dandy while you're here, out of the blue and needing our help."

He nodded. "I get it, but it's what I want…more than anything now that I've seen you. I've missed a lot, and I don't intend to miss any more. You kids are looking so grown up."

Gina squirmed, ready to get up from the table. "Let's get you those items, Dominic. It sounds as if you are a dangerous person to be around at the moment."

"Yes. You're right. It might be a good if the three of you even left town for a few days. If I get out of this, I most likely will be put in a witness protection plan. So…if you don't hear from me for a while, it's for your own good."

Gina shook her head. "The kids are in school, exams are coming up."

"Look, the people who are looking for me won't give a shit, do you follow?" He peeled a few thousand dollars off the wad in his pocket and handed them to Gina.

She nodded, finally seeing the truth in his words.

***

Gina drove Dom to the Mall she'd mentioned and purchased a cheap phone, putting the plan in her name. Dom made a copy of the files off his memory stick at an Apple Store. He gave the second stick to Gina. "Like I said, I'll text you the address where you can send this. Now, I have to get out of here."

"Where will you go?"

"I'm going to call DeRosnay. Hopefully, she'll meet me soon. Then I don't know."

"You look terrible. When's the last time you slept?" Her eyes wandered over his gaunt face drawn at the corners.

"I caught a few hours last night. I can't use my credit card to rent a room. They'll track me within hours."

"Here, take mine. Get yourself something to wear. You look like an old guy in kids clothes, where did you get them?" Her face bloomed into a wide smile for the first time.

"Benny Leahner. I have money. I'll take the card though, I can leave you another thousand to cover any charges; you can cancel the card in a few days."

She accepted the additional cash. "Let me drive you somewhere."

"You sure?"

"I called in sick, and like you say, the kids should stay low. I'll call the school to talk to the principal once we've dropped you somewhere."

"I won't let you down, and I appreciate all of this."

"Payment is you giving these kids some attention."

Both Richie and Molly rolled their eyes.

Dom smiled at all three. "Deal. Let me call Joanna."

***

DeRosnay sounded hesitant when she first answered Dom's call. "You've opened one hell of a shit storm, Doctor. I don't usually answer calls from pay phones, but I suspected it was you."

"I don't want to burn my new cell phone. This can of worms cracked open decades ago, I've just stirred it up."

"Major, they've threatened me. I don't take being threatened lightly by the State Department and the Military. Bachman called me in immediately when I mentioned you'd made contact. I'm to be at the Pentagon later today for an emergency briefing. I'm not a source of credibility anymore, the way I read things. From what you're telling me, you were never intended to succeed. It was intended that I would report to the UN that the U.S. government was doing its part. However, the act of infiltrating the Mexican Cartels was just too dangerous. Your head, the proof is in the pudding."

"You got it. It's a damned mess, though I have to say, I'm glad my head is still attached."

"U.S. officials at all levels are no different than those in the poorer countries where the extractions are being made. Same as in those countries, it starts at the bottom and works its way to the top. Doctors, nurses, morgue officials, customs, law enforcement and in this case, the U.S. Military and State Department. The wheels get greased under the false assertion that an unspoken good is occurring. People's lives are being saved by turning the other cheek. Public officials and hospital boards look good."

"Dr. DeRosnay, believe me, I get it."

She paused. "I don't want to go down as a martyr. If you can somehow find a way to see your way through this…I will be there for you in your corner. You can count on it. Until then, I'm going to have to state that I told you to turn yourself in, nothing more. Frankly, I think this is too big for one man to take on. If you don't end up buried deeply in prison, the Mexicans will get you. Word has it that Hernando Suarez has a hefty bounty on your head."

Dom sighed. "I heard. And, I accept your position, Joanna. I signed on in the beginning because I wanted my medical license back. I'll admit it…selfishly. Now that I've seen what's been happening up close and personal, I have to take a stab at this. Really, I have no choice."

"You have a good point there. You know I've read your dossier."

"Of course."

"Are you doing this because you want to be the hero? You've been accused of grandstanding in the past."

Dom felt his pulse quicken. "Admittedly, I would have said yes in my younger days. It isn't the case now. I seek justice for the poor bastards being swindled for their body parts and those being outright murdered to save the life of another. Once this is finished, I'll seek anonymity…perhaps out of necessity. Puffy altruistic words I know, but I mean them."

"Good luck, Doctor." She hung up.

***

Gina rented a room for him at the Embassy Suites in North Anaheim. He leaned into the driver's side window and put a hand on her arm as she prepared to drive away. "Thank you."

She slowly shook her head as the beginning of a tear welled up in the corner of her eyes. "You wear your feelings on your shirt sleeve, Dom. If I couldn't see that you were telling me the truth, I wouldn't have helped you. It's ironic, I knew you were playing around behind my back six years ago. You can't hide your guilt. The same trait that let me see the truth about you back then…allows me to see the truth now."

He nodded, not wanting to bring up the point she'd been screwing his best friend, prior to him messing around. "You are a good person, Gina. We're just way too different."

She cut him off. "That's okay, we need people to wage wars. I get it. I didn't want a husband that wasn't going to be there every day. I shut off, we both found something else. We don't need to rehash it. Go fight your battle, Dominic Tavano."

She laid her head on his arm briefly before driving away. Staring at the back of her car as it disappeared in the distance, he'd never felt so alone.

CHAPTER FIFTY

RICHARD BRICE PICKED UP THE PHONE and heard, "Dr. Brice, Benny Leahner's on the line." Brice could feel the hair stand up on his arms and scalp. *Christ.*

"Okay, put him through." He let the line ring four times before picking up. "Mr. Leahner?"

"Dr. Brice. No need for the formalities, Richard. I will make this short. I want ten million dollars, and I will disappear, along with your problems."

Brice felt his blood pressure go through the roof. "What makes you think you have that kind of leverage, Benny?"

"I would think you might know me better than that by now. I am not a man who likes to waste his time, as I know you feel the same. You will be exposed by a high-ranking military officer. This person, I think you might know by now, possesses a memory stick with my banking information for the past few years as it pertains to Sun Medical. In addition, I have left paper trails, documenting our many transactions."

"And if I pay you?"

"If I stop the access to my accounts, they cannot build a case; I retain this failsafe, which is important, because I know you will ask: What will stop me from doing this again? I am not a greedy man, Dr. Brice, I only want my due, and you have burned me for at least ten mil in real estate alone. At my age, I don't feel I have it in me to set up another network. I plan to disappear after you pay me. If you don't, let me further my threat. My world is very finite, Richard. I know many of the other agents who operate in the various profitable venues. I will warn them. I will monitor their transactions, exposing them if they decide to do business with Sun Medical. You know I have the capability to do so with my banking connections."

"You have to offer me a guarantee. This is a damned one-sided negotiation."

Benny laughed. "Don't be coy, doctor. You've heard about Doctor Dominic Tavano; don't tell me you haven't. As I already mentioned, he's been given information that will incriminate you. He's back in the States. Once I have received notice of payment to my Swiss account, as a bonus, I'll offer to kill him for you. I'll do it myself, no blood on your hands. If you don't pay, I'll let him loose with the information. I might just gain some satisfaction in seeing you go to prison, not ten mil worth, but close."

"You fucking bastard, Jew!"

"I'll take that as a compliment, Doctor. We must take account of our advantages. I give you two days to make payment. My Jewish bankers will notify me promptly of your payment. Moreover, if it gives you any comfort, I have a tag on Tavano, I know where he is."

CHAPTER FIFTY-ONE

DOM PUT HIS HEAD DOWN on the pillow and couldn't remember falling asleep. His dreams were riddled with the sound of metal wheels running over train tracks- ka klank, ka klank; Chantal falling, the dream kept repeating itself. Then he found himself driving, but he couldn't get to where he was going. No matter how hard he tried. He sprung awake, one of his numerous cell phones ringing. It took him a few moments to register which one it was…Leahner's. "Yes."

"Doctor, It's Benny Leahner."

Dom fought the urge to respond with sarcasm. "Yes, Mr. Leahner… It's damn early to be calling."

"No rest for the wicked. You're obviously not detained if this call is getting through to you."

"Perceptive of you."

"Now, now Doctor. Have you made contact with anyone that is unsympathetic to Sun Med?"

"My U.N. contact, but I think they are putting pressure on her."

"Do you still have the information I gave you?"

"Let me check my pants. SHIT! I lost the memory stick in the chase yesterday, I must have left it by accident on the dash of the minivan where you put it," he lied.

"This is most unfortunate, surely you jest. Is there anywhere else you could have put it?"

"I'm not trying to be funny. I swear, I don't have it. I'll need another stick, it'll have to be a hard copy. They'll have access to my email account."

Silence. "If you're lying to me, doctor, I'll have you eradicated from the planet!"

"Believe it, this puts me in a real bad spot. That intel is my get-out-of-jail-free card."

"I suppose it is. I'll text you in an hour or so to tell you where you can pick up another stick. But, I need you to get this to the right sources. Intelligence will be all over you and I wouldn't put it past them shooting and asking questions afterwards."

***

Dom rolled out of bed and made himself a coffee. He would have to wait half an hour before the office opened in Bethesda Uniformed Services Teaching Hospital opened. He needed to speak to his secretary, Robyn.

***

"Doctor Tavano! Where the heck did they send you? There were no goodbyes, we all miss you here."

"Believe me, I miss you too."

"Listen, I'll call you back soon to tell you about my new posting. For now, I need you to look up Colonel John Burrow's number with the Surgeon General's office."

"Sure thing, Major."

***

Dom bounced around several times before he connected with Burrows…precious time passing.

"Major Tavano?"

"Colonel Borrows." It still irked Dom having to talk up to the man, but he needed him.

"I can only imagine why in hell you are calling me. I will tell you though, Tavano, I feel privileged. It seems like half of Washington would like to talk to you right now."

"That bad?"

"Don't let it go to your head, I might be over embellishing."

"Colonel, if I may."

"You have my ear."

"Look, I know that there's no love lost between us, but in a roundabout way, that's why I'm calling you. I've been burned, my mission has been burned."

"Okay?"

"Colonel, all I've done is fulfill my mission guidelines. I believe it was never supposed to be completed." Dom quickly revealed the circumstances of the past few days.

"Jesus, Joseph and Mary."

"I feel the same way, and I think my life is in serious peril…They are going to kill me. Let me give you my reason behind calling. I feel if you were part of this, you would have been the first one shipping me off to Mexico."

"Good point. But seriously, if what you say is true, this is one hell of a conspiracy."

"Yes. Some high-level wheels were getting greased. Colonel, I've got no one else to go to but you. You are the only one besides Joanna DeRosnay with any in-depth knowledge of the mission. She doesn't have any authority."

"What about Williams?"

Dom thought for a moment. "My gut tells me he's right in there."

"What are you suggesting? The ramifications of this are mind boggling."

"Agreed. I lied and told Benny Leahner I'd lost some information he'd given to me. I'm going to be receiving a text soon from him, telling me where we're supposed to meet. He will be delivering another USB memory stick with the banking info needed to nail Sun Medical."

"Where are you, Major?"

"San Bernardino. I forgot to tell you, I still have the banking information and can have it sent to you if you can give me an email address where I can safely send it."

"Can I be honest with you?"

"Why not at this point."

"I figured you to be a total fuck up. I never questioned your ability as a doctor, but I did question your integrity as an officer. We hand out rank in the medical corps more because of the pay scale than the authority we intend to give to our medical practitioners. Frankly, I thought you overstepped your boundaries in the Middle East. I didn't want you out there with the authority that you'd previously been given. I didn't want you court-martialed…I wanted you pulled back, out of a position of authority. I'll tell you, I understand why you did what you did with Fields, but we couldn't condone it. If we'd let you off any lighter, it might have led to an international crisis. CNN would crucify the military over it. We hush-hushed everything; it happens. Believe me, Tavano, it could have been a lot worse."

Dom sighed. "I can see it now, and I did think about it during all of those years I plodded away in Bethesda, but I always thought you were the bad guy, the one who'd stripped my license. I thought General Williams the good guy, but he would continually step back when I questioned him about my license."

"Williams is an ass. Let me rephrase…a gutless ass. He's more concerned with his pension than doing what is correct. Dominic, I'm going to be blunt, I'm sorry for what you have been asked to do in the name of the U.S. Government. Now that I see the thing for what it is, it stinks. Let me tell you, I believe what you're telling me, I can hear it in your voice, and I did have my misgivings from the beginning. I flat out didn't want you out there with any more authority. Okay, I've been proven wrong. Now Major, I will check out the intel you've given me." Burrows gave Dom an encrypted back-channel address.

"Someone will send the information to you very soon, Colonel."

Burrows went silent. "I'm going to call my friend Alex Summers, he's at FBI headquarters. I'll let him know about Bachman and we'll get as many men out there as we can muster. I don't think we want to talk to military intel at this point. If what you say is true, we don't know who else might be involved. I'll contact you on this line Major to let you know what's going on. Try to stall Leahner if you can. It would be nice to nail him. Tavano…as much as it pains me to say it, good work!"

"My thoughts exactly, Colonel, and thank you, sir."

***

Dom took a moment to text Burrows' e-mail to Gina. He hoped that he wasn't bringing her in too deep. He took a deep breath. At this point, all he could do was wait.

CHAPTER FIFTY-TWO

"BACHMAN…."

"Sir, we just traced a call to the Pentagon from San Bernardino. The phone is unlisted and the recipient, Colonel John Burrows."

"Do you have a feed on the location of the cell?"

"Affirmative."

"We'll sync it to your onboard computer."

CHAPTER-FIFTY THREE

THE TEXT CAME five minutes later. Dom would meet Leahner in a shopping center off the San Bernardino Parkway, in front of a jewelry store near the main mall entrance. Dom immediately relayed the information to Burrows by email.

Dom called a cab. His heart raced as the taxi merged onto the parkway. The past two days seemed like a bad dream, a whirlwind. His nerves were frayed and he knew one way or another the next hour would either vindicate him, or seal his fate. He considered himself an amateur at this clandestine stuff, and felt way in over his head. The only thing that gave him any comfort, the hard lump of the snub-nosed 45 pressing against the car seat and his lumbar.

As the cab pulled into the mall parking lot, the phone rang. "Yes?"

"It's Burrows. We can get some men there soon. If you can somehow hang onto Leahner for five, maybe ten minutes."

Dom took in a deep breath. "10-4 Colonel. But I have the feeling that might be a tall order. The man is elusive."

"Do your best, Major."

***

Dom could feel his heart thumping in his chest as he entered the mall entrance. He bent over for a moment to catch his breath and ease the dizziness that threatened to overcome him. Being this early in the day, there were only a few shoppers milling about. He spotted the jewelry store fifty yards ahead to his right. Part of his nervousness lay in the fact that he didn't want Leahner to slip through his hands. The organ agent was no better than the Cartel bosses or the big business medical conglomerates.

Dom nearly jumped out of his skin when his cell rang. He picked up, hearing the now familiar voice on the other end of the line.

"Doctor."

"Yes?"

"You will find the stick in locker 88 down the corridor to your left. Try not to lose this one. This is the last time I'll do it. Any luck finding a contact?"

"As a matter of fact, yes. I've been in touch with Colonel John Burrows from the Surgeon General's office, he's the only one who didn't back me for the mission."

"Good, the key for the locker is on the seat of the table right in front of you."

Dom eyed the mall, looking for Leahner.

"You didn't think that I would be so stupid as to reveal myself, and did you really lose the original? You're an amateur in this game Domin–"

The bullet made a loud thwack as it hit the pillar behind him. Dom reflexively turned to look behind him, Bachman ran towards him with a silenced handgun pointed at him. He fired again, narrowly missing. He didn't look in the mood to talk. Dom jumped behind a kiosk, reaching behind for the snub nosed handgun in his belt. Across the hall he spied a Target store. *How appropriate.* He ran through the entrance, a bullet hitting the folding glass door as he pushed to the side of the doorway.

***

Leahner watched the gunman as he closed in on Dom. He cursed under his breath. Tavano being a military doctor, not a combat specialist, wouldn't win this battle. He liked the doctor, but he just might have to die. He knew too much and Leahner felt absolutely sure the doctor lied to him about the memory stick. Moreover, he didn't doubt the cavalry would be arriving at any moment…Benny the quarry. He took the silencer out of one pocket and quickly screwed it onto the end of his Beretta, then followed the gunman and Tavano into the department store. It was time to leave California and call it a day, but he needed to tie up a couple of loose ends.

***

There were screams coming the entrance where the first shots were fired. Dom ignored them and ran deeper into the massive store. He dove into the kitchen aisle, which gave him some protection. He stopped, hoping to catch sight of Bachman, backing into the pots and pans section, watching the end of the isle. It didn't take long for Bachman to appear, the silenced pistol held out in front of him in both hands. One of Dom's phones rang. *Dammit.* Bachman heard the noise and turned down the aisle.

Dom ran around the end of the row and headed into the grocery section at a full sprint. One of the stock boys looked up in shock as he ran by him, gun in hand. Bachman turned the corner behind him and fired. The stock boy hit the ground covering his head. The phone continued to ring, he rounded a corner putting his phone to his ear. "Yes!"

"This is Agent Briggs, FBI. What's your location?"

"Target." Dom stuffed the phone back into his pants. The FBI operatives would be here at any minute. He needed to keep evading his attacker, possibly returning to the front of the store, where he imagined the FBI would enter. He swung around back to the right. The phone call had thrown him off and he'd lost track of Bachman, which proved to be a big mistake. He appeared in front of him, a sneer on his face.

"I've had about enough of you Tavano." He pulled the trigger. There was an audible click as the firing pin slammed into an empty chamber. Bachman quickly reached into his jacket for another cartridge of bullets.

Dom pointed the snub nose 45 at him as he walked slowly in his direction. "Put it down Bachman."

He didn't listen and rammed home a full magazine.

Thwack, the bullet hit Bachman square in the forehead, a red dot of blood forming into a trickle of blood that quickly ran down over the man's nose. A look of shock came over his face as he collapsed to the floor.

Dom spun around to see Leahner standing ten feet behind him, his gun pointing at his forehead. Dom started to raise his gun hand, but Leahner with his free hand, waived his forefinger at him.

"Not advisable, Doctor. If I've read you correctly, you are a man of principle. No doubt you've alerted the powers that be, and I'm sure they'll be here in no time. I would advise you to put your gun on the ground and sit down with your hands on your head, facing away from me."

Dom remained standing, too stunned to respond. Would this be how it ended after all that he'd been through?

"Do it!"

Dom dropped the gun and slowly lowered himself to his knees.

"Now, that's a good Doctor. Did you deliver the information?"

"If not, it will be soon."

"You have fifteen seconds to say a prayer. Do you have a God, Dr. Tavano?"

Dom could find no words. His throat dry, he closed his eyes, waiting for the bullet. The silence seemed deafening, blood pounding through his chest.

It was suddenly quiet and Leahner chuckled as they heard the sound of approaching hard-heeled shoes clicking on the hard floor. Looking down at Dom now shaking his head, Leahner disappeared around the corner. *Lucky man.*

Dom heard the approaching men as well. Opening his eyes, there were four approaching from the opposite side of the aisle, guns in hand. "Don't move!" Within moments his hands were zip tied behind his back. The operatives quickly escorted him out of the mall as he tried to spot Leahner to no avail…the man truly was a ghost.

***

Leahner placed the gun into a wastebasket on the outside sidewalk after he stepped out of the fire exit. He didn't worry about the alarm that went off instantly. He stripped off the latex gloves he wore and shoved them into his pocket. He walked calmly to his rental car and slipped into the driver's seat. Maybe it was justice that saved Tavano's life. Fate dictated that the man should live. It would have been tidier to have removed Tavano. All that he could do now would be to wait and see how things turned out. He couldn't do anymore here.

If the traffic wasn't too bad he would easily make a 2 pm flight to Miami. The Ghost disappeared…as he always did.

CHAPTER FIFTY-FOUR

CARMEN SUAREZ SAT at the head of the dining room table. It was covered with an assortment of food and drink. At the table were those that she trusted most. There were not many. The stress of Camille's death caused her father Hernando to suffer a serious stroke. Carmen didn't think that he would come out of the episode alive.

While Hernando held power, Carmen and her sister learned to acquiesce and follow the man's dictate. She hadn't always agreed with his strong-fisted attitude. He could be brash and vindictive. Carmen asked herself, did she want this? Could she run Pacifico? Something awakened in her over the past days and weeks. Perhaps inherited from her father…A deep anger simmered at a low boil under her calm demeanor. Under control, anger could be a strong motivator.

She looked around the table. She'd worried that the men would have left. It was not safe to remain in a Cartel with no backbone. She could tell by the looks on their faces that she retained their respect. She'd been told that she possessed Hernando's eyes, never happy with the comparison. But on this day, for the first time, she found herself thankful.

She spoke calmly, as Hernando used to do, the calm before the storm. "By your presence here, you give me your loyalty and I thank you. Pacifico must become respected and powerful again. We must strive to control the South Coast, its towns and cities. We have suffered grievous losses." She bowed her head towards the table, slowly letting her eyes rise. "I know that you looked up to Hernando, but his time is past. Pacifico must now rely upon knowledge and clear thinking, as well as the muscle that we are known for. We will bide our time, but when the opportunity presents itself, we will eradicate the Gulf Cartel. We will eradicate our enemies, and that includes the rogue doctor. I am doubling the bounty on the man. As my father said, I want his head in a bag. There is nowhere safe on this planet."

She could see the vengeful looks on the men's faces. A smile slowly formed on her lips for the first time since her sister's death.

In unison, the men who sat around the table rose, clapping their hands together.

Carmen nodded her appreciation for the tribute. "Pacifico will rise from the ashes. We will prevail. We will be great again."

CHAPTER FIFTY-FOUR

HEARING

BEFORE THE

SELECT COMMITTEE ON

THE EVENTS SURROUNDING

THE JOINT U.S. STATE DEPARTMENT, UNITED NATIONS, FBI TASK FORCE

ON CROSSBORDER ORGANIZED TRAFFICKING

ONE HUNDRED AND FIFTEENTH CONGRESS – FIRST SESSION

HELD IN WASHINGTON, DC, OCTOBER 1ST, 2017

DOM SAT IN FULL DRESS UNIFORM. The conference room in the Longworth House office building would normally have been packed, but because the Congressional hearing would most likely lead to criminal charges, as is protocol, the hearing would be closed to the public. He breathed a deep sigh of relief as the call to order was taken. Several months passed since the showdown with Agent Bachman. Dom had been placed in a witness protection program. He would be glad to see the light at the end of the tunnel. He looked around the room and identified several familiar faces. General Williams, Christine Pendergast, and a man he assumed to be Richard Brice sat at the defendants table, their gathering of lawyers nervously sifting through stacks of papers. Colonel John Borrows and Joanna DeRosnay sat on either side of him. He listened intently as Congressman Dale Harvey of Idaho, chairman of the committee, made his address.

Harvey, an older man, probably in his mid-seventies, immaculately dressed, was well respected for his ability quickly to cut to the truth. He put his glasses on his nose and looked down at his notes. "Good morning. The committee will come to order, and the chair notes the presence of a quorum. Welcome Mr. Secretary."

The Secretary of State, Bud Simmonds nodded his acknowledgement, a stern, and very serious look on his face. "Mr. Chairman." The accusations against his Under Secretary, Christine Pendergast were serious and he felt it a reflection on his own reputation. He'd been lied to and intended to have the truth come to light.

"Welcome to each of you," he addressed the committee members.

"This is a closed meeting of the Select Committee on the events surrounding the Joint U.S. State Department, United Nations, U.S. Army task force, on cross border organ trafficking." He took his glasses off his nose. "Just a couple of quick administrative matters before we start. There are predetermined breaks, but I want to make it clear that if anyone feels that they need a break, then we will take one. I will also remind you that proper decorum will be observed at all times."

"As the ranking member, I will give my opening statement. After that, the members will alternate from side to side. Everyone in this room has been sworn in, so we will begin.

"Accusations have been made and charges laid with regards to what we shall call: The Mexico Task Force. By mandate, from the President of the United States and the State Department. Mr. Secretary, in conjunction with the United Nations and U.S. Military Intelligence, Major Dominic Tavano was given directive to attempt to discern the link between a Mexican Drug Cartel known as the Pacifico Cartel and various United States medical Institutions."

"Major Tavano," he nodded to Dom, "who is a U.S. Military physician, went undercover and true to his mandate, accomplished what was asked of him. It is my understanding that Major Tavano's findings have uncovered what equates to a massive ring of corruption which includes: The State Department, and the U.S. Army. If such allegations are proven correct, it is the committee's belief the corruption will have filtered down through the system involving more than just the administrative heads."

"Such corruption permeates the organ trade on a worldwide scale. The fact that the corruption could be so deeply seated in our great nation where we would like to think that corruption, though it will always be present, would be at a minimum, especially compared to less democratic states throughout the world. Hopefully, Major Tavano's bravery will bring to light the breakdown in the system which allows human organs, which are taken from less privileged human beings, through coercion and physical force, to be sold to more privileged U.S. citizens. I believe this to a clear and present evil within our society and societies around the world. It is this committee's mandate to clean up our own house and to make sure that The United States of America can be seen as taking a lead to end this horrific problem. Clearing up our problem will help other nations see what needs to be done. Halting the flow of U.S. dollars to countries like Mexico, Bangladesh and other nations where significant poverty exists will be doing our part in this global crisis."

"The Committee hopes to call to the stand today for precursory questioning, Under Secretary Christine Pendergast, followed by a break. If we have time, I would like to call Dr. Richard Brice of Sun Medical.

"Ms. Pendergast, I call you to the stand."

CHAPTER FIFTY-FIVE

MADDIE CHAMBERS DIARY

I'm alive…wow! I feel like I've been given a second chance to be my best and to show more appreciation towards Mom and Dad. I have someone else's heart inside me - wow. I feel like I am sharing my body with that person. I will never get used to that. I received a post card from a doctor named Dom Tavano. He's the man who brought me my heart, and appears to be a man of few words, but those few words have given me comfort. I received this letter from him yesterday.

Hello brave Maddie. I hear that you have been doing well. The heart that now beats within you comes from a strong bloodline. The donor died during an operation, which I performed.

I will say that I'm not unhappy to see her pass. I will tell you about her if I ever get the chance. Her gift in death has given you the door to life.
Keep well, Doc Dom

I have chosen to believe the doctor, but I still think it's a little sketchy. But hey - I am alive and healthy, with a beating heart. I wouldn't blame my parents for doing everything they could, because I would do the same for them. I wish things could have happened in a normal way, but then again, what's normal these days? I'm not naïve and there is still the smell of a lie in the air that nips at me from time to time. I try to ignore the feeling as best I can.

~ Maddie Chambers

CHAPTER FIFTY-SIX

DOM BORROWED A TRAY from the Tikki Bar to carry three Piña Coladas to the beach. The surf rolled in gently, accompanied by a warm breeze. As he walked, he pondered the events of the past eight months, the things that happened to Chantal, Pedro, and Carlos, and to all the poor Mexicans he'd operated on. Though he didn't like what happened, he knew they received the best medical care possible under the circumstances. Those who were involved in the corruption: Brice, General Williams and Pendergast would spend a long time behind bars. It would take time to ferret out those who were involved at the lower levels. Dale Harvey, Chairman of the Congressional inquest swore he would incarcerate "any and all" that were involved, which meant investigating the military, doctors, immigration, city morgues; the list was long.

Benny Leahner remained an enigma. He existed on the edges, always wary. It would take more than a sting operation to capture him. Dom shook his head. The man could have killed him in the end, but walked away. Perhaps he felt he owed the man, but his involvement in the process could not be tolerated. If he ever got the chance, Dom would turn him in, but the chances of Leahner emerging again were zero, at least Dom hoped so.

He worried about Gina and the kids. Through the FBI, he'd been able to let them know he was okay. For the time being, they were under surveillance, which gave him some comfort. He would make amends with them, but a lot of dust needed to settle.

The sand burned his feet and he had to half dance-walk to reach his destination. He surprised the two figures sitting with their backs to him. He'd been happy to catch an earlier connecting flight out of Hawaii; he wasn't expected until later in the night.

"Mrs. Chavez, Carlos."

Both happily accepted the cocktails, surprised by his appearance behind them. "Dominic!" Chantal said, looking back over her shoulder. She'd healed nicely since the fall from the train. Her upper leg and shoulder had required extensive surgery to repair the gunshot wounds. "Took you long enough." She wore a wide smile despite her best efforts to conceal it.

"The Congressional hearing nearly did me in…painful. But I tell you, the two of you look good…a sight for sore eyes." He leaned down and kissed her deeply. "So, this is Bali."

Carlos took a long sip from his drink. "The clinic is looking good, Doctor Dom. It's good that you are here."

"No rest for the wicked. Will the two of you not grant me at least a week to settle in?"

Chantal laughed, reaching over to give him another kiss. "I have plans for you for at least a week…which don't include…work," she blushed.

Dom couldn't contain his grin.

***

Chantal, Carlos and Dom sat enjoying the evening sunset, while another set of eyes on the beach seemed less interested in the scenery. The black-haired man tapped away on his cell phone, intent on delivering the important text message.

THE END

ACKNOWLEDGEMENTS

Gavin Literary Agency, LLP

Editing—Mary Ellen Gavin

Publicist—Shari Stauch

Assistance with medical procedures—Dr. Karen Berti

Special thanks to Perry Johnson and his twisted mind

Readers—Carmen Bowron, Bonnie Grimm, Philip Bowron, Susan Phend, Sarah Gleddie, Graham Heyes, Audrey Wright,

Jennifer Caughill, Phil Torrell, Bev Matychuk, Tamara Schaaf, Bryan Funk, Jewell Betts

BIOGRAPHY

Christopher's roots are in Canada, and his two children make the fifth generation to live in Niagara-on-the-Lake Ontario. His second home in Southwest Florida is in an area of the everglades and the ocean. Both provide ammunition for his imagination and his love of storytelling. The diversity of the everglades became the backdrop for his first published and best-selling novel **Devil in the Grass** and his recently released sequel *The Palm Reader.*

Considering himself fortunate, Chris enjoys living his own personal great story. After earning a B.A. in History and graduating from Brock University, Chris is now surrounded by a wonderful family and runs a real estate brokerage. Whenever possible, he enjoys getting away to do some salt water fishing in Florida.

Like most writers, Christopher Bowron loves a great read and possesses the rare gift to spin tales of his own. His published work describes him as a *mystery writer of dark thrillers*. His readers love how his stories leave the humdrum train station of life and travels through dark tunnels to the unknown. They may need to buckle up and hold on tight as they ride along. He stories always go the distance to the sharp edge of reality, where they often get to peer into the paranormal.

More from Christopher Bowron

"A FAST PACED, ACTION-PACKED THRILLER. HIGHLY RECOMMENDED!"
—THE COLUMBIA REVIEW

DEVIL IN THE GRASS

A THRILLER

CHRISTOPHER BOWRON

Devil in the Grass – Published 2016 Koehler Books. **Number one Best Seller**, book one in the Jackson Walker series. A tantalizing fast paced Paranormal Thriller, set in the backdrop of the Florida Everglades.

"... fantastic characters and a truly spellbinding plot—
the best book in its genre I have ever read."
—SUSAN KEEFE, THECOLUMBIAREVIEW.COM

THE PALM READER

A JACKSON WALKER THRILLER

CHRISTOPHER BOWRON

BEST-SELLING AUTHOR OF *DEVIL IN THE GRASS*

The Palm Reader – Published 2018 Koehler Books. Book two in the Jackson Walker series. Rave reviews.

"…fantastic characters and a truly spellbinding plot- the best book in its genre I have ever read."
—SUSAN KEEFE. THE COLUMBIAREVIEW.COM

"A gripping thriller, which excels in unusual twists and turns, explorations of family heritage and truths, and one man's ongoing journey as he explores new connections to his life."
—DIANE DONOVAN. MIDWEST BOOK REVIEW

CPSIA information can be obtained
at www.ICGtesting.com
Printed in the USA
LVHW04s2245041018
592473LV00001B/3/P